Lehman's Infamy

by

Leonard McClane

Cover Design by **Mark Flaherty**
(www.meandalan.cc)

Reviews for "Terms"

"If Shane Black wrote a Geordie private eye thriller for Ross Noble this would be it!"
Emily John

"An unconventional action thriller; purposefully meandering (in a good way) but when it kicks into gear its impossible to put down! It's dark, funny AND actually quite moving!"
Sarah Mitchell

"I, and hopefully a wider audience, found [McClane] quite enjoyable as a guide into the world of the P.I."
Thomas Ludlow

*"An exciting, investigative, thrill-ride where lots of stuff gets smashed the f**k up!"*
Rob Leatt

*"If you like 80s action movies, s**t soft rock, comedic ramblings about pop culture (specifically the ending of The Fugitive) and an irreverent new spin on old private eye tropes, THIS is the book for you! This is DEFINITELY the book for you!"*
James Grant

*"*****... by the time you get to the shocking reveal it is impossible to put down!"*
Helen Grover

*"It's assured in its style and sets that out from the start. I blasted through it for one reason: It's f**king good!"*
Mark Flaherty

Reviews for "Run"

"… A scarily perceptive take on the world we live in right now, dressed up in a rip-roaring private eye caper that lovingly tips its cap to the Jerry Bruckheimer blockbusters of the mid 90s!"
James Grant

"He's done it again! An absolutely gripping read right from the get go! Read the majority in one sitting.
Some brilliant characters and action packed storyline."
DJ Leighton

"The stuff with the school and the social media propaganda is so clearly well researched and perfectly utilised it actually scared me with how accurate it is and how it's probably happening to kids right now!"
Robert Gottleib

"… Plenty of laugh out loud moments, particularly if you are a movie buff. The action was ramped up to the 'Bad Boys 2's motorway chase' levels in the final act and worked brilliantly! But overall the story was the shining light; not only very sad, but very current. I literally cannot wait for more!"
Matt Williams

"★★★★★ … Brilliant! A fast-paced read with the usual Leonard McClane wit and a gift for bringing the city of Newcastle to life - a real page turner!"
Gareth Mitchell

"Lehman is back with a bang! Leonard McClane has produced a thrilling second novel; fast-paced, fascinating characters and a story that bounces you from scene-to-scene, all making it one of those books you don't want to put down… If you like your heroes tortured, your plots twisted and your mind wowed, read this!"
Lesley Renwick

For my Grandma, my wife and my boys…
… all of whom taught me unconditional love in different ways.

Because of you all I've come to learn you can dream big, believe passionately and achieve enormously when you embrace such love!

[Prologue]

or

“12th August 2013

Fake it till you make it.

That’s what the fella said at the Jobcentre mandated ‘Build Your Own Business’ seminar a year ago. Back when I was just two weeks alcohol-free, trying to get on my feet again after being unjustly fired by the police. And at the same time attempting to prove to Jane, my wife, that I was still worth something and capable of providing for our children going forward.

Which is how in some sort of whirlwind of hasty decision making halfway through 2012 I went from being a borderline bed-ridden alcoholic living on the wrong-side of a nervous breakdown to suddenly sitting my Private Investigators qualification and going all out on my own as - what movies suggest is the action movie cliché to end all clichés - a broken-down ex-cop who’s trying to scrape out a living as a private eye on the bottom rung of the ladder.

One year on from that and I was sat faking it until I ‘made’ it: Walking around the city with pockets full of cheap-looking business cards knocked up on Vistaprint during one of their 70% off sales. Pimping my wears as a private investigator in Newcastle. Selling myself with a prestigious ‘NE1’ business address in the centre of the city that, if anyone took the time to check, would ultimately reveal itself to be just a secure post office box situated in the back of a café on Grainger Street. One of those types that specialised in board game playing customers of the teenage and university student variety.

My *actual* business was physically situated at the end of the driveway of my home address: It was a computer positioned on top of an old wallpapering table in my garage. Where, each and every morning, I would head on out wrapped up in a jumper and a cardigan (because I couldn’t have the computer and a portable heater plugged in at the same time in there) whilst carrying a jug of black coffee that I’d normally polish off in just over an hour.

When I wasn’t sat in there waiting for the mobile phone to miraculously ring with a job, *any* job, I was throwing on a shirt and tie at seven in the morning to embarrass myself by going out to all the various business networking breakfasts being hosted around the region. Essentially begging for work from the variety of other business types in attendance.

There were the ones held in service station coffee shops filled to the brim with desperate businessmen not so much trying to sell you a product as much as they were trying to recruit you to sell a product for *them*. Just so they could then change their title from 'salesman' to 'manager' on their business card; juice diets, herbal pills, energy supply contracts. You know the type, right?

Then there was the excruciating pyramid-scheme ones. Where they want you to pay a few thousand a year to be a 'member' and all you have to do is introduce others to become a 'member' too. In the hope that the membership each week keeps growing until you're eventually introduced to someone of a business type that can help you. Each week you're sat there willing one of them to have a cheating spouse who needs followed or something, all whilst warding off pitches from painters and decorators or 'motivational speakers' who are just as desperate as you for a job.

Networking can be a conman's dream stomping ground and over time I began to notice two things that were of value to me: One was that those that can't really run a business properly seem to set up business networking ventures. And two, more importantly, for the sort of work I was seeking to bring in a regular bundle of cash for me each month I needed to be meeting and getting through the doors of solicitors and law firms.

On top of that, I was a recovering alcoholic with a deep mistrust of people and a hatred for the very city I was trying to find work in after what Mick Hetherington did to me. Meeting people and selling myself to them wasn't easy. That's why, bit by bit, I started to lean away from business networking events with all their overpriced memberships, pyramid-scheme style structures and shitty breakfasts. Instead I started to lean instead towards skulking around coffee shops and cafes outside of the law courts on the Quayside and the law firm buildings nearby; eavesdropping on conversations and politely interjecting with a soft "*Excuse me, I couldn't help overhearing what you were saying there to your colleague about blah, blah, blah and I just so happen to be a private investigator specialising in litigation support and...*"

A quick handshake followed alongside the gifting of one of my business cards and, fuck me, who would have thunk it but it actually started to work. Soon enough assignments for Lehman's Terms started to roll in with process serving and people tracing becoming a regular weekly cycle from solicitors around the region.

Pretty soon I was able to afford to pay for an electrician to come out and fix the garage so that I could run my heater and my computer at the same time.

After one such run of politely interrupting solicitors in coffee shops to mixed success down on the Quayside that I started my usual trudge back up to Monument metro station, heading back to Lehman's Terms HQ and that freezing cold garage, only for me to be shaken from my thoughts by the shouting of my name.

I looked back down Dean Street but saw no one. Yet still the shouting of "Jake? Jake Lehman?" continued and didn't stop until I saw an overly happy Sergeant Richard Parkinson come bounding across the road towards me.

Parkinson had been my relief sergeant when I first came out of police training. He was a good guy. He was one of the few who tried to fight the fight for me when Hetherington's screws turned tight on my policing career. He'd tried calling when I was first kicked out. Naively under the impression that I would want to talk to anyone let alone anyone at all from my policing days, but he quickly gave up just like everyone else.

Apart from my wife.

And before I could update you folks as to anything else about him, here he was right up in my personal space wrapping his arms around my panicked body and bearhugging me tightly.

"Lehman!" he bellowed. "I *thought* that was you, mate."

I smiled weakly. "Sgt Parkinson, how are you?"

"Don't bother with all that Sergeant nonsense. Not here and not now." Parkinson smiled. "How the hell are you? We've been worried about you buddy. You just seemed to disappear off the face of the earth. Where have you been?"

Parkinson shifted his feet forward, invading my personal body space just that little bit further. He was a big, gangly bloke with broad shoulders and a huge warm smile that never seemed to leave his face even under the most testing of circumstances. I'd liked the guy a great deal back in the day.

"I've still been around. Just... you know... getting on with things, really." I said.

I ignored who the 'we' could possibly be in an entire police service that turned their back on me the minute the knife landed between my shoulder blades and my body was thrown out into the gutter.

"So, what are you doing nowadays then?" he asked, before speedily adding "That was bad shit that happened to you back then, I want you to know that."

I nodded quickly whilst staring hard at the ground.

"So, what are you up to?" Parkinson pushed some more.

"I'm... I'm a... private investigator now." I said, blushing with embarrassment for some reason I could only assume was a feeling of having suffered an almighty fall from grace.

"You're kidding? Really? That's *great*!" Parkinson responded, pushing hard on the 'great'. "Come on, let's go get a beer and you can tell me all about it!"

I smiled politely and started to step away. "Thanks, but I don't drink anymore."

"A coffee then?"

I smiled and kept stepping. "I'm sorry. I can't. I'm in a bit of a hurry."

"Come on," he laughed. "Fifteen minutes, we'll nip into Costa on the corner just over there and have a quick catch-up. Believe it or not, you might end up getting some work from it!"

Parkinson winked.

I stopped in my tracks.

I really, *really* didn't want to sit and set the world to rights, so to speak, with Richard Parkinson in a coffee shop. I didn't want to risk it devolving into him wanting to rehash old cases he supervised me on or, you know, what happened to me. I didn't want his sympathy. I didn't want to hear how well all my old colleagues were doing now.

I certainly didn't want to hear the name Andy Andrews get mentioned.

But then I remembered the business had made exactly £89.75 profit for the whole of the previous month and I didn't have anything on the docket for the foreseeable future. Which was starting to make me nervous... and that's why I quickly nodded, pretended to look at my watch as if I was pondering whether I could make this work in my 'busy' schedule and then said "Okay. A quick coffee."

I have to give Parkinson his due because he picked up pretty quickly that I wasn't going to be reciprocal to throwing back and forth old police 'war stories' from my time as an officer. Nor did I want to discuss my unjust exit from the service. Instead, after five or so minutes of small talk about Jane and the kids after he sat back down at our table with a couple of coffees and delivered on his promise of potential work coming my way:

"Have you heard of Arkin Dentz?" Parkinson asked whilst stirring his cup.

I shook my head.

"He's a big money guy, played the stocks, worked as a financial consultant for some big firms. He's minted basically. I got to know him through my Masonic lodge commitments. He's a huge, hairy Jew who used to be a jocular, life-and-soul of the party type but then his daughter went missing on a gap year out in Australia sometime last year and he's gone to pieces. He came to me for help because the Aussie police have basically locked it all down and written it off. They're plagued with like... a thousand missing backpackers a year or some shit like that, you know? But obviously there's little I can do at our end here and my Chief Inspector has told me not to get involved."

"So..." I began tentatively.

"So, he's been asking me recently if I can recommend anyone to help him?" Parkinson smiled. "And I could recommend you, if you like?"

"And his name is Arkin fuckin Dentz? Seriously?" I replied.

"That's your response?" Parkinson laughed. "That's what you're going with? Not 'Thank you'? Not 'Okay, I'm interested'?"

I'd thanked Parkinson and said "Okay, I'm interested".

The next morning found me on public transport to Arkin Dentz' enormously intimidating and borderline palatial property. Tucked away in what felt like a secret estate all of its own in Tynemouth.

I buzzed the gate intercom and identified myself to the young male on the other end of it. As soon as the impressive wrought iron gates swung far enough open I began the *long* walk up the gravelled drive to the front door.

I was met at the door by a weedy-looking, well-dressed man whom I presumed I'd just been speaking to moments earlier via the intercom.

"Mr Lehman?" the man said as he extended his hand out to me.

I took it, shook it and let it go again whilst smiling and nodding.

"Hello," said the man. "I'm Marcus. I'm Mr Dentz' assistant. Please come in."

I walked in through the impressive doors and stepped into the most ostentatious foyer-come-hallway I had ever seen in my life at that point. This was an explosion of money being thrown down at... at... *everything*! Art-deco pieces? Antiques? Marble? Thick cuts of mahogany? It was all here.

I followed Marcus through this warehouse of high-end materialism into a large and airy room. Where the man himself, Mr Arkin Dentz, was sat in a deep chair that had an oxygen tank pushed up to the side of it, tubes flowing into the mask affixed to Arkin's rotund and hairy face. He lifted his bulbous hand with a giant nugget of gold squeezed onto his little finger, pulled the mask from his face and beckoned me towards him.

"Jake Lehman?" he gasped.

I nodded. "Yes, Mr Dentz. It's a pleasure to meet you."

I reached out with my hand. He clasped it inside of both of his giant mitts and squeezed it tightly whilst smiling at me.

"Thank you for coming out to see me. Our mutual friend Richard speaks incredibly highly of you."

His hand dropped back down into his lap and I could see that he was wearing a Rolex Sky-Dweller in Oyster steel and yellow gold. This was a *very* good watch. A fairly rare one too. Not in the sense of the number of them made but more that they were so expensive they could only be afforded by a very select, moneyed few so there was not a lot of them in circulation. The watch on Arkin Dentz' wrist went for around £11,125.00.

And with that the 'small talk' floodgates burst open.

He asked about my experience as a private investigator, I exaggerated my answer. He asked about my reputation in my field and how long I had been doing it, I exaggerated that answer too. He told me about himself and how his wife died five years ago and all he had left was his daughter, Maya. He explained that Maya means 'water' in Aramaic. He talked about how she was his everything. That he had planned his entire life around her excelling academically, studying for a business degree and then taking over the running of his company. His demeanour changed when he explained how he was completely torn asunder when Maya informed him she was taking a gap year. Those two specific words spat out of his mouth with the utmost contempt as he explained Maya was going to meet her best friend from school out in Perth.

"The plan," Arkin sighed. "was that she was going to go out in December just gone, meet up with her friend Anna and hire some sort of camper van or something to travel across the country in time to arrive in Sydney for New Year's Eve."

"And how did that plan work out?" I asked.

"She left Perth in the company of Anna and one of Anna's Australian friends called Sarah, along with a male from Sweden by the name of Edvin Sixten. My daughter and her friends never made it to Sydney. They were never seen again..."

Arkin broke into heavy sobs. Marcus appeared almost by magic by his side and handed him a handkerchief that looked like it cost more than all the clothes I was wearing at that moment combined. Marcus picked the oxygen mask up from Arkin's lap and attempted to put it to his face, but it was quickly batted away.

Arkin instead took a deep breath independently and continued. "... The four of them had apparently bought a second-hand vehicle to make the trip across the country in. It was found abandoned on a dirt track road in the Blue Mountains. Sixten's body was found at the bottom of a cliff there, a suicide note had been left in the car. The Australian police closed the case last month after seven months of investigation. Concluding that Edvin Sixten had murdered my daughter and her friends, disposed of them in such a way they are never to be found and then committed suicide."

I exhaled and sat back in my chair.

"Wow. Okay."

"Indeed. But I struggle to accept that. I would have very much liked to have gone out there myself because none of this makes sense to me. But my health is such that I'm told I wouldn't survive the flight or if I did, I wouldn't last in the heat. I have emphysema and... and..."

Marcus stepped forward. "Mr Dentz has emphysema and coronary artery disease. He can no longer walk unaided and his conditions have only worsened since the death of..."

Arkin's fist slammed down hard on the arm of the chair which in turn kicked off a desperate coughing fit that required two big gulps of air from his oxygen mask. He held his hand up through the whole re-regulation of his breathing as a sign no one else was to speak until he was settled. Finally, he spoke.

"*Disappearance*!" he snapped.

"Excuse me?" I replied.

"I'm sorry," Marcus said quietly. "His conditions have only worsened since the *disappearance* of his daughter, Maya."

"I have too many unanswered questions. I have tried to use any one of my innumerable solicitors to engage with the Australian police and receive these answers." Arkin said quietly. "They have thus far not agreed to commit to what they consider to be a full re-investigation of the case itself. Which is what they seem to indicate it would be in order to give me the answers I need. They have placed my Maya as just another 'lost backpacker' statistic."

Arkin wiped tears from his cheeks.

"It sounds certainly suspect that they consider answering a grieving father's questions to be akin to fully re-investigating the case itself, doesn't it? If it had been thoroughly investigated in the first place then surely they would have your answers at hand?" I said.

Arkin clasped his hands together forcibly, smashing out a deafening clap.

"Exactly!" he exclaimed. "*Exactly*! That is what I've told my representatives."

"So... what is it you think I could be of assistance with exactly, Mr Dentz?" I asked apprehensively but with a twinge of hope... and maybe a couple of dollops of excitement too.

[1]

or

"The Return of the King"

"♫♫ ... And we can build this thing together. Standing strong forever. Nothing's gonna stop us now. And if this world runs out of lovers, we'll still have each other. Nothing's gonna stop us. Nothing's gonna stop us now... ♫♫"

'Nothing's Gonna Stop Us Now' - Starship
Written by Diane Warren and Albert Hammond.
From the album 'No Protection' (1987)

I should have led in with "And now the end is near and so I face the final curtain" from Frank Sinatra's 'My Way', shouldn't I? Or is that too much of a spoiler? Would that throw too many of you into a state of sitting there thinking *"If this fucker has been telling this whole thing from the goddamn afterlife all along I'm going to lose my shit here!"*

Anyway, welcome back one and all.

Let's set about seeing if third time really *is* the charm, huh?

There's pressure anew here as well isn't there? Because if you're back then it means then our second get-together did not suck *entirely* for you but now I've got to maintain a standard and see this whole thing through to a worthy conclusion. You know, like Back to the Future Part III, Evil Dead: Army of Darkness, War for the Planet of the Apes, The Good The Bad & The Ugly and, if it's allowed to count, Iron Man 3?

What I can't be doing is dropping the ball so badly as we approach the finish line that I end up serving you all the 'private eye action thriller yarn' equivalent of The Godfather Part III, Beverly Hills Cop 3, Blade: Trinity, The Hangover Part III or, who could forget, the trauma of Look Who's Talking Now?

Do you know what all of those third efforts have in common by the way? All of them would later come to be thoroughly disowned by the major stars involved with them.

Who knows? Maybe I can land this thing *so* brilliantly and end it so perfectly – like Indiana Jones & The Last Crusade, The Bourne Ultimatum, Star Wars: Return of the Jedi, Die Hard With A Vengeance or Lord of the Rings: Return of the King – that I'll get the opportunity to come back after way too long a period of time and fuck this whole thing up with unnecessary additional instalments? That could be something to… look forward to… right?

Soooo… how have you all been?

What's it been? Six months or something? Last time we got together I was neck-deep in a missing person case that ended up with me hanging off the back of a bomb-laden train after running up against a gang of right-wing white supremacists funded by a crazed, racist millionaire – and my life has been one hell of a rollercoaster *since* then too. What about you?

Psychic and I are no longer kind of a 'big deal' in inverted commas anymore. We're the actual *real deal* 'big deal' now since saving the city from that terrorist attack. And not just in the region either – nationally as well!

They rushed out a couple of documentaries about us. You might have seen them? Not ones where we're just a couple of talking heads for a few minutes either, like that one they did about Stephanie Jason. Then we had movie studios came a-calling about wanting to obtain both of our 'life rights' in order to make a full-on action movie about what went down.

No, stop laughing, I'm *not* making this up.

In fact, where I'm bringing you in this time is quite literally just as Psychic and I were returning to Newcastle after a few days down in London. We were being schmoozed and negotiating contracts for a big money deal from Universal to make a film about us, our work at Lehman's Terms and the now famous Baadir Gadiel case. But, hang fire, I'll get back to that in a minute.

Let me catch you all up on everything else first.

Because it's been a pretty crazy six or so months:

The team at Lehman's Terms has expanded and now alongside Psychic, Holly and I, we've brought Catrina in. How could we not after she showed off those savvy IT skills and technical know-how that generated us the lead that ended up solving the whole Gadiel case in the end?

I'm talking like you're all up to speed and know exactly what I'm referring to in this short, chatty, just-between-friends manner but… well… as with last time, surely you're *all in* on my 'Jake Lehman' adventures by this point, right? You're indubitably not going to be jumping in at the end of the trilogy as your starting point of choice, surely?

Saying that mind you, Psychic once tried watching Game of Thrones via some streaming site and fell asleep mid-episode. He woke up without realising it had auto-played episode-after-episode whilst he'd slept and then spent a whole load of work-time sat in a surveillance vehicle with me having to listen to him mutter *"... And Sean Bean just seems to have disappeared into thin air without explanation and everything makes less sense than it did before and it barely made any sense then either... and now there's dragons? I thought this was a proper true-history medieval thing but there's dragons!"*

Inspector Leigh Richardson-Jones has joined our team as well. He retired on medical grounds from the police after losing his legs in the process of saving my life in that shoot-out at Metro Headquarters. He now works for us on a part-time basis as an investigator. It pains me to say this but he's bloody brilliant and he brings in a boatload of work for us with his connections too.

Between Catrina's tech-savviness raising our game and Richardson-Jones raising our client base, Psychic and I have been able to take more of a backseat and sort of enjoy the business as managers, as opposed to being boots on the ground all the time. Hell, it's been ages since I've done any process serving actually now that Richardson-Jones uses it as an excuse to "stretch his legs" (his joke, not mine, since getting fitted with two titanium limbs) and get out of the office every now and again.

This works decidedly well for Psychic because Emily is about to give birth. It works well for me too because it means I can step back a little and kind of give Jane a bit of what she wants. Which is me putting a bit of space between myself and the business now it is a success independent of me. After all, we've got movie studios throwing big money at us and, well, all of that *good* stuff.

A 'little bit' isn't enough for Jane though and I'm not going to lie things are surprisingly tough between us at the moment. Pretty damn difficult in fact. We're still in couple's therapy with Barbara and it's through that I came to learn that the whole Baadir Gadiel / nearly getting blown up 'thing' really did shake Jane up.

I pushed maybe too hard on accusing her of secretly wanting me to have taken up Chief Constable Lane's offer of a job with the police as a consultant then resenting me for taking up her own suggestion of not accepting. I questioned whether she seemingly dangled that option in front of me as some sort of 'test'.

Well *that* all blew up big time mid-therapy session.

"Hardly Jake!" she'd snapped. "Because you know something? I'm not sat dreaming about the missed opportunity of the regular income and more social hours or any of that. Do you know what I'm dreaming about now things have developed how they have these last few months? I'm dreaming of you riding the success to a place where you might become a silent partner in your own company and we can move out of this city. Because I don't know if I can survive this city kicking your fucking arse again and me having to sit by a hospital bedside wondering whether your body is going to survive the trauma this time. Let alone your mental health. Do you know what *else* I dream about?"

I sat staring at the floor.

"Ask her. Engage with her question." Barbara said softly whilst leaning forward to try and make eye contact with me.

Jane didn't wait for my 'engagement'.

"I dream about me, you and the boys packing up and moving off to some little village somewhere. Maybe over in the Lake District or something? I dream of me having some little teaching job in the village school and you just pottering around every day, cashing your royalties from whatever movie is made about you and taking your monthly wage from Lehman's Terms' continued success. I dream of the boys having a quieter life and us having a better relationship with them and I dream of you just getting to a place where you can just... *breathe*!"

"Well Jake," Barbara said. "What do you think of that?"

"I think that I dream of threesomes with Jessica Chastain and Elizabeth Olsen but you don't see me trying to force them out into reality and onto other people, do you?" I sneered.

God, I am **such** a fucking dick.

"You're such a fucking dick!" snapped Jane as she stood up, grabbed her bag and stormed out, slamming Barbara's door on the way out.

I jumped to my feet, checking my watch as I did.

"We've only been here twenty-five minutes Babs, so make sure you bill accordingly yeah?" I hollered back to Barbara as I sped on out the room after Jane.

I caught up with her as she stormed across the car park and drowned her in apologies.

"I'm sorry. I'm sorry, okay?" I gasped breathlessly. "That was out of order. I was trying to be a smart-arse and it wasn't appropriate and you deserved better than that."

"Get stuffed Jake!" Jane replied.

"No, wait…"

"No, *you* wait!" she snapped. "All I've done from the minute you got your police career stolen from you is pick you up every time you plummet, put you back on your feet and support you as you head back out again. I've helped you through your addictions, I've helped you through all the night terrors. I've changed the bandages on your wounds. I've been more of a nurse to you than a bastard wife, frankly. And *now*? Now, when I suggest we ride the wave of success to the benefit of your mental health and our family by leaving this fucking city behind and getting much needed space, you treat me like I'm a joke?"

"You're right. I'm wrong..." I attempted.

"Like that *ever* matters!" Jane said as her eyes welled up with tears and she climbed into the car, swiftly switching on the engine and moving off out of the car park at speed.

Without me in the passenger seat.

I never got the chance to get my sincere apology to land or for Jane and I to discuss things any further because she purposefully kept out of my way for a few days. I was astute to realise it would be wrong to deny her the space she needed to move past some innate need to punch my fucking head in. Then by the time I felt a respectful amount of time and distance had passed by, Psychic and I were off down to London for a few days of being glad-handed by producers and movie types who were interested in schmoozing us for our life rights.

We spent that time being wined (I drank water) and dined (I grumbled about the portion sizes) in fine restaurants around the city of London. Before we left to come home I sloped off on my own and spent an *insane* amount of money on a beautiful pair of diamond earrings to give to Jane for Christmas – along with the suggestion we start looking at putting a deposit down on a 'weekend home' outside of Newcastle as some sort of compromise.

My plan was simple: Get back home, keep my head down for the next two days and on Christmas Eve night take Jane out for a bite to eat somewhere posh – but not too pricey. Then give her my gift and my suggestion of a compromise along with an apology for, you know, me being a dick.

Psychic and I got the last train out of Kings Cross as soft, intermittent drops of snow fell on the capital. By the time we passed through Durham we were pushing against a wall of sheer white as a blizzard hit the North East hard.

We alighted at Central Station and dropped our bags at our feet in order to zip up our coats and pull up our collars in unison. Psychic snatched a quick look at his phone.

"Well, I managed to get from London to Newcastle without Emily going into labour!" he smiled.

"Not long now, huh?" I replied. "Excited?"

"I *think* I am." Psychic said.

"I am *for* you." I laughed. "You're about to have your world rocked, man!"

Psychic picked his bags up and started to walk. "You're not really going into the office tomorrow, are you?"

I nodded. "I'm just going to check in. I'm not doing a full day. I'm off most of Christmas so I want to just make sure everything's good with Leigh and Catrina… and that Holly isn't hosting Christmas raves out of our office or something!"

Psychic laughed. "Jake, she's a *millennial.* She doesn't even know what a rave is!"

"Christ, we're so old!"

We walked off towards the exit as carol singers positioned just in front of the archway echoed out around the giant expanse of the station.

"We're still catching up tomorrow night with you and Jane and Luke and his lass, if Emily's not popped by then, right?" Psychic asked.

"Yeah, of course. If Jane's not still trying to burn the back of my head out with a death glare, of course." I smiled. "Emily's got a hospital appointment tomorrow during the day, hasn't she?"

Psychic nodded.

"Well, keep us posted about that too!"

Psychic nodded some more. He then stuck out his hand and when I took it to shake, he engulfed me in a hug that caused his bag to slap me hard on the back.

"We're going to be rich and we're going to be characters in a film – how cool is *that*?" Psychic giggled.

"Very cool!" I smiled broadly.

Psychic walked off to the taxi rank ahead of me even though we were both headed in that direction anyway. I stopped and watched him go.

A warm butterfly feeling began to develop in my gut – between the city becoming encrusted in pure white snow, the sound of carol singers, the excitement at the future that lay ahead for Psychic and I in the aftermath of all that we've faced <u>and</u> the prospect of getting out of Jane's bad books with what I had planned, I felt…

… good.
I felt really fucking *good*.

[2]

or

"It All Falls Down."

The blizzard dug in almost instantly with forecasts predicting it was here for the next four days at the very least. I woke the next morning to Jane asleep alongside me, her back turned to me and her body clung perilously to her side of the bed. Which was unusual for her as she's normally tucked away under my armpit with her arm draped across my chest when I wake. I checked my watch on the bedside table and slipped out of the bed without waking her.

Jane had still been up when I got in the night before. She was two mouthfuls away from polishing off a glass of red wine and it didn't look like it had been her first of the evening. It was all the more surprising to me because she'd been running a 'dry' house for quite some time now to support me in my recovery. Something I hadn't asked her to do by the way. She made that decision all on her own, just in case you all thought I was some sort of demanding, expectant dick.

As opposed to, you know, just a dick.

We talked. A little. It didn't go *great*. The conversation lasted as long as the wine in her glass did and then she took herself off to bed.

Therefore, come the next morning I thought it best to let her sleep in with the boys and pick things up later on that day. Or maybe on the drive out to meet up with Psychic, Luke and their partners later that night.

I knew the snow had landed hard just by the white glare reflecting into our home as I came down the stairs and into the living room. Being mindful not to wake Jane and the boys, I opted out of showering or making too much of a noise. Instead I put my shit together quietly and headed out the door with the intention of picking up a strong black coffee and a breakfast sandwich once I got into the city.

The snow was very close to knee deep already and I was no more than twenty or so metres from my house when I started to come around to the notion that there's no way the metros would be running in these conditions. I was so busy bemoaning my lack of 'extreme weather' wear and how utterly soaked the legs of my jeans were, whilst arguing with myself ("Why *should* you have a section of your wardrobe dedicated to the slight possibility of Newcastle choosing to become frickin' Alaska for the day?") that I was half way up the road to the metro station with the cold wind lacerating flakes of snow across my face before I stopped and thought "Where the hell are you going Jake and how the hell are you getting there?"

After discovering with one quick phone call that everyone else bar Psychic had made it into the Lehman's Terms office, I decided I had to push on and make an effort. So I crossed down beneath the metro station underpass and grabbed a taxi into the city instead.

I trudged through the mounds of snowfall building up at a faster rate than it could subside, pushing on away from Monument Square and down into Grey Street. No matter how much weight I'd lost or how much better shape I'd got myself in, I couldn't shake the daily back pain and arthritis in my knees and hips. The almighty kicking I'd taken from Jeff Petersen on Byker Bridge last Summer had not helped it in anyway and this severe weather was sure as shit accentuating it.

It was absolutely, most *definitely*, days like this where the fight against popping a couple of Tramadol was at its hardest. I was in a secure place mentally regarding my addictions though. Making it very easy for me to flip that switch in my head and purposefully distract myself from ruminating on the past. Looking instead to the future - apologising to Jane, getting things back on track with her, eating good food surrounded by great friends later that night.

I kicked the snow from my boots as I clumped up each step to the office. Desperately shaking my arms as I climbed to try and break off the large clusters of snow that were clinging to every crease on my arms and torso. I was minus my desired coffee and Danish pastry because I was too cold from the journey to have stayed out there a minute longer. But I was just the right amount of 'arsehole' that I'd send Holly, our lovely, bubbly long-term receptionist out to get them for me instead.

I came through the main door to the sounds of Holly and Catrina mid-squabble along with the sight of Leigh Richardson-Jones sat with his head in his hands.

"Thank CHRIST!" exclaimed Richardson-Jones as he caught sight of me. "I can't put up with this a minute longer."

"What's going on?" I smiled.

"Tell him!" Catrina laughed.

"No, he already thinks I'm a fool!" Holly replied.

"I don't think you're a fool," I said. "I think you're... *unique*!"

"So, the other day we were trying to explain to Holly the difference between being naïve and being gullible..." Catrina began.

"Straight off the bat I want to be clear that I do not like where this starts nor where it is going." I interrupted.

"... And as a sort of partial, live, practical scenario yesterday Leigh suggested to Holly that she nipped out and bought some powdered ice to go in our drinks for the Christmas farewell drinks in the office later." She continued.

"There's Christmas farewell drinks in the office later?" I asked.

"We'll tell you about them later." Catrina smirked. "Anyway, Holly asked what 'powdered ice' was and Leigh said that it was this powder that you put in the ice cube tray and add water and it makes the ice cubes..."

"Oh Holly... *no*?" I said.

"No, hang on." Holly shouted. "I thought that they meant it made the ice cubes like... more... special. You know, like *fresher* or something? I knew that they didn't actually make ice because it's the cold that does that. I'm not THAT thick, okay?"

"Okay." I said. "But tell me you didn't go out looking for powdered ice around the shops?"

Holly looked to the ground.

Catrina started to laugh hard.

I looked to Richardson-Jones. "Leigh, you bastard!"

I hung my coat up on the hook and as I advanced towards my office door, I put a hand gently on Holly's shoulder. "They're a couple of dickheads, Holly. And remember, when it comes to taking sides I've always got your back because you saved my life that one time!"

Holly laughed and stuck her tongue out at Catrina.

"Hey!" gasped Catrina. "I broke the lead on your Baadir Gadiel case!"

"You did, yes. But she...you know... saved my *life*! Which is a little bit better, I guess." I replied with a smile.

"But didn't she shoot you as well or something?" Catrina said.

I turned back to Holly. "This *is* true also!"

"Don't start!" giggled Holly.

"Now, if you want to make up for the fact that you shot me by accident that one time and you still like going out and enduring the city centre shops at this time of the year for *anything* how about you go grab me a black coffee and a Danish?"

"Check your desk!" Holly winked.

I let the smile break across my face as I looked in through the door and saw she'd very kindly left both of those things there already - still with steam coming up from the coffee cup too.

"Holly, you're a bloody star!" I smiled.

"I know!" she replied.

Settling in behind my desk, I shouted through to ask if there were any messages before I got started on tearing through my email inbox.

"I need to talk to you about this Gateshead job I'm finishing up!" Richardson-Jones shouted back.

"Okay!" I replied.

"The only message is from Bobby!" Holly bellowed. "He wants to see you urgently."

I sighed. "Fuck!"

As I'm sure you will all recall, Bobby Maitland is the 'numero uno' as gangsters within the region go. He's got his hand in pretty much everything. And frankly, he's probably got a collection of severed hands in a box somewhere too from fending off anyone who's ever reached in and tried to take a piece of what he has control over. Clubs, pubs, security services, construction companies, Bobby is pulling money from all of it around the North East.

Six months prior to this particular day, and with the Mayor of Newcastle as his mistress no less, Bobby was pushing to go legit. For all intents and purposes in the eyes of the public and the law he recently actually *had*. I knew differently though - because in some misbegotten way we'd become sort of 'friends' / associates over the last couple of years. But mainly because Bobby was *Bobby* and he tended to lean less towards actioning a Human Resources investigation into his employees' misconduct and more towards just having them put in the back of a car and driven off, never to be seen again.

I doubted he'd ever change.

I knew that because as legitimate as he'd become as a businessman, he still consistently pushed up against the line of what myself or Psychic were willing to do for him as his go-to private investigators. In every situation where once told we wouldn't or couldn't do what he was asking of us because it was unlawful, he always responded "Okay, fine. How much for you to stop being little bitches and just get on with it then?" with negative effect.

And it was within the area of that very sort of scenario that Bobby and I had... well... not so much 'fallen out' in the last six weeks or so but more just let a frost descend between the two of us. Things were made all the more awkward by the fact that just a fortnight before the big 'frost', Bobby had got himself a *professional* office space. No more big oak desks stuffed away in the back of pubs that he owned. No more holding court in a hastily arranged "VIP area" of the members' bar down the local golf club. Bobby now had offices directly across the road from Lehman's Terms premises on Grey Street.

Which was *great* to start with because Bobby seems to have ADHD for the working day and never failed to call up and drag us out for a lunch (on him) that took up most of the day. But then once the "squabble", as Psychic calls it, occurred it became bloody *awkward* because I live in fear that he's going to have his righthand man Ryan or one of his other goons firebomb our office.

It's all just... just... so unnecessary.

You know how there's two sides to every story, right? Well, let me give you Bobby's side first: He hired Psychic and I to do a job recently. It *had* to be me and Psychic, no one else. He hadn't taken to Leigh Richardson-Jones at all and said he didn't trust him. As far as Bobby was concerned, we did the job and didn't deliver on what was agreed so now he was refusing to pay us what we were owed. And all told we were out just shy two and half grand on this particular job.

Now, with that out the way, let me give you *my* side of the story: Bobby had a problem with one of the guy's running a construction job on one of his many projects. A fella by the name of Dougie Carrell. It turned out that Dougie was creaming materials off the top of deliveries and selling them on the side to cowboy builders and the like. Bobby found out and went crazy as Bobby is accustomed to doing. So Dougie did the sensible thing and went to ground as soon as word spread he'd been found out.

Bobby figured he was down about £100,000 or more from Dougie's side project and because he was all "legitimate" and what not now he wanted to locate the guy so he could bring about a private prosecution. We pushed for him to notify the police and have them find, arrest and charge this Dougie bloke but Bobby was having none of it. He said that I knew more than anyone "not to trust the ol' bill".

So Psychic and I ran the usual trace work and found enough evidence to indicate Dougie was potentially hiding out at his grandfather's villa in Majorca. We indicated vaguely enough about this to Bobby for him to say that he trusted us and only us to get the evidence he wanted. He demanded hard photographic proof of the target coming and going from the relevant property out there. Which is how Psychic and I found ourselves on a mid-November trip out to Majorca, dawdling around the ex-pat bars looking for our guy.

Whilst out there on the job we came across a couple of Bobby's favoured heavies walking the same routes as us. We came to realise they'd been placed on stand-by out there in order to grab Dougie as soon as we ID'd him and confirmed his whereabouts with certainty. Suddenly things felt like they weren't being lined up for Bobby to have his day in court but instead for him to have his time alone in a room with this guy and his favourite collection of sharp implements. When confronted Bobby 'fessed up and confirmed the latter was the case.

Because it turns out it isn't that easy to take the gangster out of the legitimate businessman after all, huh?

Feeling like we weren't *cool* with the prospect of sending Dougie Carrell off to his death, Psychic and I pulled short of identifying his full location and refused to confirm any further information with Bobby. Which he quickly became irate about once his goons trawled around the whole of Majorca but couldn't uncover what we had found out as to Dougie's exact whereabouts.

My submission of our invoice for services rendered up to that point and expenses, etc. was met with an incandescent Bobby ringing me up at the office and screaming "ARE YOU TAKING THE FUCKING PISS SENDING ME THIS, THINKING I OWE YOU ANYTHING?" Things only worsened from there really.

That's why when I received Holly's message that he wanted to see me the first thing I did after my initial expletive was to peer cautiously around my office door and whisper "How did he sound?"

"Okay?" shrugged Holly.

"Did he sound like he was loading a gun in the background or slowly simmering with barely contained rage or something?" I asked.

"No, not really. He just said to go and see him as soon as you got in."

I gradually started to nod.

"Maybe he misses me and has decided our friendship is more important than money?" I theorised out loud.

"You know Bobby Maitland once stabbed a man's eyes out with a screwdriver because he tried to squeeze in on Bob's territory?" interjected Richardson-Jones. "Think about who you're talking about here!"

I sighed, nodded the head a little more vigorously and grabbed my soaking wet coat.

I suggested to Holly and Catrina that we should think about shutting up shop at lunch-time and then we could have Christmas festivities earlier. I revelled a little bit in the excited squeals this elicited from both of them. I told Richardson-Jones I'd catch up with him about the Gateshead job in thirty minutes as I headed out the door.

Grey Street was awash with a steady flow of foot traffic as people came and went from the festive market up on my right in Monument Square.

The blizzard had eased off slightly though the air was still positively caustic in terms of its temperature. I pulled my coat tight around me, dug my hands deep into my pocket and crunched across the street, through the thick snow underfoot as The Pogues' 'Fairy Tale of New York' played out from loudspeakers up amidst the market stalls.

"♫♫ ... *An old man said to me, won't see another one. And then he sang a song. The Rare Old Mountain Dew. I turned my face away. And dreamed about you...* ♫♫"

The walk across Grey Street, through the door and up the stairs into Bobby's offices was probably no more than a ninety second journey. Two minutes maximum. In that time I thought less about what it was that Bobby could want and more about breaking bread with him properly. Even if that meant taking a bit of a hit on the outstanding invoice's subtotal. Then with that out the way it could be all about closing down the office for Christmas and getting home in time for a hot shower and going out with Jane, Psychic and Emily, Luke and his girlfriend.

I pushed open the external door and took double steps up the stairs...

I missed having Luke 'Jimmy' Brody around nowadays, I'm not going to lie. It felt like an age since he made some serious fucking money (he's a millionaire!) winning a reality TV competition and moving away. He still comes back up every now and again because he's brought properties up here that he's making a killing with and he's very hands on with them all. We always catch up for dinner when he does, but it's not the same as being out on the street with him as the Kevin Costner to my Whitney Houston on the more precarious jobs.

I rounded the corner at the top of the stairs and made my way along the corridor to the office at the end that Bobby Maitland called 'ground zero' for all his business dealings, pushing open the door with a gentle tap on the glass to accompany me doing so…

Luke and I had come along way when you think about it. Just nearly three years ago we were scrapping around together. I was chucking him thirty quid here and fifty quid there and he was using it to survive on for as long as he could. Now he's got a million or so in the bank and I'm in the process of selling off my life rights to have a movie made about me and there's more than one documentary out there about me, the Baadir Gadiel case and my credentials as an investigator after what I uncovered looking into the death of Stephanie Jason.

BOOM!

My body crashed to the floor as my feet slipped out from underneath me within seconds of getting through the entrance to Bobby's office. I'd have thought I'd skidded to a crunching impact with the floor due to water or an ice patch had it not been for the blood all over my hands as I attempted to push myself back up onto my feet.

Was it my blood?

Had I walked into an ambush?

I put my hands to my head. There was no pain and it certainly didn't seem like blood was pumping from out of anywhere. I didn't think I'd been shot in the head because I was now standing back up and taking note of my surroundings. But then, to be fair, I'd never been shot in the head before so I had no point of comparison. I looked down at my feet just in case I wasn't standing up so much as I was floating away from my own corpse, murdered by one of Bobby's dickhead heavies over a £2,500 unpaid invoice.

There was no corpse beneath my feet, certainly not one that looked remotely like me.

Just a massive pile of blood that seemed to be streaming its way from out underneath the enormous antique mahogany table across the room.

No, the only corpse in the room belonged to Bobby Maitland, sat, slumped in his big, quilted office chair.

He was completely white in pallor and his eyes were widened, frozen stiff in a state of shock. A thick bloodied gash lay open across his throat from ear to ear with the stream of blood already starting to dry in around the collar of his expensive high-collared dress shirt.

"Fuck!" I gasped. "*Fuck*!"

I stared down at my hands and saw how drenched in blood they were, along with the sides of my jacket and most of my jeans too. I started to retch but controlled myself long enough to reach deep into my pocket for my mobile phone.

... which was sat on my desk back in the office.

Shit!

I stepped forward to pick up the landline telephone on Bobby's desk, cautiously trying not to slip back down into the bloodied pool that was filling out around the main space in the room. God, there was so much blood. *So* much blood.

The line was dead.

I checked twice.

Nothing.

I was just beginning to back out of the office carefully and get back across to my place to use the phone there when a heavy thud landed against the cupboard door to my right on the far side of Bobby's office. It was followed swiftly by a second thud. And a third. And then the door itself burst open and Ryan Flaherty fell out, his own blood streaming down the left side of his face from an open head wound.

Bobby's right-hand man caught sight of his boss almost immediately.

"What did you do?" he screeched. "Jake? What the fuck have you *done*?"

I tried to step towards him at the same time he tried to charge me but his own dizziness got the better of him and he fell forward to the ground.

I reached down and positioned him up against a nearby chair.

"Stay here!" I gasped breathlessly. "I'm going to go get help."

Ryan reached out to grab me but I gently patted his hand away and clambered out of the room as best I could.

I bolted along the corridor and down the stairs, ricocheting off walls and bannisters as I went. The flashing blue lights dazzled me as I burst out of the door and onto Grey Street.

"FREEZE!" came a chorus of voices.

"GET DOWN ON THE GROUND!" shouted a police officer as I skidded under foot at the sight of an armed response vehicle and a police van crunched to a stop in a bank of snow right outside the doors of the building for Bobby's office.

Guns were drawn and a laser sight appeared on my chest almost immediately.

"Wait..." I stammered. "I'm trying to get hel..."

"GET DOWN ON THE GROUND!" screamed another officer.

"TAKE HIM DOWN!" hollered a sergeant from the rear of the police van.

Before I could so much as turn my head, two officers hit me from either side and slammed me face down into the ground. The snow did little to cushion the impact and my lips popped as a result, spraying blood across the sheer white surface.

I could hear Ryan's voice screaming behind me in a furious rage, having obviously followed me down the stairs soon after my exit. "You're dead, Jake! You're fucking *dead*! What have you done?"

My arms were forcibly dragged behind my back as I looked as best I could around me to see all the Christmas shoppers starting to congregate in a semi-circle next to the police vehicles and hastily erected taped cordon that was getting set up before my very eyes. This was quite the show for them.

To give you an idea as to just how long this had all been going on for from entering the building to shocking discovery and all the way through to this wrongful arrest, The Pogues' 'Fairy Tale of New York' was only *just* finishing up.

"♫♫ ... Can't make it all alone. I've built my dreams around you... The boys of the NYPD choir, still singing "Galway Bay". And the bells are ringing out for Christmas day... ♫♫"

"Stay still!" one of the police officers spat out at me as the cuffs tightened around my wrist.

"I've been in that building less than two fucking minutes, man!" I shouted back. "Look at that scene in there. It's hours old. I'm not the bastard culprit here, for Christ's sake!"

I craned my head as best I could as the police officers continued to manhandle me and I could just make out a line of sight back up to my own offices up on the other side of the street.

Holly was stood at the window. She looked genuinely shocked.

I just caught sight of her seemingly gesticulating to Richardson-Jones and Catrina to come and look at what was going on when…

B - A - N - G !

Holly's body burst out through the window, framed as the masthead at the front of a large orange explosion of fire. The deafening sound of the blast swiftly followed, masking the thud as Holly landed in a twisted bundle of flames on the concrete ground below.

The crowd scattered in a chaotic cacophony of panic and screams.

Amidst the chaos I was dragged to my feet as a secondary detonation inside my office rang out and more flames erupted from the upstairs window.

"NO!" I screamed as police officers dragged me towards an awaiting van, my ears ringing as the uniformed officers around me sprang into action with their attention drawn now towards the devastation around them.

"Please… Please… someone get to Holly." I stammered through tears. "Get to her. She needs help."

The police van doors slammed shut behind me, locking me in the dark enclosed cage at the back of the vehicle.

[3]

or

19th August 2013.

"Let me get this straight," Jane gasped. "Are you telling me this guy is offering you an all-expenses paid trip out to Australia, a hundred quid a day per diem and a salary of three hundred pound a day on top of *that*? And all he's wanting you to do is go out there, liaise with Australian police, look over their files, make notes on anything iffy or any gaps or whatever and then come home? That's it?"

I nodded.

"And you're what? *Thinking it over?*" she asked.

I nodded again.

"Because you need to see if you can fit it in alongside what? All of the other copious cases and work you *don't* bloody have on at the minute? What is there to think over?"

I shrugged. "I don't know – maybe whether I'm the right guy for this?"

"As opposed to who?" Jane countered. "The police here have categorically stated they're not getting involved, right?"

I nodded.

"This grieving dad has had no luck from his MP or the Foreign Secretary?"

"Allegedly." I replied.

"So he comes to you. What's wrong in that? How do you think you're not the right guy in this situation? Didn't you say once you got that private investigator qualification that you were going to use it to protect the people who felt there was no one left to help them? You said that, yeah? You said that you were going to help people who felt helpless. This Arkin Dentz fella sure sounds helpless to me, Jake."

"Jane, I'm a recovering alcoholic with no specialised investigatory experience. I'm a private eye now because everything else was stolen from me..."

"You're good at what you do." Jane smiled. "Your confidence is for shit, that's all. But this could be really beneficial for you – get out of the city, go someplace where no one knows about you and this whole Mick Hetherington thing, excel the way I know you can... and Skype me and the boys every chance you get to rub all that sun and sand in our faces! We'll be here when you get back, I promise."

"I don't know, baby." I sighed. "I just..."

"Jake?"

I looked up from the floor for the first time and stared her dead in the eyes.

"Jake darling, we *really* need the fucking money!"

I sat in the departure lounge of Newcastle Airport, sipping on a ridiculously priced Diet Coke. I poured through the summary file I'd been provided by one of Arkin Dentz' solicitors minutes after the ink had dried on my signature at the bottom of an extensive Non-Disclosure Agreement they told me I had to sign before they would even look at *my* Contract of Service (which I'd stolen a template for off the internet when they emailed me a reminder to bring it to our final meeting).

From reading the summary file, the Australian police felt this was as clear cut as clear cut could be:

Maya Dentz left Perth in the company of her friend Anna Skelton and a girl Anna had been travelling with up until that point by the name of Sarah Fox. Enquiries completed around Anna and Sarah's original base in Perth indicated that they were looking to buy a cheap ride off the backpacker boards that they would be able to drive across the country. A friend of Sarah's put them in touch with someone she knew selling a not-that-old, purple-ish Holden Equinox "at an absolute steal".

By the time the girls got down to take a look, the vehicle was already getting sold there and then to a young Swedish backpacker by the name of Edvin Sixten – who was planning to use it to travel across to Sydney where he was going to look for work, according to the car's original owner. Conversation and bartering occurred and concluded before the vehicle was ever driven away and Edvin Sixten had agreed to share the journey with Dentz, Skelton and Fox, splitting the costs evenly.

They set off together in the first week of December. Over a week later, Sixten's body was found at the bottom of a cliff within the Blue Mountains on the other side of Australia. His suicide note was left on the passenger seat. Traces of Anna Skelton's blood was found in the backseat of the Holden Equinox along with the bags and belongings of Anna, Maya and Sarah, none of whom were anywhere to be found. Their respective families were duly notified.

Sydney Police led an investigation that saw search teams crawl through the whole of the Blue Mountains area, which in itself was an enormous endeavour seeing as the national park itself was 11,400 km² of steep cliffs, eucalyptus forests, waterfalls and villages surrounding the famous Three Sisters sandstone rock formation.

A nation-wide appeal was launched and aerial coverage was carried out across the whole of the route across the country the four were believed to have travelled, purposefully looking for fresh and undisturbed soil markings that could indicate shallow graves for the three women somewhere out there in the big orange expanse somewhere along the way.

A robust background check into Sixten indicated that he had been arrested in his native country at the age of eighteen for hitting his girlfriend. Charges were eventually dropped but the matter stayed on his file. Australian police saw this as an indicator of his potential for violence towards women. When no other leads were generated, despite extensive enquiries on both sides of the country the file got marked as resolved.

In the eyes of the law in Australia, Sixten had murdered three women and successfully disposed of their bodies before killing himself. Australia is a vast place. A lot of wild life out there in the outback and its various nature reserves. Their bodies are unlikely to ever be found. Etc. Etc. *Case closed.* The summary file indicated that the families of Anna Skelton and Sarah Fox had accepted these findings. Edvin Sixten's family appeared to have been left no choice but to do the same. Only Maya Dentz' father did not accept the police's conclusion as closure.

Arkin Dentz began a very expensive rebuttal against the Australian police, attempting to draw in the support of political figures within his social circles and high-ups within the police. His money was for nought and despite being rich, powerful and well-connected his demands for his legal team to be granted all copies of the entire evidence files for this case went nowhere.

His requests were argued extensively for a month straight until a compromise was reached whereby Sydney police would allow an independent investigator of Arkin Dentz' choosing to come and complete a case review with a member of their staff then report back to him.

And, with the UK police service having to diplomatically bow out on instruction from the Home Office, Arkin Dentz appeared to have reached down into the bottom of the barrel as options go...

... and found me.

I continued reading and re-reading the summary file once I was onboard the plane even though it was nothing more than a narrative breakdown, scant on actual supporting evidence.

I flew from Newcastle to London then London onto Sydney, with a stop-over in Abu Dhabi along the way, landing twenty-seven hours and thirty-one minutes later. My back and legs were in a state of cramp, my head hurt and I'd not slept anywhere close to the level I was hoping to.

Arkin Dentz had supplied me with a photograph of Maya; a cherub-faced, beautiful young woman with a black bob cut and dimples that seemed to run from below her eyes until they fell off the bottom of her face. At every difficult point in the reading of the summary file on my flights, I pulled the photo back out and stared at it hard. It preoccupied every moment when I should have been sleeping on the plane.

"This," Arkin had said as he shakily pressed the photo in my hand the night before I left Newcastle, "is why you're doing this. *This* is who you're doing it for. Not for me. Not for my peace. For this lady here. My daughter. Bring me the *truth*, Mr Lehman."

As I stood at the baggage carousel awaiting my luggage, I rubbed so hard on my eyes that I felt like I'd popped them with the force. Letting out the sigh only a broken man could deliver, I reached back into my notebook and took the photo of Maya Dentz out once more.

"Bring me the truth, Mr Lehman."

I quickly stuffed the photo and notebook away in my coat pocket on sight of my bags barrelling around the carousel towards me and grabbed them both as they attempted to pass. As the automatic exit doors speedily pulled opon I was hit with a wall of heat coming off the Arrivals lounge alone that made me not just regret wearing a coat but also in packing pretty much the entirety of the clothes I was carrying.

Remember that utter shit in that god-awful Richard Curtis movie, Love Actually? Where Hugh Grant tries to tie together some nonsense about the feeling of love and the arrivals lounge of an airport or some shite like that? Well, even if that was *remotely* true – and it isn't, there's got to be a time-based factor to that. Because I walked out into the Arrivals lounge mid-morning on a weekday and there was about ten people, if that, idly standing around with airport staff bustling around in and out around them. None of them looked loved or in the mood to love. They all looked a bit stressed and as if they all had better places to be.

Love, *actually*, was nowhere to be found.

What could be found was a very attractive red-head with a face full of freckles, standing holding a sign that said *'Jake Layman'*. She had the smile and bone-structure of a young Ellie Kemper, circa her run in the later seasons of The Office - The American version.

I stopped, squinted my eyes a little at the sign and decided to take my chances regardless.

I walked over to the woman holding the sign, dropping my bags on the ground either side of me.

"That's not quite my name but I think you might be looking for me?" I smiled.

"If it's not your name then I doubt very much I'm looking for you!" came the curt reply.

"I didn't say it wasn't my name. I said it wasn't *quite* my name."

"Is it your name or not?"

"Well, I'm Jake Lehman. L-E-H and you have it as L-A-Y..." I attempted.

"Ok, so you're the guy then?" the woman shot back.

"Unless you're rather amazingly waiting for a Jake Layman who came in on the same flight as me and who..."

"You're the private investigator from the UK, correct?"

"I am, yes."

"Then you're the guy!" she snapped as she lowered the sign and tucked it under her arm.

I smiled weakly. "I'm your guy!"

"I never said you were *my* guy. I said you're *the* guy!"

"This is going well, huh?" I said, extending my hand. "Jake Lehman, nice to meet you."

She took it and quickly, forcibly shook it. "Detective Constable Rachel Casey. I'm your liaison during your time here. You have your luggage, I see. Great. Let's go."

Rachel turned and started walking briskly without looking back to see whether I was behind her or not. I quickly grabbed my bags and took off after her, taking note of the very athletic build she carried beneath her smart trousers and dress shirt.

Because I'm married but not blind.

The drive out from the airport to the hotel was no less contentious than our initial introduction in the Arrivals lounge.

Combative didn't quite cut it as a description of her character.

It appeared that every attempt at a conversational ice-breaker was an affront to her in some manner. Before we'd even hit the halfway mark on our journey she'd already come to feel that I was "latently sexist" and "casting aspersions" on her professional experience.

I tried changing tack by asking about the bush fires that were raging on the other side of Australia, heading down the coast line towards Perth. There'd been stories on it on the news before I left and coverage of it was all over the screens at Sydney airport on my arrival.

"They'll have it under control." Rachel muttered. "It always looks worse on the TV and to you guys overseas who aren't used to that sort of thing."

I half-heartedly nodded and said "I guess."

As she pulled into the drop off point of the hotel, I smiled politely and asked what time she would like me to be ready for the next day in order to introduce me to the rest of her team.

"What team?" Rachel said sternly.

"The investigation team that worked this case?"

"I think you're terribly confused. Let me get you up to speed in case you've been misled by your client, Mr Lehman. You've been granted access to a case review with the relevant officer assigned to this *closed* case. That officer is <u>me</u>. You come to my office where all the files are waiting, you read through the files, you make notes but take away no copies of any one single page and then we are done. Are we clear?"

"Listen," I exhaled as she brought the car to a hard stop outside the hotel entrance. "Have I done something to offend you from the outset? I don't really get this whole instantly abrasive thing you've got going on towards me. Normally it takes people a good two hours or so to realise I'm a dickhead. You've been kicking my arse from the *minute* I walked up to you."

"I don't like my time being wasted Mr Lehman and I feel like this is a waste of my time, frankly." Rachel responded. "And what's more, your very being here feels like you're out to try and make our police service look bad by showing us how we fucked up on a job we were extremely thorough and attentive with. I'm sorry that I didn't have a bloody marching band and fireworks waiting for you."

I let out a little laugh. "Please call me Jake here on out, okay? And listen, I'm not out to sweep the legs of you or any of the other investigating officers on..."

"I wasn't one of the original investigating officers, Mr Lehman." Rachel interrupted. "I'm just the officer assigned to watch you read files and that's it. If you've got any more questions designed to complicate matters greater than that can you save them for tomorrow? I'll be outside here at eight-thirty am!"

I unclipped my seatbelt and started to clamber out the passenger seat as best I could whilst peeling off my sodden shirt that had been stuck to the back-rest with sweat.

"You know something, DC Casey?" I grinned. "I think this is the start of a beautiful friendship!"

"It isn't." Rachel fired back. "I assure you."

"Do you know who once said that too? Murtaugh about Riggs! Are you familiar with the Lethal Weapon films and..."

"Get your bags out the back or I'm driving off with them."

"Okay. Okay. We'll talk tomorrow." I laughed, swiftly pulling open the rear doors and grabbing my bags.

She pulled away within half a second of the back doors closing on her car.

As I turned to look at where to go a sudden a haze fell over my vision and my head started to feel like it was inside of a vice.

Is this what jet-lag felt like?

I had no point of comparison because I'd never been on a journey that long before. It certainly felt dangerous to me because the next thing I knew I was sitting down on the edge of the bed in my hotel room, minus any recollection of how I'd got here or what I'd done downstairs to actually check in.

My mouth felt so dry and my throat was stiff. There was a bottle of water in my bag. I just need to find the energy and steadfastness to stand up, go over there and take it out. Instead my eyes fell upon the minibar in the corner of the room. Like a Terminator zeroing in on a target, I scored sight of the mini bottles of Jim Beam lined up on the second shelf down almost immediately.

The corners of my mouth felt like they'd crusted up instantaneously on sight of the bottles and I swallowed hard whilst running my fingers through the stubble on my chin and up onto my lips.

I blinked furiously and stood up, grabbing my laptop alongside the water bottle from my bag as I did and then flopped straight back down onto the bed.

It felt like a twelve round boxing match just to power up the laptop and activate Skype.

[4]

or

"Welcome to the Game."

Custody suites had changed considerably since my time in the police. Everything was much more streamlined nowadays. Like a factory conveyor belt. Within seconds of being brought through the pin-coded access doors, I'd been dropped down onto a hard mental bench, picked back up again, brought up to the custody desk before a weary-looking Sergeant, had my handcuffs removed, reminded of my rights, told I would get access to a phone-call in due course, had all of my clothing removed and bagged in secure/sealed evidence bags, strip-searched and hit in the face with a packet containing a paper all-in-one suit and told to "Put it on NOW!" by the observing police officer. Then I was pushed all the way down along a corridor of cells and politely guided into one by a gaoler who had zero interest in my protestations to be allowed to make a phone call before they slammed the steel door shut behind me.

The click of the lock and the closing of the small observation gate in the centre of the door dialled my panic levels up and, trust me, I was *seriously* panicking.

Not just about being arrested for the murder of Bobby Maitland. But... but...

... My team? Holly, Richardson-Jones and Catrina? That explosion was *huge*. No one could have survived that. Holly certainly didn't. I saw her burning body fall. Did Richardson-Jones and Catrina get out in time through the fire exit? Had anyone notified Psychic?

What the FUCK was going on?

I paced.

I relentlessly paced.

Back and forward. Back and forward. Over an hour passed.

Maybe two.

I had no concept of how long I'd been in there.

The door to my cell clicked and opened and the same gaoler that put me in there now beckoned for me to come out. I exited and walked back up the corridor into the main custody suite where two plain clothes police officers were waiting for me.

A man and a woman.

The woman pointed at a nearby bench. "Take a seat. We'll be with you in a second."

I flopped down on the bench, lowering my head but keeping myself locked in on listening to the woman as she finished up her conversation with the man stood next to her.

"We work chronologically, okay?" she said quietly. "Dentz was discovered first, so we hit him with that. Then Maitland. Then..."

She looked down at the paper in her hand.

"... the three from his office, we don't have ID's on them yet, is that correct?"

The man shook his head. "Nor do we know if the explosion was something we can tie to him either."

I went to stand up. "Excuse me, go back a second, did you just say the name Dentz just then? As in Arkin Dentz?"

Two police officers rushed me and pushed me back down into my seat.

The woman spoke assertively. "Please keep in mind you're under caution, Mr Lehman. I suggest you save anything you have to say until we press record on our interview."

"Someone needs to tell me what is going on?" I replied. "Please?"

"I'm under the impression you've waived your right to legal representation at this time, is that right?" the woman said.

"I'm sorry but who are you?" I snapped.

The woman stepped forward and closed the gap between the two of us. "I'm DS Lisa Clarke and this is my colleague DC Gareth Mitchell. We're going to be speaking to you about why you've been arrested today..."

"Are you confirming Holly, Leigh and Catrina are dead?" I said quietly. "Is that what I heard you two talking about just now?"

"Three bodies have been recovered from the explosion at your office earlier today. We have yet to identify them. I suggest we continue this in a more formal interview setting under caution and..."

"I want my phone call." I said through tears. "I want my fucking phone call now."

Suddenly the security door on the far side of the custody suite buzzed loudly and swung open as Chief Constable Jessica Lane pushed her way inside, flanked by two uniformed officers either side of her.

We'd become fast friends since Emily first introduced us and she came to head up the police service this side of the river. We'd become even closer over the last couple of years in a social capacity and my rejecting of her Consultant Investigator job offer hadn't done any damage whatsoever to our relationship.

I gasped a little at the sight of a friendly face at such a fraught time.

"Detective Sergeant!" Lane said as she approached. "Can I have a word urgently please?"

Clarke smiled, nodded and stepped towards Lane.

Whatever Lane had to say it was said quietly and conspiratorially into Clarke's ear and it made her eyes widen and do a double-take in pulling away and meeting Lane's eye line.

Lane moved her head affirmatively.

The look on her face and the size of her eyes strongly indicated this wasn't good and as she turned to come my way there was a very clear, very distinct feeling that my awful, awful, hellish day was about to get so much worse.

She placed her hand gently under my arm and lifted me out of my seat, guiding me carefully to a nearby room where she and a Chief Inspector I'd never seen before entered after me and closed the door behind them.

"Take a seat Jake." Lane said softly.

"I'll stand."

"Take a seat Jake." Lane reiterated, pushing harder on each word.

I sat.

Lane pointed at the Chief Inspector. "This is Chief Inspector Brest. He's here at my short-notice request to come and observe our conversation so I can't be accused of unfairly advising you or interfering in anyway. I want you to know that I cannot comment on what you've been arrested for. I've come here as a friend because there's been reports come through that there's been a fire at your home..."

I felt right away like I'd been cut in half and my body was reacting to searing pain.

"My... home... is on... fire?" I stammered.

"Jake, listen very carefully. There's been a considerable fire and your property has been burnt to the ground. I've had it confirmed no bodies have been found but..."

"What about Jane and my boys?" I cried as tears fell hard and fast.

"No bodies have been found but the scene examination process hasn't been officially concluded. I myself haven't been able to get a hold of Jane and..."

"WHAT ARE YOU SAYING?" I screamed.

"Jake, you need to listen as best you can and try and focus on the facts I'm giving you." Lane said as her eyes welled up. "There's been a fire at your home as well as at your office and Jane and the boys are currently missing. They're not answering their phones and..."

I stood up shakily to leave

"Don't!" Lane said. "Don't do anything to worsen this situation Jake. Please. I beg you. I don't know what is going on. I know that it doesn't look good, but you have to trust me here. I will make sure everything is done to gather all of the facts and try and get to the bottom of this whole thing - because it just doesn't make sense. I mean... I knew you and Bobby were going through a rough patch and..."

Chief Inspector Brest leant across and whispered "Ma'am, be careful."

Lane stopped herself and nodded.

She cleared her throat and stood up.

"I will keep trying to make contact with Jane, I promise!" she said before walking quickly from the room and wiping a tear from her eye as she went.

Brest was not far behind her but before the door could close, DS Clarke entered with DC Mitchell by her side.

"Mr Lehman, further to your arrest on suspicion of the murder of Robert Maitland I am now further arresting you on suspicion of the murder of Arkin Dentz. You do not have to say anything. But, it may harm your defence if you do not mention when questioned something which you later rely on in court. Anything you do say may be given in evidence. Do you understand?"

"Wait... *What?*" I gasped through my sobs.

Prior to the interview beginning, they'd allowed me to make my phone call.

Of course I made sure it was to Jane.

Her number rang out.

I clicked the phone back down into the holster and swiftly picked it back up again and re-dialled before anyone could spot me or tell me I couldn't. Her number rang out again.

There was no voicemail.

There was *always* a voicemail. I knew the lilt and inflection on every word of Jane's voicemail recording, I'd left messages on it so frequently. But it was not there.

I attempted to squeeze in an attempt to change course and call Psychic but the custody sergeant spotted me and ordered me to put the phone down.

"It's not a 'ring-around your entire contact book' process, thank you very much!" he shouted.

I stepped away from the phone and allowed myself to be led to Interview Room 3.

"You're an accomplished investigator, aren't you Jake?" Clarke said as the interview got underway under the whirl of a recording device far more impressive and up-to-date than the old double-deck cassette recorders I used as a police constable. "You're essentially world famous now because of the Baadir Gadiel and Stephanie Jason double-whammy, right?"

I stared at her without saying a thing.

"So you tell me as a world famous investigator what you'd think here. The landlord of your business property is found murdered in the early hours of this morning with a fresh partial match of your fingerprints found at the scene near the body. Hours later, Bobby Maitland is found murdered in the same manner with what we believe is the same weapon and you come running from the scene covered head to toe in his blood. We learn from Maitland's closest associate that there was some tension, or 'bad blood' if you will, between you and Maitland lately over an unpaid invoice and now he's dead too. There are more fresh partials of your fingerprints on a weapon found at the scene..."

"We're awaiting results from tests to see whether there are strands of Arkin Dentz' blood on the knife too." Mitchell interjected.

Clarke nodded and continued. "... And CCTV footage from Grey Street and Maitland's property itself show that nobody else went in or out in the time leading up to Maitland's murder. Come on Jake, this is *not* a good look at all is it?"

"What would the infamous Jake Lehman think if he was presented with these facts on a case he was leading the charge on?" Mitchell smiled officiously.

"Was there some dispute with Arkin Dentz too?" Clarke said. "Was he planning to evict you or put up the rent or were you in debt to him or something? Is that why you went round there and cut his throat?"

My eyes widened.

"The first... I fucking knew... that Arkin Dentz was *dead*... was when you fucking arrested me... for his fucking murder!" I snapped.

"Then how were your fingerprints found fresh at the scene? When were you last around at his property?" Clarke replied.

"I'm just... I'm... just... not doing *this.* Get me a fucking solicitor." I shouted.

"Oh. You want a solicitor now?" she smirked.

"Are you having some sort of psychotic breakdown, Jake?" Mitchell sneered.

"What did you just say?"

"You heard me. Are you having some sort of breakdown that has set you loose on a campaign of revenge against everyone you feel wronged by? Because right now, your house is burnt to the ground with your family nowhere to be found, your landlord has been found murdered and nine miles along the Coast Road your business associate who you've recently fell out with has been found dead in the same way. And we're not even touching on the three dead because your office has mysteriously blown up as well. What happened there Jake? You just spat your dummy out and decided to wipe them out too. Why? Were they repeatedly late? Took too long a lunch break? Why did they deserve to die too?"

I jumped to my feet. "GO FUCK YOURSELF! HOW DARE YOU? HOW FUCKING DARE YOU? I DON'T KNOW WHAT IS GOING ON BUT I KNOW THAT I HAVEN'T KILLED ANYBODY. I NEED TO GET OUT OF HERE. I NEED TO KNOW THAT MY FAMILY ARE..."

Clarke slowly rose to her feet and gently raised her hand. "You need to calm down and put yourself back in your seat. You're not helping matters behaving like this. Do you understand? We'll suspend this interview at this juncture and allow you the opportunity to access legal representation, okay?"

I flopped back down in the chair next to the custody suite telephone and looked to my left and right to see how closely I was being observed. Not feeling like there was any one particular set of eyes gawking down on me, I leant in and dialled Jane's mobile phone number one more time instead of the number above me on the board which identified how to access a duty solicitor.

It rang.

And rang.

And rang.

And then the line clicked open which caused me to inhale hard in anticipation of hearing her voice on the other end.

Instead a digitised voice spoke out down the line. Unidentifiable as either male nor female, it played out instantly without giving me a chance to speak first.

"Hello. Jake Lehman. What we do in life echoes out. Our actions reverberate and create consequences and effects we must own. It is time for you to be responsible for your own reverberations... Welcome to the game! Your wife and children are in my possession. If you alert anyone to our contact your wife and your children will die. If you show disobedience or disrespect to the game your wife and your children will die. If you fail to achieve the objectives of the game set for you within the timeframe given your wife and your children will die. If you achieve all of the objectives laid out over the course of the game then your wife and your children will be set free to continue their lives. The game will be explained to you in greater detail at the start of the next round should you make it that far. Round One begins..."

The digitised voice fell silent.

"... Now! A mobile telephone has been placed within your belongings currently held in police custody. This mobile telephone only accepts incoming calls. You cannot call out on it or send text messages through it. If you attempt to circumnavigate such communication restrictions then your wife and your children will die. This phone will ring again at seven pm this evening. By the time it rings you must be free from police custody and ready to move quickly into Round Two. Good luck in your efforts and I look forward to meeting with you in due course."

The line clicked and went dead.

I staggered up onto my feet but my legs wouldn't work properly and I felt like I was going to faint. Mitchell and Clarke walked towards me and Clarke looked at me with an expression of concern.

"Are you okay?"

"They've got... They've got my..." I stopped myself.

"Good news for you anyway, Lehman." Mitchell interrupted. "You've got a bit of extra thinking time for your bullshit before we go again - your pal Chief Constable Lane has requested you be transferred down to Middle Engine Lane and put in custody there for the time being!"

The clock on the custody suite wall showed the time to be 16:35.

[5]

or

"The Great Escape."

Have you ever seen the 2008 action movie Eagle Eye?

Most people who have will tell you that it sucks. But let me bravely stand alone here and tell you that Eagle Eye is actually pretty fucking great, and frankly the only reason people say that movie sucks is because of its reveal / ending. Let me back up a second:

In Eagle Eye Shia LaBeouf - back when Shia LaBeouf was a big, mainstream commodity - plays this deadbeat slacker type called Jerry who gets entangled up with this complete stranger called Rachel, played by Michelle Monaghan. Then they both receive these random mystery phone-calls from this emotionless voice demanding that they complete a series of increasingly dangerous tasks throughout the US or their lives and their family's lives are at risk.

It's a bonkers movie and I *really* recommend it. Or at least two thirds of it anyway. Because in the back third of the movie - and SPOILERS for a decades-old action blockbuster here by the way - it is revealed that Jerry and Rachel are being called and instructed by a supercomputer that has become sentient in order to carry out a political assassination. Or something.

Let me tell you lot this for nothing - if it turned out all of this hell involving my family being at risk was down to a sentient bloody 1980s Sinclair ZX81 or whatever I would be very, very vexed indeed. So, I get that reaction to Eagle Eye. I do.

This *isn't* Eagle Eye.

I promise.

I thought about Eagle Eye for some bizarre reason that only the very deep parts of my brain will ever be able to fathom as Mitchell handed me over to two uniformed police officers who were going to be guarding me on the transportation between Forth Street police station and Middle Engine Lane police station.

"See you at the other end, Superstar Private Eye!" laughed Mitchell.

I looked down at myself, still clad in the paper suit I'd been made to wear since arriving in police custody.

"Hang on," I said. "You're not seriously making me travel like this are you?"

"Your clothes have been taken away to have tests carried out on them. You can go naked if you like?" Mitchell smirked.

"There's a fucking blizzard going outside. Knee-deep snow. Sub-zero temperatures. And you're going to make me travel like this?"

One of the officers dragged me backwards and away before Mitchell could say another thing.

"Stop your whining," he laughed. "We'll turn the heating up in the van."

The access door to the custody suite buzzed open and I was pushed off down a ramp to an awaiting police van with the rear cage doors open, readily awaiting my arrival. Two police officers either side of me set the pace a little faster then I probably would have preferred. Another officer, the driver of the van stood smirking on sight of me as I was dragged towards him.

"What a fall from grace, eh?" laughed the driver who I immediately christened 'Burt Reynolds' in my mind because he was a fat, pale lookalike of the late actor. "You were hero of this bloody city... what... like three weeks ago or something? Now you're going round murdering people?"

"I don't know," grinned the police officer to my right, who we're going to go with calling 'Steroid Steve' for reasons I'm sure are clear to readers as astute as you. "There's a lot of people out there that would see murdering Bobby Maitland as still quite an heroic act."

Burt Reynolds took hold of me at the bottom of the ramp and pushed me into the awaiting cage. "This murderous twat right here cost my brother his job in CID thanks to him running his mouth off about the Hadenbury shit back in the day. There's *nothing* heroic about him."

"Has anyone ever told you that you look like Burt Reynolds?" I said. "Only more like if Burt Reynolds had taken time off from 1985 onwards to just sit and eat lard all day?"

Burt slammed the doors, locking me inside.

I could hear Steroid Steve and his colleague laughing at the jibe to Burt Reynolds from inside my cage.

I started to think fast.

I needed a plan and it had to be better than just taking my chances of kicking out at these guys the minute the cage opened at the other end because I knew all too well I'd already be locked inside the custody compound at Middle Engine Lane by the time these doors opened again.

Maybe fake an illness? Collapse or something and force them to take me to hospital where I'd have a better shot at getting some sort of escape going from there? Perhaps.

I was shaken from my thoughts as Steroid Steve and his compatriot climbed inside the main body of the van and slammed the door behind them.

"Do you have the time?" I shouted.

"Ten past five!" Steroid Steve shouted back. "Now shut up buddy, okay?"

I nodded and smiled.

I looked through the panel off the cage and strained to see through the windscreen up ahead as the sound of the internal gates rolled open and Burt Reynolds started to slowly move out into the dark night air.

Walls and walls of relentless white snow careered down and the police van's windscreen wipers were working in overtime to try and keep them clear.

Muffled somewhat as it was to my ears inside the cage itself, I still heard well enough as Burt Reynolds shouted back to the rest of the van and hit the red button to activate his blue lights at the same time:

"Batten down the hatches, ladies and gentlemen. Newcastle Council have given up the ghost on clearing or gritting the roads, we're in a state of gridlock along most stretches of our intended route, it's rush hour and we're heading out into sixty mile an hour winds and what looks like an avalanche falling from heaven! ... This should be *fun*!"

The wheels of the van spun under the texture of the surface outside as we headed into the blizzard.

The more the body heat rose inside the van the more the windscreen steamed up and added another barrier to Burt Reynolds' visibility as he valiantly tried to battle on through heavy traffic. The limited visibility upfront drastically reduced my ability to keep my bearings as to where we were at any point on our route out of Newcastle and down to the main police custody suite inside the headquarters in North Tyneside.

Jesus Christ, this was some fall from grace. Who could argue with that?

Earlier this same year I was sat in the Chief Constable's office at the very top of the building, being feted for a job with the police service. A mere month after that I was being lauded as a hero and brought back into the same office to be commended for my actions on what was meant to be Newcastle Day. Now I'm being driven through a snow storm to the very same building in order to be dropped into the bloody custody dungeon regarding murders I know I didn't commit.

What the hell was going *on*?

Steroid Steve was in no mood to play satellite navigation with me either.

"Where are we?" I shouted as I banged on the internal wall of the cage.

"Shut the fuck up! That's where we are!" he bellowed back.

"That's not a place. That's just a statement." I replied.

"Okay. How about 'Shut the fuck up street' south of 'It doesn't matter where we are avenue'? Is that any better for you?"

"Sort of!" I sighed.

Steroid Steve shook his head at me and went back to checking his phone.

The lights ahead of us and the manner in which moments later the interior of the van lit up as we passed into them gave me a strong indication that we were going into the underpass at Jesmond and would be coming out the other end down in Jesmond Dene and then up the embankment onto the Coast Road.

"Listen..." I fake slurred as I banged my head purposefully against the cage wall. "I'm not... feeling... very well... I need some... help here!"

"SHUT UP AND PACK IT IN!" screeched Steroid Steve's colleague who wasn't distinct enough in any way for me to garner him with a nickname.

"I'm not feeling... well." I mumbled as I fake-fell out of my seat onto the ground.

"Hey!" shouted Steroid Steve. "He's passed out back here!"

"For real?" I heard Burt Reynolds shout back.

"I don't know." Steroid Steve responded. "But he's on the bloody floor right now!"

"We're ten minutes out from Middle Engine Lane and conditions are bad. Let me call it and have some people on stand-by to help. We'll just have to get there. There's nowhere safe for me to stop along the Coast Road."

"You better not be faking, you little shit!" shouted Steroid Steve's pal.

I mumbled a bit more of what I presumed someone would sound like in their death throes.

I could hear Burt Reynolds on the van's radio asking for urgent medical assistance to be waiting at Middle Engine Lane police station. I could hear Steroid Steve too, positioning himself closer to the cage wall in order to look through at me as I lay on the floor.

"He's still breathing." Steroid Steve shouted. "I can see rise on his chest."

I kept my eyes closed and let my jaw hang loose.

The plan was that I was going to let myself go floppy the minute anyone tried to pick me up out of the van on arrival, let my face droop, slur about chest pains and hope an ambulance was called. I'd worry about fighting my way out of the ambulance further down the line. But it was going to be a hell of a lot easier to free myself from an ambulance than fighting my way out of a secured police 'meat wagon' that's certainly for... ...

Suddenly my entire body contorted against its will and I was twisted in a way that caused my head and shoulders to slam hard against the roof of the van as my legs and hips came crashing down into my face. Then I was lying on the roof as the seating and floor beneath me was now fixed above my head. The sounds of metal crunching and impacting in against something was genuinely horrifying and...

BAM!

Another spin of the van itself saw me rotated against my will again, now smashing repeatedly off the floor, the ceiling, the seating block... round and round I was spun.

I caught sight of Steroid Steve as he came flying at speed into the cage wall but he was soon gone from sight again just as fast as he appeared when another deafening crunch led off another tumultuous turn of our surroundings.

Then it all *stopped.*

The surface beneath me felt uneven and warm, thick blood started to pour down into my eyes. Soon the hooded collar on my paper suit was drenched in red. Pretty soon the cuffs and stomach area of the suit began to darken with blood seepage too.

I stared out into the darkened depth of the main body of the van but could not make out any one person or any one thing.

"Is everyone... okay?" I tried my best to shout.

There was the soft cackle of the police radio up ahead.

I could feel myself starting to fade out when the back end of the van itself started to abruptly lift, sliding me a few inches forcibly into the internal cage wall. The front end of the van started to bear down into black and I heard the crunch of tree branches and gravel beneath me.

"Woah! Woah! WOAH!" screamed someone within the van in a state of terror and then...

The van started yet another tumble. This time it wasn't horizontally across hard concrete terrain which is what the last few spins had felt like. This was *down.* This was a plummet which was met with a hard and sudden impact with ground below.

Smoke immediately blasted loose from the engine block right back up into the main body of the van and I began to panic as the area I was trapped within slowly started to fill up with dark grey, stinking fumes. I began to cough.

The panic was short-lived only because the black slide around my eyes arrived and I slipped into unconsciousness.

The first thing I saw through my blurred vision upon coming back round again a few minutes later was the bent and buckled cage doors at the rear of the van as I lay on the ceiling, upside down inside the battered police van. There was enough damage to possibly get the doors opened with a little bit of coercive force on my part.

I just didn't know whether I had the effort in me.

Blood from somewhere on my head continued to flow down, obscuring my vision. My chest and legs ached and my right hand was very close to being completely numb.

I pushed hard on the door as best as I could. It wasn't enough. I leant back onto the ceiling that was now my ground and kicked out at the buckled door. It just about gave way, certainly enough for me to reach into the gap I'd made and press the clasp down to free the cage doors completely.

I crawled out and landed in the cold, wet sludge of a semi-frozen stream of water with a high snow-covered embankments either side of me. Pushing hard to gather my bearings, I looked up at the smashed terrain down into where we'd come to rest and I started to figure we'd come up off the Coast Road at the old bridle path next to St Peter's Field in Wallsend.

But how? We were travelling on the other side of the dual carriageway. Burt Reynolds must have lost complete control for us to have not only crashed but to have smashed over the central reservation, skidded as far as we had and plummeted down into this embankment.

This had clearly been the very sort of crash that if you'd been watching it in a Michael Bay movie you'd have thought "Well I'm sure everyone is absolutely fine and will only need a quick second to have their hair restyled!" even though the vehicles flipped over thirty-two times and burst into flames twice, but if you'd watched it in reality you'd definitely have gasped "There's no WAY anyone could have survived that!"

And yet here I was.

Surviving.

Just.

I couldn't yet bring myself to completely stand so I pulled myself as best possible through the cold and wet beneath my hands and knees to get to the main body of the van. The side door was half open. I could see before I pulled it all the way that the expressions on the faces of Steroid Steve and his colleague were motionless and their contorted bodies definitely indicated they could not possibly have survived.

Up top on the road above us a commotion of sorts was heard and headlights that appeared at the broken fence line indicated someone or some people had pulled up at the scene. I tried to shout out to them but the pain was too much. Instead I pulled myself into the main part of the van where Steroid Steve and his partner lay dead and I grabbed the evidence bag at Steroid Steve's feet containing my belongings, fingering through it from the outside to make sure that there was a mobile phone inside like the digitised voice of command had stated.

I could see from inside the van that Burt Reynolds was hanging upside down and bleeding quite badly but he was still breathing. He suddenly became more thoroughly lit in the position he hung from when a small fire burst from the engine and flames started to gently peak from the broken dashboard of the van.

"Hey?" I whispered. "Hey, are... you... okay?"

"We... were... rammed." Burt slurred.

I heaved myself from the mid-section of the wreckage and dragged myself round to the driver's side door and started to work at pulling the door open. It wouldn't budge. I relied on the smashed window to reach inside and help free Burt. He unclipped his own seatbelt and fell into a crumbled heap into the footwell. I could no longer get to him from where I clung.

Burt turned himself around whilst screaming in pain and I was able to take hold of him under his arms and pull him through the window.

"My ribs! My ribs!" he screamed as I did so.

"I know. I know. I'm sorry." I whimpered as I grimaced through the pain.

I dragged him as best I could to get to the furthest point of the embankment away from the burning vehicle and then collapsed down next to him, my paper suit now torn in various places and soaked through with blood and dirty stream water. Rigid, sizeable flakes of snow continued to plummet all around us. We'd fallen to the ground in exhausted agony as the fire built, both of us completely unaware of the two dark figures slowly making their way down the makeshift stairs at the top of the embankment.

"Do you... do... you have a... phone?" I said shivering.

Burt Reynolds slowly nodded and pointed to the zipped pocket on the breast of his illuminous stab-vest. I reached over and set about removing the phone.

"The pin code?"

"Use... my... radio!" Burt stammered.

"The radio is smashed." I said, guessing.

A loud gunshot unexpectedly rang out. Amidst the sound of panic and scattering from the usual rubbernecks up top on the Coast Road, a voice was heard to shout out "JAKE LEHMAN!" through the darkness.

"Come out, come out wherever you are!" another voice followed. "If you've survived the little meet-cute with our cars that is!"

I looked at Burt Reynolds.

"This... isn't... good, is... it?" I spluttered.

"Friends... of yours?" Burt replied.

I reached down and pulled the asp baton from Burt's holder on his stab vest whilst shaking my head and pushing his mobile phone into my other hand.

"I need your... pin code... for your phone." I whispered. "Because... I need to get...help. Whoever... they are... they're *not*... friends!"

Another shot rang out.

"This is going to be the easiest ten grand ever earnt!" one of the voices laughed.

Then there was another shot.

"Stop wasting shots, Wayne." The other voice said through the darkness more quietly.

"Fuck!" I snarled, extending the asp baton and using it to push myself up to my feet.

The van exploded out a small ball of fire that indicated a build was starting to occur and the whole thing was going to go up any minute.

The fire lit up enough of my surroundings for me to be able to get bearings on where the two men were before they got sight of me. I pushed myself into some nearby undergrowth and excruciatingly held my breath in deep.

The first man passed me by and as soon as he did I bit down hard on the inside of my mouth to swallow the pain and pushed out in order to fall in behind him. As I did I lashed out with the asp on the back of his legs and knocked him to the ground. Before he could turn I hit him twice across the back of the head with the asp, knocking him unconscious.

A fast rustle was heard to indicate the second man was coming this way quickly and I grabbed onto which direction he was coming from just as the night sky seemed to light up with the spinning blue sirens of approaching emergency service vehicles.

I grabbed the first guy's shotgun and fell backwards off balance just as a bullet slammed into the ground beneath me from an oncoming attack.

I pulled the trigger twice in quick succession as I slammed down into the ground.

There was a groan and then a scream from maybe ten metres away.

I got myself agonisingly to my feet and stepped over to the second man, now lying on his back with his head tilted down into the stream. Blood bumped out of a large wound on his right shoulder. He was tattooed up to the eyeballs and couldn't have been more than twenty-five years of age. If that.

"Who… are you?" I said.

"Fu…ck!" the young man stammered back.

"Who sent you? Why… are you… after me?"

The man said nothing.

I raised the shotgun and pressed it against his eye socket.

"Do you… know… what… pisses me off?" I garbled through the pain, hoping he'd be in too much shock to remember the barrels of the gun were empty after two shots. "Unanswered… questions!"

I started to squeeze on the trigger.

"You… killed Bobby… Now there's a price… on your head. Ten… grand to… whoever… clips you!" The man coughed and blinked rapidly.

A hit out on me for a murder I didn't commit? That was fast. But with Bobby gone who the hell stepped straight in and put that together?

"Who put… the price… down on me?" I asked as the sirens drew closer.

There was no response.

His eyes had rolled back into the side of his head.

Fuck!

I dropped the gun and reached down to check his pulse. It was still there, thankfully. I felt his breath under his nose too. I pulled his jacket from off of him and made my way back over to Burt Reynolds who was now looking a deadly pale colour.

"Just to be clear…" I stammered as my teeth chattered with the cold. "They were… alive… when I left them… okay?"

Burt stared back at me without saying a word.

"You tell them I rescued… you, okay? Promise?" I said as I pulled the man's jacket on around me. "I didn't… have to… do that. I could… have been long… gone by now."

Burt nodded slowly "1-1-0-2…"

"That's your phone code?"

He nodded again.

The police van finally gave out and exploded into a larger fireball.

I stuffed the evidence bag containing my belongings inside the jacket, pushed Burt's mobile phone and police asp into the pocket and zipped everything up.

I knew if I got up the embankment and onto the path on either side of the stream then I'd be leaving thick, clear and bloodied footprints in the snow as I went and that would be far too easy a tip-off for the arriving police. Instead I stuck to the stream, pushing myself on to stumble painfully as quickly as possible along through the dark, dirty and semi-frozen water beneath my feet.

I fell out eventually into the expanse of Burnside Dene nearly ten minutes later, struggling to breathe and get my bearings through the darkness. I knew I didn't have much left in me and that if I pushed myself on too much further I would collapse out in the open. I hastily crossed over to my right and made my way to The Crow Bank that led from Wallsend Green into Burnside Dene itself.

There was a thick nest of trees and bushes off to my left at the bottom of the steep embankment. I clambered inside as best as I could, covered myself with foliage and shakily dialled Psychic's number.

There was no answer.

I could feel myself fading as the clock on the smashed mobile phone screen flashed over to 18:03. I did everything I could to hang on just long enough to dial one more number before my head lolled back against my will and I started to pass out due to the pain.

I wanted to believe I got enough information out about my location and circumstance before I fell into unconsciousness. But I couldn't be sure.

[6]

or

21st August 2013.

The jet-lag had left me in such a state where I think I could have brought myself round to semi-consciousness and a reasonable functioning state after perhaps another day's worth of sleep. Maybe a day and a half?

Instead I'd had just shy of ten hours. All because I read some stupid bloody post on the internet before I left the UK that said the 'trick' to combating jet-leg "instantly" is to force yourself to stay awake if you land during the day and sleep only in line with the country's night time where you've landed. So I ended up spending the previous afternoon pottering around the hotel grounds, going for a walk in a circle around the block where the hotel was based, dozing off in the hotel gym's jacuzzi and then eventually falling asleep in the chair in my hotel room whilst watching some awful Australian drama about bicycle police or whatever they were meant to be.

I rose with the alarm the following morning, washed under the force of a power-shower that made me feel like I was being assassinated by a million blasts of wet machine gun fire, shaved and dressed then sat down to a breakfast in the hotel restaurant that was meant to be the "fried breakfast" option but turned out to be a plate of some meat I didn't understand the concept of what it was trying to be and scrambled eggs buried beneath a pile of mushrooms and tomatoes.

I *detest* mushrooms and tomatoes so pushed the plate away and downed black coffee like it was cold water delivered to me in the centre of the Sahara desert instead. I grabbed a couple of Danish pastries too.

By the time I was done Rachel was idling in her car outside the hotel's reception and I walked out to meet her with the warmest fixed smile on my face that I could muster.

"Good morning!" I beamed falsely.

"Morning!" she said without turning to make eye contact with me as I climbed inside her car. "How's the jet-lag?"

"Refusing to go away!" I said as I tried to click my seatbelt into position.

She sped off out the car park before I was done.

We arrived at the Sydney police station I'd be working out of over the next few days and I was suitably impressed. It looked more like the sort of glass-panelled high rise you'd expect Wall Street brokers to be working out of. Once we had parked, I followed Rachel through the main doors into this big, open expanse of office spaces that span out into an upwards rotating vista, floor after floor.

I stopped to take it all in.

Rachel saw that I had and came back to get me.

"Don't get too attached. The department you're working out of isn't any of these." She said before pulling me on a bit.

"What are all these then?"

"These are... well... everything, really." She replied as she pushed me to walk to the elevators at the far side of the ground floor atrium. "You've got your neighbourhood units, your serious crimes, arrest warrant teams... they're all somewhere up there. *We're* not though... so come on."

"Where do the actual prisoners go though?" I asked.

"There's a custody suite one floor down."

"And where are you based?"

"One floor below that!"

I saw a flicker of a grimace across Rachel's face as she pressed the button for the elevator which arrived in a matter of seconds. We walked inside and her finger dropped below the 'basement' button and pressed hard instead on the one marked '-1'.

"And what's your department again?"

"We're the 'Cold and Closed Case Review Team'." She said as the elevator dropped. "But I use the term 'we' very loosely."

The doors pinged open and we were immediately met with a darkly lit, windowless open plan room. There was no door to enter into it. No corridor to walk up. Just a room, filled with desks that had no one sat at them and computer monitors that didn't look like they'd been switched on in a while.

In the far corner was one desk that had a flickering light coming from the rolling screen-saver on an active computer screen. Files were piled up around the legs of the desk.

Next to it was a wooden table and chair, cleared of anything.

I looked around slowly, taking it all in.

"Who did you piss off to end up here?" I said wryly.

Rachel strode on over to what I had assumed correctly was her desk.

She pointed at the boxes.

"These right here represent the entirety of the investigation carried out into Maya Dentz and her travel companions. All statements, all police enquiry reports, all forensics, all exhibits... they're here!"

She lifted the first box and dumped it loudly on the wooden desk near to her.

"You can read through them at whatever speed you like. You can't take anything. You can't copy anything. You *can* make notes. Before you leave our legal department has asked that you let us make a copy of any notes you do make. If you have any questions, ask them. That's what I'm here for."

"You'll be around to help then?" I said.

"No. I'll be around to watch. If I *have* to help, I will." She responded coldly.

"And you'll be..."

"Right here!" Rachel sighed, flopping down into the chair at her desk. "Watching you!"

I sat down and opened the first box.

Nothing was filed in any particular way or with any sense of organisation that was going to be remotely helpful to me. I reached in and pulled out the first piece of paper that lay across the top of everything else.

It was a photocopy of a small piece of notepaper. The corner of the photocopy had all the relevant police evidence codes and filing information on. I took in the body of the note itself – a scrawled one sentence missive that simply said *"I'm sorry! It got out of hand!"* with the dots on the exclamation marks replaced with hastily drawn circles instead.

"What's this?" I asked.

Rachel leant forward, studied the piece of paper in my hand for less than a second and then exhaled hard and with a sense of the over-dramatical. "That's Edvin Sixten's suicide note, found on the dashboard of the vehicle."

I nodded and placed it to the side of the box.

"Will you be doing this with *every* sheet of paper that you bring out of the boxes?" she said. "Because this could extend the time my superiors have projected for this piece of shit assignment if that's going to be the case!"

Flash forward three days.

Yes, *three* days.

Three days of sitting hunched over box after box of paperwork, scribbling notes down of things that were interesting to me or things that I wanted to ask follow-up questions about.

... Three days of thinking to myself over and over that this room really needed better lighting and a stronger wattage of bulb.

... Three days of letting my eyes fall to my right for just a second only to find Rachel sat sprawled in her chair either staring intently at the side of my head or checking something out on her phone but never anything other than the former or the latter.

... Three days of dropping hints that it would be good to get out of the building and take a lunch-break somewhere 'interesting' because I'd never been to Australia before, only for Rachel to walk away and come back from the canteen with a shitty sandwich of her choosing and a bottle of iced tea. (The beverage was a real fucking nipple-twister of consternation frankly because I told her after the first day that I don't like iced tea – so you can understand I was beginning to think that Rachel was actually just a full-on bitch, frankly.)

... Three days of diving deep into every single fact and every single lead that the Australian police had secured on this. And you know, Arkin Dentz was probably not going to find this easy to hear but during this initial period of looking through everything it certainly did seem like the police *had* been very thorough.

But then I went and ruined it all by doing something stupid like... starting to find the holes in the investigation scattered throughout.

I was attempting to intersperse my work with futile attempts at rapport building with Rachel as she sat burrowing a hole in the side of my head. I tried mutual interests in television programmes. That didn't work because the shows I liked she said they didn't get over in Australia. I tried films we both might have a shared enjoyment of. That failed too because according to Rachel she "didn't have time" to go to the cinema.

I'd taken it upon myself to turn the radio playing quietly in the corner of the room to some 'greatest hits of the 80s and 90s' type station and every so often I'd click my finger and point in the direction of where the song was coming from and say things like "This? You must know this? This is a *classic*!"

She would just shrug and accuse me of being an 'old man' even though I was probably only about eight years older than her.

On one particular day where I managed to draw Rachel into saying more than two or three sentences the whole bloody day by getting her to talk about some Australian band called Last Dinosaurs or something, I came across a series of photographs of Edvin Sixten that had been printed off and bundled together.

"What are these?" I asked.

"Those are the most up-to-date photos of Sixten, last uploaded to his social media account, in the immediate lead up to his suicide." Rachel replied, leaning over from her desk to look.

"He sure does love that hat, huh?" I said as I pulled a magnifying glass from my bag and focused in on in the grey porkpie hat he seemed to religiously wear in every shot that he was featured in. On close-up examination I could see that the hat appeared to be covered in distinctive patch-badges for various places. Front and centre on the brow was a stitched badge that represented the colours of the Swedish flag. "He appears to sew a badge on to represent every place he's been to."

Rachel shrugged and sat back into her chair.

"Was he found with the hat?"

Rachel looked at me quizzically before finally replying "He was found in an exploded pile of his own self at the bottom of a very high cliff, Mr Lehman."

"*Okay*," I sighed. "Do you know if they fished that *hat* out of the bloodied pile of gloop that used to be Edvin Sixten then?"

"What's your fascination with the hat? What are you thinking there?"

It was my turn to shrug. "I don't know, probably nothing. It's just it doesn't seem like the guy has been far from the thing from the minute he left his home country and now I'm not seeing it listed on any of the property records for what was found at the suicide site or what was found in the abandoned car and... well... as I said, I don't know. But that's intriguing."

"I have no answer for you and unless you give me a direct line of evidential enquiry relating to the hat specifically then there's not a lot I can do. But who knows? Maybe he got blood splatter on it whilst killing one of the women so he buried it somewhere in order to hide the connection to him."

"Legitimate line of thought," I replied. "However, he certainly didn't bury it in the Blue Mountains did he? Because according to these investigatory records, you guys had sniffer dogs rip that place apart in all its vastness and they'd surely have picked up *that*, don't you think? And secondly, why would he need to hide the 'connection' to his crimes? He's essentially admitted to it in that note and then killed himself as far as your investigators are concerned. He doesn't have a single fuck to give thereafter, right?"

Rachel leant forward again and propped her head on her hands as she placed her elbows forcibly down on the corner of the desk between us, clearly smelling the sense of sarcasm I'd laced my previous statement with.

"Is this your plan of attack then, Mr Lehman? To not only look for areas where evidence has failed to be explored by our police - which is what I was told your agenda was going to be anyway - but also to diminish the grounds we established our suspect on?"

I sighed and rubbed my eyes and the corner of my temple.

"What if there is no agenda, DC Casey?" I replied wearily. "What if I was just out to chase the facts wherever they take me – and if that takes me back to the UK with no further lines of enquiry or established fact to give my client then so be it? What if that was all there was to this?"

Rachel smirked. "Hmmm. Bull*shit*."

I pushed the photos to the side and picked up a file I had been looking at earlier.

"I was just shooting the breeze with you on the hat thing, one investigator to another. But if that wound you up I don't know what you're going to think to the question I had from earlier this morning."

"Go on..." she responded.

"You ascertained that for where Sixten's car was found in that particular area of the Blue Mountains it would have had to pass along a specific stretch of road where a ranger station was based, is that right?"

"That's correct."

"And that ranger station has an external CCTV point with the ability to cover at least the registrations for all vehicles going up that road, with partial coverage for them coming back down."

"Correct." Rachel said.

"And the lines of enquiry conducted determined that in the twenty-four hours alone leading up to the discovery of Sixten's body, the positioning of his vehicle, track depth or whatever you have it explained as in the summary, there was a total of one hundred and sixty-six vehicles pass along that road."

"That's what the records show."

"Have they been run through any systems? Have they been checked and drivers identified etc?"

Rachel grabbed the nearby summary page and scanned it with her eyes. "Long answer? If it doesn't say so on here then no. Short answer? No."

"Why not?"

"Because no one considered it to be necessary at the time, obviously. They clearly thought it irrelevant to the evidence that was presenting at the scene. And I cannot see any superior would sign off on me doing it now?"

"You need something as basic as that to be okayed now? You can't just fire up some police national computer or vehicular database and me and you can roll the registrations?"

"Something as 'basic' as that huh? What are you getting at Jake..." Rachel snapped.

"Oh. Sorry. Now I'm Jake?" I snapped right back, a little bit perturbed that something that felt standard to me hadn't been done then and yet now would be fairly hard to justify.

"What? You want to waste the rest of the time you have here sitting and doing data entry on one hundred and sixty six bloody car registrations in the hope that one of them was stupid enough to register the vehicle under the name '*Shhh. I'm Maya Dentz' real murderer. Please don't tell anyone*'? Is that what you're suggesting?"

"I'm not suggesting anything. I'm *asking*. I'm asking you as the best liaison I've been gifted in representing the Australian police to explain to me why this wasn't done as standard just for the value of potential unexplored witnesses alone."

"And *I've* told you that I wasn't one of the original investigating officers and I'm not going to second guess them as..."

"Yeah," I sneered. "You keep reminding me as to what you're *not*. But what actually *are* you in this process? Because so far, you hold a detective constable rank yet you seem to only have the skill set of a fucking librarian who's watching a customer read a really rare book in order to make sure they turn the pages softly enough!"

"Oh. You're shitting on *my* rank and standing within the police service?" Rachel gasped in mock indignation. "You who... what... judging from your age lasted all of five minutes in the police service before deciding to hang his hat out there as some Jim Rockford wannabe."

"That's an old reference for someone as young as you. Normally I get Magnum PI." I half-smiled.

"They show re-runs of The Rockford Files on a weekday afternoon here. It's a good show. It holds up."

"I know, right?" I started to say. "It's..."

"No. Wait. Fuck *you* Jake." Rachel snapped.

"No, *you* wait. We're starting to bond now." I tried.

"No, we're really not. Trust me. Find your own way back to your hotel."

She turned and walked away towards the elevator, smashing her knuckle hard into the button to call it down and it seemed to take an age to arrive to let her get in it and away from me.

"This is awkward," I shouted. "Shall we make small talk until you get the chance to leave or shall I just stand here silently and watch you go?"

"I don't give a fuck. You seem to know everything Mr Lehman, so *you* choose."

The elevator arrived.

I made my way back to the hotel that evening via a taxi and I arranged my way back to the ostentatious police station the next morning too, careful to secure receipts to match up with the daily per diem spends Arkin Dentz had granted.

Reception staff at the police station were indifferent enough to any real security measures of weight and buzzed me through to take the lift down to Rachel's dungeon pit all on my own.

By the time Rachel showed her face a good ninety minutes or so later, I'd been hard at work tearing through the files soundtracked to some choice musical hits from the late 1980s into the early 1990s. Without her around I'd taken the liberty of turning the radio up high and I was chair-dancing whilst writing to Phil Collins' sublime hit, 'Something Happened on the Way to Heaven' when she exited out of the elevator into the workspace.

"♫♫ ... How many times do I have to say I'm sorry, yes I'm sorry. How can something so good go so bad. How can something so right go so wrong. I don't know, I don't have all the answers. But I want you back... ♫♫"

I mouthed along to the next bit whilst looking directly at her and smiling. "How many times can I say I'm sorry?"

Rachel stood on the spot and put her hands on her hips.

"Phil Collins!" I shouted, pointing back at the radio. "Surely you can't hate Phil Collins? Nobody hates Phil Collins. *Nobody*. Not even his first wife – and he divorced her via fax back when faxing was a rich person's thing!"

Rachel was unmoved.

"This is my favourite Phil Collins song!" I continued. "And Phil Collins has done a lot of amazing songs so that is saying something. He is great, man. He really is. Did you know that this song was written for the movie The War of the Roses?"

Rachel's eyebrows burrowed.

"Have you seen The War of the Roses? Oh God, that is a masterpiece of a film. It is so dark but yet so funny."

Rachel looked over to my desk.

"♫♫ ... We've had our problems but I'm on your side. You're all I need, please believe in me, oh yeah. I only wanted someone to love. But something happened on the way to heaven. It got a hold of me and wouldn't let go ... ♫♫"

I pushed out my chair, got up and walked over to the radio and turned it down slightly.

Turning back to face her, I hit Rachel with the information tsunami I'd been waiting for the last forty-five minutes to land on her.

"You know Sixten's vehicle? The purple Holden Equinox he purchased in Perth?" I started. "The vehicle has 18,197.9 miles on the clock, right? The log book he signed ownership of on the day he took the car off the previous owner's hands shows that this was the mileage at the point he took the car on. That's documented here, okay?"

I slid a copy of the vehicle's registration documents and service history across the table to separate them out from the pile of paperwork I had going on.

"... And by the estimate I've just done here, Perth to the Blue Mountains is a trip of 2,385.5 miles right? So that would mean that even with side-trips, possible detours, getting lost and all of that, the minimum mileage we should be looking at is around 20,583.4 by the time the car is found abandoned. Wouldn't you say?"

"♫♫ ... We had a life, we had a love. But you don't know what you've got 'til you lose it. Well that was then and this is now. And I want you back. How many times do I have to say I'm sorry, yes I'm sorry. You know you can run, and you can hide... ♫♫"

Rachel wouldn't say anything. Her hands did not budge from her hips and her eyes did not move from burning directly into my skull.

"But it's not. It's not 20,583.4 at a rough estimate." I said. "It's 18,966.1."

I clapped my hands together as if this was the quintessential mic-drop moment.

There was nothing but silence in the room.

"Okay... well... '*So what are you saying Jake?*' I hear you want to ask me but find yourself unable to do so for some reason" I pushed on. "Well Rachel, thanks for not asking but secretly wanting to anyway. I'm saying either one of three things - the mileage has been tampered with or rolled back before they set off or since coming into police custody OR at around seven hundred and sixty miles, give or take, into their journey they hit a ramp high enough and fast enough to fucking fly the rest of the way across the country OR that car didn't make that trip from Perth to the Blue Mountains in the conventional way we're thinking it did!"

Rachel turned on her heels and walked straight out, this time not waiting for the elevator to arrive but instead kicking open the fire exit door tucked away in the far corner and storming off up the stairs out of sight.

[7]

or

"If This Has Been Written Well Enough So Far, This Is The Chapter You'll Need In Order To Catch Your Breath A Little Bit."

The priest said "You may now kiss the bride!" and I leant in so quickly to kiss Jane because I was so overcome with how beautiful she looked and, just as our lips were about to meet to the sounds of cheers from our friends and family, it all flashed white and…

… and … and… There I was suddenly back in the Metrocentre, battling it out with Jason Grant in a fight to the death. I grabbed the nearest piece of cabling and started to furiously wrap it tight around his neck, pulling tight as I went and causing shards of broken fairy light glass to embed into his skin and small lines of blood start to emerge. "This? *This* is how you hang someone, you sick fuck!" I screamed. And with that I pushed myself over the railing and took Jason with me.

Then *FLASH*… I was bouncing along in what seemed to be the back of a vehicle as who I could only just make out to be Luke 'Jimmy' Brody drove at speed through the darkness, slipping and sliding along the road as snow pummelled every inch of the car and Luke's voice cried out to me as I shivered beneath what seemed like piles of covers and duvets. "Stay awake Jake, mate. Stay awake. Talk to me."

My eyes rolled back and… there was my boy Jack in my arms, wrapped in a soft baby blanket, no more than an hour old. I couldn't stop kissing him. I remember that. It was the same when Jonathan was born. I couldn't stop kissing him either from the minute he arrived on this earth and then… *FLASH* … I was right there in the room as baby Jack was pulled from between Jane's legs and instantly placed upon her chest… *FLASH*… There I was, sat on Jonathan's bedroom floor threading string through the bottom of two paper cups so we could make 'telephones'.

"Talk to me Jake. Talk to me buddy." Luke shouted.

I was dying.

This had to be the whole life flashing before your eyes bullshit, right?

It had to be because now I was on Byker Bridge, with Jeff Petersen raining punches and kicks down upon me. "Traitors will NEVER supersede patriots!" he screamed manically as he pushed himself to his feet and slammed kick after kick into my torso. I shrieked in pure agony as the third kick audibly broke my rib cage and thumped me through the railings and, just as I thought I was about to plummet to my death, I realised I was hanging backwards over one of several workmen's cages fixed to the low side of the metro overpass.

... FLASH!

There was Jane, lying naked in bed post-sex, laughing.

... FLASH!

There was the fine dust-like dirt of the Australian outback falling through my fingers.

... FLASH!

"Help... me..." I heard myself say as street-lights lit up the interior of the vehicle momentarily and Luke spun a hard corner in hazardous conditions, desperately trying to keep control of the car.

... FLASH!

Rachel Casey was stood in front of me. She winked at me and reached out her hand, revealing an ice cold bottle of Coopers Pale Ale in her grip.

Then the white went black and I was... *gone.*

I came round to find myself lying on a sofa in an unknown location with the sound of the sea smashing hard into rock. I heard a female voice rattle me even further awake with a shrill shout of "He's up!" and I struggled to sit up.

I was surrounded and covered up to the neck in piles of duvets that had been wrapped both around and on top of me. I could feel that I was wearing proper clothes now and I hazily reached down under the blankets and felt with my hands, discovering the feeling of an ill-fitting long-sleeved t-shirt and a pair of jeans that were maybe a couple of sizes too big around the waist.

Luke appeared in front of me and helped me gently into a better seated position.

"If it isn't Dr Richard Kimble himself!" he smiled softly.

A gentle punch landed on Luke's arm and he stepped aside to reveal Psychic stood next to him. A heavily pregnant Emily was sat behind him in a nearby chair, drying her tears. And in front of me was Luke's girlfriend, Jennifer.

Jennifer Howard was an old school friend of both mine and Luke's that I had not seen in a long time. Hers and Luke's was a grand on-off love affair that was a story in and of itself. But, of course, now is not the time for any of that is it?

"Where… am… I?" I grimaced quietly through agonising pain.

Luke had invested a lot of his freshly acquired wealth in various pathways and one such route was in buying up property and having development teams do them up, rent them out and bring him a tidy little return each month. He had some apartments scattered around the North East. He had some stuff down South, a couple of properties over in the Lakes and a nice little place up in Edinburgh that he'd locked down a couple of months back.

The boy had come a long goddamn way from the brain damaged Neanderthal 'thumper' everyone had written him off as even as recently as just a couple of years back.

"You're in one of my properties in North Shields, mate." Luke replied. "I got you here as quickly as I could the minute I found you down in Wallsend."

I nodded. "Thanks. I wasn't… sure… I'd got the call through before…"

"Crashing out? Yeah, you did thankfully." Luke smiled. "You're not good Jake. I've done the best I can stitching you up and what not but I was never much of a cut-man, you know that right? I was always more the guy getting cut."

I half-smiled as best I could.

"I've stitched up your head and I've dressed your wrist as tight as I could. I think it's fractured. Your ribs are broke too. You're going to have to get properly checked." Luke continued.

I shook my head. "There's no… time. Where's the… the… phone?"

Psychic held up the police property bag with my belongings in it. "This?"

I nodded. "What time is it?"

"It's nearly seven o'clock." Jennifer responded first.

I reached out with difficulty and took the property bag from Psychic and leafed through it to find the phone that the 'voice' would call me on any minute.

"What's going on Jake?" Psychic said.

"Does he even know about Holly and the team?" Emily said as tears fell again.

I nodded as my own eyes filled up. "It happened right in front of me."

"So what's going on then?" Emily said. "What the hell is going *on*?"

I took a deep breath and tried to cover everything as quickly as I could or at least as quickly as the air in my lungs would allow me to through the pain. The more I talked the more ridiculous it all sounded and I could see that by the widening eyes of all the people listening to me.

Any one of these things on their own could be the plot of a preposterous straight-to-DVD B-movie Nicolas Cage would likely be asleep at the wheel of as he continued to still pay off his tax debts. Or a bad Saw sequel, made long after anyone stopped giving a shit about them – starring a barely conscious Nicolas Cage who was only in it to pay off those tax debts. But put *together*? Jesus Christ, I sounded like a mad man… Finding Bobby dead, being arrested, the office blowing up with our team inside, being told Arkin Dentz had been murdered and my prints were at the scene and then the voice, the creepy fucking voice…

By the time I got to the disappearance of Jane, Jack and Jonathan the silence of my audience was finally punctuated by the sound of Emily breaking down sobbing and Psychic gasping as he fell back into a nearby seat and covered his hands with his mouth.

"Go back a second – Arkin Dentz? Our silent-landlord Arkin Dentz?" Psychic queried.

I nodded. "I'd not seen him in years. Everything just ticked along. We'd share occasional emails and phone calls but that was about it."

"So how are you fingerprints at the scene of his murder?" Emily asked.

"I don't know Em'. I don't bloody know."

"And what?" Luke chipped in. "We just sit back, waiting for the phone to ring and for this mysterious voice to give you the next command?"

"This is some proper Die Hard with a Vengeance shit!" Jennifer said.

Our heads all turned and looked directly at her.

"What?" she said incredulously. "Don't act like you all haven't seen that film, yeah? The phone calls demanding that Bruce Willis has to complete all these tasks or…"

Her sentence finally trailed off as if she'd finally found it in herself to read the room.

"Sorry!" Jennifer said. "But in my defence I came up here for a night of fine dining and bullshitting with all you guys and now? Now we're in a real life version of… of… what's the name of that Die Hard 3 knock-off with John Cena in it, babe?"

She looked over to Luke. Luke in turn slowly shook his head and put a finger to his lips.

"A computerised voice?" Emily said, forcing the conversation back onto the required track.

"A computerised voice!" I confirmed.

Emily slowly shook her head.

I started to talk about the van accident and the young men with guns who claimed there was a price on my head for the murder of Bobby Maitland.

"Who the hell has sat down in Bobby's chair before its even gone cold and started putting out orders like that?" Psychic asked. "It's not likely going to be one of his big rivals from the other side of the river is it? They'd be *applauding* you."

I shrugged.

"Ten grand isn't massive money for that sort of task amongst the heavy-hitters either." Luke offered. "Let me make a call or two to people I think will be able to shed some light on this. In fact, fuck it, I'll just call Ryan Flaherty and ask him directly. I came up on the amateur boxing circuit with his younger brother, Mark. He's a really good kid. He'd vouch for me if Ryan starts acting like a dickhead."

The vibration came first and the ringtone quickly followed as the phone inside the property bag lit it up and I attempted to move quickly to pull it free and answer it. I daren't risk putting the call on speakerphone in case whoever was on the other line picked up on that and assumed I was in a room with the authorities. Instead Psychic leaned in with his own phone and tried as best as possible to record what was going through the earpiece.

The minute I clicked to accept the call the voice started in without giving me a chance to speak once again:

"Hello. Jake Lehman. Welcome back to the game. Congratulations on completing Round One. You did not pull any punches in your completion of Round One and this shows a commitment to the game I hope will continue. As a gesture of goodwill for the impressive manner in which you have conducted yourself in Round One, you have earned one proof of life."

There was silence.

And then Jane's voice broke out over the telephone.

"Jake? Jake baby, the boys are okay. I promise. We're okay. I need you to..."

The line clicked and Jane's voice was gone.

"JANE!" I screamed through a voice swollen in anger and emotion as tears cascaded down my face.

"Round Two begins now. Your task is to return to the scene where an individual known to you as Stephanie Jason was found dead. Upon arrival at this scene you will be granted a meeting with me in person and you will be given a new phone. You will also be given new instructions regarding Round Three. You have sixty minutes to…"

I began to scream over the top of what I assumed was an automated recording. "Fuck you! Fuck YOU! I don't give a shit about some quick recording of my wife you're trying to pass of as proof of life. I want *actual* fucking proof of life, you sick piece of shit. Put her on the phone NOW!"

The digitised voice was gone by the time my interruption had finished.

There was just quiet.

Nothing.

Psychic looked worryingly over his shoulder to Emily.

Jennifer looked up from her seat at Luke.

Jane's shaking voice came on the line and everyone including me seemed to exhale in union.

"Jake?"

"Jane? Jane darling, is that really you?"

"It's me. Listen I'm not being given long. We're all alive and unharmed. I promise."

"What time is it Jane? Tell me the date and time quickly?"

"It's just after seven pm. It's December 23rd. And I love you."

"I love you too. I'm so sorry Jane. I'm so sorry that…"

The line clicked and the digitised voice kicked back in.

"I am not a recording Jake Lehman. You are talking to a human being and you will respect me. I will not tolerate bad manners. As a result you have received your first sanction and you now only have forty-five minutes to appear at the previously described location. If you alert anyone to our contact your wife and your children will die. If you do not come alone to the previously described location your wife and your children will die. If you show disobedience or disrespect to the game your wife and your children will die. If you fail to achieve the objectives of the game set for you within the timeframe given your wife and your children will die. If you achieve all of the objectives laid out over the course of the game then your wife and your children will be set free to continue their lives. As promised, the game will be explained to you in greater detail at the start of the next round should you make it that far. Round Two begins… now!"

The line clicked again and the call was over.

I let my head drop into my hands as the phone fell down on the sofa next to me and I began to sob even more heavily.

"Who the heck was THAT?" Jennifer said.

"Maybe one of Hadenbury's old foot soldiers, newly released from prison and out for revenge?" Psychic offered. "Think about it, Round Two is dragging you back to where Stephanie Jason was found. That Stephie Jay case was what brought Hetherington, Hadenbury and all their guys down... That could be a link?"

"Someone out for revenge against you guy's is a foregone conclusion for the type of cases you two have solved but this is very specific to Jake." Emily rebutted. "I've not been taken. He wants Jake and Jake *alone* involved in this game. This is about *him.*"

I looked up panicked and confused and made eye contact with Emily.

"So you don't think it's one of the Knights of George then?" I asked. "There's a lot of them still hiding out there in the shadows."

"And they could have some residual money belonging to Bill Collins to fund whatever this is because whoever it is has got a long-game planned, surely?" Psychic added.

"Then why aren't you Player Two?" countered Emily.

"Maybe I'm going to be? Maybe I'm going to get buzzed into this sick game in Round Three or Round Four?" he replied.

"I'm due to give birth any fucking minute Robbie Dayer!" snapped Emily. "Why would you say shit like that?"

And then the classic Psychic-Emily squabble kicked in.

"There's no time for this!" I shouted as the room fell silent.

"I can't just be reactive to this guy. I have to get myself two or three steps ahead of him and try and find out who he is because if I don't there's nothing to say I'm going to just do everything he asks and then he's going to kill Jane and the boys anyway. I need to get in a position to derail his plans and get my family free."

"If it's a man." Jennifer offered.

We all turned to look at her once again.

"Not now, Jen honey." Luke whispered.

Emily exhaled and placed her hands protectively on her baby bump. "I'm going to try and open up a discreet line of communication with Jessica Lane and alert her to this killer-from-the-Saw-movies wannabe and try and get the police onside."

"Good luck with *that.*" Psychic said.

"And I'm going to start ringing round and see what we can do about this price on your head and who the hell put it there." Luke proffered.

I struggled up and onto my feet, finally getting my bearings within the top floor apartment we were situated in near the mouth of the Tyne as stormy seas lashed outside and snow smashed against the window. I kept a tight grip of the waist of the jeans as they nearly dropped down. "Luke, do you possibly have any better fitting clothes then this… and maybe a weather-appropriate coat?"

Luke smiled and started to leave the room.

"I need to borrow your car too" I shouted after him.

Psychic looked at Emily with a look of alarm.

Her face twisted and then she eventually nodded her head.

"I'll drive you." Psychic said.

"No. No way." I immediately countered. "I have to go alone and you need to stay here with Em'!"

"It's fine." Emily replied. "I'm going to stay here. Jennifer can keep me company. Luke isn't going anywhere and he's an even better bodyguard than my man here could ever be…"

Psychic playfully flicked her the finger.

"You are in no fit state to drive," Psychic said. "I'll get you where you need to go and I'll stay out of sight and… well… if Emily's waters break, I'll abandon the shit out of you, I promise!"

[8]

or

"This Chapter May Upset You".

We drove out of North Shields in silence, Psychic wanting to take the long route in Luke's gun-metal grey Land Rover Defender 2022 into town and over the Tyne Bridge to get to Hebburn instead of cutting straight through North Shields town centre and down through the Tyne Tunnel to the other side of the river. He was paranoid that we'd get picked up through the windscreen on their new and sophisticated toll booth camera system or spotted by some of the security staff there and come to be pinned inside the tunnel itself by an ambush blocking us in at either end.

He was probably right if I'm honest but it didn't help my anxiety as we were cutting it fine to get to Hebburn by quarter to eight, especially driving in these conditions when traffic flow was all but at a snail pace on nearly every road.

I'd popped paracetamol and ibuprofen before leaving the apartment. They hadn't make a single bit of difference to the cluster of injuries I now carried. The only positive that could remotely be etched from all of this was that the pain in my ribs and my wrist was so intense that it at least distracted a little from my usual back ache and hip discomfort. If I'd only known they were to be the start of a long night collecting physical harm to my person I probably wouldn't have griped so much.

Luke had loaned me a pair of his jeans and there was something a little disconcerting that his skinny-fit style was the perfect semi-baggy fit for me. He'd paired them with a quilted Superdry military style jacket that I pulled a little tighter around me as we pushed on through Jesmond. Johnny Matthis' version of 'Do You Hear What I Hear?' played quietly in the background on the radio, both of us sitting pretending to listen to it but really just lost in our thoughts.

"♫♫ ... A star, a star. Dancing in the night. With a tail as big as a kite. With a tail as big as a kite. Said the little lamb to the shepherd boy. Do you hear what I hear? Ringing through the sky shepherd boy. Do you hear what I hear... ♫♫"

Nobody calls Johnny Mathis' version of 'Do You Hear What I Hear?' by that name anymore do they? They all call it the 'Gremlins Song' because of how indelible it is to that movie. It was so effectively used in that film that it could never shake off the attachment. Not to anyone I know anyway.

Eventually I leant forward and clicked the radio off.

"Shit sticks, you know?" I said.

"How'd you mean?" Psychic responded.

I didn't bother leading in with my Johnny Mathis / Gremlins analogy. I just got straight down to it. "Even if I come out the other end of this, which isn't looking likely, and even if I clear my name it won't ever be truly *clear* will it?"

"Like Michael Barrymore?" Psychic offered helpfully.

I stared at the side of his head. I think he could feel me doing so as he very carefully mouthed the word 'Sorry!' and I continued.

"Everything's gone now, hasn't it? Let's be honest." I said forlornly, looking out the window as we took the underpass down through Manors towards the Tyne Bridge. "I don't know if I'm ever going to see my wife and my boys again. The business is blown to bits. They're not going to be going ahead with that option on a movie about us now and..."

"They've made films about worse people who did worse things than anything you've been accused of, Jake. Look at Hannibal Lecter."

"Hannibal Lecter wasn't a real person." I said quietly.

"Bullshit! Of course he was." Psychic gasped.

"Nope. Total fictional creation."

"Jesus, really? Okay, well what about Ted Bundy or... or... the Zodiac killer, you know?"

"I don't think either of them got the royalty cheques, if you know what I mean?" I countered.

As we crossed over the Tyne Bridge I couldn't hold back any longer and I started to sob uncontrollably.

"I can't not see Jane and the boys again, Psych'. I can't." I cried. "I don't know how to live without them being a part of my life day in and day out."

"That's just not something you need to be thinking about." Psychic said assertively. "Because it isn't going to happen. Listen, if this is it and this is us having to escape from everything being burnt down around us by some sick fuck with a grudge then let's go hard on one last ride together and grab this bastard and pull him down into the flames with us, okay?"

I wiped the tears from my eyes.

"I could do with a more sedate change of direction once the baby arrives anyway." Psychic smiled. "So let this be my last high octane hurrah before I go to work in a call centre or something."

I half-smiled.

Psychic reached into the back with one arm as he drove and pulled his kit bag from the rear footwell, dumping it into my lap in one fluid motion.

"Now, here's what I'm thinking," he started. "I drop you on the outskirts and circle the area and look for any sort of van that this twat might have used to get to the old Hark Roy building. I'll sneak up on it and if Jane and the kids are in there I'll break them out and run, if they're not I'll slam a GPS tracker on it and then let it play out so the hunter becomes the hunted."

"I don't know mate." I replied. "I don't think whoever this guy is will make it that easy and if we get caught doing this he'll kill my family."

Psychic changed direction. "Okay, what about this? You stick one of the covert button-hole cameras on and you record your interaction with him. You try and coerce an admission out of him about Dentz and Maitland... Hell, get him to confirm he blew our office up too. And then no matter what else happens, I'll make sure the footage gets into the hands of the police."

I looked down at the bag and back to Psychic.

"That *could* work." I said with a grin.

Callerton Industrial Estate was all but a ghost town when Stephanie Jason's body was found there, a result of the economic free-fall that had hit the UK back then. Whilst there'd been some financial stability in the region since it hadn't helped the Callerton site in Hebburn and the association to the Stephie Jay tragedy definitively killed what business was left for the remaining biggest warehouse units in the North East. Nobody wanted to be associated with it for fairly understandable reasons.

The minute you passed through where the security gates once stood, manned by Bobby Maitland's long-since-left Blue Light Security company you could see, even in the pitch black of this devastatingly cold winter's evening, that the warehouses all looked like the broken up ruins of some post-apocalyptic wasteland. It was crazy how bombed out the whole place had come to look in such a short space of time.

We had little time to spare on arrival and I utilised it to get hooked up with Psychic's button-hole camera unit, run a test on it all, stick a pocket flashlight into the side of my coat and begin the long, freezing cold limp up the dark path towards the old Hark Roy site.

I wasn't just trembling with the cold and the pain. I was shivering with discomfort. This was my first time returning to the scene of where Stephanie Jason had been found and it felt all the more traumatic now, having full knowledge of what had *truly* happened to her and how she'd come to be found here. And what on earth could whoever was doing this to me and my family have with the Stephanie Jason case? Why were they forcing me back here?

I stopped outside the old, rusted and ruined loading bay door and bent down, retching with the pain as my mind flashed over the prospect that I had possibly got new private security mercenary buddies of Jason Grant and his team on my tail now.

That made sense. Slightly.

If anything it was just about crazy enough to fit in with the sheer insanity of everything I was caught up in right now.

I finished vomiting and picked up a handful of pure white snow from the ground nearby, forcibly wiping the thick frozen clump around my mouth to take away some of the awful taste I was left with.

Taking a deep breath, I clicked on the flashlight and cautiously slid through the broken door into the interior of the building.

My torchlight bounced hesitantly and with uncertainty around the huge dark breadth of the warehouse. I was finding nothing until the clanking sound of an old door was heard off in the far left corner, followed by shuffling footsteps making their way across the dirtied concrete floor.

I quickly scanned my flashlight over to the sound and fell backwards on my feet in shock at the sight of a bright white ceramic mask bobbing out of the darkness. As the light eventually formed more steadily around the rest of the shape I came to realise the figure was clad head to toe in black attire and the mask was the centrepiece.

The figure danced.

They fucking *danced*.

There was a skip into a twirl and they came to stop twenty or so metres across the expanse of the warehouse from me. They finished off with old style jazz hands before reaching up to their neck and pressing down on a small circular black device they had fastened there with a thick strap.

"Hello Jake Lehman. It's wonderful to finally come face to face with you!" the digitised voice familiar from the previous phone calls emitted out from the neck device. The mask rose and fell ever so slightly as the words came out, confirming to me that whoever was in front of me was speaking the words that the device released. *"This moment has been such a long one coming. I'm excited that it is finally here. I truly am."*

The figure drew a small handgun from the back of their waistband and playfully dangled it from their hand. *"Just in case you were thinking of rushing me or anything like that, Jake Lehman. I know how you like to play all the hallmarks of a have-a-go hero."*

I stood frozen to the spot.

"Why are you doing this?" I finally said.

"Such a cliché of a question don't you think, Jake Lehman?" came the digitised response.

"Really? I'm the fucking cliché here? You're out here dressed like the killer in a bad 80s slasher movie, pulling off some scam you ripped from one of the Saw sequels and putting me through the ringer like some Bruce Willis action sequel... but *I'm* the cliché?"

The figure danced from one foot to the next.

"It amazes me that you can still be so feisty with me, Jake Lehman. I thought you would have understood your place in these proceedings by now."

"And what's my place exactly?" I snarled.

"Your place is to do as you are told to by me and to keep doing what you are told until I am finished with you. And I will be finished with you when I feel you have reached your end. Physically, mentally, emotionally. When I feel like you are done and you can't walk another step or think another thought, I will end this game. At the game's completion my need for collateral will have expired and therefore my need for your family will end and they will be released."

"How do I know that you will do that? How do I know you're going to let them live?"

"They will live because that is the agreement I have made with you. And I will stick to that. You have my word. My word matters."

"Your word doesn't mean shit to me. There's nothing stopping you murdering them like you did my friends or Bobby Maitland or..."

"All of those people were necessary machinations in order to set the tone of the game. They were required to show you who it was you were playing against. Regardless, they were all associates of you and because of their poor taste they were completely expendable."

Please be recording... Please be recording... Please be recording...

I fought the urge to adjust my coat lapel to be sure the angle for coverage was *just* right because that would be a dead giveaway. No one can pull that shit off inconspicuously, can they?

"You really have some sick fucking blood lust for me, don't you? What'd I do? Expose you as a cheat to your wife? Get you sent to prison for some stupid fraudulent scheme? Come on, what?"

The figure did the most eerie, excited little dance.

"There's so much still left to unfold isn't there? You've led such a life that you can't figure out who your greatest nemesis could possibly be in these circumstances can you?"

"Greatest nemesis?" I fake laughed. "Have a bloody word with yourself. You're this week's villain of the week at best!"

The figure flicked the handgun back up into a controlled grip and pointed it right at me. *"You don't get to be so flippant with me, Jake Lehman. You don't get to live the murderous life of an unchecked vigilante, choosing who should die at your hands and receiving no consequence for your psychotic behaviour. You have no idea how long I have lay quietly under your skin, living your life alongside you and learning everything I need to know about you in order to use your weaknesses against you and expose you for exactly what you are - you're a treacherous hypocrite who hides behind the cloak of someone who demands that he is lauded for grand acts of heroism when really such acts are selfish attempts to dilute or diminish all the sins you carry upon your soul."*

"Wow. That was overwritten. How many drafts did you do on that? Be honest? Because I think you thought you were hitting some sort of Shakespearean tone there. But really? It was kind of like a bad Thanos speech from The Avengers films. I know you said this moment was a long time coming for you and everything but I want you to know that you *blew* it. You blew it badly because that sucked."

The figure stood motionless. I could see the eyes beneath the ceramic mask flicker and twitch.

"You know, when you first spoke to me back in the police station I was worried that you were doing an Eagle Eye on me. Have you seen that movie? I was concerned you were just a super computer or something, you know? But you're obviously not, are you? Though I kind of wish you were because a computer would have drafted up something a little better than that bullshit you just spilt. So... which one of your friends' deaths do you think I'm personally responsible for then?" I continued, trying best to hold everything together just long enough so that I didn't take my chances and charge this piece of shit down whilst he pumped me full of bullets.

"How many people have you indiscriminately murdered such as it is that you have come to lose track? Furthermore, I understand that you have built this glib, action hero stream of waffle into your personality, Jake Lehman. But as we move forward you will come to understand that it only serves to work against you because I will not be disrespected." The figure pretended to check their watch and then flicked the gun to their left. *"Bring your light over here please, Jake Lehman."*

I slowly moved the torchlight over to where I was directed to and space on the far right of the warehouse was suddenly lit up well enough to reveal a small plastic table on which was placed a large metal serving platter covered with one of those old style lids. Behind the table were two chairs, seating two trembling figures with hoods over their heads and their arms bound excessively with thick black electricians tape.

The figure moved into position behind the two figures and I trained the light onto the ceramic mask, utterly disinterested as to how the beam would be affecting them.

"Please come and join us, Jake Lehman."

I took a step forward.

"Closer please. You're entering into the final stages of Round Two. Time is of the essence and you cannot afford to mess up at this stage."

I didn't move. I pointed instead at the two figures, one of whom could just about be made out as female. Her hands felt somewhat familiar to me but I couldn't place them. They certainly weren't Jane's I knew that much.

"Who's under the hoods?"

"Move closer, Jake Lehman. Don't get ahead of yourself. Lift the lid, please."

I apprehensively moved one step closer and lifted the metal lid that covered the serving platter. There beneath it stood a sealed bottle of Jim Beam and next to that lay a handful of tablets I instantly recognised for obvious reasons to be Tramadol.

"Round Two, Jake Lehman. You have two minutes to consume half this bottle of Jim Beam and four Tramadol tablets..."

"Fuck you, you sick bastard." I sneered. "If you do know anything about me at all you'll know I'm a recovering bloody addict. This isn't funny."

"I do know you, Jake Lehman. I know you and your past and your weaknesses too. And I know that if you want to successfully survive Round Two you will re-embrace your demons."

"No. I won't." I aggressively spat back.

The figure nodded, stepped forward and whipped the hood from the seated figure furthest to my right. There, under torchlight sat the dishevelled figure of Margaret Jason, Stephanie Jason's mother. Her mouth was taped and her eyes were clustered with ruined make-up from crying and sweating. She looked at me desperately and her eyes widened.

The figure stepped off to the side and removed the other hood to reveal Matthew Jason, Stephanie's father, who's mouth was also taped shut and who looked as if he had been held in a captive state against his will for some time.

"Your time starts... now!"

"I can't. I can't. You don't understand, that mixture could actually kill me. What's the point of having this long game if I'm never going to see Round Three. Or was that your plan all along?" I garbled quickly and manically.

"My due diligence indicates that this amount of pills and that amount of alcohol will not be pleasant but neither will it be fatal." The figure replied in their digitised voice.

"So... So... So... you're setting me up to fail then? You are handicapping me so that I'm incapable of being able to complete whatever you have planned next?"

"Forty-five seconds!" The figure barked in their electronically-enhanced way and then with that said they stepped forward and placed the gun nuzzle down on the top of Matthew Jason's skull. Matthew's eye's burst wide in panic at the exact moment I screamed out for the figure to stop.

I staggered forward and grabbed the pills. My hands shook as I forced four tablets into my mouth. I snatched the bottle and my fingers quivered as I yanked desperately to burst open the lid and I gagged pouring the contents into my throat, washing down the tablets in the process.

Where once Jim Beam would have felt like a smooth, thick velvet sliding down my throat, now it burned and tears fell from my eyes. I gagged but pushed on and when I thought I had hit the required mark I slammed the bottle back down on the table.

"Let's see how frequent your little comedic action hero quips are here on out, Jake Lehman."

"I DID WHAT YOU ASK..."

The figure pulled the trigger and Matthew's jawline exploded as the bullet exited out the bottom of his skull and he forcibly bounced in his seat before flopping to a halt off-centre of where he sat, tipping the chair and falling lifelessly onto the cold concrete floor.

Margaret's eyes magnified in agonising shock. Her screams muffled by the gag but still noticeable in their pained anguish. She'd lost her daughter in horrendous circumstances and single-handedly fought to bring her husband back from near total collapse in the aftermath of that – only to see him so brutally and coldly murdered right here and now in front of her, two metres from her face.

This wasn't right.

This wasn't fair.

Why was this happening to *them*?

The black-clad person before me stood, slowly tilting their head whilst staring at me from the darkened area of the warehouse floor. I stood staring back. My breathing struggling to gain control of itself. There was an eerie silence.

Matthew lay bleeding out on the floor with the bottom half of his head missing. Margaret's screams continued trying to burst out from behind the gag across her mouth. It felt like I was being dared to make a move as the Jim Beam started to rise back up in my throat.

"Please, Jake Lehman, do tell me if you feel THIS is a little overwritten too!" the figure said as they calmly pulled a large knife from the back of their belt-line and stabbed Margaret Jason in the neck.

Then again. And again.

Her head lulled forward as blood sprayed out all over the figure's waistline.

"NO!" I screamed.

"She never needed to die, Jake Lehman. I wish to make this abundantly clear. I intended to kill one and let you rescue the other in order to give you a sense of achievement you could use to spur you on. That was going to be my gesture to you. Alas, she has served as your punishment for mocking me. You must learn that this game is to be respected and <u>I</u> am to be respected. Margaret Jason died because you don't know when and how to shut your mouth. Her death is on you. Now, do you have more quips you'd like to make about films or do you want to complete this round?"

I stood silently, seething as tears built up in my eyes and I blinked them away. The only sound now was the deathly gurgles of Margaret Jason as she bled out in the chair in front of me. Her eyes desperately flickering away. Until they fell to a slow stop along with her breathing.

The figure tilted their head and took a paused look at the bottle's contents.

"I'll let you off a couple of centimetres, Jake Lehman." They pointed down towards Margaret's body. *"She wouldn't have been much good in this world without him anyway. It was a mercy killing, I'm sure you'll agree. She'd been through enough as you well know. Now, congratulations on passing Round Two, Jake Le..."*

I made a rush for the figure as my head buzzed hard from the sound of the gunshot and my eyes blurred from tears and what felt like almost instant intoxication.

The figure twisted the firearm and effortlessly fired two shots at my feet, missing but causing me to fall backwards onto my backside.

"It may serve you well to prepare yourself for the fact each round will now grow in its intensity, Jake Lehman. Round Three will require you to attend a place very personal to you. At ten pm this evening you need to be at the place you once tried to take your own life. There you will find a replacement phone. It will ring and you will be provided with further instructions. If you are not there when the phone rings, your wife and your children will die. If you alert anyone to our contact your wife and your children will die. If you do not come alone to the required location your wife and your children will die. If you show disobedience or disrespect to me or the game akin to what you have just now, your wife and your children will die. If you fail to achieve the objectives of the game set for you within the timeframe given your wife and your children will die. If you achieve all of the objectives laid out over the course of the game then your wife and your children will be set free to continue their lives."

The figure then completed a ballet-twirl before stepping back into the darkness and when I moved my torchlight to refocus on their new position they were gone.

I wobbled to my feet and pushed myself out through the door, falling into the deep snow outside. I quickly pushed my hand down into my throat and vomit appeared with ease, spraying up all over my hand and then down onto the ground around me. It seemed to burn a hole in the snow as it landed.

I vomited again.

Then when I was done, I pushed my hand back in again and painfully retched.

I got to my feet and staggered back down the path to the gates, falling multiple times and crying with pain and shock each time I had to get back up again.

And then just at the exact moment I didn't think I had it in me to stand back up again no matter how many times I forced myself to picture my wife and sons, headlights appeared as they turned left off the junction ahead and the gun-metal grey Land Rover Defender 2022 came to a stop right in front of my crumbled, heaped form.

[9]

or

26th August 2013.

Rachel didn't come back at all.

I pushed on through the files regardless and took an early finish mid afternoon because my head was starting to pulsate. Too much reading, too much heat and too little air conditioning to provide any sort of circulation of fresh air. I reached a point of being completely fed up with repeatedly freeing my soaking wet shirt from being stuck to the back of the chair I was sat on, so on the umpteenth time I stood up to free myself and shake out a bit of the clinging moisture, I simply didn't sit back down again.

Instead I took a taxi back to my hotel where I showered under a chilled blast, changed my clothes and then got a second taxi down to Walsh Bay. My hotel receptionist had recommended both an early evening walk around The Rocks Market and then down to a little restaurant near the Barangaroo Reserve, which was apparently "one of the best kept secrets as eateries in the city go".

I was willing to bet she said that to all the guests.

It was a gorgeous evening and I returned back to my hotel fully appreciative of the beautiful sights I had taken in and the surprisingly tasty kangaroo steak I ate at the recommended restaurant – which was every bit as great as the receptionist indicated. I Skyped with Jane for a while and had a bit of a whinge about how difficult DC Casey was to work with, if you could actually call what we were doing together 'work'. *One* of us was definitely working. What she had been doing was more akin to 'creeping' on what I was doing.

I lay on my bed reading over my notes that I'd taken up until this point with Australian prime time TV playing in the background. Aussie television had a much weirder set-up than our television scheduling. In the UK you knew exactly where you stood when watching something with adverts in – programme started, ad break at the halfway mark, back into it, ads at the end and then onto the next programme. Here it was like there were advertisement breaks every ten minutes in one hour long programme. And then, get this, five minutes before the end of a bloody show they pause for MORE adverts and when it comes back they play the end credits and it goes straight into the next programme.

"This programme is really getting in the way of all these adverts!" I muttered out loud to no one but myself, as I become disconcerted about the incessant interruptions to some Australian medical drama I wasn't even paying proper attention to anyway. I looked around the room and stupidly became a little disappointed that there was no one here to catch my witticism.

A knock at my hotel room door pulled me out of these random thoughts and I jumped up and made my way to see who it was. Upon looking through the peep-hole I sighed so hard that the person on the other side could not possibly have missed out on hearing it and I opened the door wide with a jaded and weary expression across my face to find DC Rachel Casey herself stood out in the corridor.

In one hand she held a six pack of bottles of Coopers Pale Ale and in the other a music CD of some kind that I could not make out.

"As much as you wind me right up Mr Lehman, I couldn't let you go another night sat alone in my home country drinking tap water beer like Fosters so I bought you some of the *proper* good stuff!" Rachel smiled as she held out the beers.

I'd not seen her smile properly before. She had a really delightful smile with perfect teeth and a couple of tight little dimples in each cheek when she did so.

She held this smile and kept her arm outstretched with the beer pack dangling on the end of her hand. The silence was a little uncomfortable.

"I'm an alcoholic in recovery." I finally spoke.

"Pull your head *in*!" smirked Rachel. "Deadset? ... For real?"

"For real." I rebutted. "Very much an alcoholic."

"Wow!" she laughed nervously. "Well, now I feel like a right dickhead so these beers are for me then and *this* is for you..."

She dropped the beers back down to her side and the glass bottles clinked recklessly off one another as she did. In their place she raised up her other hand and offered up a CD of Phil Collins' 2004 compilation album, 'Love Songs: Old & New'.

"You don't have this one, I hope?" she said.

I cautiously took it from her, turning it over in my hand to look at the track-listing on the back whilst slowly shaking my head.

"I do not." I replied. "Thank you."

"Good. Good. And you're welcome."

We stood looking at one another.

"Can I come in?" she asked in a tone that suggested a nervousness and vulnerability from her that I'd not encountered since we'd come to be in each other's company.

I silently stepped aside to make space for her to pass into the room.

"This is a nice room, Mr Lehman. You're choosing to spend your client's money very well I must admit."

"How about you cut the intermittent Mr Lehman shit finally and just call me Jake consistently?" I said.

Rachel nodded. "Okay. Okay. Jake it is from now on."

"And then how about you jump straight in with why you're here?"

She flopped down into a nearby chair, pulled a beer from the pack and held it up. "Are you okay with people drinking in front of you?"

I gestured affirmatively.

She patted the bottle from her left hand to her right and slammed it down on the edge of a nearby table. The bottle's lid sprang with gusto up into the air and she caught it in flight with her free hand whilst pumping the neck of the bottle straight into her mouth before so much of as a millimetre of froth escaped anywhere. This appeared like a well-practised process for her and she came across like an expert in it.

"We got off on the wrong foot and I'm here tonight to put us on the right one."

"And how are you going to do that?" I asked.

"By being straight with you?" Rachel shrugged.

I sat down next to her.

"Listen up, Jake. My directive was to give you access to what had been legally negotiated for you to have access to. But my superiors made it very clear to me from the outset that this was a fishing expedition on your part with a view to you finding neglect in our investigatory methods for the purposes of your client bringing an expensive lawsuit against us. I was not only told that I wasn't to give you so much as a centimetre of a helping hand but also that the investigation into those girls' disappearance was airtight and thorough."

"I don't think it was." I interjected.

"And you know what?" Rachel replied. "I don't think it was *either*. And I don't know why I thought to trust these bastards ever again. I think I'm getting thrown under the proverbial bus over it too. I think I'm being set-up."

"How so?"

"You've seen where I'm working, right?" she sighed. "Come on, that's not the dream posting is it? I'm clearly stale dog shit to the people up top that make the decisions."

"Why?"

"Well that's a long story Jake. And I'm not sure you've got the time to hear it but I'm certain I don't have the energy to tell it. Let's just say, my posting to the 'Cold and Closed Case Review Team' was their way of punishing me without it seeming like I was being punished if that makes sense?"

"No. It doesn't. Of *course* it looks like you're being punished – you're in a windowless, airless sub-basement beneath two other fucking basements working in a department that consists of you and you alone and... and..."

"Okay. Yes. It's very *obviously* a punishment posting. But the posting down there is punishment enough don't you think? I don't need to be stitched up any further and that's what this is starting to feel like – you're asking me questions that, and I agree with you, are very basic from an investigatory point of view and I don't know why the answers aren't there but I have a sinking suspicion my superiors are going to lay blame at my door for their absence."

"Are you here tonight asking me to bury this and go back to the UK pretending I'm empty handed so you don't end up in trouble?" I clarified.

"No, not at all." Rachel answered. "I wouldn't have spent most of the day doing what I've been doing if that was what I was shooting for."

"And what have you been doing most of the day then?" I smiled.

"The Holden Equinox is still in police storage, held in situ because of Mr Dentz' legal proclamations. It's in one of our lock-ups over in Parramatta. I got one of our mechanics to drop in there and run an assessment. He is claiming that there are zero signs of Sixten's car having had its mileage tampered with or reset. Ever. At *any* time. He says he would attest as such in court under oath – the mileage on the vehicle is legitimate."

"Okay." I said quietly. "So how did that car make a 2,385 mile trip in around 750 to 760 miles then?"

"*That* I don't know. And I'm not at a point where I'm willing to go with the fact it flew the rest of the way like you suggested. I left that alone and decided as an act of contrition to you to have all of the 166 vehicle registrations ran through the system and, well, this is going to sound incredulous but I think I might have found *something* that brought me back round to the mileage discrepancy."

"Go on..."

"First of all, do you know what a road train is?"

I shook my head.

"They're also called 'land trains' and when you get right up into the territories they're known as 'LCVs' which stands for 'long combination vehicles'. Standard trailer trucks pull one trailer but these are designed to move road freight much more efficiently around Australia, using two or three trailers. Some push it all the way up to four. They're used to get stuff around rural and remote areas of the country. Though it's kind of insane for one of them to be hitting the roads around the Blue Mountains because those are a lot of tight, thin, poorly surfaced and tourist-laden routes."

"I'm not following..." I said.

Rachel put her drink down on the table and pulled a notepad from her pocket. "There's not a lot of interest in the vast majority of the 166 vehicles I ran because nearly all of them are registered or associated to South Australia or New South Wales but there was one that intrigued me – a road train registered to a facility that specialises in making and selling them that's based out in Nullarbor."

"Right... *still* not following?"

"If I was to take a map right now, okay? And on that map I was to measure out a scale of the miles we think that Sixten's car covered from Perth then draw down a barrier line as the cut-off then it's obviously far from exact but it would put that car closer to the vicinity of Nullarbor than either Perth or the Blue Mountains, yes?"

I slowly started to nod.

"... And I had the mechanic out at Parramatta run the numbers for me and the measurements on the Holden Equinox versus the measurements of the make and model on that road train indicate that the former could be placed inside most trailers attached to the latter." Rachel continued.

"So you think the car was intercepted and then taken the rest of the way as cargo then dumped in the Blue Mountains?" I asked.

"It's pure conjecture but it's a hell of a lot more plausible than your flying car theory isn't it?"

"I guess. I mean, I saw this film a couple of years back called Wolf Creek. Have you heard of it?" I said.

"Yeah, but don't talk to true blue Australians about shite like that. Anything that perpetuates the whole missing backpacker, murderous 'Ocker' Aussie thing is not something we're fans of frankly." She half-laughed.

"Rachel?"

"Yeah?"

"Just to remind you – I'm out here looking into a missing backpacker and the sturdiest theory the two have us have managed to land on involves them possibly getting picked off by someone driving a road train in the middle of the Outback."

Rachel now started to fully laugh.

"Wolf Creek is looking like a fucking documentary right about now."

"Fair point!" she grinned.

"What now?" I queried.

"Well," Rachel said, finishing off her bottle of Coopers Pale Ale and dropping it down on the table between us. "I was thinking we head in tomorrow morning, first thing, and we push for a meeting with my DCI. The easy thing would be for us to give this place in Nullarbor a quick call and find out if they have any information on who the owner or driver was during that period leading up to Sixten being found. But what I'd like to do is just land on them and catch them on the backfoot."

"You want to go out to Nullarbor? How far is that?" I enquired.

"It's a quick flight, two and half to three hours, no big deal. The big deal is going to be getting my DCI to sign off on us doing just that." Rachel replied.

"And do you think they will?"

"Fuck no. Not a *chance*!" laughed Rachel.

The next morning Rachel picked me up and we took the same drive to the police station and parked in the same spot and walked into the same building and across the same open foyer in the same formation we'd done on every other day, her on the right me on the left, before stepping into the lift on the far side of the concourse.

Only this time instead of going down, we went up. Gliding silently floor after floor past the various departments until we were exited out, two levels from the top.

"I put in my request late last night and we've been granted ten minutes." Rachel said in a hushed tone.

"Any tips?" I replied.

"On what?"

"On how to make the best impression with this fella then?" I whispered as we stepped out and made our way along the corridor.

"First of all, don't assume it's a man." Rachel smirked.

"Is it a man?"

"It's a man, yes." she laughed.

"Shut up then!" I teased. "Anyway, what would you like me to do to help?"

"Don't speak!" she laughed before becoming immediately stony-faced. "Novak and I used to be good mates a while back. He was one of my trainers and mentors when I first landed in the job. We'd drink together, do barbies, the whole thing. Before he learnt it wasn't in anyone's best interests to be pally with me. Now he's risen as fast as I've fallen. The walking definition of how well you can do in this job when you shut up and nod."

Our bums didn't touch the seats outside DCI Novak's office before his door opened and he barked "Get in here!" in our general direction.

He was a podgy man who'd clearly been softened by time spent predominantly behind a desk and he carried a well-coiffed old style military side-parting on his thinning black hair.

Rachel and I walked towards the door of his office and as she went through it, he slammed it shut in my face leaving me outside. I backstepped a couple of paces and sat back down in the seat, taking full advantage of the walls being thin enough and Novak's voice being loud enough for me to hear everything anyway. At least everything *he* said.

"Are you absolutely one hundred percent for real?" he screeched. "Where on earth do you get off sending an email like that to me?"

I could not make out what Rachel was saying in response but he shut her down midway through regardless.

"I don't care. Excuse me but I don't give a single *fuck*." Novak bellowed. "You had one job and that was to watch that man out there read a set of case files and then put him back on a plane to wherever he came from."

Rachel spoke inaudibly.

"I FUCKING KNOW HE'S FROM THE UNITED KINGDOM, DC CASEY!" he screamed incandescently. "How do you get from observing him reading a set of case files and then bundling him back onto a plane having ensured he hasn't stolen any of our documents to putting in a permissions and expenses request to go to..."

She finished his sentence by presumably filling in the location.

Novak jumped out of his seat and barrelled round his desk and across his office to the door, which he yanked open with force and barked "You! In here! Now!" at me.

'Hey. I'm not one of your staff, you soft-bellied fuckstick! Talk to me like that again and I'm going to snap a chair leg off, stick it up your arse and wave you around this bloody building like you're a goddamn Greenpeace sign!'

... is what I thought but never, *never* said. I internalised it all and smiled meekly instead. I stepped forward and entered his office noting that Rachel was stood so I opted to stand too, taking a position in the left corner across from Novak's desk.

Novak wilted back into his seat and buried his face in his hands. He let out a muffled scream and then sat back up to stare directly at Rachel.

"Why couldn't you just have the dignity to bloody resign, Casey?" he finally said.

Rachel stood in front of him and did not respond, widening her stance and pulling her hands tight around her back.

Novak sat back and folded his arms across his drooping man breasts that stuck out either side of his dress shirt. "Fine. Walk me through this."

Rachel began to talk. And talk. And talk. She did not pause once. It seemed that not only had she rehearsed this speech repeatedly that very morning before picking me up but that she'd practised doing it all in one breath so that no space was left for Novak to try and take her argument down before she was done.

She covered everything – the mileage discrepancy spotted, the absence of checks completed on vehicles in that area in the lead up to the discovery of Sixten, the lines of enquiry open as a result of both and the one area of investigation that permission was being sought to explore *in person* out in Nullarbor.

"For all that is holy PLEASE tell me that between you and Inch High Private fucking Eye here, you both have better than counting out the miles you *think* Sixten and these missing women drove and then drawing a line down a map and saying 'Right. That's where they are then'!"

'Nope. That's actually pretty much it, I reckon. But fuck you on the Inch High Private Eye jibe you fat shit. I'm six foot two and three quarters!' I thought but... again... absolutely did not say out loud because, you know? Tact, and what not?

Rachel kept pushing on.

"Why in person?" Novak asked, reasonably. "Why can't you email or call the site?"

"Because if there's even a small possibility that the road train was involved..." Rachel started.

"... which it wasn't because this is, to put it bluntly, *bullshit*!" Novak interjected. "Road trains travelling the outback snatching up backpackers is the stuff of shitty Ozploitation horror movies we sell off around the world to gullible idiots!"

"... if there IS a possibility though, we'd like to catch them on the backfoot and perhaps get a look at the vehicle properly if it's there and..." Rachel tried to valiantly push on but Novak wasn't having it.

He spun his chair to direct his full attention to me.

"And *you*?" he sneered. "Are you just going to stand there? Do you *speak*?"

"I speak." I smiled, laying it on thick. "But I don't speak half as well as I read a room, sir. And frankly, reading this room I get the impression you'd prefer for me to shut the fuck right up and not say a single thing because you'd have preferred even more to have never had to encounter me at all, let alone make time for me this morning."

"You read a room very well." Novak smirked.

"Thank you." I replied. "May I say just one thing very quickly and only one thing please sir?"

"I *like* this guy!" he said, side-eyeing Rachel before reinvesting me with his full attention. "You may. Go ahead?"

Let the bullshit flow forth...

"I had no issue whatsoever with the investigation in the manner it was carried out and I am drawing up no criticism of it..."

"Well, considering you're in here telling me our officers' conclusion may be up for debate and there's holes you would like filled in on what we have put forward in our findings I'd say what you're suggesting is not the truth, Mr..."

"Lehman. Jake Lehman." I fake smiled again. "Please understand that I am not the enemy here. I am not out to try and take you or your police service down in any way. Actually, quite the opposite. I have to report back a full and honest account to my client and I have to report back information I would be prepared to discuss under sworn oath if necessary. And I know that if I reported back even just one 'i' on a document that hadn't been dotted then my client would jump on that, regardless of whether there was legitimacy or not. I spotted this mileage thing and alongside the unchecked vehicles I brought them to DC Casey's attention and she rightly agreed with me that this was an exploitable and vulnerable area my client's legal representative could take advantage of. Rather than risk perjuring myself at a future date by hiding it, I suggested to DC Casey that we seek clarification on this and she did some investigating and found an avenue that we could explore and then close off before bringing the reporting back around to its original conclusion as posited by the original investigators. She feels that this would be a good way of protecting your police officers, firming everything up and giving me the peace of mind to close off my enquiries and head home."

Novak sat back in his chair; a grin started to form across his face.

"They say that you sit behind a desk long enough and the nerves in your arse will dull eventually." He said. "But my arse nerves aren't so numbed out yet that I don't know when someone's stuck their face between my cheeks and started giving me a good old licking!"

I looked at the back of Rachel's head to try to get a measure on how she was reacting to this then back to Novak, unable to mask my grimace.

"That's... good? I *guess*?" I awkwardly replied.

"When you get to my rank, receiving a bit of an arse-licking every now and again isn't that bad. You kind of assume you deserve it more frequently than you actually get it." Novak continued. He looked directly at Rachel now. "*You* should keep that in mind. In fact, I think you could benefit a great deal from learning the tricks of the trade from this fella right here. And the best way to do that is to stay in his company a bit longer because then we have ourselves a win-win situation, do we not?"

"How so?" Rachel replied.

"How so *sir*?" he snarled.

"I'm sorry. How so sir?"

"Because you win by getting what you want and this station, your colleagues, if not this entire fucking city wins by benefitting from *you* not being around." Novak laughed. "I will grant your request. I think it's all set to be a spectacular failure but regardless... You have permission to fly out to this facility in Nullarbor, make your relevant enquiries and return here to this office within 48 hours. Is that clear?"

We both nodded.

"And when you return to this office it will be to close off this entire stupid, pointless affair and see Mr Lehman back off to the UK on the first available flight, is that also clear to you both?"

Rachel did <u>not</u> fuck around.

Within four hours she had us a private plane arranged at emergency notice running off a side-strip at Sydney airport. She'd dropped me at the hotel to grab a carry-on bag of whatever I needed whilst she sat outside with the engine running. I didn't even have time to Skype Jane and give her the latest updates and where I was heading off to. Rachel said it wasn't needed. I'd be back at the hotel in the early hours of the next morning all being well and according to her that would time out well with calling Jane at a more appropriate hour. I didn't really know what to pack, so I hastily threw my cameras and deodorant into a small shoulder bag with some paper and pens.

Before I stopped my head spinning around with the stress and the speed at which we were all suddenly moving, we were up in the air in what felt like the world's smallest plane, made from the thinnest possible materials on the planet judging from how much we shuddered and shook.

This was *crazy* – earlier that morning I was in the Sydney police headquarters and now I'm off flying into the great unknown, quite literally actually because all that lay ahead of me up in the distance was one enormous orange haze. Hell, in true 1980s action buddy movie style, last night Rachel was just some obstacle in my path who was nothing but rude to me and twelve hours later we're bonding like crazy and united under a common cause.

'You know what's even crazier?' I said to myself. 'A couple of weeks back you were sat in your garage on a rainy day, thinking about Pabst Blue Ribbon, wondering where the next pound was coming from and wishing there was more to life than this. *Now* look where you are and what you're doing!'

A voice shattered me from this thought.

"That shit back there in Novak's office?" Rachel shouted at me over the roar of the small plane engine, even though we were sat side by side with one another. "That was some gold standard bullshit. I am impressed. You can certainly lay the chuff on thick when you want to, can't you?"

"What's 'chuff'?" I shouted back.

"You don't have 'the chuff' over there in merry old England, huh?" she laughed. "That must be an Aussie thing – chatting and bluffing; 'chuffing'? It's expert level bullshit delivery in order to advance your course!"

I laughed. "Chuffing! I *like* that. I'm stealing that one!"

We passed out over Melbourne and Adelaide and just shy of three hours later we clumped down on a dusty orange, dirt track and decamped.

I immediately started coughing from the harsh heat that met me the minute I stepped out into the spread of Australian dust that surrounded this tiny airfield.

Rachel pushed me on the shoulder in the direction of a dirtied, worn jeep in the corner by a building across the way.

"That's ours!" she exclaimed, striding off towards it. "The pilot called ahead and sorted it for us with a mate of his. We've got it for a few hours."

"How far away is this road train place we need to get to?" I coughed.

"A couple of hours maybe?"

She overshot her estimation by thirty minutes. Having bumped along a mixture of gravelled dirt roads and smooth open highways for nearly an hour and a half, we then found ourselves at the security gates of Ashton Carriage Ltd – a massive vista of various lorries, tractors, trailers, heavy duty tires and broken-down vehicle chassis.

Rachel pulled the vehicle to a stop next to a side building with 'Reception' etched in faded paint across the roof ridge in a swampy green coloured paint. She reached into the back and retrieved her small bag and from it she took her police ID and a firearm in a leather clip-on holster.

"Wait. You have a gun?" I gasped.

"Don't *you*?" she smirked back.

"No, I don't. You know I don't. Should *you* have a gun?"

"I don't know." Rachel giggled. "Probably not. But they were giving them out back at the airport and I thought 'Hey, I've always fancied having a gun' and... of *course* I should have a gun. I'm a police officer for one. And for another thing, I'm a female out in the bloody sticks with you and you've not proven one bit how good you are in the shit, you Phil Collins loving question mark. So, damn right I'm going to bring my gun."

"I preferred it when you were a sullen barely communicative moody bitch!" I replied.

She laughed.

We entered the reception building and asked to speak to the duty manager.

The duty manager was out "at a meeting".

We asked to speak to the next person in charge.

The elderly lady behind the reception desk looked slightly panicked.

Rachel identified herself as a police officer whilst I took a couple of steps back.

Calls were made. A radio missive was put out on the antiquated CB system stacked up in the corner of this dusty, aged out building. Eventually a morbidly obese mountain of a man wandered in and pushed his way behind the desk.

"The buck starts and stops with me; how can I be of assistance?" he said in a thick Australian accent.

Rachel pulled out her pocketbook and flicked it easily open to the relevant page she sought. She succinctly explained the context for her enquiry and read out the details on the road train she was interested in.

The mountain of a man pushed his head to his chest and squinted down at a computer monitor on the reception desk, tapping away on the keyboard with his massive log-sized fingers before standing back up fully straight again and twisting the computer monitor round so Rachel could see the screen.

"We built that thing, but it isn't one of ours anymore. We reconditioned it nearly four years ago and sold it on to the boys up on the Brennan site."

"What's the Brennan site?" Rachel replied.

"*Where's* the Brennan site?" I interjected.

The mountain of a man turned unsteadily on his feet and faced the giant map of Australia pinned behind him on the wall of his reception building.

His big fat fingers landed instantly on where Nullarbor was situated and traced left and up, past the marked point for Plumridge Lakes nature reserve, up past Yeo Lake and Neale Junction nature reserves too. His finger came to rest on the wide empty space that sat there on the map with nary a mention of anything nearby except what looked to be a tiny speck of a place called Warburton that was still way, way off from where his finger had stopped.

He then tapped that empty space on the map twice for effect.

[10]

or

"Face Off".

"It was back towards the end of 2013. A month or so before we met. Maybe a little longer." I said quietly, almost to myself as I sat shivering in the passenger seat of the gun-metal grey Land Rover Defender 2022 Psychic had pulled to a stop in an alleyway off some street in the back ends of Jarrow. "I wasn't in a good place. I'd fallen off the wagon again with the drink and I'd just started taking painkillers for all the physical damage I came back from Australia with. That was some heady mixture, you know? And I could feel Jane's disappointment along with her parents' judgement. I could *feel* it physically burrowing away into me. And, well I guess I just felt like a burden to them and a failure to myself and my boys."

Psychic sat silently, clutching the handheld video monitor in his hands he'd just used seconds earlier to watch the covert footage I'd recorded, listening and watching me furiously wrench at my fingers as I spoke.

"I always had such lovely memories from my childhood of Tynemouth Priory. My grandparents used to take me there a lot in the school holidays and we'd picnic up on the hill with fish and chips from just up the road and then when we were done we'd either go down onto King Edwards Bay beach or take the old footpath all the way down onto the fish quay and walk around all the markets. I loved it." I continued as tears easily fell. "And one night I found myself back there as a grown man. Alone. I couldn't get these images out of my head that just kept flashing into my mind against my own will – I kept seeing her lying there in the outback, bleeding out. The fire raging and all those men reaching out and grabbing at me and... and... before I know it, I was a bottle of Jim Beam down, standing smoking Lucky Strike Lights, hitting warm cans of Heineken like they were pop and looking down into the darkness below where the sea could be heard smashing into the rocks."

"And then what happened?" Psychic asked softly.

The back of my gullet felt stripped bare from repeated vomiting. I couldn't tell what was shock and what was minor affects from what I'd ingested moments earlier and not been able to jettison from my system.

A lump emerged in my throat and it became painful to speak. "Then I remembered that she died so that I could get home to my boys. She used her last dying fucking breath to urge me on to get back to them and I thought to myself that if I committed suicide there and then it was an utter disservice to her memory!"

Psychic smiled and nodded. "A wise thought!"

"So, I stepped back from the cliff edge… pissed my pants and passed out by the old wooden bench up there. And do you want to know what *really* fucking disturbs me the most right now?"

Psychic didn't speak.

"What REALLY has got my head twisted mate is that up until this point no one knows just how close I got that night or what Tynemouth Priory represents in my personal history bar one person and that's the cognitive behaviour therapist I confessed it to a couple of years back. I never told you, I never went into such detail with Jane… so how the hell does that psychotic masked bastard *know*?"

Psychic slowly exhaled. "And there was only that one time? There can't be any confusion here about the place he is wanting you to be at?"

I shook my head. "I assure you it was a one time, one location thing."

Psychic sighed some more.

We sat in silence once more until eventually he tapped the monitor in his hand and smiled. "We've got him though, Jake. We've *got* him. Let's get this into the hands of the police and then they've got to change tact here and accept you're innocent."

"I'm not going to hand it in though mate." I replied. "I have to be free to answer that phone up at Tynemouth Priory."

"It's cool. I'll check in with Emily and hopefully she's got a hold of Lane and we can arrange for her to view it and then pass it down the line to every single officer in her force that you didn't kill anyone or blow up anything. Then whoever this piece of shit is who's got this grudge is going to get the shock of their life because if you've managed to keep pace with them up until this point with the police on your arse, just wait until he sees what you can do without that to worry about!"

"The… The… Jason's, man." I said quietly as I struggled to find the words. "I don't understand… I just don't… *understand.* I just know… I'll never, ever be able to forget the sight of the both of them before he murdered them the way he did."

"You said he told you that you live the life of a murdering vigilante or something and that you choose who should die without any consequence for your behaviour, is that right?"

I nodded.

"And he drew Margaret and Matthew Jason into this, yeah? So… what if we're dealing with one of Jason Grant's army mates or any of his Black Box mercenaries? If he did what you described, then he's got some ease with killing indiscriminately and that would tie in with how Stephanie Jason's parents have been dragged into this too. They were the ones that kickstarted you down the path, after all?"

"You know, I was thinking pretty much the same thing too." I said. "Or, you know, the fucker putting me through all of this is my cognitive behaviour therapist?"

We took what little time we had to pause, lie low and catch our breathes a little. The only good thing about having been forced to ingest the bourbon and the pills was that the edge had been dulled on my agonising pain for the first time since the crash. I wasn't anywhere near as intoxicated as I would've expected. Maybe the instant vomiting had been effective after all?

Psychic tried to make a couple of calls. Luke wasn't available to talk to as he was apparently in "deep" conversation with someone regarding my *other* predicament. He spoke with Emily briefly though. She was waiting on a call back from Chief Constable Jessica Lane, but she was delighted that we had secured footage of my aggressor as good as confirming they were responsible for the carnage so far.

It still felt a little *too* easy though. The covert camera hadn't been spotted so we throw the footage at the police, they apologise, release me from my charges and help me find this person and get my family back? Surely it can't go down like that, huh? What would we talk about for the other thirty-something chapters if that was the case. This isn't a spoiler, necessarily. Not when it's me we're talking about. When have you *ever* known for *anything* to be simple when it comes to me?

We stayed hunkered down for another twenty minutes after that - me downing water Psychic had picked up from a nearby petrol station and pissing it back out again as quickly as possible in order to flush my system, him listening intently to the local radio stations as they reported in on the police van crash off the Coast Road earlier in the evening and my escape from custody. The news was reporting not just that two "members of the public" were caught up in my getaway and left seriously injured at the scene but that, as I'd suspected, Steroid Steve and his colleague had died. Burt Reynolds went unmentioned.

The report had a little hastily buttoned-on soundbite interview with Police & Crime Commissioner Janet McKinley at the end of the news bulletin because, well, there isn't a camera or microphone that woman won't push herself in front of or any sort of regional event she won't appear at in order to maximise her exposure. She really should have been flushed out alongside Hadenbury and Hetherington way back when, yet she seemed to find just the right amount of career-specific glue to keep herself where she was. Though she was up for re-election imminently, so it'd be interesting to see where that goes...

"The public need to forget whatever they previously thought of when it comes to Jake Lehman." McKinley was heard to say. "The media may well have built him up as a hero following events earlier this year but representation in news articles should not supersede hard facts and at the moment hard facts avow that at the time of what appears to be a violent escape from police custody Jake Lehman was under arrest for two murders, the whereabouts of his family are unknown at this time and he was on his way to be interviewed under caution for several other serious offences that were resultant in the death of three other innocent people. The public are urged not to approach this man and instead to contact the police urgently."

I sighed. "I fucking *hate* that woman."

"Me too!" Psychic replied.

"What's the play here?" Psychic asked as we travelled slowly down Front Street in Tynemouth and swung the gun-metal grey Land Rover Defender 2022 right down onto Pier Road which led to the cliff edge and parking area up over to the right of the old Priory ruins. Despite the temperature and horrible weather conditions Front Street, a popular social haunt full of bars and restaurants, was still packed out with people moving around from eatery to pub as the night wore on.

"I'm not sure we need one." I responded. "Get in, get the phone and get out? Whoever this twat is they didn't specify I had to do anything else other than answer the phone. And I'd hate to be pinned in up there. One road up to a cliff edge? If shit went south our options are limited."

Psychic nodded as he slow-crawled along the road.

I checked my watch.

It was just after quarter to ten.

The snow had eased off for the first time and whilst it was still hard to push on through all that had landed and formed as far as the eye could see, there was at least a reprieve from the disastrous and restricted visibility that came with the incessant snowfall.

The car park down on our right used to be an infamous 'dogging' spot. If you are of the naïve persuasion who assumes this has anything to do with walking your dog than I will pause right here and give you the opportunity to hit up an internet search engine and improve your understanding. I apologise in advance for educating you on such an activity.

... You done?

Good.

Again, I'm sorry.

Okay. So just off Pier Road on the right was an old, torn up and worn down car park that was used as a dogging site and there'd been an occasion a few years back, before the Stephie Jay case, where Psychic and I ran a surveillance operation down there trying to catch out a cheating husband who was involved in this 'scene'. I recall Psychic commenting on me being out of sorts that night and I am guessing now he can work out why - because only a few metres further up on the left was the car park and cliff edge where I'd reached my lowest possible ebb a couple of years earlier.

We pulled to a slow stop inside the car park and both of us took a long, studied look around from within the vehicle to check out through the darkness whether we were being watched or if there were any other cars in the vicinity. We appeared to be alone. The lamp posts were all non-functioning.

"Do you think he did that?" Psychic whispered.

"Who did what?" I replied.

"The street lighting up here - do you think 'mystery man' arranged for them all to be off. It certainly adds more of an obstacle to proceedings, doesn't it? You could fall off the edge of the cliff up there if you're not ca..."

Psychic stopped himself.

"Sorry. I wasn't thinking." he said.

"It's okay. It's fine. Don't worry about it." I smiled. "Anyway, we're going to have to give this fucker a name for the time being, aren't we? I can't keep calling him 'fucker' and I really don't like 'mystery man'."

"Ooooh. Who was the guy that played the evil mastermind in the Saw movies?"

"Tobin Bell?" I asked.

"Yeah. Yeah. *That's* the guy. Let's call him Tobin."

"You keep saying 'him' you know? It's very sexist." I replied.

"Well, you've been up close and in the same room as this person. Did they have boobs?"

"What?"

"Did you see any titties? And not like man-boobs. I mean, like very obviously lady breasts?" Psychic grinned.

"No." I half-laughed. "But it *was* dark."

"Then for the time being I will continue to assume that this psycho is a man and that until I'm presented with evidence as to his real identity, I'm going to call him Tobin!"

"*Tobin*? Really?"

"Really!" Psychic laughed.

I sighed and opened the passenger door, delicately sliding myself out as my ribs sent shockwaves of pain up into my brain. I stood unsteadily, zipping my coat up to build a barrier as best as I could against the bracing cold wind, and then moved off falteringly to try and get a sense of my surroundings as to where the new phone could be. All the while I pushed myself to listen intently for any ringtone that might give the position away.

A worn wooden bench was set out close to the lip of the cliff edge up in front and it stood there almost as some sort of twisted monument to the exact spot I stood on years back when I contemplated ending my life.

How did this son of a bitch know about *that*?

I stepped up to the bench and looked across its seat. There was nothing there that I could see. I dropped myself down into the snow and started to feel underneath the wooden beams, eventually coming to rest my hand against a cold wet plastic bag taped to the underside of the seat. I pulled it free and could just about make out the shape of another mobile phone.

The same make and model once again.

I slowly and painfully pulled myself back up onto my feet and no sooner was I vertical the phone buzzed alive and started to ring inside the bag. I tore at the plastic, freeing the phone and quickly pushing it up to my ear.

The voice once again kicked in straight away without pause.

"Welcome to Round Three, Jake Lehman. I understand it may be difficult for you to stand on this spot once again because of what it represents but it's important for you to do so because Round Three is going to be demonstrative of a physical, mental and emotional escalation in order to teach you the most important lesson you will ever come to learn – that what you do in this life echoes!"

"You mean there's more escalation than being forced to watch you murder two innocent people you sick fu..." I snapped.

"You really are not learning the dangers of disrespecting me are you, Jake Lehman? Interrupting is disrespect. How many more people need to unnecessarily lose their life because you cannot behave appropriately? Do I need to take Jonathan Lehman and blow a hole in the back of his head in front of his mother and brother?"

I stood silent. I could feel my grip tightening and tightening with anger. My face curled and I bit down on hard on the inside of my mouth, desperately forcing myself to just shut the fuck up no matter what.

"As I was saying, what you do in this life echoes. It pushes on as a ripple through the lives of others and causes untold consequences. And there **has** *to be consequences, Jake Lehman. That is the nature of life. Every action births a reaction. That is the fundamental underpinning of everything. For too long you have contravened this datum and that is unacceptable. It must be rectified no differently than in the way the Grim Reaper himself catches up eventually with those that have a near-miss with death. I am your reckoning. Your sins are now being tallied and your penance is finally catching up with you."*

"I want to speak to my wife AND my boys now. I want proof that they're still alive." I said sternly into the mouthpiece.

"I'm not unreasonable, Jake Lehman. This is perhaps something that could have been afforded to you but unfortunately you showed ill-manners towards me at the start of this call and therefore your behaviour will be sanctioned. You will not be receiving proof of life at this stage. Now, please listen carefully. Round Three is generously spaced out in order to give you the best chance of success. You will find £10,000 by any means necessary over the course of this night and you will be ready at nine am tomorrow morning to receive a call from me on this number with instructions as to where to meet and hand over the money..."

"And that buys my family their freedom, does it?" I interjected. "Is that what this has all been for? Ten bloody grand?"

"STOP INTERRUPTING" screeched the digitised voice at an ear-piercing pitch. *"WHAT IS WRONG WITH YOU? DO YOU HAVE A DISABILITY? I TOLD YOU IF YOU SHOWED DISRESPECT TO THE GAME YOUR WIFE AND YOUR CHILDREN WOULD DIE. I MADE THAT CLEAR DIDN'T I?"*

"You did. You did. Look, I'm sorry. I'm sorry, okay? I apologise for interrupting."

I fell silent again.

Yeah Jake, what the fuck *is* wrong with you pal? Then again, at least you're proving you can really throw this criminal mastermind off-kilter, huh?

"It was already set in stone that I would be raising the intensity level on this round straight out of the gate." The voice continued in a lowered tone. *"But thanks to yet another interruption requiring yet another sanction I'm going to add another layer of difficulty. A call will be placed to the police giving your current vehicle details and your exact location as of right now. Prior to their imminent arrival, you will have my original obstacle to deal with..."*

Headlights suddenly lit up off in the distance at the entrance to Pier Road. Two sets. Both snaking their way down the twisting road towards us. I pushed the phone to my chest and shouted to Psychic. He stepped out of the driver's seat and I clicked my fingers and pointed off towards the approaching headlights behind him.

"... Your back is well and truly up against the edge now, is it not Jake Lehman? I will call again at nine am to ensure you have successfully completed Round Three and that more importantly you have survived the night. You will then be provided with further instructions. If you are not able to answer when the phone rings, your wife and your children will die. If you alert anyone to our contact your wife and your children will die. If you do not come alone to the required location your wife and your children will die. If you show any further disobedience or disrespect to the game your wife and your children will die. This is your final warning on this matter. If you fail to achieve the objectives of the game set for you within the timeframe given your wife and your children will die. If you achieve all of the objectives laid out over the course of the game, then your wife and your children will be set free to continue their lives. Good luck Jake."

Psychic swung the gun-metal grey Land Rover Defender 2022 round and up close to where I stood, slamming into an embankment of snow and scattering it everywhere.

"Get in!" he shouted.

It didn't matter whether I did or I didn't. The first car was through into the car park and the second one pulled itself sideways to block any chance of us getting out. To our rear and our right was a plummet straight off a cliff edge into a pile of rocks below. To our left a giant snow-covered grass incline that dropped right off into a small declivity ostensibly leading to the foot path along the North Shields Quay. *Or* the River Tyne itself if you were to overshoot it.

Three men alighted from the first vehicle and stood in front of the headlight beams. The light illuminated their entire shapes and I could make out the range of baseball bats, hatchets and the like that each carried.

'Think Jake! *Think*!'

The man in the middle spoke first through the darkness. "Let's not make this a whole *thing*, Lehman. Come over here and get in the car!"

"I don't know you. 'Stranger Danger' is still a very real thing even as an adult you know?" I shouted back.

'Think Jake! *Think*!'

I peered down quickly into the gun-metal grey Land Rover Defender 2022 and made eye contact with Psychic. "Do you still have that stupid sound effects thing on your phone?" I whispered.

"Yeah. Why? Now's not the time for fake farts, is it mate?" he mouthed back.

"Can you do gun fire with it?"

"Erm… yeah… why?"

"Sync the fucking thing with your Bluetooth to the car stereo and turn the volume up really loud, okay?" I hissed. "I'll distract them."

I stood back up to look at the men again.

"Don't fuck around Lehman. We have someone who wants to meet with you and talk about what you did to our friend Bobby." The male shouted.

"Who's that then?" I responded.

"You know damn well who it is," he bellowed. "The same guy throwing money down to make it happen. Ten grand to kill you. Fifteen grand to bring you in alive. There was a tip off that you were down this neck of the woods and it looks like we were the first to get here. Now, get in the fucking car and come with us before some other twat turns up and tries to steal you off us."

"Fifteen grand? The price is going up." I smiled. "That makes me feel good."

The man started to walk forward.

"Wait!" I snapped. "Don't move. In the interests of total transparency, it is only fair to all of you that I explain you've come to this confrontation woefully underprepared."

The man stopped in his tracks.

I looked down at Psychic.

"Not yet. Not yet." He snapped as he feverishly tapped away on his phone. "A couple of seconds…"

I sighed and went back to my attackers.

"Have you guys seen The Untouchables? The Kevin Costner film? It's a classic. It really is. There's this scene in a church where Costner and Sean Connery, who's doing another one of his no-attempt-at-anything-other-than-a-Scottish-accent performances, are sat talking about how they're going to get Al Capone once and for all. And Connery says 'They pull a knife; you pull a gun. He sends one of yours to the hospital, you send one of his to the morgue. *That's* the Chicago way!' and I'm looking at you all here before me and I'm reminded of that scene whilst looking at your knives and what not because... well... we've got *guns*!"

The man turned and looked at his two compatriots.

They looked panicked.

"Bullshit!" the man eventually snapped.

"*True* shit!" I smiled and banged my hand down twice on the roof of Psychic's car.

The air was instantly filled with the sound of gun fire.

Machine gun fire, in fact. Rapid, relentless machine gun fire.

These guys must be dumb as fuck, if I'm honest.

Because they scattered all over the place whilst the car at the rear beat a hasty reversed retreat back down Pier Road, crashing into a nearby fence line as they did. The three men in front of us gathered themselves and dived into their car as Psychic hit the button on his app a second time and blasted out more fake gunfire through the Land Rover Defender 2022's stereo system.

Then the army of blue flashing lights started to emerge out of the darkness as police units appeared on mass at the bottom of Front Street and began the twisted route in towards where we were positioned.

"Erm... Jake?" Psychic said.

"I see them." I replied, quickly pushing myself into the passenger seat and strapping on my seatbelt.

"Okay. So... what now?" he shouted as he pulled the Land Rover Defender 2022 back round again to face the direction we needed to leave by but which was currently filling up with police vehicles charging their way towards us.

"We go!" I shouted back. "Got to go! Got to go! Got to *go*!"

"Where? We go bloody *where*? Straight at them? Back off the cliff? *Where*?"

I frantically looked around.

"Drive!"

"WHERE?" Psychic screamed.

[11]

or

"Jake Lehman: Public Enemy Number One".

The police entered the car park at roughly the same speed at which Psychic and I tried to exit it and their manoeuvring on the long thin road suggested they thought a) we were pushing for a game of 'chicken' and b) that *they'd* win it.

"Pull left! Pull left!" I shouted.

"*Where* left?" he responded hysterically.

"Through here!" I said as I reached out, grabbed the wheel and yanked it down to the left.

We hit the snowy embankment and burst up through it, crunching through the fence line with surprising ease and demolishing our way into a grassy field completely swathed in white as far as the eye could see. Deep, thick, totally untouched white devoid of any interaction with man nor beast from the point it had landed.

The incline was immediate and we barrelled downwards at great speed, leaving behind the flashing blue lights up top on the car park because it would appear that no matter how desperate the police were to get me back into their custody, they weren't *so* desperate as to want to replicate this utter stupidity.

The snow smashed up against the sides of the Land Rover Defender 2022 and made awful grinding noises as it churned rapidly through our wheels. We were hitting such a speed and the incline kept rising as we travelled that we made light work of the snow whilst struggling to keep the back end of the vehicle on the ground.

"I need to know the next stage of this plan, Jake!" screeched Psychic.

"This *is* the plan!" I stammered as I bounced in my seat, struggling to hold myself steady. "Everything now is improvisation!"

"What's ahead? Do you even know what's at the bottom of this hill?"

"A big drop and then… the River Tyne?" I shouted unhelpfully.

A human sized piece of ice rebounded up from the ground and smashed into the windscreen leaving an impressive crack right through the middle.

"Have you ever jumped out of a moving car before?" I asked.

"What? NO!" Psychic fearfully replied.

"No. Me neither. But... well... come on, if this is our last adventure let's tick it off eh?" I said as I quickly unclipped my seatbelt and got to work on the door handle to my left.

"No! No! No! No!" Psychic screamed whilst following my actions.

We timed our forced exit from the sides of the car at the exact moment it hit a stone wall three-quarters of the way down, crunched into it and the back end flew up with the impact. The Land Rover Defender 2022 flipped over the small stone uptick and plunged out of sight down a ten foot drop just as I slammed face first into the snow and felt the bottom half of my body twist into the impact with the ground.

I felt a warm floor of blood rise up from the back of my throat and down out of my nose at the same time that waves of sheer physical anguish coursed through my body.

I heard Psychic groan but anything else he attempted to follow through with was drowned out by the sound of the Land Rover Defender 2022 exploding into a ball of flames ten foot down from where we lay.

I needed to take a minute.

I was beginning to regret expunging all that tramadol and bourbon a couple of hours ago because I could have really done with them in full effect right about now – the slow numbing of my ribs that had started to take hold was completely gone now and I was back to searing agony, my right wrist had swollen to twice its size and my vision was completely shot. Not to mention the blood that seemed to be flowing out of every orifice on my face.

I'd just close my eyes for a couple of seconds and...

"Get up Jake. You've got to get up mate, come on!" I heard Psychic say as he reached down, slowly turned me onto my back and began to gently pull me up onto my feet.

He was bleeding from his nose and that appeared to be the worst of it for him.

"How do you... keep getting off... so lightly... on *everything*, man!" I stumbled.

"God likes me!" Psychic smiled as he took hold of my belt at the back of my jeans and the collar of my jacket and did his best to frogmarch me on down the rest of the hill. He did what he could to help me down the drop onto the North Shields Quay pathway where the Land Rover Defender 2022 lay as an upside down flaming wreck but there was no way that dropping down ten foot wasn't going to hurt like hell for someone in my condition.

Psychic grabbed me again in the same position and pushed on along the path.

"Luke's apartment is up there on the right, two streets back. We've just got to keep going." He said.

I half-nodded and set about concentrating on keeping one foot going in front of the other as the sounds of police sirens and their flashing blue lights circled up above us from where we'd just came, snaking down as far as they could between the last stretch of Pier Road and the footpath it turned into.

We could hear enough commotion to indicate there was officers out on foot now racing to get down onto the path we made our way along. Psychic pulled us both right on the footpath up along the tree lines near Collingwood Monument and out near Northumberland Terrace. A police car sped past us on that exact street and we both ducked back into the bushes just in time to avoid falling into the driver's line of sight.

"*Fuck*! That was close!" whispered Psychic as he pushed us a few feet back towards where we'd just came from. "Okay, come with me."

"I can't..." I found myself slurring. "I need... to sit... down."

When my eyes opened again, I was lying back down on the very same sofa inside Luke's apartment that I came around on earlier this very same evening. I would come to learn that I'd passed out back on Northumberland Terrace, but Psychic picked me up and carried me the rest of the way to safety here.

Man, I *truly* love that guy.

The first thing I heard as I came back to the land of the living was Jennifer asking where her car had been left.

"Oh. It was *your* car?" Psychic replied.

She nodded. "Luke got it for me. Where is it?"

Psychic ushered her to the window and pointed far out, down towards the mouth of the River Tyne.

"Do you see that little orange flame glowing away in the distance?" he said.

"Is it parked all the way back there?" Jennifer asked.

"No. That orange flame *is* your car unfortunately!"

"It better bloody not be!" screeched Jennifer as she stormed from the room just as Emily waddled into it clutching her oversized belly with one hand and a bag of ice with the other. She passed the ice to Psychic who instantly pressed it against the bridge of his nose and flopped down into the sofa chair opposite me.

Luke came and sat on the arm of the same chair and looked across to me.

"Did you blow up Jennifer's car?" he said whilst looking disappointingly at both Psychic and I.

"In my defence we thought it was *your* car!" I whispered.

"That's not much of a defence is it though?" Luke replied, shaking his head. "She was after a new one anyway but it's not the point."

I straightened myself up in my seat a little and looked out to everyone in the room. "This guy on the phone..."

"Tobin!" Psychic unhelpfully interposed.

I sighed. "This guy on the phone who Psychic here has randomly nicknamed Tobin has given me until nine am tomorrow morning to put ten grand together and have it ready to hand over to him!"

"Wow! That's it? All of this has been a play to get you to hand over... *ten thousand pounds*?" Emily asked.

"That's what I originally thought but I don't think it's that simple after all." I countered. "I think the ten grand is just the start of him bleeding me and turning the dial. I mean, come on. Where am I going to be able to access ten thousand pounds between now and nine am on Christmas Eve?"

"What denomination do you want it in?" Luke said with nary a pause.

"You what?" I exclaimed.

"Yeah, how do you want it?" he replied. "Listen bud, he's given you the night to draw it all together and have it ready for him like that's going to be a task and half, right? Well, fuck that. I can walk out right now and go get one of my property managers up out of bed and draw that sort of cash together from the safe in no time. I've got shit like that squirrelled away *everywhere*, man."

"I can't ask you to do that, Brody!" I smiled warmly.

"You're not asking me, mate. I'm offering it up. Jane and the kids are my family too in a funny old way. This guy wants to exhaust you and push you that little bit further through the night to get this done? Well fuck him. You get your much-needed rest and let me sort this for you, okay?"

"You're going to need your rest anyway Jake because things are... messy!" Emily offered up nervously.

"You don't think things are *already* messy?" I asked.

"Ok. Let me rephrase then." Emily sighed. "Things are *messier*!"

"How so?"

She turned in her chair and pointed at Luke. "You go first."

Luke cleared his throat. "I called Ryan Flaherty to see if he could help lift this hit that's been put out on you, Jake."

"*And*?" I pushed anxiously.

"And it turns out *he's* the one that put the hit out on you in the first place so you can imagine he's pretty unwilling to lift it."

"What?" I gulped. "He's a two-bit fucking thumper for Bobby Maitland. He's got no authority whatsoever."

"Looks like he didn't need it though, did he?" Luke replied. "He wants Bobby's death avenged and he's obviously got access to the man's money to be able to fund it."

"But I didn't bloody kill Bobby Maitland!" I shouted.

"Don't you think I know that, Jake?" Luke fired back. "That man was like a dad to me when I was growing up. He threw money down when no one else would to sponsor my journey from shitty fights in horrible banquet suites at rundown hotels back in the day to getting a shot at going professional. When I blew it all, he was the fella who along with yourself made sure I still had a few quid in my pocket to eat. When this entire city turned me into a laughingstock and give me the 'Jimmy Riddle' nickname, he pushed me to own it and start staring people back down. Do you know how I turned my prize money on that TV competition into millions more than I initially walked away with? I got floated the money to bet high on myself and it paid out big time. Guess who put the money up and took back only what he loaned me with no interest? So, trust me when I say this Jakey boy - if I thought for *one second* there was the *slightest* chance you harmed Bobby in anyway, I wouldn't be helping you I'd be holding you face down in the river out there. You get me?"

I nodded.

"I vouched for you with Ryan. I gave his brother Mark a call and got him to turn the screws on Ry' a bit. It didn't matter one jot. I offered to pay out on the price and buy him off. He wouldn't have it." Luke continued. "In fact, now I'm hearing Ryan's upped the bounty to fifteen kay if they bring you in alive so he can tear you to pieces himself."

"Yeah, I heard that too." I grimaced.

"I've done some digging and apparently the word has spread through every pub, bar and gutter in the whole of the city. Every scumbag and their nana have stepped up to have a pop at putting you six feet under."

I nodded. "And judging from what we've just encountered up there at the Priory, this Tobin fella is using it to his advantage somehow too."

Luke shook his head. "I've called in every favour I can and got as many of my old contacts to stand down and leave this well alone. I don't know what else to do mate. I'm sorry."

I smiled. "You've done more than enough Luke. Thanks for trying."

I looked to Emily. "You're right. It has got messier."

"No." replied Emily. "That was only half of it."

"You're *kidding*?"

She reached over as best she could with her giant baby-filled belly blocking her way and picked up the TV remote from the coffee table. Slouching back into the chair, she clicked the TV on and bounced through the tabs on screen to the 'recordings' section.

"This," she said as she pressed on one programme, "was the BBC Look North bulletin just a few hours ago. Pay attention."

I watched as a press conference played out in front of a gaggle of reporters hastily arranged around a conference table in the foyer of police headquarters at Middle Engine Lane. Behind the table sat Deputy Chief Constable Cary Falk flanked either side by Police & Crime Commissioner Janet McKinley and Mayor Eve-Marie Benchley, the latter of whom looked visibly upset.

As I struggled to listen in, Emily said "Are you seeing Falk's name card on the table?"

I squinted and leant in closer to the large widescreen TV mounted on the wall of the living room. On closer inspection I could see that it clearly said *'Acting Chief Constable Cary Falk'* on it.

I looked in shock to Emily. She slowly nodded her head whilst biting her lip.

I concentrated on the TV again.

Falk spoke clearly and assertively, stating that two of *his* officers have died and another is in critical condition resultant from my "brutal escape" from police custody. He reiterated that there was strong, corroborative evidence indicating my arrest on suspicion of two murders was "just" and that I was now wanted for questioning in relation to the explosion at my business premises and an "attempted attack upon a place of worship" his officers thankfully intercepted. He said that he regards me as a clear and present danger that should not be approached but that notifying the police as a matter of urgency should be the number one priority.

"Wait! What the fuck? What did he just say about a place of worship?" I gasped.

"Hang on. We'll come back to it." Emily responded, shushing me.

Mayor Benchley sat silent alongside Falk, staring down at the table.

McKinley spoke next. "As I said earlier, it concerns me that the public may not be acting quickly enough in disassociating themselves from whatever they previously thought of in relation to Jake Lehman. He is NOT a misunderstood hero. I believe we could potentially be looking at the possibility that Mr Lehman has had some sort of mental breakdown due to past traumas he suffered in highly stressful situations the media have previously copiously covered..."

Falk attempted to intercede and pull her away from saying more.

McKinley was only picking up speed and was not going to be silenced easily.

"... It worries me that we may be looking at an unstable individual who blames this city from his mental traumas and is exacting some sort of revenge. I actually encourage, under the circumstances we're all now aware of, to draw *absolute* inference from the fact that when faced with the facts and the charges against him, Jake Lehman has chosen to harm others in order to break free and run rather than let the truth play out."

"Okay. Thank you everyone." Falk interrupted. "Thank you. There will be no questions I'm afraid."

He stood up from the table and I dropped my head just as Emily switched the television off.

"I've had hype-men at some of my fights that haven't done as good a job at riling things up as she's just done!" Luke said.

"What is this shit about an attack on a place of worship?" I blurted out angrily.

"Aafeen Taif apparently called in a suspicious package to the police earlier this afternoon that he found on the grounds of Central Newcastle Mosque on Grainger Park Road. Allegedly your fingerprints are all over the device." Emily said quietly.

"What the FUCK?" I shouted. "How have you heard that?"

"I got in touch with Jessica Lane," Emily replied. "As you may have gathered from Falk's hasty retitling, she's been quietly removed from duty with immediate effect. According to her, McKinley questioned why you ever needed to be moved stations in the first place and why Lane put that into effect. She basically put her powers into full force to examine whether Lane's personal friendship with you was a factor in her facilitating your escape from custody and McKinley has pushed her out!"

"Unless it was Chief Constable Lane who rammed that police van off the Coast Road and down into that bloody ditch at the bottom of St Peter's field then she had sweet fuck all to do with me getting free!" I blasted out to the room.

"No one believes she did. I don't even think McKinley believes she did." Emily countered. "But it's very obviously a powerplay isn't it? You've got to keep in mind McKinley is a holdover from the Hadenbury era and she was very much mentored into that position in the first place by Hetherington with a view to bigger, grander roles in the political landscape. She is not 'good people', if you catch my drift?"

"What do we do now?" I said as tears filled up in my eyes.

"I go get your money!" Luke said, standing up.

"I copy up the footage you've got of Tobin so far and hand it off to Lane somehow for her to do her best with!" Emily offered.

"And *you* rest!" Psychic said, pointing directly at me. "Something tells me this is a momentary calm before the storm circles back around!"

"Well, *I'm* going to go lie down and start shopping online for a new car!" Jennifer exclaimed dramatically whilst exiting the room.

[12]

or

28th August 2013.

"You don't want to be heading up there and sticking your noses through the gatepost at Brennan, trust me! They're an uncultured lot, they are!" The sweat-covered mountain of a man at Ashton Carriage Ltd had said, before turning his attention to me. "And *you* definitely don't, my friend. They fucking *hate* pommy-bastards up at Brennan!"

I don't think I'd said a single word the whole time we'd been on site at Ashton Carriage Ltd. So now, my paranoia being what it was, I found myself slumped in a seat in some cowboy's saloon of a dive bar in what constituted a 'town centre' in this part of Nullarbor, nursing a foul-tasting lemonade and allowing myself to get paranoid about whether I had some sort of "English gait" in the way I walked or whether there was a "pommy-bastard scent" in my sweat.

Rachel was sat tapping furiously on her phone, occasionally slamming it down on the table in frustration at the piss-poor wi-fi and general awful signal she was getting. Eventually she reached a point where I think she'd gathered enough facts and information to hit me with her pitch.

"I think we should take a drive up to this Brennan place!" she said a little too excitedly for my liking.

"How long is that going to take us and what do..."

She never let me finish.

"It's a twenty-seven, maybe thirty-hour drive west from here. I reckon I could get us up there in no more than twenty-five." Rachel began. "I think we should head up there, fake our way inside, have a nosey around and see if we can land sight of this road train. Or, even better, see whether your Maya Dentz lady is hanging from some cage in their compound or partying it up in there like a saloon floozy!"

"Thirty fucking hours?" I gasped hard. "Your pal Novak would never, ever sign off on that!"

"He doesn't need to know, does he?" Rachel countered. "By me being right here right now with you he's already agreed to me going out of my jurisdiction. I'll just wander on out a little further and we'll be a *little* bit later getting back to him. You in?"

I took another repulsed sip of my lemonade. "What the hell happened to you in the last twenty-four hours Rachel Casey?"

"I *woke up*!" she grinned. "Now, do you want to keep letting my bosses dictate the terms and make you phone this whole thing into your client or do you want to get your hands a bit dirtier doing some actual *investigating*?"

Brennan – or "Last of the Independents" as it sold itself – was a coal-mining facility 831 kilometres (or 516 miles, if you will) from Nullarbor, past the Gibson Desert in Central Western Australia.

Australia is the world's leading coal exporter and it's mined in every state of the country except the South with over fifty percent of what's mined going on to be exported, mainly to Eastern Asia. Did you know that 193.6 million tonnes of... *What*? Why can't Wikipedia be my friend here?

What I'm trying to get you to realise is that even in this day and age coalmining is still huge in Australia. And the international billion-dollar company Bagnall-Farina Inc. pretty much have the monopoly of it all. They're running every mining site around the world. Unless you happen to still be inexplicably running one of the very few independent mining corporations in today's age. In which case Bagnall-Farina Inc. will crush you into falling under their wing with financial buyouts often four times your worth and therefore *impossible* to ignore.

According to Rachel's rushed Googling, every currently functioning mining site in Australia was one of theirs or a subsidiary of BFI, as they market themselves around the world. Brennan was a firm hold-out against the mighty Goliath and proudly stated themselves as such with "Brennan: Last of the Independents" being unofficially emblazoned wherever the team up there could paint it.

Brennan had survived miraculously for just under seven decades by this point. Even with BFI crushing them down at every turn, they found a way to keep their heads above the water line. Their whole time in existence they'd always been a pulled-together-with-rope-and-tape type of operation; hard-working men putting in long shifts in insanely uncomfortable weather conditions where things like "Health & Safety" went unspoken and there wasn't an HR representative or a company-logo embroidered baseball cap or t-shirt anyway in the vicinity.

It came into existence in the late sixties to early seventies when three men – William S. Gilmore, Walter Gallo and Charlie Berenger – took a chance at their own expense on an illegal and low-level exploratory dig out in the Australian desert. They struck lucky on discovering a reserve of coal in that area unknown to (and therefore untouched by) others. Pulling their money together and floating the entire endeavour on stacked bank loans, they bought a small patch of land together out in the desert and got to work.

They named it 'Brennan' after Berenger's dog, who came to a stop on the very spot they first dug down on. They became successful over the course of the first five years; small teams splintered to work night and day, a live-in base of operations for all employees. Gilmore was the first to jump ship with his cut of the initial wave of profit. Berenger bought out his share. As the decades ticked on, greed consumed him and he eventually pushed Gallo out too and ended up with full control of the company.

Tragedy and bad luck would see Gallo eventually fall from partial owner to working the mines. His ties to Brennan ran so deep that even when he became too old and infirm to work there anymore, he still hung around the site day-in-day-out. Pitching up a caravan a few miles down the road and drinking in the makeshift watering hole the miners used when not on shift. Every day babbling away to anyone and no one like he still had an opinion that mattered.

By the tail end of the 1990s, Brennan was struggling as big industry types took an even stronger stranglehold of coal mining in the country. They could no longer realistically compete. Instead all they could do was desperately hang on. And that's all Brennan has done since. Ticking away, turning a dollar here and there where it can, sometimes running at a loss for months. The men sometimes missed a pay-day but they were loyal and stuck to the place. Most of them were working there as a 'last chance saloon' for personal and professional reasons with nowhere else to go.

Charlie Berenger died in 1997 and his son Sid took it over, having worked there himself for nearly fifteen years. In time his own son, Danny, would make the journey up into the desert and come to work alongside him and eventually become his second-in-command.

The best images you could find of the place online were shabby photos of a bunch of clustered shipping containers and portacabins dumped in a circle out in the middle of nowhere with a fuel tank and observation tower perched next to a mining point at the other. It looked less like a functioning business and more like someone had abandoned waste in the Australian outback that they no longer wanted.

... And DC Rachel Casey wanted to drive out there and go look at *this*?

We knew it was a piss-take to try and push the loan of our current vehicle on a journey deep into the Australian desert. So Rachel handed it back to the pilot's friend as originally agreed and hired out an alternative. Which turned out to be an old and beat-up jeep from an ersatz rental place on the edge of town that specialised in catering to those planning on driving the Nullarbor Plains.

It was hitting 37 degrees as we headed out on the long journey over. The rental place owner warned us we'd be facing the mid-forties as we passed the Gibson Desert. "The hottest on record!" apparently.

The roof of the jeep was pulled back and the windows rolled down as we stormed off the tarmacked "civilian" roads and out deep into the dusty terrains. Rachel pushed forth her theory that we should go in as if we were representing Bagnall-Farina Inc. and wanted to talk to them about a buy-out.

"And you don't think that would just have them shut the gate in our face?" I asked over the noise of the engine and tyres smashing down hard into crunched up stones and rock. "I'm not sure that's the best approach. From what you've said so far they're not exactly friendly towards the big guns in the industry!"

"It's a lot better than getting up there and me flashing my police badge and then asking for a look around their facility without a warrant!" she shot back without her eyes ever leaving the road.

"What if we said we were news reporters?" I countered.

Rachel's eyes briefly looked over at me and her smirk sort of emerged on the side of her mouth for a very short moment.

"We could say that you're a reporter and I'm your producer and we're looking to do a story about Australian success stories and the whole David versus Goliath thing in Australian business or something, you know?" I continued.

"That could work!"

On we drove.

Very occasionally the radio in the jeep would break clear enough for us to receive a good run of music from whatever station we could pick up. Terry Jacks' 'Seasons in the Sun' got short, sharp disinterest from Rachel but I was able to coerce her into giving patience and a little respect to Earth Wind & Fire's 'Fantasy' when that broke through and I danced a little in my seat to its tremendousness.

"God, you really are an old man, aren't you?" Rachel laughed. "Is your wife into this sort of shit music too?"

"No!" I laughed right back. "She's even less tolerant than you are!"

"Are you trying to be like fake ironic-cool in saying you like this stuff or something? What is it with you?" she said. "You're only a few years older than me. Can't you have some taste in indie bands or soft rock?"

"I like soft rock!" I replied sheepishly.

"What's 'soft rock' to you though?"

"You know, Journey? Styx? Chicago? Bon Jovi? Survivor?"

"Oh Christ!" she giggled. "*Stop* talking. You really have no concept of what's good music and you really have no clue as to what makes great travelling singalong music!"

Jeeee-sus! Two days ago, I couldn't get this woman to say more than four words to me. Now I couldn't get her to stop stripping me bare with her criticisms.

"So, what's a great travelling singalong song then, Ms Casey?"

"You know? Something like Bryan Adams' 'Summer of 69'?"

"Oh no argument there. That is a *sublime* song!" I nodded.

"Something that comes through the speakers and immediately induces a big, joyous communal smile on everyone's face, forcing everyone to burst into song alongside it. Everyone knowing every word and every beat and just loving the shared moment... And do you want a really deep cut choice in that regard too?" she asked. "That one hit wonder boyband from your country who sang 'Crazy For You'? Me and my old school buddies love busting that one out when we're together." She burst into song without a moment's hesitation: "... *'Cause I feel that you know, you've got me just where you want me. I'm crazy, crazy for you. And there's nothing that I won't do. I'm caught by the look in your eyes. And it's all for the love of you!"*

She then started to laugh.

"Wow! Let Loose? I do sort of semi-ashamedly love that song, but I did not know that they were big enough to make it over here!" I chuckled.

"They charted at sixty-seven in the summer of 1994." Rachel blushed. "I had their picture on my school folder for... like a *week* or something!"

"Why would you know THAT fact!" I laughed.

On we drove, endlessly pushing straight forward along a road situated on an expansive stretch that never seemed to change. As the sun started to lower the radio crackled clear again and out of the speakers came:

"♫♫ ... Looking in your eyes I see a paradise. This world that I've found is too good to be true... Standing here beside you, want so much to give you... This love in my heart that I'm feeling for you ... ♫♫"

Rachel looked at me. I looked right back.

We both started to grin.

You can fight against it. You can lie to yourself and deny it. But the truth of the matter is that by the definition presented as to what makes a truly great travelling singalong song, Starship's 'Nothings Gonna Stop Us Now' was possibly the greatest of all time.

"Don't fight your feelings Jake. Come with me." Rachel smirked as she launched into song. *"... Let 'em say we're crazy, I don't care about that. Put your hand in my hand baby don't ever look back. Let the world around us just fall apart. Baby we can make it if we're heart to heart..."*

She took one hand off the steering wheel and held it out to me. I laughed and took it. I didn't hesitate for a second, diving right in so that in unison we hit the chorus hard:

"♫♫ ... And we can build this thing together. Standing strong forever. Nothing's gonna stop us now. And if this world runs out of lovers, we'll still have each other. Nothing's gonna stop us. Nothing's gonna stop us now... ♫♫"

We both burst into laughter as we passed out of Rawlinna and headed up towards the Plumridge Lakes nature reserve. Rachel thought with night falling it would be good to bed down for the night and she had done enough pre-trip reconnaissance to vouch for a tiny little cabin rental out in the sticks.

We landed there at dusk and climbed from the jeep, both of us walking like rigor mortis had set in on both of our bodies. Our clothes felt crusted solid with dried sweat, dust and dirt. The absence of our change of clothes was decidedly problematic and just one of the many flaws in leaving Sydney thinking we'd be gone only half the day.

Rachel's impulsiveness was coming around to bite us on the backside it would seem.

We found ourselves in a tiny wooden cabin, one of eight on the grounds of a small little alcove on the outskirts of Plumridge Lakes nature reserve. Cash rental only, extra for blankets and towels; outdoor shower with a couple of chairs and a picnic table provided next to a rusted up old fire barrel. Most thankfully of all though, it provided two *separate* canvas camp beds on opposite sides of the small hut.

I stayed inside and tried to get some shut-eye whist repeatedly trying to get enough signal on my mobile phone to send a text out to Jane to let her know I was okay. It was probably going to cost me £35.00 per text if it did get through. Then all of a sudden, I started to worry all ten attempts would land at once and I'd get financially hit for an astronomical sum.

Meanwhile, Rachel washed in the outside shower, drenched her clothes in there with her and washed them down as best possible with the hand soap she'd found underneath the sink in our cabin. Once she was done, I followed suit only to find the both of us in a rather uncomfortable position of each sitting wrapped in nothing but a towel whilst our clothes dried in the humid night air.

We sat around the fire I started in our assigned barrel and stared out into the night. Rachel talked about her love of Will Smith ("both as a movie star and as a legitimately great actor") and then about the wildfires that were raging down from the territories.

"They won't affect us, will they?" I queried.

"They will if we go much further up than where we're going, I reckon." She replied. "The news before we left says that it's sweeping down from the Northern Territories onto the West Coast but last I heard it wasn't anywhere near the likes of Karlamilyi, so I think we're good."

I nodded like I remotely understood anything she'd just said as we fell back into silence and stared up at the stars, shining out from one of the clearest night skies I'd ever seen.

"We're bonding, right?" I eventually said. "I mean, we're sitting here as close to buck-naked as either of us are willing to get. We've had a good old singalong on the way up here. I'd say we're pretty tight right about now, wouldn't you agree?"

Rachel smiled and concurred with her head. "We're like B-F-F's. And I *mean* 'forever' too!"

"So how about you let me in on what that whole shit was with Novak and why you're down there in the sub, sub, sub-basement of police HQ?"

She sighed and adjusted herself in her chair to make sure her towel was maintaining its position and doing the job required of it.

"You're an ex-copper, right Jake?" she said after a long, thoughtful pause.

"Yeah?"

"Shit before the shovel then, buddy. What's the context for the 'ex'?"

It was my turn to activate the considered pause. I stared down at my feet, slowly coming to the realisation that outside of Jane and her parents, I hadn't talked out loud to anybody about what happened to me and that suddenly didn't feel... correct. Then I came to sadly acknowledge that just the sheer amount of time and space it had taken up rolling around in my head again and again had duped me somewhat into thinking it was a well-worn story with everyone. And it wasn't.

And before I knew it, I was talking for the first time properly about it. About it *all*. I talked about my discovery of Madeline in that car down in Jesmond Dene... about Andy Andrews' devastating betrayal... about Hetherington and the power he yielded and how he only seemed to be getting more powerful and more influential. I talked about how I leant into alcohol as a crutch... *why* I did and how it made me feel. Soon I was talking about things I'd never even said to Jane – about how I felt abandoned and embarrassed and how even now I feel a great shame in describing myself as a "private investigator" because it felt like such a last-chance-saloon of a job by a desperate individual not considered good enough to be a police officer anymore.

"I took this job from Arkin Dentz because I'm on the bones of my arse, but I don't know what the fuck I'm doing, if I'm honest. I was a damn good police officer but it's not like I had a whole heap of experience under my belt before Hetherington stole everything from me." I found myself saying. "And I'm so clueless as to what I'm doing or what I'm meant to be doing on this job that I'm just hanging on to your coat-tails... and somehow that's led to you dragging us out into the middle of the fucking outback!"

Rachel laughed and then leant back in her chair and mouthed the word 'Wow!'

"I've got to be honest; I was totally going to shaft you regarding divulging my shit!" she giggled. "I was going to hear you out and then yawn and say, 'Time for bed!' and just bugger off to sleep but... man, you really delivered there. So much so I can't do it to you, can I?"

She cleared her throat once again and looked at me nervously as the floodgates opened.

She'd been an experienced police constable with several commendations under her belt and she had been seconded to the State Crime Command (SCC), getting made Acting-Detective rank in the process. Celebratory drinks with her new team of Detectives allegedly took an ugly turn when the Detective Inspector in charge of her unit got a little 'handsy' as the night wore on. Her resistance to his suggestion that they snuck off and got a hotel room was met with more forceful physical aggression and pretty soon Acting DC Casey found herself bustled out of a fire exit door down the side of the bar they were in and quickly forced down onto the ground out of sight of everyone.

She was drunk but not so drunk she wasn't fully aware by the way this guy was pulling at her jeans that he was about to try and rape her from behind. She did what she had to do to kick out and get him off. The harder she kicked, flayed and punched, the harder her assailant (and *boss!*) punched back. At the point she thought she was about to lose consciousness, a member of staff from the bar came out and disturbed the DI's intentions, causing him to flee.

Rachel woke the next morning unable to see out of one of her eyes for the swelling and her lips had been burst due to the impact from this shithead's fists. She pulled herself together and called it in to her own police service. The initial response was swift in that a report was taken and concern was expressed... but then came the 'door knocks' from her new colleagues. Originally there to say how "sorry" they were and how "worried" they'd been but then also to "sort of make it clear" that she'd "got the wrong end of the stick" with this DI; that he was a "good bloke", a "married fella" and he "didn't deserve to lose his job" or "go to prison over this". He'd had "too much to drink", he "wasn't normally like that", things just "got out of hand". One guy even took the approach of "Well, I heard you were hitting him just as much as he hit you so..."

Her meetings with their respective superiors was a flurry of distancing, denial and dirtied inducement as full detective rank and a move across to a "better" SCC was offered if she just "played the game". It appeared corruption ran deep in every police service. No matter the country.

Rachel didn't take the promotion-bribe nor any of the pressure. She held firm in her belief that someone like that DI had no place in the police and was a danger to women everywhere. Her stance was unwavering and eventually the rumour-mill mutated outside of the closed ranks of the police service and towards the media. Who, like sharks circling spilt blood in the ocean, started closing in on identifying who this violent wannabe rapist DI was and who within the SCC was his victim.

The upper echelons of the police acted swiftly and threw the perverted DI under the bus with a dismissal for gross misconduct. And a negotiated settlement with Rachel Casey in return for a Non-Disclosure Agreement her police union representative pressured her into signing.

She earned her full Detective rank on her own terms and abilities but it was meaningless professionally. Because no matter how hard she worked or how many high-profile and statistic-strengthening arrests she made, the ranks around her with fellow officers - especially in a predominantly male environment - closed off, squeezing her on a daily basis further and further out.

"You know the saying whereby someone is 'the poster child' for something?" Rachel sneered as she picked at the skin on her hand anxiously. "Well that was quite literally *me*! They had my fucking face on their promotional materials at one point when I was a uniformed officer. There was a point you couldn't get on a bus or a train around Sydney without my big red head beaming back at you, promoting the police service... and then BAM! All of a sudden I'm this disease everyone needed to distance themselves from just because I wouldn't take a drunken fuck from some Detective Inspector and be thankful for it?"

She sighed and stared into the fire. I smiled at her and felt a shared bond with her build right there and then.

"You know what was probably the *most* infuriating about that prick DI though? I was never the promiscuous, flirty type. I hadn't had the many boyfriends. One-night stands weren't my thing. At that point I was career-*obsessed*." She continued. "I wouldn't have known how to seduce a man if you'd paid me to, so it wasn't like I was out there drunk, giving him the big inebriated cock-tease, you know? He was just an entitled prick who thought I needed broken in or initiated onto his team or something... and didn't THAT back-fire on him?"

I sat in silence.

What could I say? I felt like the best I could do was listen respectfully and most certainly not offer her up pity. She deserved better than that.

"It became fairly obvious that the instruction from up top was to keep turning the screws until I quit but to be subtle so that obvious grounds for me taking them to an employment tribunal weren't there, you know?" she resumed once more. "They still let me apply for promotion. They just always moved the goal posts so that I never got anything and never went anywhere except sideways, further and further into shit postings. And I never reacted. *Never*. Even now, sat in an airless windowless room down below the basement, they're not going to force me out."

"I'm pleased to hear you say that." I offered quietly. "I'm worried by going quite literally off the reservation though, you're leaving yourself open to a shit storm from them."

"No, don't worry about that. Do you know why?" Rachel smiled. "Because something fucking stinks about those missing women and the Edvin Sixten thing. Rather than have them spin this around and say *'Well Rach', it was your case to review and you dropped the ball on this so fuck you, you're fired!'* we're going to get to the bottom of it and drop it right back on them. And do it in such a way it can't be ignored at a risk of your client raining negative exposure down on the whole of the Sydney police service. And I'm going to use the spotlight it creates to free myself of the shitty narrative they've applied to me!"

"Okay." I said assertively. "I'm in. I think."

Rachel laughed. "Of course, you're in, Jake. You're *here*. You were 'in' the minute you let me into your hotel room and heard me out."

"I guess *so*." I replied. "But do you really think the answers to my missing girl and her friends lie up at this mining site?"

"I don't know for sure but I do like the prospect of getting up there, dropping our initial cover and asking who the driver of that road train was around the time Edvin Sixten went off that cliff in the Blue Mountains and taking a read of people's reactions when I do."

I slowly nodded my head at the prospect.

"Sounds good." I said.

We fell into a comfortable silence.

Between the humidity and the warmth from the fire, there was a cosiness I wouldn't have ever expected from sitting out in the open like this. Both of us in nothing but towels.

Rachel yawned and stretched her arms out above her head, the towel around her chest slipping only ever so slightly but still enough to reveal more of the curve of her breasts than I probably had any right to see.

I looked to the ground and rubbed my eyes.

"I don't know. We're out here in the middle of fucking nowhere and I'm bored to high heaven because there isn't anywhere to get a beer round here it seems, not that you would be a good drinking buddy anyway – no offence?" Rachel said.

"None taken!" I smiled.

"So... I know that I've not exactly set the mood with that whole sorry story I've just landed on you and I really don't want you to think ill of me Jake but... I'm super-bored and a little bit horny and you're about to get a full close-up reveal on just how terrible I am with the whole flirting and seduction thing so... what do you reckon... do you want to have sex or something?" she proffered in one rather random stream of consciousness, almost distantly whilst staring off into the night across our little fire.

I froze with my head only half-raised back in her direction.

"Or... Or... *something*, I guess." I stammered. "Because... you know... I'm married?"

Rachel nodded and laughed. "And you don't want to exercise your 'different continent, different rules' marital small print, no?"

My mouth moved but no words came out.

"It's okay, Jake. You can say no. I wouldn't be offended. I'm offering something to kill the time, not the suggestion you up sticks and leave your wife!" she laughed.

I smiled.

She cleared her throat.

"Are you *happily* married, Jake Lehman?" Rachel winked, clearly changing her approach in order to try and achieve her aim from a different direction.

"I'm married. Of course I'm not happy." I laughed nervously. "It's *marriage*. By its very design it prevents me from having sex with extremely attractive women like you! And that's like... you know... a full-on *crime*!"

She laughed hard. "Why thank you."

"Seriously though?" I said. "For all my bullshit, I'm very flattered you would think of me as an option to while away your evening out here in the middle of nowhere. Especially with no other penises available to you as possibilities. But I do love my wife *very* much and all joking aside I'm extremely happy."

She moved her head affirmatively and stood up, tightening her towel around her chest again. She took one step closer and bent down, kissing me very softly and briefly on my mouth.

"You're a lovely man, Jake and your wife is a lucky woman. I think you made a wise choice but know this – I would have rocked your world! ... Goodnight!"

She turned and stepped off around the fire and into the tiny cabin behind us.

I looked down at my erection as it made itself known beneath the towel around my waist and let out the longest exhalation of air until it felt like my lungs were empty.

"Goddamnit, Jane!" I muttered.

The next morning existed firmly as if the manner in which Rachel and I parted the night before was to be considered alongside the conversation that preceded it as a complete figment of my imagination. To put it more bluntly, we behaved like last night's conversations never happened.

I rose early and pulled on my jeans and short-sleeved white t-shirt that had now taken on the discoloured tone of a garment tie-dyed in rust and I made my way out of the cabin to try and source us some breakfast.

The old lady in the cabin marked as a reception booth was kind enough to sell me half-a-loaf of bread and a couple of eggs from her fridge. Walking back to the cabin, it struck me how completely ill-prepared Rachel and I were to be this far out here with such little food, money, water and even a change of clothing. Especially since we were about to head off further into the Australian desert to go digging around on a half-baked notion.

Rachel just kept charging fuel and snacks to the credit card tied to the police department she was the singular member of as we plunged deeper and deeper into the desert.

I kept that all to myself though whilst I quickly made us scrambled egg on toast over the fire barrel and Rachel filled up the giant jugs of water from the back of our jeep. Then we were off.

Ten more hours of further driving, mixed in with stupid games, banter and intermittent improvised singalongs filled the void left by an unclear radio signal. We started to build into a slow and steady incline up a hill with waves of sandy dust particles blowing down against us from the crest of it. The breeze would have actually been welcome if not for the dirt it was kicking up. Despite it only being midway through the afternoon the sky way off in the distance appeared a darkened grey that infringed on the giant, blazing ball of sun just above our heads.

"How's it getting so dark already?" I asked.

"That's smoke." Rachel replied. "The fires must be a few hundred miles further up now, I reckon. And it must be a real bastard if it's blacking up the sky so much we can see it from all the way back here."

Before I could say another thing, we hit the peak of the incline and my stomach lurched as the front end of the jeep made it over. Rachel slammed the brakes on and brought us to a heady and instant stop on the dirt track.

She pointed down to the base of the very road we sat stationary on.

I looked out to a fence line in the distance that curled round an enormous cluster of corroded and tarnished containers and portacabins. The sound of mining equipment echoed out of a large tunnel on the far side of the compound.

"Well Jake..." she pronounced dramatically. "Welcome to *Brennan*!"

[13]

or

"I Just Want Us To Have A Moment To Breathe Out".

The night before I'd left for London wasn't a *good* one. Deep in my sleep I found myself reliving the sight of Tracy Blythe's head splattering across the touchscreen metro route map inside the metre headquarters as a single gunshot rang out, swiftly followed by multiple bursts of more as every CCTV monitor in the room was obliterated, catching two or three staffers in the cross-fire at close range and spraying their heads and torsos with bullets. I flashed back once more to Richardson-Jones grabbing my arm and yanking me to the ground, diving on top of me as gunfire ricocheted off things and obliterated the room. I saw Hicks striding towards us both once again, firing as he went and screaming "FOR THE COUNTRY!"

I'd woke gasping for air, drenched in sweat and - regardless of the growing tension between us – Jane was right there next to me, helping me prop myself up in bed and regulate my breathing.

"It was a bad dream, Jake." Jane whispered. "You're awake now."

My eyes darted around the room.

She gently caressed my shoulder whilst yawning. "Come on, lie back down and just take some deep breathes. It's okay…"

The next morning we were back to barely being on speaking terms again. I had struggled more than most other mornings getting out of bed that day and I didn't look forward to the prospect of a long train journey down to London. My lower back hurt and all my joints felt like they'd been cemented into a locked position. It kind of killed me a little to concede that I was going to have to come around to where Jane's point of view was on my/our future because I really didn't know how many more serious 'kickings' my body could realistically take and by now you and I know each other well enough for it to be acknowledged that I *attract* beatings. It killed me even more to make such a concession because I'd built my original stand-offish position from such a place of admitted absolute dickishness.

I'd returned from London to find Jane still up and working through a bottle of wine when I got back home. We made small talk and I tried to keep things light, but she worked the conversation back round to the difficulty we were facing, rather effortlessly too considering the alcohol she'd consumed.

"Maybe it's my fault overall?" she'd said quietly, almost to herself. "I was the one who sat by your hospital bedside six months ago and gave my approval to walk away from the police job because people needed the likes of you and Psychic to support them. But saying that was kind of irresponsible because it was in denial of my own concerns about your approach to how you *deliver* that support to people."

"I'm not sure I know what you mean." I'd said.

"Oh, come on. You're absolutely an 'all in' type of guy, aren't you? These last six months, do you know what I've started to understand about you? You didn't *have* to go smashing your way into the Metrocentre that night. You didn't *have* to jump on the back of that train. You *needed* to do those things. There's this something missing inside of you that you're trying to fill or replace. There's this right you need to wrong but it never seems righted no matter what you do. I think you've got an addictive personality, Jake. I'm not sure you yourself would deny that and the alcohol was a crutch that you replaced with the pills and the pills got replaced by you becoming consumed with work and some misbegotten weird marriage between needing adrenaline hits and needing to right wrongs. If I'm honest, I truly thought the way things developed in the aftermath of the Stephanie Jason case you were finding that inner peace you deserved and the right balance mentally and then the Baadir Gadiel case shows up and... BAM... we're all getting dragged right back into the gung-ho bullshit alongside you."

"I don't know if I'd agree wi..."

Jane didn't let me finish. "I think you're phoning it in with all this therapy stuff, Jake. It certainly feels that way with our couples counselling, if I'm being truthful with you. You spend more time and energy on thinking up ways to wind Barbara up than you do giving honest answers to questions asked about our relationship. I think no amount of talking it through or processing or rumination-avoidance techniques is having any effect on the very simple fact that you think you've got some whole heap of debt in your ledger and you're doing everything you think you have to do to get it erased or evened out. That's where I'm at on this whole thing. That's what I think. It's very clear you consider what went on in Australia as..."

"We *don't* talk about Australia!" I'd snapped.

"No, we bloody *don't*, do we?" Jane had snapped right back. "We just lock it right down, buried really deep, and then stitch you up or stand you back up each time you go about destroying yourself in some ill-conceived attempt to escape or evade it. And I think you've got this insane routine perfected in your head, so much so you've got complacent and you've started to take me for granted. You seem to think I'm here to change the bandages from your wounds and pat you on the back for another reckless act of heroism you think is righting wrongs from your past. Where's *my* reprieve? Where's *my* escape from the exhaustion that comes from being the dutiful wife who's meant to cry by your hospital bedside every few months when some other random bad shit has beaten you to a pulp? Because the way you've selfishly reacted to the merest suggestion of such an escape or a reprieve has pretty much appalled me, Jake. I just want us to have a moment to breathe out *finally*. And you're acting like this is a total affront to you."

"And moving away, kicking back in the countryside with money in our pockets and a slower pace of life? That's what you want? That's your reprieve?" I'd asked, genuinely.

Jane stared at me.

There was an uncomfortable silence.

"Oh fuck off, Jake!" she sneered as she jumped up and stormed out of the room.

I guess this is the problem with being an acerbic dickhead ninety percent of the time. When you bring a moment of authenticity to the table the other ten percent no one believes you.

I thought about that conversation over and over again as I sat staring out of the window in Luke's apartment, watching the harsh blizzard conditions kick back in after what had only been an hour or so's reprieve. I sipped carefully on my third cup of pitch-black coffee within the last hour, trying to avoid the various internal and external cuts around my mouth.

I could still just about make out the blue police lights flashing around way off in the distance further back down towards where the quay path curled round to the Priory. They hadn't given up just yet and clearly had no idea that I had pitched up and remained so close.

I took a long, deep breath and gently ran my fingers around the lumps that had now fully swelled up on the front and sides of my skull. Eventually I let my head drop into my hands and I just let the tears fall. That couldn't be the last proper conversation I ever have with my wife, I said to myself over and over. It just couldn't.

'Why didn't you go up those stairs after her, Lehman?' the voice in my heard snarled at me. 'Why didn't you catch her on the stairs that night and pull her round to face you and kiss her and tell her she was wrong, and nothing was more important to you than her and her happiness? What the fuck is WRONG with you? You could've given her the present early. You could've woken her the next morning and done it then! What? Were you just expecting her to phone in the affection on your night-out with friends and then you were going to ride that wave? You're a dick, Jake. You don't deserve her!'

"Jake?"

I was shaken back into the room by Emily approaching me and taking a seat delicately alongside me, resting both her hands on the side of her baby bump as she did.

I smiled as warmly as I could muster.

"Are you okay?" she said in an almost whisper.

I shook my head. "No."

Emily gently nodded. "No, I didn't think so."

We sat in silence for a bit.

"Do you have any idea at all who this Tobin, for want of a better name, is?"

I shook my head again.

"Robbie seems to think it's some special forces man affiliated to the Black Box guys from the Stephanie Jason case?" she proffered. "What do you think?"

I shrugged and quietly murmured "I've made a lot of enemies, Em'!"

"You *are* a somewhat disagreeable sort; it has to be said." Emily smiled mischievously.

I tried to raise a smile.

"Listen," she continued. "You're amongst friends who love you. We're going to get Jane back and we're going to get the truth out. I promise. Your boys are going to make wonderful surrogate brothers to my baby girl. That just *has* to happen."

I slowly nodded and my eyes filled with tears.

"I'm waiting on a call back from Lane. I'm going to really push her to take control of this footage and do something with it fast. If not? Well…" Emily paused.

"You want to throw it all over to your pals in the press, right?" I clarified.

"Not if it'll worsen the prospects of Jane and the boys coming back alive obviously!"

"As long as the game is in play and they're still being held by him, that footage getting handed over to the media would kill them all. *Guaranteed*!"

Emily nodded just as Luke entered the room, undoing his coat and dusting off the layer of snow that had accrued around his arms and shoulders. He dropped a large, thick padded envelope down on the windowsill next to Emily and me.

"Right!" he exclaimed. "That Tobin cunt or whatever his real name is can get fucked! There's his ten grand! Round Three is done. Let's go to bed and set the alarm for Round Four!"

I smiled and reached out, offering him my good hand.

He shook it and nodded.

"Thank you." I said.

"No worries." Luke grinned. "Let's just start closing the net on this bastard."

Maybe I should have been more on the ball than I was to spot that those blue lights off in the distance were drawing a little too close for my liking. But, hey come on now, I'd just been smashed off the Coast Road and sent upside down into a small ravine in the middle of a blizzard AND then took a head-first high speed dive off a car park down at Tynemouth Priory – with forced consumption of bourbon and opioids in between. Cut me *some* slack.

"Does no one else find it a little bit weird that Tobin is asking for the same amount as what Ryan has put on Jake's head?" Emily asked.

Suddenly Psychic burst into the room as the ground floor car park below lit up in a sea of blue lights. I stared down and saw that several police units were pulling to a stop and storming into this very apartment block.

"Police!" Psychic shouted.

"SHIT!" bellowed Luke.

[14]

or

"Run".

You know, for a fella whose brain has been apparently punched into granola pieces over the last couple of decades Luke Brody was the sharpest and fastest thinker of *all* of us in that room as the blue lights flickered into the night several stories below us. And Emily has two degrees and a masters so...

A neighbour had apparently seen Psychic carrying me into the building late in the evening, made an assumption that I'd been beaten up in some drunken kick-off over on Front Street and commented to her husband that such 'types' and behaviour were not welcome in this particular complex. It was another local news bulletin in the early hours of the morning whilst she couldn't sleep that forced her to make the connection and call it in. My saving grace was that there had been so many false sightings called in around the region that between manpower issues and the hazardous weather conditions, the police were struggling to wade through them all at the speed they would have preferred. They got there in the end though. That's why just after two am, what I presumed was every police unit in the entire region descended on the apartment building.

"Emily, give Jen your car keys!" barked Luke. "Jen – they don't know you or are aware you have any association to Jake so get your fucking coat on quick and casually walk on out of here. Em', tell her where your car is parked!"

He spun round and lifted me to my feet, grabbing the jacket he'd loaned me off the back of a nearby chair and thrusting it into my aching chest. "They've got this building surrounded and they're going to start hitting every apartment. They won't have the next building over surrounded though so get the fuck upstairs and get out!"

"Wait, what? I stammered.

"Psych', you go with him." Luke continued. "Get him down the other side and take Rivers View under as much cover as you can through to Tanners Bank – Jen, you meet them there!"

Jen nodded and started to pull on her coat.

I looked at Psychic. He smiled at me and shrugged then turned to look at Emily. "Keep our little girl in there until I'm back, okay?"

"Just make sure you come back!" Emily nodded. "Don't go falling off the roof of a high storied building in the middle of a snowstorm. That's such a Robbie thing to do!"

"Fuck *you*! ... I love you!" Psychic smirked as he bustled me out of the apartment door and out into the corridor. I rammed Tobin's phone into one pocket and the envelope full of money into another as we went.

We sprinted down to the fire exit door at the bottom of the communal hallway and out into the stairwell. I snatched a look and could see ten or twelve floors down that there were uniformed officers making their way up the stairs.

"Got to go! Got to go! Got to *go*!" I exclaimed as I grabbed a hold of the bannister and forcibly pulled myself up the stairs.

One flight up, Psychic smashed down on the security bar across the door panel for the roof and we stumbled out into an immediate smash of freezing white hitting us both at high speed as jet black surrounded us instantly when the door closed behind us. Psychic lit up the ground as best he could with the torch from his phone, scanning frantically until he eventually landed on a rather thin concrete and steel decorative girder that ran from our building over to its sister building maybe two-hundred or so feet away.

It was difficult to make out against the blizzard-drenched nocturnal panorama that wrapped around us as it was so entrenched in matching white.

"You have got to be shitting me!" Psychic muttered.

"Have you seen the movie Birds on a Wire with Mel Gibson and Goldie Hawn?" I asked quietly. "What about the Emilio Estevez B-movie Judgment Night?"

"No, Jake. No, I *haven't*. Do I need to have in order to know this is a terrible idea?" Psychic fired back at me.

I shook my head and put my hands on my hips. "It's probably best you haven't. That's all I was going to say."

"Scissor Paper Stone as to who's going first?" Psychic said as he held out his shivering fist towards me.

I moved my head side to side again and exhaled. "No, this is on me."

"Don't fall off okay?"

"Erm... okay. I'll try not to, dumb-arse!" I snapped.

"There's no need to be short with me. I'm trying to be encouraging. I don't *have* to be out here, you know."

"Are we *really* having a domestic right now? Now? Honestly?"

"Fine. Sorry. Look, I was just struggling to think of the right thing to say Jake." he sighed.

"I find that you say it best when you say nothing at all." I smirked as I tentatively made my way up onto the ledge and lay down onto it.

"Wait. Did you just quote Ronan Keating at me? Are you bloody serious?" Psychic said.

"Life's a rollercoaster!" I laughed as I started to shimmy myself along the beam on my stomach, gripping tightly to either side of the concrete as I went. The thick layers of snow ploughed their way free as I pulled myself along whilst keeping my legs locked straight together, drenching my top but also sending mounds of it plummeting down below in the very direction I was praying I would not go myself.

"That seems quite an effective method. Should I copy that?" hissed Psychic from out of the darkness behind me. "I just hope all the snow you're knocking off isn't landing on police below because that would be quite the giveaway to..."

"Psych'!" I snapped in a theatrical whisper. "Will you *please* shut the fuck up for a second?"

He didn't reply.

He'd already bitten the bullet and started sliding out behind me, replicating my moves to the letter. A high wind hit me hard three-quarters of the way across and I wrapped my arms around the concrete beam like I was hugging Jane again. The velocity lowered just as I heard Psychic exclaim "Jesus Christ!" behind me.

I did my best to look back and check that he was still there and then I slid onwards.

We both made it to the other side and fell into a soaking wet mound on the cold dark roof of the other apartment complex. I reached my hand out to Psychic. He took it and we shook hands whilst silently nodding our heads in unspoken appreciation of one another.

"Do you know something?" he finally said. "The thing I probably like about being in business with you is that not one day and not one case is really the same, you know?"

I nodded. "It's just a shame they're most likely going to void that deal for our life rights and not make the film about us in the end?"

"They already made this film, Jake." Psychic smirked. "It was called Taken 3. And it was rubbish!"

Psychic got up and prized the roof door open with a piece of metal.

We made our way down the fire exit stairs for a couple of levels and then took the elevator the rest of the way when my legs started to give out.

We got out the rear door to the sister complex easily enough and through the area where the communal bins were kept, each helping the other up over the boundary wall and down into the bushes on the other side.

I felt a warm liquid start to coat the roof of my mouth and congeal around the sides of my lips. I reached up and wiped it away on the sleeve of my jacket, noticing as we passed under a streetlamp that the sandy coloured sleeve was now marked with red.

A dark red.

This wasn't good.

But nor was this the time to raise it as a priority.

We passed by the school on Rivers View and stuck to the cover of darkness wherever possible, eventually pushing out through some undergrowth out onto Tanners Bank just like Luke suggested.

We could see the rear headlights for Psychic and Emily's car fifty or so metres up and made a dash for it as quickly as we could. I wasted no time in yanking open the back door on the passenger side of Psychic's off-black Audi Q8 and lying down across the seats.

Jennifer jumped in shock. "*Jesus* Jake!"

Psychic walked around to the driver's side and opened the door. "We'll take it from here, cheers Jennifer!"

"Wait. I'm not coming *with* you?" she said.

Psychic shook his head.

"And you're not dropping me back off?" she added "I'm going to try and walk back through a blizzard to get back into a building surrounded by police and without the car they saw me leave in?"

"That does sound complicated, doesn't it?" Psychic replied.

"Okay... Okay... So, I'm sorting this out myself?" she grumbled as she unclipped her seatbelt and climbed out of the driver's side. "I'm going to kick Luke right in his dick when I get back. What bullshit plan was this? There's a bloody blizzard raging and its two in the morning and..."

Psychic shut the door on her as she continued her rant.

He sped off leaving her standing in the middle of the road.

"I'm sorry, I know that was rude, but we'd have been there all night otherwise!" he said as he pulled his seatbelt on and adjusted the mirrors as he drove.

"I meant to ask you." I said from the back seat. "How much is this car setting you back a month then?"

"Don't *start*, Lehman!" Psychic sneered.

Let's press pause and roll out a quick quiz before we head into the final stretch of this whole sorry saga, okay? Let's separate those who've been paying attention from those who have just been scanning the pages looking for tips on *great* music. And screw you to those who went on 'Good Reads' and had a bit of a bitch about the fact that I gave a shout-out (pardon the pun) to Lulu's cover version of 'Mighty Quinn' last time round, by the way.

Question 1 of 1. Finish the following 'Jake Lehman' proclamation you should all know by now: *"Newcastle is a big ... ?"*

What's that?

Yes. That's correct. Newcastle <u>is</u> a big city but a small place - all roads lead into each other's pockets in one way or another.

And because this assertion is true, Psychic and I found ourselves parked up and tucked away at nearly three am on old farm grounds situated on the edge of Rising Sun Country Park that belonged to a friend of his dad's, us both having bombed up the A19 and out of North Shields to leave behind the high volume police search for me.

I'd climbed out from the back of Psychic's Audi and had joined him in the front. We couldn't afford to run the engine in order to keep the car heated so we sat together shivering. After an hour or so, with neither of us unable to cope with the chattering of each other's teeth as snow cascaded heavily down around us, he relented and turned the engine over and blasted out the heat for a bit. With it came the radio which Psychic instinctively went to switch off.

"Leave it, just turn it down." I said quietly to him through the darkness in which we hid. "There might be another update on the news soon that we could do with hearing."

Psychic nodded.

'Little Drummer Boy', the Bing Crosby and David Bowie version, played out gently in the background:

"♫♫ ... Come they told me. Pa rum pum pum pum. A newborn king to see. Pa rum pum pum pum. Our finest gifts we bring. Pa rum pum pum pum. To lay before the king. Pa rum pum pum pum. Rum pum pum pum. Rum pum pum pum... ♫♫"

Psychic looked out into the nothingness that surrounded us. Just trees and some rusted up farm equipment left to ruin inside of an old stable area that had long since fell to bits. Way off in the distance was a construction site as more new houses got built on any and every inch of land the property development companies could pull away from the independent farmers and landowners that existed or used to exist around the edges of the Rising Sun grounds. The friend of Psychic's dad being one of those types who'd long since taken the cheque and abandoned what he once had here. What was left standing would be imminently bulldozed to the ground and built on top of.

"The sun will be up soon." He said quietly.

I nodded. "That's going to add an extra layer of difficulty."

"I guess so, yeah." Psychic replied. "I was talking to Emily back at the flat though and she's really going to push hard on getting some clandestine meeting with Chief Constable Lane arranged, putting a copy of our footage into her hands and getting her to call off the dogs, so to speak."

"Hopefully it will be that easy."

"♫♫ ... Little baby. Pa rum pum pum pum. I am a poor boy too. Pa rum pum pum pum. I have no gift to bring. Pa rum pum pum pum. That's fit to give our king ... ♫♫"

"But there's still the matter of Ryan turning the entire criminal underworld loose on me." I said forlornly as I tapped my fingers on my legs gently in time with the song.

"Yeah, I don't know what to do about that. I honestly thought Luke was going to have a breakthrough there." Psychic said. "I just can't believe Ryan has been able to do that. Is there no sort of respected structure to this...? I don't know... 'gangster' way of life? The man at the top dies and his fucking coffee boy just steps in and takes his place and starts barking orders?"

"I guess it's difficult when you were as monumental as Bobby Maitland was. He wiped out pretty much all of his rivals so I don't know who would see his death as something they could maximise the opportunity to expand out and take advantage of. There wasn't really anyone left. The void would have to have been filled with someone stepping up from within I suppose." I pondered.

"♫♫ ... Pa rum pum pum. Pum pum pum pum. Mary nodded. Pa rum pum pum pum. The ox and lamb kept time. Pa rum pum pum pum ... ♫♫"

"You'd think one of the small-fry lot from south of the river would step up though?" Psychic countered.

"There's still time. His body's not yet cold if you think about it!"

"He had everyone in line in a lot of regards, but he still had a couple of dissenters. Bobby was always moaning about the shitheads over in Gateshead fucking things up for him by not getting in sync with his operations and..."

"Wait!" I interrupted, twisting painfully in my seat to look at him. "Say that again?"

"Which bit?"

"All of it!"

"What? That one of the smaller families down in Stockton or Gateshead might want to step up? What I mean is that surely it shouldn't be as easy as Ryan fucking Flaherty just stepping over the big boss' corpse and saying, 'I'm the captain now'!"

"I think you've just put an idea in my head buddy!" I smiled. "How much time do we have left on the clock?"

"It's just after three am. We've got time. What are you thinking?"

"I'm thinking about pulling a 'Yojimbo Method'!" I grinned.

Psychic and I worked on a commercial malfeasance / corporate espionage job a few years back and it was a little bit difficult because our client knew that something was amiss and that an employee had breached confidentiality and started trading company secrets to business rivals but it was difficult in getting to the bottom of just which one of said rivals had entertained the notion and which one had gone right ahead and bought the stolen materials for their own game. So we rigged a scenario that put some high value materials of our clients' into a *controlled* black-market sale and then played both of these rivals off against one another in order to out which one was the one dealing in the stolen stuff and who their mole/handler was within our client's company.

And it worked a *treat* and I'd love to sit here and brag about it in more detail and tell you exactly how we pulled it off, etc. but... well... my wife and children are still kidnapped, I've got a ten grand hit still on my head, a psychopath out killing anyone associated with me and the whole of the local police service hunting me down so it's best if we stay focused here, okay?

"You're thinking about pulling the 'Yojimbo Method'?" Psychic said with a look of confusion. "Who the hell are you going to play *that* with?"

[15]

or

30th August 2013.

The first thing I noticed as we neared the bottom of the descent down the old dirt road towards the gate for the Brennan facility was *not* the giant decrepit sign fastened with chains above the entrance in the fence line that broadcasted '*BRENNAN – Last of the Independents*' in badly painted, rusty red letters across a decaying white background. No, the first thing that my attention was drawn to was the sound of Smokey Robinson's 'Tears of a Clown' blasting out from inside the grounds, the tinny low-quality acoustics of it rattling across the barren desert wilderness that surrounded it.

Rachel and I were still squabbling about the approach we were going to take as we drew closer and closer... and *closer* still to the entrance gates of Brennan itself.

"I think we should go with the TV production thing!" I proffered quickly.

"I don't know. That's risky. We haven't really thought that through!" she countered.

"It's no more or less thought through than claiming we're from Bagnall-Farina Inc." I fired back. "I can blag my way through being a TV producer. I don't know the first bloody thing about being a... being a... I don't even know how to describe what role I'd have at BFI!"

Rachel smiled as she slid through the opening where it appeared that a locked gate once stood. She pulled the car to a stop and turned to me just as two men started to approach.

"Okay. *Fine*. We'll go with the TV thing, yeah? 10 News First on Network 10, yes?"

"Wait." I exclaimed. "*What?*"

"We're producers from 10 News First on the Network 10 channel. Okay?"

I nodded just as a dirt strewn man with a quizzical look approached and shouted "How are you going? Can I help you folks?"

"Don't tell me you're lost?" laughed his colleague, a big round fella with no neck.

"No, I think this is where we're meant to be." Rachel smiled. "This is Brennan, right?"

The no-necked fella pointed back to the sign above her head on the other side of the fence line. "That's what that thing says, eh?"

His colleague laughed.

Rachel grinned and nodded. "I'm from Network 10. I was wondering if I can speak to the site manager, if that's possible?"

"Have you got an appointment or something? Is he expecting you? Because it seems you've taken a hell of a chance just driving out here on a whim!" asked the sweat-strewn dirty man.

"My bosses were meant to have rung ahead and sorted a meeting out, yes." Rachel chuffed.

"You sure of that, girl?" No-Neck said, leaning it and propping himself against her side of the car. "I'm not sure the phones have worked up here since Malcolm bloody Fraser ran the country!"

The dirty workmate laughed at an inside joke that I was clearly destined never to get.

"It'd be great if I could talk to somebody about why we're here. We've come a very long way you see and..."

"Where you both come from?" The dirty workmate jumped in with.

Rachel fixed her grin solidly to her face. "Sorry, what's your name?"

The dirty one stuck out his muck-stained enormous hand. "My name's Harv'. This big useless bugger here is Rodge."

The no-necked man I now knew as 'Rodge' smiled and threw Rachel and I a quick salute.

Rachel and I nodded and smiled back in unison.

She took Harv's hand and shook it warmly.

"Hi Harv'. I'm Rachel. We're both from Sydney and we represent 10 News First on Network 10. We're looking to do a story on Brennan and how it has survived as this 'David' of the coal mining industry against all the 'Goliaths' out there. This is my colleague, Jake."

I reached over Rachel and extended my hand.

"Hi Harv'." I said warmly. "It's nice to meet you."

Harv' didn't take my hand. Instead he clapped his hands and shouted "Hey Rodge, I think we've got a bleedin' pom here!"

It was *that* instant.

Rodge moved round to Rachel's side of the car. "Our boss is a bloke called Sid Berenger. You'll find him up in the main tower over there!"

He pointed off to the far right of the compound at a rickety looking wooden tower with a small cabin affixed to the top of the immense vertical beams, accessible by what looked like a thin metal ladder driven into the wood. Next to that? A giant metal rig structure that disappeared into the very hole in the ground eliciting clanging and rattling that could be heard all around the compound. A steel cage attached to a lift pully hung precariously over the open hole.

"I'll go get him down for you guys if you just go pull your car in down there on your left." Rodge continued as he pointed at the enormous faded yellow steel receptacle further down on the left, near to the tower itself. "Be prepared though, he's not going to be interested in shite like that."

Rodge walked off and Harv' banged on the side panel of Rachel's car as we moved off slowly to where we'd been directed to. I tried to take in as much as I could as Rachel curled the car round to the left.

There was the aforementioned tower up ahead of us with the giant yellow petrol pump near it. A row of battered shipping containers lined up along from the tower. As they went on, they became stacked two containers high. Opposite to them on the other side were portacabins, some made of wood and some put together in that old-fashioned aluminium siding type of material.

Smokey Robinson finished up 'Tears of a Clown' just as my eyes fell on the ground levelling downwards off on the furthest corner of the left where there were more containers and parked amongst them a series of trucks and discarded vehicle parts.

We parked up and alighted from the vehicle, both of us stretching our bodies out and making the same groaning noises in harmony, each spinning on the spot to take in our surroundings as we stretched out. A few hundred metres or so off down towards the portacabin and the cluster of trucks we could see a small group of men making their way across the orangey dirt terrain from one end of the grounds to a cabin on the other side.

A breeze was kicking up and throwing dust aloft, creating a knee-high haze on the terrain up ahead. If it wasn't for the fall out from causing a few too many dirt particles to fly close to my eyes and nose, I'd say that such a light wind was both otherwise welcome and pleasant.

"Maybe we should start counting heads?" I offered. "So, we know what we're up against if they start getting shitty with us?"

"I don't know, Jake. Harv' and Rodge seemed positively delightful." Rachel smiled.

I ignored her. "Them, plus the five I just saw cross over down the other end of the site? That's seven."

"Good counting. Is this your Sesame Street audition?" she giggled.

We didn't get a chance to go any further with this because striding towards us was a broad shouldered, leather-skinned man with a look of consternation on his face and a poorly buttoned flannel shirt that had seen better days.

"How are you going? I'm Sid Berenger. This site is mine. Can I help?" he shouted before he was even in close proximity to the both of us, Rodge wide-stepping alongside him to keep up.

Rachel fixed on that fake grin of hers tightly once more and met him halfway towards us with her hand extended. She hit him hard and *instantly* with the whole 'chuff' about being from Network 10 and wanting to do a piece for 10 News First about "the true, dedicated Aussie independent miners standing off against the international billion-dollar industry titans trying to crush them out of the game".

Sid smiled knowingly. "I wouldn't go that far but you sure do make us sound good. I'm not sure we'd be interested though."

Rachel pushed on.

Sid pushed back. "What's your name, girl?"

Rachel introduced herself and then me, just as she had to Harv' and Rodge.

"Here's the thing, Rachel. We do well because we're out here in the back of bourke right in the middle of the never-never. We run a small, tight ship of just a few tradies who like hard yakka and we survive by keeping ourselves and our methods cheap and close to our chest, if that makes sense? We do well because we're secretive about how we do what we do. Putting it out there on your telly show is a risk. It's also a risk I'm pretty certain most of my blokes just wouldn't be interested in. I know, Rodge said your boss had made a call beforehand but I didn't get any call. I'm sorry because if I had I could have stopped you making the trek up here."

I doubted just how secretive they truly were up here at Brennan seeing as their gate posts were decidedly lacking in an actual *gate* or any sort of security checkpoint. We did, after all, drive straight in here. I was thinking about saying some smart-arsed variation on this when I became instantly distracted by something sticking out from between the last two containers on the far side of the compound, down towards where the mining point was situated.

"Could we... still... maybe grab a tour... as long as we promise not to record or photograph anything, of course?" I found myself saying distantly whilst my eyes fixated on what I thought looked like the front of a huge lorry.

Sid's eye burrowed down deep onto me. "Where you from, lad?"

"Me?" I stuttered as I refocused back on what I should been focused on all along. "I'm from the UK originally but I've been out here a few years now working for Channel 10."

"Network 10!" Rachel swiftly corrected. "These poms and their weird turns-of-phrase for things eh, Sid?"

Sid half-smiled but kept his eyes on me. "So, there was no news-man jobs in England then? You had to come take one off an honest, hardworking, true blue Australian then?"

"Well no... that's... not... what..."

He didn't let me finish. "I'm just gammin', mate... I'm *kidding* with you."

The lack of smile and the unchanged expression on his face indicated he wasn't.

I slowly nodded.

We stood looking at one another. Sid's eyes took to checking me out, up and down. His gaze switched to Rachel. The silence was awful and uncomfortable. She kept smiling no matter what. The only sound was the clanging coming from the mine and a sudden and unexpected whistle from the wind picking up.

"Looks like we're going to have a bit of a sandy nip!" shouted Rodge.

I looked across to Rachel and semi-shrugged with confusion.

Finally, Sid spoke. "Ah fuck it. You two have come a long way. Let me walk you both around and let you stretch your legs before your long journey back down to..."

"Sydney!" Rachel grinned.

"Sydney? Right..." nodded Sid as he started to walk off.

"What's a 'sandy nip'?" I asked as we followed him and Rodge tucked in alongside us.

"Sandstorm!" Rodge replied matter-of-factly.

Sid walked us through the main open grounds of the facility, giving us the potted history of the place and how long it had been going for and explaining that it was a fully-functioning live-in site with all of the men taking residence in one of the specially adapted containers where they bedded down at the end of each shift.

"We've even got our own pub!" Rodge interjected with a smile, pointing back to a container back up next to where our car was parked. "Serves proper grog too!"

"How many people have you got on site?" I asked Sid.

He turned as he walked and snarled "Why do you want to know how many people I have on the lurk, pom?"

He stopped in his tracks and looked at me hard. "What didn't you understand? You've been here a few years, yeah? You have the lingo down, right?"

I slowly nodded. "Yeah?"

"Lurk *means*?" he quizzed.

Rachel stood behind both his and Rodge's line of sight and mouthed the word 'job' at me.

"It means *job*!" I responded with faked confidence.

Sid eyed me suspiciously and moved on.

An old man who looked two steps away from the grave staggered on with two fellas walking either side of him, both of whom looked so dirtied I could not determine what their natural skin colour actually was.

"Here! Hold up!" shouted Sid, bringing us to a stop directly in their path. "This fella right here is who you want to be doing your story about!"

He stopped and put his arm roughly around the shoulders of the old man.

"This old bludger right here is 'Goodjob Walt'!" Sid exclaimed. "He's one of the Brennan *originals*. The last of the last of the independents, if you get me. Say hello, Walt mate!"

Walt smiled and offered his hand first to me and then on to Rachel.

"G'day. How are you going?" he said. "Who am I saying g'day to and what's a couple of young 'uns like you two doing out here?"

"They want to do a story about us, Goodjob Walt!" Sid smirked. "They're from some news network down in Sydney. This one right here is a job-stealing *pom*, can you believe it?"

He pointed at me. His smile didn't seem like it was selling the concept of 'banter' all that successfully.

"You want to do a story about Brennan?" Walt grinned though his eyes seemed to suggest something else entirely. "Well isn't that something!"

"*You* don't still go down the mines though, do you?" Rachel asked.

"What you saying? I'm walking cactus or something?" Goodjob Walt laughed before shaking his head. "Nah, nah. My days of that sort of lurk are long behind me, girl. We had a fall-in here about... ninety-nine... was it?"

Sid stepped in. "No, Walt mate. The fall-in was *long* after that."

Sid's eyes burrowed deep into the side of Walt's head.

"What's a fall-in?" Rachel inquired.

"It's a tunnel collapse that has a domino effect and brings everything down beneath it and on all sides of it. It pulls down everything in its vicinity. It's the *big* 'un!" said one of the men standing next to Walt.

"Sorry, where's my manners eh?" Sid said, putting his arm on this man's shoulder. "This here is John Kalinda and the man to his left is his big brother, Scott. They're another couple of longstanding Brennan grafters."

Hello's were exchanged, comments made about how Brennan breeds loyalty, etc. and amongst it all I started to struggle to maintain my count. Were these men part of the group I saw earlier crossing the grounds? Are these new to my existing count or to be added on top of the seven I have stored in my head already?

Scott seized the introduction as an opportunity to takeover. "Yeah, we were lucky to only lose one bloke that day. Goodjob Walt saved the day though. Hence the nickname, you see? He got us all out. We lost decades of work. That whole thing fell in on itself and to this day it's just a big unstable mess down there we have to swerve around when working now."

"Wow!" Rachel gasped. "Maybe *that's* the story right there!"

"As I said," Sid growled. "We're not really looking for *any* of the stories about Brennan to get told. Come on, let me walk you back around to your car."

Walt slowly nodded his head whilst staring intently at Sid.

Nah, *something* didn't seem on the level here. I just couldn't put my finger on it.

This was driven home mere minutes later when we curled off to the left as we headed down towards the mining point and I saw a cluster of small trucks and lorries parked in a scatter behind a batch of containers. The end of one of them was what had first captured my attention before we'd set off on this 'tour' of sorts.

The vehicles blocked the path of a three-carriage road train that to my eye looked exactly like the one we had identified as being in the vicinity up in the Blue Mountains around the time of Edvin Sixten's death.

"Man *alive*!" I exclaimed overly dramatically whilst pointing over to the road train as a means to make sure Rachel's attention had been fully drawn to it. "That's some *beast* you've got there. Is that what you use to get the coal you mine delivered all around the country?"

The Kalinda brothers had long since broken off and Goodjob Walt was lingering around somewhere a few feet back. Rachel looked at the road train then back to me and smiled knowingly. She eventually brought herself back round to look directly at Sid.

"Can we go look at that up close?" she said, putting on a little girlish type smile. "This is going to make me sound like a complete nerd, but I'm *really* into trucks and shit in a big way and I've always wanted to see a straight-up, legit road train in the flesh?"

"Are you serious?" Sid asked quizzically.

"God yes! I hear that they have reinforced driver's cabins and some serious sets of wheels on the under carriage and..."

"Hey, fill you boots!" Sid shrugged.

I hung back and dawdled a little in order to inconspicuously put myself a bit closer to Goodjob Walt himself.

"You're one of the last of the original crew then, eh Walt?" I enquired.

"Sid likes to undersell me," Walt replied as he spat a big clump of thick, discoloured saliva out onto the ground by his feet. "I was one of the *founding* bloody members of this site. Me, his dad and another fella. He likes to try and cut that bit of the story out though, does young Sidney."

I nodded and faked a look of being impressed. "So, it started out just the three of you? How many work the mine now?"

"Sid's got twelve lads now, including his boy Danny as his second on site. Fourteen if you count Sid himself and me but I'm just a handyman nowadays. I do bits and bobs to get my packet at the end of the week... just to be able to keep the lights on, you know?"

"I thought that would all be included with the live-in arrangements?"

Walt shook his head and pointed off in the direction of eleven o'clock to where we were standing. "I've got my own little sweet spot up over the hill a few miles towards Warburton. I'm too old to be putting up with the noise these lads make when they've clocked off."

"Fascinating." I muttered.

"You'll never get him to go on record about this place by the way. For one, you're English and the Berenger's don't do business with anyone that's not true-blue Oz through and through."

"That must be hard when they're exporting coal?" I smirked.

Walt ignored me. "For another, he's got a tight little ship here that he's not going to want to shine a light on."

Sid himself suddenly barked loudly across at us. "What are you wittering on about, Walt? 'Pommy Bastard' get yourself over here!"

The 'Pommy Bastard' was me, it seemed.

I walked over as Sid came back down towards me, Rachel walking a few steps behind him with a huge wide-eyed expression on her face she was directing right at me.

"It pains me to say this but it's not looking safe for you two to go trying to travel back down today!" Sid said with his hands on his hips and the dust scattering up around his feet. "This sandstorm is coming in too fast and you'll be going straight into its path if you leave now. You'll not be able to see the nose on the end of your face and it'll probably put the two of you upside down and on your arse. Try and go around it and you could end up getting lost in the smoke blowing in off the fire up in the territories. You've basically created a *right* mess for yourselves."

Rachel and I looked at one another with concern.

"Come back down to my office and I'll sort you out with a couple of beds for the night and you can get yourselves off first thing in the morning." Sid offered, as he strode off once more totally uninterested in hearing our response.

"Sounds like the best plan!" Rachel said loudly before turning back to me and conspiratorially whispering "The road train is *our* road train!"

"What?" I gasped.

"I will check my notes when we get a discreet minute," she whispered, "but I'm pretty damn sure that the reg we *want* to find is BTF-936 and the reg we have on that thing over there matches that!"

"Fuck!" I muttered.

"What are you two whispering away about?" Sid shouted back at us. "You're not worried you're going to get murdered in your sleep, are you?"

"No!" we both sang out in unison.

"Don't be stupid!" Rachel buttoned on the end.

Though that was absolutely and unequivocally exactly what I was worried about frankly, so much so the concern drew all my attention away from noticing the three Brennan men checking out Rachel's jeep up close as we rounded back in order to head up towards where we'd originally parked.

[16]

or

"The Yojimbo Method".

For those not in the know, Yojimbo is a 1961 samurai movie made by Akira Kurosawa. There's a lot of people that consider it Kurosawa's best movie and there's some that consider it to be his best *samurai* movie. Both of those sets of people have clearly not watched Kurosawa's Seven Samurai - the goddamn granddaddy of action cinema - and should be treat with caution, if you ask me. And I say that as someone who recognises Yojimbo as an absolute masterpiece too but still, let's try to be reasonable here.

Yojimbo stars the magnificent Toshiro Mifune as a Ronin (a masterless samurai) who lands in a small town where two rivalling crime lords are at war for supremacy and he sets himself up in a manner where both rivals each want to hire the Ronin as a bodyguard for themselves and Mifune's character plays both sides off against one another in order to wipe them out and save the villagers from the effects of their criminal behaviour and constant warring.

This all might sound familiar to those that didn't realise that Sergio Leone's A Fistful of Dollars with Clint Eastwood and Walter Hill's Last Man Standing with Bruce Willis are in fact direct Westernised remakes of this Kurosawa classic. Oh, and by the way, there's a lot of clueless dickheads, wanting to appear more educated on Kurosawa and world cinema than they are, who identify 'Yojimbo' as the main character's name and that's bullshit. Yojimbo is the Japanese word for 'bouncer' or 'bodyguard'. Mifune's character is *actually* called Kuwabatake Sanjuro…

I digress. I apologise.

"I get your intention. I know what you're referencing and I will never forget you forcing me to watch the film itself," Psychic said. "But I'm just saying I don't know who you're talking about playing off against one another here? Ryan and the police? How the hell are you going to do that? Who else?"

"Do you remember how Bobby used to talk about those fellas up in the 'shit-hills' of Gateshead, as he called it? How he used to always say they'd be the first to gun him down in the street to take so much as one slice of what he's established?"

Psychic stared at me open-mouthed as if he knew where I was going but didn't like it very much nonetheless.

"Well, if we're being really pernickety about all of this than everything Bobby established is up for grabs isn't it? Why does Ryan Flaherty get to say that it isn't? If there was a stand-out war for control now Bobby's gone, and Ryan ended up the victor then so be it. But that hasn't happened. Bobby's dead. Ryan has said I've done it and…"

"To be fair, *everyone's* saying you did it, mate." Psychic offered.

"Focus!" I retorted.

"Sorry. I apologise. But are you seriously sitting here and telling me that with what little time you have left between rounds on this stupid, deadly game Tobin has going with you and with the lives of your wife and children at stake, you're going to sneak past every scumbag out there trying to do you in for ten grand AND the entirety of this region's police to go stir things up enough between Ryan Flaherty and the Barton boys… The fucking *Barton* boys?"

I stared out the window and took note of the snowbanks deepening up around us. I exhaled hard and discreetly wiped away more dark blood before it had a chance to seep out the corners of my mouth and then I looked across at the clock on the driver's side dashboard of Psychic's Audi Q8 and watched as the digits changed right before my eyes over to 03:30am.

My head slowly started to nod.

"I'm going to tiptoe past the police, creep around all these goons out to try and off me for ten thousand quid and I'm going to go start a war between Ryan Flaherty and the Barton boys… and I'm going to do all of that and be back onboard to start Round Four at nine am!"

"Aww Jake, *man*!" Psychic sighed as he switched on the ignition and started to grind us out of our hiding spot and through the heavy snow.

There's a major problem with trying to be desperately inconspicuous when you're wanted at the level I was and yet in one of the only few cars stupid enough to be out on the road in these precarious conditions and at this time of the morning too.

Psychic drove cautiously but with purpose and tried to not pull panicked or desperate counter-manoeuvres on sight of approaching police vehicles. By just after four am we'd hit the A695 and were heading down into an old housing estate near Blaydon Burn where we knew the entire Barton crime family lived, scattered across multiple ex-council houses in the same street that they'd bought, expanded and decorated in that horrible, overly ostentatious style people with vast disposable / questionable income but no discernible taste often did.

We knew where Paul Barton lived for definite. We'd completed some surveillance on his address about a year after we broke the Stephanie Jason case. Bobby Maitland had suffered a break-in at one of his warehouses and he'd heard a rumour that the Barton boys were responsible. Whispering on the street suggested a small section of said stolen goods would be getting delivered to Paul Barton's house over the course of the next week.

There were several options I could take here in terms of how approaches go. Psychic and I had discussed most if not all of them on the drive over. I'd opted, time being what it was, to just go with walking right up to the man's front door, knocking him out of bed and asking to have an open and honest conversation with him.

Psychic thought I was mad, but he couldn't offer me a better alternative. I didn't want to even get close to discussing with him that my pain was starting to get too much and the thick, dark blood coming up from inside clearly suggested things weren't looking good for me in there. I was bottling down just how frantic I was feeling about the possibility of dying before I could get Jane, Jack and Jonathan back.

I had to use this pain as fuel and push on. No matter what.

Psych' was right to worry about my approach because Paul Barton was not the 'friendly' sort if his reputation was to be believed and he certainly wasn't the type to be any more friendly from having been knocked out of bed at four in the morning:

Paul was about ten or fifteen years younger than Bobby Maitland. They'd always been in each other's circles and there was once a period of time when Paul worked as a 'heavy-hitter' for Bobby way back when the man himself was first on the rise in the North East.

Do you remember a while back I told you all about when local head-honcho crime figures Alfie and Roy Woodruff were shotgun blasted to death in the car park of The Charnwood back in 1998 and it was always thought among certain circles that Bobby Maitland was one of the two shooters that night as part of a power grab against the Woodruffs, though it was never proven. Well, what *was* proven was that the other shooter that night was definitely Paul Barton.

There was a fundamental difference between these two men that neither could see past. Bobby believed in extreme violence as a *rarity*, to be brought out and used sparingly for maximum effectiveness against the most necessary of situations. Like murdering your crime bosses so you can take their place. As a result, the mere threat of it could be effective without it automatically being required. Paul was the opposite. He fucking *loved* violence. He lived for it and would force through any excuse to beat, bite, burn and bury anyone he could for any infraction he envisaged, minor and upwards. That's why he was never out of prison for pretty much three decades straight, apparently.

In the eyes of Bobby, Paul Barton was a loose cannon he didn't want anywhere near his businesses and he distanced himself accordingly. The level to which this bothered Paul dissipated in time. Especially as his brothers, Freddy and Ricky, soon rose up 'on the wrong side of the street' and joined him on his rounds of armed robbery, drug dealing and general thuggery.

They became a major headache for Bobby and the closer Psychic and I got to him in these last few years, he was never backwards in coming forwards in spitting fury about them. After years of having them smacked around by a few of his blokes, barred from his establishments and marks placed against them should they ever target any of his businesses, Bobby apparently eased off a little. He came to regard them as 'small fish' and subsequently let the Barton boys "fuck around" in the pubs and estates in Gateshead as long as they respected *his* major territories in the region.

And yes, you're absolutely right – Ricky Barton *is* a ridiculous name when considered up against the existence of a certain Latin American gay popstar turned actor. But I'll let you go and tell Ricky himself that. Do you know why? Because eight years ago, someone thought it was funny to play 'Living La Vida Loca' on a pub jukebox in Swalwell every time Ricky went in there for a drink. By the fourth time, ol' Ricky cottoned on to what was being done and ended up embedding two-pint glasses in the guy's mouth and eyes.

All that being said, you can understand my nervousness as I pulled myself from Psychic's car and staggered towards Paul Barton's front gate.

"I'll wait here." Psychic had said.

"And what?" I'd replied incredulously.

"And... if it all goes south, I'll beep my horn really aggressively and make my disapproval known. How about that?"

"Yeah, that sounds good, dickhead. Just make sure you press on your horn really hard so that I can hear it whilst Paul is stamping on my skull, okay?"

I took a deep breath and knocked on the door.

The lights upstairs didn't just go on almost immediately, the lights across the street did too. And two doors down from that hit their lights as well. Before I knew it, all these doors on the estate started opening up and half-dressed figures crunched haphazardly through the snow towards me.

"Erm... Jake?" Psychic shouted at me from the comforts of his car.

As these bodies blasted through Paul Barton's gate and up the drive towards me, the front door opened and there stood Paul himself - in all his greying, sagging, tattooed and thoroughly naked glory save for a very thick terry-towelling dressing gown that he could / should have tied up around his waist. The belt was right there, dangling away right alongside a penis that really didn't have the sort of physical heft and impressiveness to make it worthy of being put out on display. No matter the hour.

"WHO THE FUCK ARE YOU?" screamed Paul.

"What you doing knocking on the man's door at four in the morning?" hollered one of the several male voices surrounding me on the doorstep.

One muscular, tattooed arm reached out amongst the throng and grabbed my head, pushing it up against the wall with a force I didn't have any resilience to fight against.

"Uncle Paul! Uncle Paul!" bellowed another voice. "This is that lad off the news, isn't it?"

"YOU WHAT?" Paul shouted.

Suddenly I was off my feet and being pushed hard to the ground. Paul didn't have time to move backwards so my face smacked off his aged penis as I was taken to the floor. I was incredibly *not happy* about this, as you can well imagine.

I could just about make out Psychic's voice as he tried to reason with people left, right and centre. If at this point you're all screaming *"How's your car horn method working out Psychic, you utter bastard?"* then good on you. I'm right there with you.

"This is that Jake Lehman bastard, Paul. There's ten grand on this fucker's head, do you know that?" interjected the man I recognised as Freddy Barton. "That's what I was hearing late last night anyway!"

"Are you telling me I can take this cunt's head off and get ten kay for doing it?" shouted Ricky Barton.

"Or you could hear me out for three minutes as to why I knocked on your door in the middle of a blizzard at four in the morning and make millions instead!" I shouted right back from below the angry horde of Barton family members.

"WHAT DID HE JUST SAY?" screeched Paul as he reached on down and grabbed hold of me by the neck, yanking me right up onto my feet. "What did you just say?"

I was nearly sick with the pain as he did so.

"Uncle Paul!" hollered one of the younger male's voices in the group. "I definitely think this is the fella all over the news. He's wanted by the police and he escaped from a police van or something. But he's definitely wanted!"

"Aren't we all!" another voice said to a communal burst of laughter.

"I *am* Jake Lehman, yes. I am wanted. But wanted for something I didn't do. I'm not denying that. There's a ten-grand price on my head, I'm not denying that either. But if you ignore that, focus on the long game and help me out over the course of the next four hours then you and your family could be pulling in *millions* instead." I offered.

"How'd you reckon that then?" Paul snarled.

"You heard Bobby's dead, right?" I murmured as his grip tightened around my neck.

"Wait!" Freddy said as he pushed his way in further to get alongside Paul and look at me dead in the eyes. "That's *really* true? Maitland is dead?"

I nodded as best as I could with my head held in Paul's hand. "Bobby Maitland is dead. That's who's murder I've been framed for. That and... well... that and *one other*... but... okay... that's not important. Let me back track... Ryan Flaherty is trying to frame me for Bobby's murder but that's only to distract from the fact he's pulling an instant takeover of the man's whole empire without paying the proper respects."

Paul's grip slackened just ever so slightly from around my neck.

I took my chances.

"Ryan didn't come up with Bobby. *You* did." I said pushing my forehead forward in the direction of Paul Barton. "I don't know who killed Bobby Maitland, but I damn well know it *wasn't* me. It could be you or one of your family for all I know. To put it bluntly, it is fuck all to do with me. The only thing I know from talking to Bobby and working for him these last few years is that he had a *code* and he believed there were rules to live by. Ryan Flaherty just stepping over his corpse before it's cold and taking control of everything; barking out orders and putting out hits on anyone who disagrees with him goes against *all* the codes and *all* the rules that were important to Bobby."

Paul dropped his grip completely and took a step back. He waved off the men pushing around me and they made enough space so that I could see Psychic was up the drive and trying to get closer to where I was stood.

"I don't know who gives a shit, but *I* believe in Bobby's code and I believe you and your family don't deserve to be cut out of consideration. I've worked these streets in various capacities over the years and I know that deep down Bobby respected you and your family and how self-made you all were whilst existing within the same code." I lied.

Chuff. Chuff. *Chuff.*

Chuff like your life depends on it, Jake. Maybe because it bloody well does.

"So... you can smash my head in right now or cut my throat or whatever then dump my body on the doorstep of Bobby's office that Ryan is now claiming as his own and pocket ten grand for doing so." I continued. "Hell, you can tape up my hands and bag my head then dump me there with a pulse still in my veins and claim fifteen from what I'm hearing now. Or... Or... you can help me keep Bobby's code of ethics alive amongst you gentlemen and in place by seizing your chance to take on the businesses he's left behind and reap millions. I can help you get those millions and I only have *two* conditions."

Paul looked over my shoulder to his brothers.

I didn't think I'd nailed it entirely as well as I needed to.

I could still see by the furrow in his brow that there was an uncertainty.

"I mean... well... at the end of the day, Paul... do you want to finally own this city or not?" I stammered desperately.

BANG! That was *it*. I saw the effectiveness of that last sentence land like I'd hit a bullseye.

Ricky Barton stepped right up into my face and started looking me up and down.

I could hear Freddy in the background lean into Paul. "I don't know if we need to rush on this. Bobby's not even six feet under yet. Let's be patient. Let's throw this twat back into the sea and let some other predator nail him. We can walk out tomorrow, next week or next month and take this city anyway."

Ricky started to smile whilst staring directly at me. "I don't know brother, I have always really, *really* hated that smarmy Ryan Flaherty bastard!"

Paul stepped forward and wrapped his arm around Ricky's shoulder, a smile broke wide across his face as well. "Me too, Rick! Me fucking *too*!"

He turned to look straight at me. "Okay. What are your conditions?"

"We have to act really fast and you have to wear clothes!" I smiled.

[17]

or

"Big Feet / Small Boots".

"I hear you want me and you're willing to pay anywhere from ten to fifteen thousand pound to get me." I snarled at Ryan Flaherty through Paul Barton's mobile phone whilst sat in the man's living room, surrounded by him and his family members.

I was sat underneath his ginormous flat-screen TV that took up most of the wall it was mounted on - but which could have done with taking up *all* of the wall to hide the hideous wallpaper made up of tiled prints of the Tyne Bridge and the Newcastle skyline.

"*Lehman*?" Ryan's voice spat back down the phone line. "Is that really you?"

"How many other people have you put out hits on within the first twelve hours of jumping into Bobby's chair?"

"You know there's nowhere you can hide that I won't find you, right?" Ryan fired out at me. "You know you'll never be able to out-run me?"

"You know I'm not hiding, right?" I replied. "I was just biding my time."

"You better be calling me to tell me *now* it's time for you to face proper justice for what you did." He said, each word curdling with fury.

"I didn't kill Bobby Maitland." I said more loudly and with more assertiveness.

"Bullshit!" Ryan roared back. "You took a cheap shot on me from behind like the coward you are and then slit his throat. And you're going to pay for it."

Paul Barton clicked his fingers and rolled his fingers around in a circle in the internationally recognised sign for 'Wrap it the fuck up!'

I nodded and took one big deep breath. Because as far as I was concerned, we'd reached the moment where Ryan Flaherty was going to show an interest in the true facts or such a lack of interest was going to possibly cost him his own life.

"I have footage of someone confessing to Bobby's murder. Not just his murder but the murder of other people associated to me. I'm willing to give it to you and prove to you that I'm telling the truth."

Ryan exhaled down the phone and there was an uncomfortable pause. "I would be interested in taking a look at that, obviously. But I'm not confident it's going to change a thing. I've never liked you, Lehman. And that runs deep."

"Let's see what it changes. You. Me. Six am at the old boat yard off Kingfisher Boulevard down in Scotswood. We're going to settle this once and for all."

And *that's* how I found myself sat in the backseat of Psychic's car, Ricky Barton pushed in alongside me to my left and Ricky's eldest boy, Ben Barton, to my right at just after five am. We drove on through the slicing snowfall back over to the north side of the Tyne in a convoy of three cars to set ourselves up as per Paul Barton's very specific directions.

Ricky sat pushing shotgun cartridges into his pockets whilst Ben carefully loaded the barrel of his shotgun with ammunition.

"You 'member what I told you about that thing, aye?" Ricky said to his son across me. "It's no good from fifty odd feet away or anything like that. Especially in these winds. You want to get yourself tucked away where you can pop up close and blast them arms distance from their head."

Ben nodded.

I gulped a little to try and keep the vomit down.

Ricky's definition of bonding and teaching life lessons to his son was clearly very different to what I'd ever done with Jack or Jonathan.

On arrival, Paul pulled his vehicle to a stop on the other side of the road adjacent to the old boat yard. We convened there around his vehicle and he wound his window down to speak to us. When you're the head of a crime family, low level or not, you don't step out into the freezing cold blizzard unless you absolutely want to.

"Dump your cars further down the road and hurry back to get in position. I don't want multiple car tracks in the snow giving the game away." Paul barked from inside his car.

The encircle of eight or so men, including Ricky and Freddy, all nodded whilst shivering and pulling their coats a little tighter around them.

"Tuck yourselves away tight but make sure you've got them surrounded. Don't let this mouthy shit-turd here get hit. That's the agreement." Paul continued, as I nodded slightly to show my appreciation that he was still thinking of me.

"Thanks Paul but shit and turd are the same thing so you cou…"

I stopped talking as I saw his face twist into a snarl and his eyes narrow.

"Sorry." I smiled weakly.

"When his hand goes up, start shooting like it's the bloody O.K. Corral." Paul continued. "As soon as I hear it all go off, I'll come in through that road over there and cut down any escapees, right?"

The murmurs all concurred with what Paul was saying.

I truly hoped there was a way Ryan was going to act reasonably and not make a move against me so that everyone could walk away unscathed, but my gut told me this was unlikely. The truth of the matter was I'd laid this up in such a way where I knew I'd put him and several others in a position where they were walking in on something they wouldn't be walking out on. It didn't sit well with me, but I really felt out of options by this point. I knew I didn't have anything left to survive 'the game' physically or mentally AND deal with this shite Ryan Flaherty had decided to rain down on me.

Something had to give and *this* felt the one out of the two that I could possibly control.

The conversation was over and Paul drove off further down the road out of sight.

Psychic stood looking at me.

I couldn't bring myself to look him in the eyes.

"You're not sure about this are you?" he said softly.

I shook my head.

"No, me neither!" he proffered. "It is what it is though. These guys were destined to come and butt heads anyway. You've just expedited it, I guess."

"Thanks for helping me justify this, Psych'. I needed that." I swallowed down on the nausea. "There's still a chance he might call this whole thing off and…"

"Jake?" Psychic interrupted a little more forcefully than when he last spoke. "He's coming here to kill you and I don't think that's going to change. So just promise me that when the bullets start flying you get low, okay?"

I nodded.

Take the darkness of the winter morning, add the perilous blaze of snow smashing and slashing against my skin then multiply both with the one lone security light seemingly only half-functioning and you have the fact visibility was *bad.*

Thankfully Ryan was considerate enough to pull in off Kingfisher Boulevard and into the old boat yard, front and centre in the middle of the concrete space with his headlights on full beam.

He climbed from his vehicle, zipped up his coat and looked around the yard slowly and cautiously. He squinted a couple of times into the dark recesses of the yard before eventually turning his attention back to me.

"Did you come alone?" he shouted.

I nodded.

"Where's that idiot sidekick of yours that's always standing off to your right?"

I shrugged. "Probably in bed. He's no good in the cold."

"I'd say he's no good full stop if he's hanging around with you, Lehman."

"Are we going to stand here freezing our nipples off, carrying out a performance review on my business partner or are we going to deal with what we're really here about?" I shouted.

"Oh, we're going to deal with that, trust me!" Ryan smirked as he turned slightly and banged his fist down twice on his car roof.

The backdoors of his car opened up and three men climbed out the rear. One went around to the back of the car and unclipped the boot, freeing a fourth man from where he'd been lying covertly. Each had a firearm of one type or another. I couldn't clearly make out what they were. Most of them looked like shotguns. But then you know by now that I'm no connoisseur when it comes to guns.

The men spread out in a line and came to a stop directly behind Ryan.

"You know that even after you've struck me down for something, I think you know deep down I didn't do, you're still going to have to face off against a wave of people wanting a piece of Bobby's empire. That shits been out of reach for decades. It's all up for grabs now."

"*Is* it though?" laughed Ryan. "From *who*? Most of Bobby's biggest threats died out years ago from old age or from falling down repeatedly into sharp implements. Everyone left is well looked after enough to know which is the right side to stand on and not fuck with the status quo."

"There's the Barton family!" I offered.

Ryan dialled his laughter up to fake, purposefully over-theatrical levels. "The Barton's? The fucking *Barton's*? Are you for *real*? Have you seen those Wrong Turn films about the inbred hillbilly psychos? That's based on them. Did you know that? The Barton's can come at me for what I'm going to be doing with Bob's empire, but they'll probably trip and blow their own heads off coming through the bloody door."

I nodded. "So, do you want to take a look at who really killed Bobby? He's wearing a mask, but I still think it's important that you hear what he says and then…"

"Here's the thing, Lehman. I'm going to be running things now. I think it's important someone who has a strong understanding of Bobby's affairs jumps straight in and lays some instant stability down before the vultures' circle and start trying to pick off his bars and nightclubs or his construction sites and stuff. And I'm really not talking about the Barton brothers either. That's just hilarious. It can't be business *entirely* as usual though. Bobby got soft in the last few years. Anyone close to him could see that. The fact he had any sort of friendship or arrangement with someone like *you* is proof of that. And he always talked about his worries regarding one day being on the wrong side of one of your pursuits, you know? I remember him saying he wanted to keep you close because if you could take down the mayor and the head of the police, he was scared what trouble you could make for him. Me? I'm not going to live every day worrying about that, mate. I think it's easier just to have you gone if you know what I mean? And, well, come on… tying it in with the idea you were responsible for Bob's death and that I avenged that, it just makes things… *neater*!"

"So, you're not going to take a look at this?" I said, holding the SD card in my hand.

Ryan shrugged. "Yeah, I'll watch it and I'll probably cut off the head of whoever's on there bragging about murdering Bobby. At the end of the day, *someone* smacked me in the back of the head and knocked me out cold that day. I'd like to know who the fuck that was for my own peace of mind and to know who to retaliate against. But that doesn't change my plans for *you*."

He raised his hands and his four men started striding forward with their antiquated looking sawn-off shotguns.

"I really wish you'd not been the *exact* sort of dick about this that I expected you to be, Ryan!" I growled, raising my own hand painfully up into the air.

Ricky and Freddy were first to pop up like gophers from the ground, slamming their respective firearms into position against the upturned boats they hid behind. They'd hidden directly parallel to where Ryan and his men stood.

Three more men jumped out of the darkness to the rear of where Ryan's car was parked.

Ricky's son, Ben, and two of his pals rolled out from underneath a broken up old boat to my right and bounded onto their feet like this was the most exciting night of their lives.

"Looks like the inbred hillbillies got the jump on you, Ry' mate!" shouted Freddy Barton.

"Drop the guns and let's turn the pressure valve down on this whole situation." I begged Ryan whilst holding both of my hands up in the air.

Ryan contemptuously spat on the ground and flicked his finger in my direction.

"Take these bastards out!" he sneered over his shoulder to his men.

They nervously hesitated. The Barton boys didn't.

The three men to the rear opened fire immediately.

Ricky and Freddy followed with one of the two of them landing a clear blast to the side of Ryan's torso as he ducked for cover, detonating him right off his feet and into the front grill of the car he arrived in.

I threw myself to the ground but the gunfire had ceased before I'd even managed to bite down through the pain and raise my hands above my head. I gingerly raised my head and caught sight of Paul Barton's car slow crawling into the boat yard.

It came to a stop and he alighted from the vehicle just as his men were circling around the fallen bodies of Ryan's men, prodding them to see if they were still alive or not.

Paul started to walk towards where Ryan lay, half propped against his car and bleeding heavily into the dirtied snow beneath him. Freddy caught up with him and handed him his sawn-off shotgun which he'd carefully wrapped a scarf around its handle.

Paul pulled a handkerchief from his pocket and pushed it inside of the trigger guard, maximising the protection against leaving his own fingerprints anywhere on the weapon. He pulled the shotgun into a tight position against his torso and aimed the barrel end down at Ryan's face.

"What did he say about us?" he shouted back over his shoulder to his brothers, revealing he'd been listening in through an open mobile phone line the whole time.

"He said we were inbred mountain men or something like from those Wrong Turn films!" Ricky hollered back.

Paul nodded. He didn't take his eyes off Ryan.

"I've not seen them. Are they any good?" he asked with a look on his face that indicated he really could not have given less of a shit about such movies.

"The first two are great but the rest are rubbish!" Freddy offered sincerely.

"How many are there for Christ's sake?" Paul replied.

"I don't know." Freddy responded. "Eight or nine or something?"

Paul tutted and concentrated. "That's just overkill isn't it? I mean honestly, how many inbred mountain men films do you *really* need?"

Ryan went to speak. He stammered and he coughed but he couldn't get his words out.

"The thing about you, Ryan, is you forgot your position on the totem pole. You've got big feet but very small boots, son. With people who get too big for their boots too fast, they tend to be incapable of learning the important things before it's too late. Like *respect*. And if you've stood to the right of Bobby bloody Maitland all these years and not learnt the importance of respect by now, you're never going to so..."

Paul pulled the trigger and obliterated Ryan's head at close range.

I pushed my face deep down into the snow at too late of a second to avoid seeing the full, horrendous gratuity of a human head exploding in such a manner.

My ears still rang from the close proximity to the cavalcade of blasts that had occurred minutes earlier. I felt a foot press down painfully on my shoulder and I turned slowly in the snow to lie on my back and look up at who was standing on me. Paul Barton stood towering over me.

"You're a free man, Mr Lehman. I'll make sure the right word spreads correctly and quickly. You'll have no trouble here on out in terms of that stupid hit being put out on you. You're as free as one person can be with the entire police force chasing you down!" He smiled, offering me his hand as he pulled me up onto my feet with zero sensitivity to the fact my ribs were now starting to push through my skin and that I was slowly dying from internal bleeding.

Paul kept a hold of my hand and wrapped his other hand over the top of it, squeezed it tightly as he leant in close to me. "Did you have a beautiful friendship with Bobby, Jake?"

"What?" I replied.

"Did you have a *beautiful* friendship with him?"

"You keep pushing up on the word 'beautiful'. What am I meant to take from that? Are you asking did I suck him off or something? Hand jobs under his desk at every meeting or what?"

Paul laughed hard. "I understand why you'd be thinking that's what I'm talking about since I had my dick out in front of your face within the first minute of meeting you, pal. But no, I'm suggesting that whatever you had with him you'll be required to replicate the same level of warmth with me."

He let go of my hand and started to walk away.

His brothers and the other attending Barton boys all followed suit.

"Take care, Lehman!" shouted Ricky Barton.

[18]

or

30th August 2013.

Sid led us up a small set of wooden stairs into a beaten-up old portacabin made of wood that seemed to curl up and out at every corner point that wasn't fully nailed down. On the roof outside was a huge bank of speakers and amplifiers poorly wired up and running down into the portacabin itself. Clearly this was the means through which Sid DJ'd for the rest of the facility? Inside the place was a slovenly mess encumbered by random pieces of broken tools, storage boxes with discoloured paperwork and various pieces of maps for the surrounding area pinned or taped to the wall with scribbles on each that were only decipherable to whoever wrote them.

I took note of all of this as Rachel and I walked in behind him. He stomped over to a big plastic box he had pushed into the base of a broken cupboard in the corner of his cabin and bent down to dig into it. I noticed a huge chalkboard that had been leant up against a wall in the far corner and on it was a list of names down one side and various hours in columns under days on the other side.

I spotted 'John Kalinda' on there, 'Scott Kalinda' too. There was 'Harv Taylor' and 'Rodge Silver' listed on there amongst others, making up a run of fourteen names in total. With Sid's back to me I quickly slid out my mobile phone and discreetly grabbed a quick shot of the board with the in-built camera. My phone was back in my pocket just as Sid turned back round with two tattered blankets in his hands and passed them across to Rachel.

"If you cross back over the other side of the stretch to the two units directly opposite this one and take the ladder up to the top one, you two can bunk down there. There'll be beds and shit."

Rachel nodded and smiled.

"This is far from ideal, I get it." He continued. "But I can't in good conscience let you both head back out knowing the conditions coming in around you."

"And we appreciate that." I said, smiling warmly.

Sid didn't even look in my direction.

"Get yourselves settled over there and then when the day shift ends come across to the grog pit up the top end and have a drink with me and the boys, yeah?" Sid said. "But don't be digging away under anyone's skin about stories and trying to sell them on doing a news piece with you or any of that shit, okay? That *won't* go down well."

The door behind us opened and a dark-haired muscular male in his late twenties came in, his hands and forearms dirtied jet black and his face seemed to have a look of infuriation chiselled into it.

"Dad, you're going to have to come and have a look at the..." He stopped himself on sight of Rachel and a lecherous grin formed across his face that dropped as instantly as it arrived the minute he clocked me standing off to the corner. "Sorry. Am I interrupting something?"

"No, no. Hang on son." Sid replied. "This here is Rachel and her workmate Jake. They're from Network 10 down in Sydney. Be warned though Jake is in a dirty pommy bastard."

The male slowly nodded in both of our directions, but his expression had some sort of twisted concern that felt very similar to the one I saw from Goodjob Walt just a few minutes earlier. He then leant forward and offered his hand first to Rachel and then to me.

"Hi, I'm Danny!" he said.

"Danny's my boy. He's second on the board up here and he'll be taking over the place in a couple of years just like I did with my old dad, isn't that right?"

Danny nodded distractingly whilst his eyes darted back and forth between Rachel and I. "Has he told you we're not interested? Media attention up here with what we do isn't for us."

"Yes, your dad's explained." Rachel replied.

"I'm letting them bed down for the night over in the spare unit across the way." Sid said. "There's a stand storm coming in and it's not safe."

Danny stood silent for a second and then changed the direction of the conversation forcibly. "Ok, well anyway the lift is playing up again and it looks like the main turn is going to need replaced and replaced *quick* before the day shifts need to come up otherwise it's going to jam them halfway. Can you come take a look?"

Sid nodded and started stepping towards the door. "You two go get yourselves settled and I'll come get you in a bit and bring you over for some drinks at our watering hole."

"It'd be cool to watch you work if we could? That'd be fascinating." Rachel proffered but Danny visibly rejected the suggestion instantaneously.

"No, we can't be having that." He said straight out the gate. "I don't know whether anyone's explained but since the big fall-in ten years ago we've never really been able to stabilise the ground up there as good as we would like. You've really got to know your shit and where you're walking when up near the entrance to the mine. On top of that we've got some flammable cannisters near the neck of the entrance way so..."

"... That all sounds like a recipe for disaster, huh?" I said, smiling before instantly regretting opening my mouth.

Danny stood staring at me.

"I guess it does." He replied sourly. "Sorry, who exactly are *you* again mate?"

"I'm a producer for Network 10." I lied.

"Hmmmm." Danny murmured whilst still staring me out. "And you're British, right?"

"That's right, yeah." I responded.

"That'll explain your sense of humour then!" he said. "Anyway, Dad? Are we going to go check out this main turn on the lift?"

Sid nodded and moved off, ushering us both towards the door to his portacabin as he did. "Go get yourselves settled. I think we've only got a couple of hours before this wind picks up."

We exited and Danny picked things up with Rachel as soon as they stepped down onto the ground outside.

"You had the tour?" Danny asked. "Has he showed you his weird little set-up that Brennan has here?"

"As good a tour as we could have, with your old man wanting to play his cards close to his chest." Rachel replied.

"So, he hasn't taken you through his painful daily playlist from the sixties and seventies that he makes us suffer from three times a day up here just because he can?" Danny smiled.

"Oh, you dig sixties and seventies music huh?" Rachel smirked before pointing towards me. "You should hang out over drinks later and talk to this guy, Sid. He's really into all that sort of stuff!"

Sid looked at me.

"She's serious." I smiled encouragingly. "She thinks it's a criticism of me. But it really isn't."

"How old are you? You can't be out of your thirties at least? What are you doing listening to stuff from my era?" Sid sneered.

"All the best music came from the sixties and the seventies." I offered back in the face of his condescension.

"I hit these boys up at the start of every morning shift, bait time and at clocking off points with a proper bit of music from my collection..." Sid explained.

"I heard your Smokey Robinson choice on the drive into here earlier on." I replied.

"So, hit me with your pick for what I should clock the day shift off with then. Come on, pom? Impress me." Sid smirked.

"Crispian St Peters." I smiled. "The Pied Piper."

"What year was that?" he quizzed.

"1966!" I replied with confidence.

"Impressive!" Sid nodded with an expression that indicated he might have thawed out a little towards me. "Summer 1966. It hit number 5 on the charts over here that year. I'll put that one out dedicated *just* for you later, how about that?"

"That'd be great."

We started to break away when two more men approached, both around my age. One topless with a torso weathered from harsh sunlight and the other in a dirtied singlet and a grey porkpie hat covered in badges.

"Hey Dan," the topless guy spoke as if we weren't there. "Ron and Jim have just radioed up and asked if the lift is going to be sorted for quittin' time. I said me and Chris would give you a hand to get things sorted."

"Cheers Michael!" Danny replied.

"I'm pretty sure I can source a main cog in storage, if that's what you're looking for?" the man that must be Chris (by the process of elimination) said.

"Let's go have a look." Danny responded as they all walked off down towards the mine.

Chris turned on his heels to sneak a look back at what I presumed was Rachel's rear end. I seriously doubted that it was mine. That's when I got a clear sight of all the distinctive patch-badges for various places that covered the main body of the hat.

Rachel and I took a walk back up to the car and we grabbed our bags and our water ampoules from the boot. The heat was still intense but the wind was picking up, spreading warm tiny clusters of dust and dirt up into the air that would stick to our skin. We walked purposefully back down the main avenue stretch to the container Sid had pointed out to us, pushing our heads down to our chest and holding our free hands up against our face to block fragments of airborne dirt from getting in our eyes and nose.

We climbed the ladder to our 'accommodation' for the night and found a couple of water cannisters and a bucket on the immediate right of the container and two canvas camping beds pushed up against either wall further down. There was a workman's light affixed to the interior beam of the container with a thick wire running down to a foot pedal.

I slammed the small steel door shut behind us and Rachel stepped on the pedal, flicking it on and offering a modicum of luminosity to our surroundings.

"It smells of piss!" she moaned.

I nodded, crossing the room and flopping down into a seated position on the canvass bed on the right of the container. I pulled my phone out of my pocket and quickly flicked it open. There was eleven percent battery power left.

Before I could get a chance to speak, Rachel jumped straight in.

"The road train is here!" she began. "The road train is *here* and nobody seems that particularly thrilled about us being here alongside it, even with our bullshit fake story. That old guy... what was he called?"

"Walt? Goodjob Walt?" I suggested.

"Yeah, him!" Rachel exclaimed. "Him and Sid's son both looked like they wanted to curl up and die on finding out we were supposed to be press."

I nodded. "I'd really like to get Walt on his own and have a proper chat with him. He was as gregarious as anything until Sid shut him down."

"You're picking up the vibe overall though too, right?" she queried. "It's not just me? There's something *off* here?"

"No, I'm totally in agreement with you. But are we going to touch on the biggest and more glaring issue of concern?"

"Because I've got to be honest, the clues that led us here are all admittedly iffy circumstantial shit when you look at it on paper but..." Rachel rambled on with little notice of what I'd just said. "Jesus Jake, they led us *here* and that has to mean *something* surely. If it... Wait a second. Go back. What do you mean 'the biggest and more glaring issue of concern'?"

"Chris Marlee?"

"Which one was he?"

I spoke quickly. "I grabbed a shot of the staff board in Sid's office. Their full names are all on there so by the process of elimination, we can strike Sid and Walt off because we've met them. We've met the Kalinda brothers. We've met Harv Taylor and Rodge Silver, obviously. Danny Berenger, we've just met. And I'm guessing that from the name's dropped outside we've just met Chris Marlee and Michael Merindah."

"So, who does that leave us to put a face to before they kick us out of here?" Rachel enquired. "And what's so special about Marlee?"

"Young Lowanna, Alf Cloke, Ernie Dewar, Ron Petrie and Jim Clancy are left to be identified. I think Ron and Jim were just referenced as radioing up from down in the mine. But it's Chris Marlee that I'd like to talk to."

"*What's* so special about Marlee, goddamnit?" asked Rachel.

"I want to ask him why he's wearing Edvin fucking Sixten's hat!"

[19]

or

"People Like Us".

It looked like the sun was finally starting to rise as Psychic and I sat parked up in the loading bay of a derelict shopping centre in Westerhope that had been hit fatally by the economic collapse a few years back and been left to die.

The unit a few hundred metres down from where we hid out was known to be an unofficial hangout / improvised homeless hostel and Psychic and I had been in there a couple of times in the last year or so whilst making enquiries or looking for a specific individual. What was once a thriving hardware store was now just filled with a sea of people trying to keep warm, steal sleep and use whatever had been left or abandoned by the retailers as makeshift bed frames or chairs. The intent to do something about this building and take it back from the homeless masses had slowly lost priority and I definitely didn't think in this fragile political climate we were currently in, any local councillor would want to be seen to throw a hundred or so vulnerable people back out into the middle of the blizzard.

The homeless types went in and out of the unsecured rear door that was the only entrance and exit into the building, minding their own business and showing zero interest in the Audi Q8 parked up tight in the corner and hiding in the shadows. We intended to return the same level of interest but both Psychic and I found that whilst one of us snatched sleep for twenty minutes at a time and the other kept watch, the comings and goings of this lot was our only form of entertainment.

It was just after eight thirty when Psychic stirred and found me staring out into the white expanse, Tobin's new mobile phone placed on my lap, completely lost in thought. I'd switched the radio on and had become absorbed in Curtis Stiger's 'People Like Us':

"♫♫ ... Baby I know, you hear a lot of talk about the bad times ahead. That I'm the wrong kind of man, what you need is a doctor or a lawyer instead. Well I know that I'm not made of money. And God knows I'm a fool... ♫♫"

This was our wedding song.

And out there in the great white vastness of the loading bay area, as snow fell all around us, I watched Jane and I dance as the silhouettes of all of our friends and family made out into a circle around us.

I got to see Jane's wedding dress again and how she'd wore her hair down but braided round the sides so it was all captured by a flower pin at the back that matched her bouquet.

I remembered her softly whispering "Are you counting your steps?" as we danced.

And me discreetly nodding as I concentrated on not fucking up because dancing wasn't my forte at all.

"♫♫ ... *People like us got no business in love. Yeah, that's what the people say. But people like them got nothing better to do, than chase our dreams away. Well I've finally found you and I won't let go ...* ♫♫"

I remembered her leaning in and kissing me softly on the mouth and whispering, "Don't overthink it baby, just sway with me."

"I'm not going anywhere!" I'd said back to her. "I'm here forever. I promise."

"Sway!" she giggled. "*Sway*! Not stay!"

Psychic stirred and twisted back around in the driver's seat to straighten himself back up after napping against the window.

I remembered how I had such a firm idea of what her wedding dress was going to look like because of how many folded pages in wedding magazines and saved website pages I'd snuck a look at as they were left open around the house. I remember being initially disappointed when she started walking down the aisle because her dress was nothing at all like any of those pictures I'd seen.

I remembered most importantly how beautiful and nervous she looked.

Jane and I danced on together as this sickness rose up in my stomach. *'How could you have ever let her think you wouldn't be prepared to give up everything and go anywhere on this earth just as long as you were with her, you absolute plank Jake!'*

"I definitely think twenty-minute bursts of sleep is worse than actually no sleep." Psychic suggested, pushing his way into my flashback. "You can't really get *under* in twenty minutes, you know?"

"Depends on how tired you are, I guess." I countered half-heartedly as I desperately tried to keep myself visually connected to Jane and me on our wedding day, never wanting to lose sight of her there and then in this dreamed haze in front of me in case I had lost her forever in reality.

"Well I'm exhausted mate and I couldn't drift off properly for all the money in the world. Have you slept?"

I shook my head. "I can't. I can't switch off at all."

"Understandable!" yawned Psychic.

It was too late. She was gone; faded in amongst the sea of white out there in the car park. I sighed hard and pointed down at the radio between us.

"This? This was mine and Jane's wedding song!" I said as my eyes welled up with tears.

"♫♫ ... things may not get better, before they get worse. They've all got their reasons why we can't survive. They'll quote you chapter and verse ... ♫♫"

Psychic watched the tears fall and gently reached over and switched the radio off, causing the car to fall into silence. Up ahead a cluster of homeless types came wandering around the corner and a couple of them started making a go of prizing open the door to access the abandoned building they would be able to bed down inside. The sun broke through the clouds and provided a clearer view of just how profuse this snowfall actually was.

"Don't do that to yourself Jake," Psychic smiled, patting the radio. "This is all hard-enough mate."

I sat in silence.

"So... are we going to address the fact that your Yojimbo method didn't exactly work because one side is still standing and now we've probably just handed the region over to the Barton brothers... who it seems you're now indebted to?" Psychic proffered.

I turned my head slightly to look in his direction and quietly said. "No. No we are not."

The silence continued.

"Anyway, have you thought anymore about who Tobin could really be?" he said.

I shook my head whilst wiping the tears from my eyes.

"I want you to hear me out about something, okay?" he continued. "What about Australia? What about the possibility this is something to do with *that*?"

I didn't turn to look at him. I kept staring out of the window. "Everyone's dead to do with that. *Everyone.* And if those bastards were the sorts to have families or friends that gave a shit to the extent this guy does, they would have jumped out long before now, surely."

Very few people knew the truth about Australia.

Those that know anything about it only know the 'toe-the-party-line-bullshit' the Australian police pitched me to sell in the aftermath of it all. The only people that truly knew the truth were Jane and, in time, Psychic. And they knew enough to know that the truth stayed buried like it was meant to and that my interest in talking about it ever again was to be buried alongside it.

At least I *thought* Psychic knew this well enough.

"Maybe. But didn't you and Jane have that whole thing with the secret code word and the immediate escape because you were so afraid that relatives of those men from Australia would come over here looking to get you?"

"That all died with the drinking. The fear faded in time. They're *all* dead." I snapped whilst staring off into the dark. "Every *single* one of them. I watched the aftermath of that play out initially. I didn't see a whole lot of grieving relatives come forward then as much as the thought of it scared me and I certainly can't see any vengeful ones stepping up now. It's been over ten years, Psych'."

"To me, it's the only logical…" Psychic tried to state.

I shut him down coldly. "Is it logical? *Is* it? Is the idea that I'm out here in this position because I'm being taunted and hunted by a fucking ghost *logical*? That's what it would *have* to be, wouldn't it? A ghost? Or a bloody zombie? Because they're all bloody dead Psychic. All of them. I watched them die in front of me. I see each and every death roll around in here…"

I slammed my finger hard against the side of my head.

"… every time I close my eyes and first thing again in the morning when I open them. And they're revisited in between both those points whilst I sleep too. They're FUCKING DEAD and if they had a mad, sad and bad brother or father or uncle or whatever they sure as shit wouldn't have waited just over a decade to come do something about it!"

Psychic looked down to the footwell and the silence engulfed the both of us.

The clock in the car struck 09:00 and the phone in my lap instantly vibrated and started to ring. I jolted with a shock and grabbed at the phone, clicking the line open and placing the earpiece to my head as Psychic pushed himself across to get close enough to listen:

"Welcome to the conclusion of Round Three and the start of Round Four, Jake Lehman. I hope the last few hours have not proven too stressful to you in achieving your objectives and that you have been successful. Your task now is to get to the Metrocentre. You're obviously familiar with this location. You will be required to retrieve a new phone from under the customer information board upstairs in the Red Quadrant. You will also be very familiar with that location too I imagine. That phone will ring at eleven am and give you the location as to where you must take the ten thousand pound. Is all of this understood so far?"

"It is, yes." I replied quietly.

"Your listening skills have improved greatly, Jake Lehman. Well done."

"I would like to ask a favour, please."

"I'm afraid I'm not particularly in a favour-delivering mood, Jake Lehman. But you are welcome to ask." The digitised voice responded.

"I want to speak to my boys, please. Just for a second." I asked.

"I don't think I can do that, Jake Lehman."

"Listen... Please, okay? *Please*? I've done everything you've asked of me so far. I've lost people I care about a great deal. I've spent the night getting the money together that you've asked for and on top of all of that I'm about to wander into one of the busiest shopping areas on the last weekend before Christmas whilst wanted by the police for crimes I didn't commit. You know the likelihood of me being able to get in and get out of there clean is pretty microscopic which means the chances of me being able to get through to the end of your next round is low. I'm waking up to the reality I'm not going to survive this or see my family again. I don't think this whole thing was designed to, if I'm honest. So please, just let me have a moment with my boys. One minute? ... Thirty seconds? ... *Please*?"

"You sound very vulnerable, Jake Lehman. You sound like the exhaustion and the pain and the fragmenting of your mental health under the stress and strain of the reality you're facing are breaking you open to a new truth – a fresh perspective, if you will? I respect this."

The line clicked and went completely silent.

Psychic and I looked at one another, wondering if Tobin had hung up.

Then Jonathan's voice echoed out of the other end of the line.

"Dad?" he said nervously.

"Baby Boy!" I exclaimed, using the same nickname for him I'd never stopped using through the years from the day he was born. "Are you okay? I love you. I love you *so* much. Is your brother there with you?"

"He's here. Mum's here. We're okay. He's not hit us or anything. What's happening Dad? When are we going to get to see you again?"

"Son, I promise you will see me again. I *promise*. No matter what." I said as my mouth curled with a sudden newfound resolve and burst of strength my mind and body had lacked for too many hours now.

The line clicked again and Tobin was back.

"... Do you see what your respect earns you, Jake Lehman? I will call again at eleven am to ensure you have successfully completed Round Three and are ready to begin Round Four in full. You will then be provided with further instructions. If you are not able to answer when the phone rings, your wife and your children will..."

"You need to understand something," I snarled. "I've decided that never seeing, holding or talking to my wife and children again is just totally unacceptable to me. And the only thing standing in my way from me doing those things is *you*... and right now, that's the most dangerous place in the world to be stood!"

I clicked the call off and dropped the phone back down into my lap.

[20]

or

"Run Faster".

All 2,200,000 square foot of the Metrocentre still stood, even after the economic collapse that shuttered the doors of most of the big retail outlets once housed there and *even* after I drove a pea green coloured 1987 Zastava Yugo 513 up one of their multi-storey car parks and through the top floor of one of their (then) prestige department stores. You remember that, right?

The Metrocentre had hung on in there as a much more streamlined and less high-status destination for shopping and entertainment. It now survived as the home to cheap outlet stores and £1.00 bargain shops, scattered randomly around the series of coloured quadrants. The high-end restaurants had all long since vacated and there was now just a glut of fast food kiosks and eateries, piled up on mass on top of each other.

People still came here in their droves. Especially around Christmas. Money was still tight within communities around the region and it was the perfect place to grab a bargain, catch some free entertainment in one of the many quadrant squares and get a cheap bite to eat with your family. Doors opened at ten am across the whole site so by the time I arrived, it looked like there was already a fair few hundred people milling around the shopping walkways.

Psychic pulled up outside the main Red Quadrant doors and stopped in one of the assigned drop-off bays.

"Have you got a hat or a hood or anything?" he asked.

"No. Do you?"

He shook his head. "I don't think you'll get as much as ten feet in there before someone jabs a finger in your direction and screams for the police. You're all smashed up and covered in dried blood. You don't exactly blend in."

"This is a serious boost to my confidence, mate." I smiled. "Have you ever thought about going into coaching kids sports or something?"

"Have you ever been back here since…"

"I have not, no." I interrupted.

"Not at all?"

"Not at all!" I confirmed.

"Not even just avoiding that one spot?" he pushed.

"Not even then."

"What about to go to the cinema? They've cut the price of tickets to try and stay afloat, you know? Me and Emily sometimes go to a Tuesday matinee where the tickets are only two quid and..."

"*You* told *me* you're going to business networking events on a Tuesday morning?" I gasped. "Psychic, you're a lying bastard!"

"Damn!" he smiled. "I may have just dropped myself in it."

"Where are you going to be when I come back out?" I asked, pushing things back on track as I realised we were up against the clock here.

"How about just around here? You're going to just walk in and walk straight out with the phone, right?"

"That sounds easy so yeah, I'll probably just do *that* then!" I smirked.

"Good luck!"

This was my first time back at the Metrocentre since that night. As I walked through the main doors I could've looked up if I wanted to and saw the exact spot four stories above me where I'd jumped from the old Debenhams site. I didn't though. I kept my head down to the ground and walked fast and purposefully towards the escalators.

The Metrocentre was every bit as busy as I assumed it would be. People were still flocking here even in the middle of a blizzard. George Romero's Dawn of the Dead was more on the money in its pointedness than you potentially realised.

I strode up the steps of the escalator and pulled myself round at the top, heading off towards the area I knew the phone would be hidden – right on the very spot where Sue George had died from a gunshot wound to the artery in her leg - once I'd walked by the exact place where I'd wrapped the cabling around Jason Grant's neck and pushed him off the walkway to his death.

How did this psychopath know to direct me back to this exact spot for the purposes of the game? How did he know what went on here? Andy Andrews, for all his ills, kept to his word and buried anything a CCTV camera might have captured. The only surviving witness was Holly and she's dead.

This guy was aware of this and he knew something as intimate as where I'd once went to try and end my own life. He knew of my connection to Margaret and Matthew Jason too and where their daughter had been found dead.

I just couldn't get my head around this. Who could be connected to all of that in my life?

The cold sweat was pouring off me, dripping down my back and off my forehead into my swollen eyes. I wiped my eyes as best I could and clenched my teeth together.

Jonathan had a football match between Christmas and New Year's next week.

Jack needed to be taken to buy razors and taught how to shave.

I pushed myself to focus on anything I could that was important to me – just to not think about the events involving my confrontation with the Black Box team around this very point in the Metrocentre a couple of years back.

I flashed to the wide, panicked gaze on Jason Grant's face as the shards from the cabling pierced his skin and tightened around his neck…

… I blinked fast and forced myself to focus as I walked closer to the customer information board situated at the top of another set of escalators where the Red Quadrant met the entrance to the Green Quadrant. This was the exact spot where I watched Sue George die. It was happening right there all over again right in front of me.

I blinked again, rubbing hard on the sides of my swollen temples and I could see the eyes of various shoppers start to zone in a little. I realised that I'd probably have no more than a minute or less before someone pulled the *"Hey, isn't that…"* and then screamed for security.

I reached under the board and found the taped bag there just like under the bench up on Tynemouth Priory. I looked at the time on the phone's screen contained inside the bag and saw that it said 10:57. A quick glimpse over to my right out of the corner of my eye revealed two women talking to a Metrocentre security guard and pointing over in my direction.

Fuck it, I wasn't prepared to wait. I'd take the call on the move.

I started walking fast, pulling the phone from the bag as I paced.

The Red Quadrant was out as an exit option seeing as there were security guards with their ears to their radios at the only walkway out of there on the ground floor and the guard directly behind me up on the second floor was moving in on me fast.

I could not allow myself to get taken down before I'd received this call.

That was *not* an option.

The phone rang and I clicked to accept the call immediately as my pace quickened even faster:

"Welcome to Round Four, Jake Lehman. I did not appreciate being hun…"

"I'm really sorry to interrupt, I know you hate that probably as equally as being hung up on but I'm in as much shit here as you probably expected and if you want me to stay in the game past this point then you're going to have to talk really, really quickly." I gabbled breathlessly. "I have your money. I have this new phone. Tell me where you need me to be and..."

"Bring the money to the exact place you found Baadir Gadiel, Jake Lehman. And bring the money by twelve pm!"

I took a quick glance at the phone screen to check the time and then pulled the phone back to my ear again. "That's only about fifty-five minutes away. Come on, please be reasonable. I can't get out of here, get all this heat off me and get down to Shiremoor from Gateshead in that time and in these conditions. It's just..."

"You should not have hung up on me, Jake Lehman. Your time has been sanctioned because of such behaviour. We will meet again in person at twelve pm. You will then be provided with further instructions. If you are not able to answer when the phone rings, your wife and your children will die. If you alert anyone..."

I stepped quickly inside of a store on my right, bent instantly behind a display stand and as soon as I saw a security guard pass by seconds later, I stood up and strode out.

"... to our contact your wife and your children will die. If you do not come alone to the required location your wife and your children will die. If you show any more disobedience or disrespect to the game your wife and your children will..."

I landed straight into the path of another security guard. He reached out for me but I moved his hand off to my right, stepped to my left and kicked out his knee causing him to fall off balance into a group of passing people. It hurt like hell to do with all the ailments I was now carrying but...

Jesus Christ look at you Jake – you goddamn Jason Bourne wannabe!

"... die. If you fail to achieve the objectives of the game set for you within the timeframe given your wife and your children will die. If you achieve all of the objectives laid out over the course of the game, then your wife and your children will be set free to continue their lives. Good luck Jake."

"See you at twelve!" I said, clicking the call off and stuffing the phone into my pocket.

I kept my head ducked down and tried to maintain being as unassuming and low-key as possible even though it was apparent all eyes were slowly beginning to land on me. This is even less easy when you're a walking mess of bloodied bruises, dirtied clothes and, well, you're public enemy number one.

My hands were burrowed deep into the pockets of my jacket, one clutched tightly around the new phone and the other tightly coiled into a fist ready to strike out again if need be.

I got myself out of the Red Quadrant and walked on along the second-floor walkway towards the Blue Quadrant area, noting how many heads were turning and whispered choruses of suspicion and identification were rising up amongst the various clusters of last-minute shoppers idling around the retail causeways.

I needed to get downstairs fast. All of the exits were on the ground floor level. And boy did I need an exit *fast*. Up ahead towards where the walkway branched off towards the food concourse and the restaurant district, I saw a security guard talking to a uniformed police officer and pointing in my direction.

Shit!

I veered right and caught sight in the mirrored reflection of one shop front that there were another two police officers marching up on my rear.

Fuck!

I turned the corner, pushing myself to think fast about the best way to get a straight run out of here and to wherever the hell Psychic would be with the car. I was panicked enough already without having to worry about where Psychic was going to be and how I would be able to get in touch with him to let him know that I'd had to abort the Red Quadrant as an exit point.

I bumped straight into none other than Richard Parkinson, in full police uniform, as I rounded that corner. With a second police officer coming up behind him to join where he was stood. I staggered backwards a couple of steps and froze on the spot.

I looked directly at Richard, noting the inspector epaulets on the shoulders of his uniform. He'd aged well. Still slim and broad shouldered, with his hair and beard now greying out evenly.

I slowly took stock of the full circle around me. A bench within reaching distance with a bannister running at the back of it all the way round to the elevators behind me and the escalators up ahead. Below me on the ground floor a Christmas craft market was set out in the open floor space. Three police officers spread out behind me. Two more up ahead on my left. Inspector Parkinson and his colleague right in front of me.

"Hi Jake." Parkinson said guardedly.

"Hey Richard. How's it going? You've got a beard now huh?" I smiled warily.

"It hides the double-chins!" he half-smiled.

"Nonsense. You're looking very trim." I said, meaning it too. "The salt and pepper look really works for you as well. It's very 'George Clooney'... I see you're an inspector now?"

"Yeah, I have been for a while. I seemed to have stagnated recently though. The kids have got in the way of my studies and… life dictates your priorities to you, you know?"

"I'm sorry to hear that but yeah, it can be difficult compartmentalising your time when you've got kids and what not." I said as I eyed the police officers around me, slyly taking note of Parkinson's hand gesture that indicated to them he wanted them to hold back.

"Sorry to hear you're having a tough time of it yourself." Parkinson said seemingly sincerely.

"Me?"

"Yeah."

"What have you heard?"

"Oh, you know - just the usual; you murdered our old friend Arkin Dentz and Bobby Maitland too, blew up your own home and your office, escaped police custody… Did I *miss* anything?" Parkinson smiled.

"No, that about covers it." I sighed.

"Thought so! Sounds like you're having a very bad day. And that's saying something considering your past."

"Yeah, you know, this is probably the worst I've had. And just this Summer gone I was hanging off the back of a train loaded with explosives so…" I trailed off.

My eyes started to close in on the bench to my left. My ears picked up the sound of police boots slow-stepping closer towards me from behind as Christmas shoppers were warded off from coming any further this way.

Think Jake! *Think*!

"Are you going to take your foot off the accelerator and come in with us?" Parkinson said quietly as he took one step closer.

I shrugged. "I can't do that."

"Sure you can."

"I can't. I'm sorry."

"Listen, I like you Jake. I always have. I'm not sure I'm fully onboard with everything you've been accused of, matey." Parkinson smiled, taking another step thinking I hadn't picked up on him doing so. "But I sure do know it'll all be a *lot* easier to get to the bottom of down at the station with us on your side then out on the street with us on your tail."

"I wouldn't be so sure of that." I exhaled.

"They're waiting on my word Jake. Don't make me give it. Just lie down, put your hands behind your back and come in without resistance."

"It was good seeing you again Richard. It's been too long buddy." I gulped down as much air as I could and held my breath.

And with that I turned and took five speedy steps straight towards the bench. One of the police officers behind me dove at my feet to try and tackle me down but I was already airborne, landing feet first onto the seat of the bench and using that in turn as a step to push up onto the bannister and then…

Parkinson screamed "JAKE!"

… I exhaled all the air back out again as I jumped and let myself crash down onto the market stall roof ten foot below, landing with an excruciating thud into the canvass top that didn't break under my weight and instead bounced me straight back off and down to the ground. The market stall tipped on its side spreading all of its content out onto the floor.

Everyone's attention zoned right in and I pulled myself achingly to my feet as blood fell from my mouth.

"Bomb! Bomb! He's got a *BOMB* strapped to him!" I screamed manically pointing back up to the second floor I'd just jumped from.

All eyes darted up to the direction I was pointing at. The shoppers put two and two together against the sight of the police officers leaning over the bannister above them, looking down at where I'd just jumped from.

And then the screaming started.

The frenzied running followed promptly.

The crowd of maybe sixty to eighty within the areas of the craft market scattered in three different directions and I ducked down amongst one such cluster of runners and moved in motion with them. As soon as I was suitably out of sight of Parkinson and his team, I grabbed one unfortunate fella running and yanked him by his neck into the doorway of a closed-up jewellers.

I punched him twice in the face and when he fell to the ground, I screamed for him to remove the black old-styled sailor's coat he was wearing.

He did this without hesitation.

"Your phone!" I shouted. "Give me your phone!"

"It's… it's in the… coat pocket!" he stammered as he handed over the coat.

"What's the security code?"

"9898!" he replied fearfully.

"Thank you. And I'm sorry." I said, lifting him back up onto his feet.

I pulled the man's coat on over the top of my own and threw myself back in amongst the throng of scared, sprinting shoppers making their way towards the nearest exits like they were taking part in the running of the bulls.

I accessed that poor man's phone and dialled Psychic's number.

He answered immediately.

"I'm coming out the Blue Quadrant exit in two minutes!" I hollered.

"I'm parked in the Red Quadrant though?" he fired straight back. "Wait. Where are you calling from Jake?"

"Forget about that. Get to the Blue exit!" I shouted.

"What are you doing coming out of the Blue one, Jake? We agreed *Red*?"

"I had to fucking improvise, Psychic. I'm sorry. But *this* is the improvisation!"

"Hang fire. I'm on my way!"

I ran out of the doors on mass with thirty to forty people all screaming and immediately turned right and ducked behind a small enclave in the brick work.

There, just off in the distance, I could see Psychic's Audio Q8 struggling to worm its way through heavy traffic and move around the outside of the Metrocentre.

I started running as best as I could but the minute I did I realised my legs weren't capable of holding me up like they would have done normally. That, plus the nearly knee-deep snow and sludge on every surface, caused me to fall and stumble every few steps.

There was a sudden scream of "FREEZE LEHMAN!" from back behind me.

I didn't look back. I kept ploughing on as best I could through the snow and into the car park, ducking between cars for cover and pushing myself to get up towards where Psychic was.

Police cars started to encircle the entrances to the car park.

I reached the embankment and started to desperately climb, pulling at the frozen plants and furiously digging my feet into the thick mounds of snow to try and get leverage upwards. One stumble gave me cause to look back and see a horde of police frantically running and stumbling towards me.

I frenetically pulled myself upwards as dark bloody mass dropped from my mouth onto the snow below. My ribs now started sending shockwaves up my body, creating blinding flashes in my line of sight.

I reached the top and threw myself over the partition barrier just as Psychic's car pulled forward approximately ten to fifteen metres away. The passenger door flung open and I dragged myself up and towards it.

"Get in!" he screamed, slamming his foot down on the accelerator before I was even properly inside. He yanked the car onto the side of the road, crunching up against every stationary car lined in traffic. Each brunt of his vehicle against theirs forced more and more space for him as he pushed through.

Blue lights flashed behind us.

Blue lights flashed ahead of us.

"Well I'm definitely a fucking accessory *now*!" he shouted.

The car broke through the block of traffic, jumped a red light and headed towards the line of police cars positioned as a barrier up ahead towards both north and south slip-roads for the A1 motorway.

"I guess now is the wrong time to ask whether you picked me up one of those cinnamon pretzels you know I like?" Psychic bellowed.

[21]

or

30th August 2013.

The wind was picking up some force as it swirled around the grounds of Brennan. I knew this because it whistled and slammed against the side of the container Rachel and I were situated inside of. After one particularly fierce slam, followed by the sound of dust and dirt scuttering along the metal roof we lay under, I looked across to her with concern in my eyes.

"This thing is fastened down to *something*, right? They haven't just plonked this one on top of another one?"

She shrugged. "Nothing about this place suggests health and safety or attention to fine details is particularly paramount!"

"That's what I'm worried about. What if we get blown away or something?" I asked, sitting up on the edge of my canvass bed.

"It's a sandstorm, Jake. Not a tornado. And anyway, you're already in the land of Oz!" she winked.

"Not funny!" I replied.

"Come on, that was a *little* bit funny?"

"Aren't you glad I stopped you sneaking out to have a poke around the grounds though?"

"No, Jake." She smirked, whilst flicking me 'the bird'. "You're no fun at all."

"I can't get a read on you at all, Rachel Casey. Ten days ago, you wouldn't so much as smile at me if I said hello to you and here we are now off on some grand adventure like we're Romancing the fucking Stone!"

"Has it really been just *ten* days?" Rachel gasped. "Wow. I feel as if we've been BFF's for so much longer than that!"

"Nope. Ten days. Just *ten* bloody days. And you've changed your personality four times or thereabouts in that time!"

Rachel laughed and then sat up on the edge of her bed to meet my eye line.

"Can I ask you something?"

I nodded. "As long as it's not for sex again?"

"Oh, that ship has well and truly sailed for *you* now Jake Lehman. Look at all these big, strong, strapping, 'Ocker' Australian penis options I'm surrounded by now." She giggled. "No, seriously. Let me ask you this – that paedophile councilman who got your job in the police taken away... Why didn't you fight back?"

I sat silent.

No one had asked me that before.

"Listen, maybe there isn't an answer." Rachel continued. "And maybe I'm the wrong person to be asking the question seeing as all I do is spend my days fighting back against the wrong done to me and I'm genuinely exhausted by it. But you? I'm interested to know what was behind your choice."

"I didn't know how to fight back, I don't think. It was all so insurmountable..." I sighed. "Actually, that's bullshit. I didn't have any fight left in me. *That's* the truth. I was scared shitless of taking these guys on and losing because I knew another loss would finish me off, so I slinked off... like a frickin' coward!"

"And what about now? Have you found the fighting mentality since?"

"Let me tell you a little secret Rachel. This whole PI thing? Everything I've ever done since? It's ALL been a fight back against what happened and maybe stopping it from ever happening to someone else. It's still early days, I guess. But do you know what I dream about in such obsessive and unhealthy detail on an almost daily basis?"

"What's that?"

"That one day I cross paths with Mick Hetherington again and I show him what a fight with me looks like now!"

"I don't think that's unhealthy. Then again, I'm absolutely the wrong person to be making that call, aren't I? I'm living purely off the entire Sydney police services' total hatred of me!" Rachel smiled. "It's good to hear you've got some fight in your belly though, because you and I both know this whole thing right here and now stinks and if shit is going to go down, I need to know that you've got my back. Come the morning, we're not just driving out of here and hoping Novak will bite the morsel we feed him."

She then reached into the bag at her feet and pulled out her firearm in its holster.

"Does shit *need* to go down though?" I asked anxiously. "They're wearing the dead guy's hat. The road train seen in the vicinity is up here. It's not a lot but it's enough to fuck off out of here the minute this sandstorm slackens off and then get back to your boss to..."

"I want *more*." Rachel butted in as she stood up and used a piece of spare shoelace pulled from inside her bag to thread through the holster. She lifted her shirt, tied the holster around her waist, positioning it to the base of her back and then readjusted herself back to how she was dressed before. "I want to ask a few subtle questions and see if we can dig some more stuff up. And I want to know whether your girl and her pals have been tied up somewhere on these grounds for the last God knows how long. I'd never live with myself if we drove off and..."

The metal door to our container flung open and hit the side of the wall with an enormous, echoing bang. In stepped Sid with a handkerchief tied around his face and his exposed areas of his arms and torso dusted with debris from outside. The wind railed around outside and he pulled heavily to close the door behind him.

Pulling his handkerchief down to expose his face properly, he smiled whilst counting to three on his fingers and then clicking them.

Through the side of the container's walls whilst the wind clanged aggressively against it I could just about make out the sound of Crispian St Peter's 'The Pied Piper' blasting out around the grounds.

"♫♫ ... You. With your masquerading. And you. Always contemplating what to do. In case heaven has found you. Can't you see. That it's all around you ... ♫♫"

"A promise is a promise, pom!" Sid smirked. "Now, I'm sorry I left you here so long but as you can probably hear, there's a right dust-up gaining strength out there and on top of that I've had to get down the neck of the mine to sort out a broken cog otherwise we'd not get the day crew up or get the night crew down. But we're sorted now, and we're going to have a bit of grog and wait out this gust if you two want to come and join us?"

I looked hard at Rachel.

Rachel nodded back at Sid.

"It's not a far walk at all but it might be a bit... intense. Just cover your nose and mouth with something and walk behind me. It's not up at full steam yet anyway."

"♫♫ ... So step in line. Hey, come on babe. Follow me, I'm the Pied Piper. Follow me, I'm the Pied Piper. And I'll show you where it's at. Come on, babe. Can't you see. I'm the Pied Piper ... ♫♫"

We climbed the small ladder down and walked speedily across the orangey terrain towards the rusted container over on the other side. The sandstorm had kicked up a wall of dust that was rolling dirt back up on me at about chest height. I placed my hand over my nose and mouth and squinted my eyes to a semi-closed state.

A few minutes later we were bustled through the same type of metal door as the one we'd left our own container through and Rachel and I stumbled into the *most* crudely executed bar you could've imagined just as 'The Pied Piper' seemed to fade to its end on the tinny speakers outside. Well, of all the bars that had been thrown together inside an old, rusted up shipping container, this was *one* of the more crudely executed.

A big long lump of three to four foot high weathered wood ran along one corner of the bar and behind it were two huge trough-like metal drums filled with ice. In one there was piles of lager bottles and tin beer cans. In the other bottles of spirits. Up above them both on the backboard of the container was a piece of cardboard with 'Sid's Saloon' scrawled in thick, black marker pen.

A very young looking male with a mop of surfer blonde hair was stood behind the wooden bar front. On a tattered, unsteady-looking high stool in front of him sat the old guy I recognised as Goodjob Walt. He was slurping on a bottle of Victoria Bitter.

Behind him was a set of cheap plastic garden furniture; a worn table and three chairs.

Clustered out from there were more mismatched plastic tables and chairs with a stereo tucked away in the corner on a separate smaller table. The wires running from it dove down into a worry-inducing cluster of extension cables and generator packs.

Two men sat together, drinking and talking. One of them was Harv' Taylor who we met on our arrival. He spotted Rachel and I and raised his glass of beer in our direction.

"I see you found the best spot on the whole site!" he bellowed gregariously at us.

Rachel smiled.

"Go get yourselves some amber and get settled," Sid urged, pushing us both towards the bar. "The day crew will be cleaned up and heading in here any minute. You want to get yourselves sorted ahead of them."

We both walked towards the wooden bar as Rachel whispered "Don't ask for a fucking water. Just get the same as me and don't drink it."

I nodded.

The surfer boy smiled as we approached. "What can I get you two?"

"Young Lowanna," Goodjob Walt smiled warmly. "These are the posh journos from the news station over in Sydney."

"Hi I'm Rachel."

"I'm Jake." I said, offering him my hand which he leant across and shook.

"What can I get you both?" Young Lowanna replied.

"I'll take anything that's coldest, thanks!" Rachel said.

"Me too!" I smiled.

He reached behind him and pulled two cans of VB from the cooling drum and slammed them down onto the wooden surface.

"Thanks." I said, turning and taking a seat at the plastic table next to the bar.

Rachel quickly joined me and Goodjob Walt seized his chance, grabbing his drink and following her over.

"Has Sid told you to get stuffed with your story then?" Walt smiled.

"As good as, yeah." Rachel grinned back.

"Heading off in the morning with your tail between your legs huh?" he guffawed.

"Something like that." She said.

I kept looking around the container. There was only the one door in and out and that was right up the top end where we'd come in. And to the left of it was that table with the stereo on it and the dangerous pile of cables that I worried were going to blow any minute.

Harv's drinking companion caught me looking around and shouted over "This place not posh enough for you, pom? Do you need a fucking saucer with your drink and... and... one of those frilly net things you all have?"

"Alright, Jimmy. Calm down." Harv' laughed.

Jim Clancy – I mentally ticked another name off the list.

I turned my full attention back to the table. Rachel was deep in conversation with Goodjob Walt about coal mining.

"How *deep*?" Walt was saying. "Well, we're not surface miners up here. BFI have got all that wrapped up. We do old fashioned deep mining here at Brennan. We're working at about two hundred feet down at the moment but that's on the fresh route we had to find after the fall-in."

"How deep were you at on the other mine when it fell in?" Rachel asked.

"Oh, that was a big one." Walt explained. "That was close to two-eighty. You can fuck around thirty feet down on that spot now and you'll soon fall two hundred and fifty feet straight down to Satan's living room!"

"Wow!" Rachel gasped.

I nodded.

"Pull ya head in, Walt!" Jim Clancy shouted from across the makeshift bar. "Stop talking our business to strangers – and fucking journos at that!"

Rachel and I looked at each other with a little bit of shared concern.

The tension was alleviated slightly by the arrival of Sid back in through the door, bringing with him a gust of wind and a spray of dusty dirt.

In one hand he carried a slap of questionable looking meat with a large knife sticking out the side of it. In the other was a tin foil tray full of bread rolls.

He walked over to the wooden bar slab and dropped both down on the counter.

I was starving but between the dirty hand that had just carried the meat uncovered through a sandstorm and then dumped it straight onto a mucky, stained and drink-soaked surface I was... willing to opt out.

"Get yourselves dug in!" shouted Sid, just as the door burst open again and two men I didn't recognise came barrelling through at several hundred miles an hour of urgency.

"Sid!" screamed one of them.

"Give me a minute man, Ron!" replied Sid.

"Nah mate, nah!" the man I'd come to know as Ron hollered back. "You need to get over here and have a word with Alf... right *now*!"

Sid exhaled hard and took a walk over to where Ron and the other man were standing. The two men started talking to their boss in a hurried and manic fashion. A couple of times the man I quickly deduced was Alf Cloke would raise his hand in our direction and Sid would reach across and slap it down.

Goodjob Walt looked across at them. "They've probably found out who you two are and what you're after up here. They'll not be happy. Too many secrets buried up here for journalists to be wanting to shine a light on."

"Shut the fuck up Walt!" snapped Young Lowanna from behind the bar.

I kicked Rachel's leg under the table.

She looked to me and discreetly nodded.

"Time to go?" I mouthed.

"Be cool!" she whispered back.

The door to the container opened again and in walked the two men I had seen earlier on outside Sid's portacabin, Chris Marlee and Michael Merindah. The latter went to close the door behind them just as Danny pushed his way in with a look of concern on his face.

Michael looked across to Ron and nodded.

Chris turned and started to lock the door and then lean against it. I could see that jutting out of his trouser pocket was that grey porkpie hat I knew belonged to Edvin Sixten.

Michael leant over and pressed on the stereo, turning the volume up high as he did so.

Overly amplified sound blasted out and ricocheted off the metal walls as 'The Happening' by The Supremes smashed painfully off everyone's ears.

"♫♫ ... Hey! Life, look at me, I can see the reality. 'Cause when you shook me, took me outta my world, I woke up. Suddenly I just woke up to the happening. When you find that you left the future behind. 'Cause when you got a tender love you don't take care of... ♫♫"

"What the hell man?" shouted Harv' dropping his beer everywhere in startled shock at the noise.

Jim put his hands over his ears just as he caught sight of Sid and the men circling in tight together, deep in conversation.

I looked to Rachel and my mouth curled into a snarl.

She winked and dropped her eyes down in the direction of where we both knew her gun was stored.

"♫♫ ... Then you better beware of - The happening. One day you're up, when you turn around. You find your world is tumbling down. It happened to me and it can happen to you. I was sure, I felt secure until love took a detour. Yeah! Riding high on top of the world... ♫♫"

Danny was arguing hard with his father.

The men I'd come to assume to be Ron and Alf looked to be butting in and seemed really quite riled.

Jim stood from his table and staggered over to where they were all stood. Within seconds of standing with them, I distinctly heard him shout "They're WHAT?" over the music.

"♫♫ ... Suddenly it just happened. I saw my dreams torn apart. When love walked away from my heart. And when you lose a precious love you need to guide you. Something happens inside you - The happening ... ♫♫"

"They need to turn this shit down, man!" screeched Walt. "I've barely got any hearing left as it is."

"Let me go do that for you!" Rachel shouted, standing abruptly up and causing the cluster of men to suddenly scatter out.

"♫♫ ... Now I see life for what it is. It's not of dreams, it's not of bliss. It happened to me and it can happen to you... And then it happened. Ooh, and then it happened. Ooh, and then it happened. Ooh, and then it happened ... ♫♫"

Ron hit the stereo and the music ceased.

"Thank Christ for that!" exclaimed Walt.

Sid and his men, minus Chris and Michael who stayed guarding the door and Danny who appeared rooted to the spot, all started slowly walking forwards.

I pushed my chair out and stood up alongside Rachel.

"Do we have some sort of problem here?" she said. "Because if I didn't know any better, I'd say that you all look as if you are priming for a good old-fashioned gang-rape and I'm really sorry to disappoint you all, but that's just *not* going to happen."

"You're a producer for 10 News First on the Network 10 channel, right?" Sid said looking Rachel directly in the eye.

"That's right, yeah." She replied.

"And you?" Sid said, turning to me. "You're 10 News First on the Network 10 channel too?"

"Correct!" I responded whilst furtively eyeing the number of men - one behind the bar, Sid in front of me within reaching distance and three behind him. Three more by the door, Harv' and Walt in chairs nearby. That's ten...

... Yeah, we're *fucked.*

"You see the thing is," Sid started saying before stopping and correcting himself. "Actually, no. Ron, *you* explain."

Ron stepped around Sid, his giant beer-belly sticking out beneath a stained AC/DC tour t-shirt clearly two sizes too small. He pointed back to Alf. "Alf here and a couple of others had a snoop over your jeep when you first got here and no sooner did he do that then he goes and smells a rat because you're out here with no camera equipment or nothing then..."

Alf jumped in. "My mate Ernie made a call down to his ex-brother-in-law at the Ashton site to order in some engine parts for when he's next on the rounds and..."

"Get to the point!" Sid snapped.

"... and... and... Ernie's ex-brother-in-law reckons they had a couple of folk from the Sydney police down there just a day or so ago asking questions about the bloody road train we've got and asking where Brennan was. He said they hired a jeep matching that one out there and it looked to him like they were heading up to take a look. He reckons one of them was a good-looking red-headed Sheila and the other was a wet-looking pom!"

Ron took back over. "So, I've called in my mates down there in the Nullarbor and they confirmed you two hired that jeep from them the other day and that you used your police card for ID... You're Detective Rachel bloody Casey, mate. You're not a fucking news producer at all. You're a ruddy copper!"

Sid grinned as his hands formed up on his hips. "I don't want anyone getting aggro unnecessarily here, but I guess the question is what the hell Sydney 'blue' is doing toodling up into the never-never, sticking their little beaks in our business whilst pretending to be someone they're not. What's *that* about?"

Chris Marlee smirked to Michael and then took a couple of steps to a dartboard fastened in the far-right corner near to the door. He picked up the chalk for the attached blackboard and wrote 'FUCK OFF PIGS!!" across the dusky surface.

Now did not feel the appropriate time to identify myself as *ex*-police and actually currently a private investigator. The manner in which he drew a full circle above the 'I' and below the exclamation marks interested me greatly however, and I dropped my eyes to look quickly in the direction of Rachel who was staring intently at the men in front of us.

I smiled.

"What you grinning at, you British shitbag?" snarled Alf. "You think this is funny?"

"I don't think is funny at all." I replied. "But I *do* think I've found the author of that Swedish kid's suicide note and while we're at it I'd like his hat back too please!"

The fuse was already lit, frankly. But that? *That* was definitely the petrol that expediated the burn down into a full blown and immediate explosion.

Chris stormed forwards towards me and I tried to delay him getting to me by grabbing my chair and throwing it off in his direction. He ducked to avoid getting hit and instead stumbled and slammed into the table holding the stereo, which in turn knocked the music back on exactly where it had left off – once again at wall-shaking, full volume.

"♫♫ ... Is it real? Is it fake? Is this game of life a mistake? 'Cause when I lost the love I thought was mine for certain. Suddenly it starts hurtin', I saw the light too late when that fickle finger of fate ... ♫♫"

Young Lowanna pulled the knife from the slab of meat and attempted to dive over the counter with it, onto Rachel's back. I pulled his feet out from underneath him and let him fall full force onto the wood bar, pulling the knife from his hand and throwing it clear of him.

Sid and his men charged as Rachel slammed herself backwards, sticking her hand into the back of her shirt and bringing it back out with her grip tightened around the handle of her gun. Ron got to her first and she swiftly pumped a bullet straight into his kneecap and just as he dropped to the floor screaming, she fired a second one into his shoulder and sent him reeling backwards. The sound of it left a deafening double-echo off the container walls still audible above the bone-shattering volume of the music.

"♫♫ ... Yeah! It came and broke my pretty balloon, I woke up, suddenly I just woke up, so sure I felt secure until ... ♫♫"

Chris Marlee got to me and threw a clean left hook towards the side of my head. I ducked it and punched him twice in return, once to the ribs as I came back up straight and again to the side of the head which served to knock him back over the plastic table.

"Stop! Stop! Hang on a second!" shouted Danny over the chaos.

Alf and Harv' now grabbed at me and forced me down to the floor. As my head slammed off the ground I could just see Sid wrestling Rachel up against the container wall to get the gun free from her hands.

Harv' attempted to punch me and I deflected the blow towards Alf's crotch, causing Alf to fall back in agony alongside Ron who was now crying on the floor whilst his blood flowed out.

"♫♫ ... 'Cause when you got a tender love you don't take care of, then you better beware of - The happening ... ♫♫"

I punched upwards and got good, clean contact with Harv's chin, knocking him sprawling backwards on top of Alf.

Rachel's gun dropped to the floor as Sid wrapped his hands around her throat. I made a dive for the gun as Michael surged forward towards me, slipping in Ron's blood as he did and knocking himself out on impact with the floor.

I grabbed the gun just as Danny smashed his fist into the stereo, finally knocking the music off. Goodjob Walt remained pressed up against the wall looking terrified.

Young Lowanna made a move once again so I span round and cold-clocked him directly in the centre of his face with the handle of Rachel's gun. I then turned quickly back and pointed the gun at the whole of the Brennan crew that was before me.

I saw Sid twist Rachel around so she had her back to him and his arm was tightly wrapped around her throat. In his other hand he held the knife I'd taken from Lowanna and thrown away.

"You... should... never have... let them in here. Let... alone... put them up, you... stupid... bastard..." gasped Alf.

"Shut up Alf!" screamed Sid. "Pull your fuckin' head in, mate!"

I flicked the gun's direction from left to right, making sure each of them knew I had them all in my sights. What I must not let them know is that this was my first time holding such a thing and I had no clue what I was doing.

'Point and shoot!' the voice in my head sneered quietly. 'It's not overly complicated.'

"Drop the gun, pom!" Sid sneered as he pressed the tip of the knife to Rachel's throat.

"Don't you drop that gun, Jake!" screamed Rachel.

"Drop the gun or..." He pressed the knife tighter against her skin and I started to see a trickle of blood.

"Throw the gun here!" Michael shouted.

"*Don't* you drop that gun!" Rachel screamed.

"Drop it!" Sid bellowed.

"Dad! Dad!" Danny shouted from the back of the container. "Listen to me. For Christ's sake, *listen* to me. We have to bring ourselves back from the brink here. They're fucking *blues*, man. It would have been risky to off them and dump them if they were TV producers but they're bloody *police*. Police give a shit when police don't come back in. You know they do. We can't have them not..."

"And my superiors know exactly where I am!" Rachel interrupted through the guttural tension applied to her throat. "If I don't check in with an update by tomorrow at nine then..."

"Shut up!" Sid interrupted. "If your partner doesn't drop the gun then you're definitely going to miss the check-in, Red!"

Again – timing wise, it was *still* feeling inappropriate to point out I was in fact not police. Though a little part of me did wonder whether there was a possibility I'd get off with less of whatever they were planning if I identified myself as a private investigator instead. Maybe like *half*-murdered instead of *fully* murdered, perhaps?

"Kill her!" Chris shouted.

"Drop the gun! Final warning!" Sid reiterated.

"Don't you drop that gun, Jake!" Rachel cried. "If you drop that gun, we're *dead* twenty seconds later. *Both* of us."

"Fuck it!" sighed Sid as he drove the blade a little deeper into the side of her neck.

Blood started to drench the collar of Rachel's shirt.

"Okay! Okay! *Okay*!" I hollered as I let go of the handle and allowed the gun to flop around upside down in my hand. "Okay... Let her go!"

I slowly bent down and placed the gun on the ground.

As I stood back up, Chris Marlee dove forward and hit me across the forehead with something hard and heavy.

The black descended down around my eyes instantly.

[22]

or

"Drive Like You're In A Goddamn William Friedkin Movie".

"Don't even *think* about touching the stereo!" Psychic shouted as he swung himself around the hastily placed cordon of police vehicles by upping the pedestrian island on the left, crunching through the plastic bollard in the middle and grinding the car across the debris, on through Hollinside Road. "We don't need a bloody soundtrack right now!"

"I wasn't going to!" I spluttered as the car painfully bounced back onto even ground.

"A1 northbound or southbound?" He exclaimed as the sounds of police sirens lit up in pursuit.

The car slid around precariously in the slush and ice and Psychic did the best he could to keep us straight as the windscreen wipers worked overtime to keep a clear line of sight ahead for us.

"North! *North*!" I shouted back. "We've got to get to Jeff Petersen's warehouse?"

"What?" he replied. "You have *got* to be kidding me?"

"No. He said I've got to be at the place we discovered Baadir Gadiel by twelve!"

"It's twenty-five past eleven now," Psychic said in a panic as he blasted through another set of red lights and attempted to take a hard-right down onto the A1 from the overpass. "We'll never make it by… *SHIT*!"

He took the corner too fast on far too perilous a road surface and the Audi Q8 skidded out on the back end and slammed into the snowed-up embankment on our left, bouncing me hard out of my seat and against the passenger door.

One police car tried to take advantage of this by pulling up alongside us as we skidded on down the road out of control towards the A1 motorway but at the exact moment Psychic regained command of the steering, he pulled left and rammed the police car off of us.

The pursuing car hit the embankment on the other side and wedged itself in with its backend sticking out into the road, causing another police unit to slam into its side and block up the road with an almighty crunch.

"Woah! Holy SHIT!" I screamed, painfully twisting in my seat to look back at what happened.

"Aww man," Psychic whimpered. "I'm in *so much* trouble now. I just slammed a police car off the road and caused a crash!"

"No, that was 'rubbing'!" I replied.

"What?" he yelled, pulling the car right as it slipped dangerously onto the A1, just about making the space between a worrying sea of vehicles that should've known better than to be travelling in such hazardous driving conditions.

"I was paraphrasing Days of Thunder!" I responded. "It's from this bit where Harry says to Cole 'You're wandering all over the track!' and Cole replies 'Yeah, well this son of a bitch just slammed into me!' and Harry says 'No, no, he didn't slam you, he didn't bump you, he didn't nudge you… he rubbed you. And rubbin', son, is racing!' And then…"

Now, you all know me well enough by now. You know *all too well* that this would be the exact moment in which I would break into a detailed (and ultimately correct) distillation of how Days of Thunder is a vastly superior film to its 'Tom Cruise cinematic bedfellow', Top Gun. Soundtrack comparisons aside (Top Gun wins out there!), Days of Thunder has *better* acting, an *actual* plot, *real* dramatic stakes, a *superior* love story, a *vastly* more likeable protagonist, a *much* greater climax and… I could go on. But anyway, think about where we are right now, what's at risk and just how out of our depth we are and, well, show some decorum and let's maintain focus here, *okay*?

"Jesus Christ, Jake! Shut the fuck *up*!" screamed Psychic.

He weaved the car in between two other vehicles on the middle and outside lane, causing the vehicle we passed in the centre to panic at the proximity and speed at which we passed. They slammed their brakes on but started to skid immediately out of control.

Two police cars came speeding up at the next slip-road on our left and effortlessly intertwined themselves into the traffic, picking up speed behind us almost instantly.

"Shit!" I shouted.

"Any advice right now would be appreciated," Psychic bellowed back. "Not movie quotes. Just advice!"

"Drive like you're in a goddamn William Friedkin movie!" I screeched.

"That's quoting movies, Jake!"

"It's the best I've got right about n… Wait a second!"

"What? Come on, quick. *What*?"

"We've just got to find a way to outpace them enough to get out of their line of sight!" I replied. "It's too treacherous up there for them to put out an aerial unit to track us, they're never going to lay down a stinger across the motorway in these conditions with traffic flow this heavy!"

"You know that for certain?"

I shrugged. "I *think* I'm certain. It's been a long time since I was a police officer. Things may have changed. But I'd be really surprised if…"

A police car suddenly loomed into view alongside us and started trying to edge its way in front.

"They're trying to box us in, Jake! He's going to get in front and hit the brakes whilst the other guy clips our back end!" Psychic screamed, holding steady on the steering wheel.

I looked to my right past Psychic and then back to the second police car looming up behind us, trying frantically to get into the exact position my driver had predicted.

"Do you think you can steer out of a hard spin?" I asked as an idea formed.

"Wait. What do you mean? How hard a spin?"

"A really, really *hard* spin?" I replied.

"Hang on. What's a 'hard spin'?" Psychic said as the police car on our right tried to inch a little further ahead of us, spraying even more sludge up onto our windscreen.

"Hit the pace car!" I shouted.

"What do you mean 'hit the pace car'?"

"There's this bit in Days of Thunder when…"

"Will you *shut up* about Days of bloody Thunder," Psychic screamed. "For the love of God…"

"No, listen!" I countered quickly. "There's this bit where Harry says, 'Hit the pace car' and Cole says, 'What for?' and Harry replies 'Because you've hit every other goddamn thing out there, I want you to be perfect!' so… *hit* the pace car!"

"Which one is the pace car then?" Psychic clarified.

I pointed across to the car on our right. "Slam the brakes hard, let the rear car hit us and take itself out and as you brake, steer into that car right there!"

"That's the stupidest frickin' thing I've ever heard!" Psychic replied.

"*One*, no it isn't and your trashed Audi R8 from that metro chase is evidence of that and *two*, okay fine, forget it. Let's just go with your idea!"

I sat back and folded my arms in a sulk.

"Fine! Fine! Fucking *fine*!" Psychic shouted.

He hit the brakes hard and we were immediately shunted under the crunching sound of the police car behind us hitting our rear end. We started to spin almost immediately, so much so Psychic didn't need to steer into the police car on our right. We simply thumped into it anyway - sending it skidding into the central reservation, spraying high volumes of snow into the air as it lost control and twisted around, back down the A1 and right into the front of its accompanying pursuit vehicle.

Psychic and I screamed in unison as our car continued to spin out at a crazy speed we had no control over whatsoever. We hit a snowy ridge on the slip-road for the Westerhope turn off and came to a hard stop that slammed the both of us out of seats and to the left. The forced retracting lock of the seatbelts doing their job ricocheted us back into position.

I groaned agonisingly as more blood fell from my mouth. It dropped down unimpeded onto my lap and Psychic looked at me with genuine concern.

"Jake, are you..."

"Just get going," I groaned. "I'm no more worse than I've been these last sixteen hours bud. Come on... We've got to go!"

Psychic turned the engine over and we pulled away with a crunch, leaving behind part of the Audi Q8's front bumper as we did.

His mobile phone started to ring and he pointed down at it.

"Get that for me and stick it on speaker for me please?" he asked.

I did as instructed and Psychic shouted "Hello!" as soon as the incoming call connected.

"Hey Robbie!" Jennifer's voice trilled. "Are you okay to speak?"

"Yeah, yeah. You're on speaker-phone!" he replied as we got off the A1 at Cowgate and started to take a less prominent route through to Shiremoor.

"Okay, well I've got good news and great news and I'm just going to hit you with both in one fowl swoop - We've got the footage into the hands of that Chief Constable woman you lot were all talking about and she's apparently going to get all over it, she's doing that as we speak in fact allegedly..."

Psychic and I looked at one another and started to smile.

"Was that the good news or the great news?" he shouted in reply.

"I guess, the good?" Jennifer replied.

"What's the great news then?"

"Emily's waters have broken. Luke's rushing her up to hospital right now."

[23]

or

"Madeline".

I asked Psychic to stop the car the minute we passed through the gates of the industrial estate in Shiremoor where we were all too familiar with knowing Jeff Petersen's old warehouse to be. I had no idea who, if anyone, had taken it on or come to occupy it in these last six months but I definitely knew it *wasn't* Petersen - a couple of police sniper bullets to the chest and a long fall downwards from a few hundred feet off the Byker metro bridge into an obliterated mess below will sure hamper your ability to maintain ownership of business premises, regardless of whether you have a millionaire, racist, architect of domestic terrorism like Bill Collins paying your rent for you.

"Stop here? Why?" Psychic asked as he pulled the car over.

"We can't let him see you," I replied. "Remember, I've got to come alone. Anyway, it's really important you get going buddy. Emily's in labour. This is it. *This* is the big one for you. Trust me from experience, you are not going to want to miss a single moment."

"There's *time*. Honestly, I have a little bit of time. We can..."

"Psychic, listen to me mate." I sighed. "Listen, *please*. This is important. I appreciate everything you've done for me. I really do. But this is my shit. *Mine*. You have a life and you have a family to be thinking about now. I want you to know that you've done enough. You really have."

I slowly lifted up my bloodied t-shirt and showed him the deep purple bruising that was already started to darken past my ribs and head up towards the centre of my chest.

"Jesus Christ!" he gasped.

"I don't know how much longer I have left, Psych'," I said as my eyes filled up with tears. "But I know that *this* isn't good and there's definitely something wrong inside of there. I'm out of fuel to keep pushing on so I'm going to have to go *all* the fuck *in* from here with everything I've got left."

"What does that mean?" he responded quietly.

"Nearly twenty-four hours ago I was bleating on that I couldn't be reactive to this son of a bitch and that I had to get myself two or three steps ahead of him and find out who he is and I've achieved jack-shit other than slowly getting more and more ground down by his sick game. He's never let me get put in a position where I could take stock of any clues or pull any leads. He's just made sure the foot stayed pressed down on the accelerator from the minute I discovered Bobby. I can't keep going."

"So... what's the plan because from everything you're saying so far, it certainly doesn't sound like you can go this alone."

"I've *got* to. I've got to." I cried. "He says we're going to meet face to face again in there. So, when we do, I'm going to have to roll the dice and try to get the upper hand on him enough to get the whereabouts on Jane and the boys and... and... and... then kill him!"

The sweat was pouring down across my face and I could feel the skin on my face tighten around my skull.

"Jake... think about what you're saying. You could kill him right there and then on the spot, but it might mean you never discover where he's got Jane and the kids."

I shook my head. "I don't think he designed this game for me to *ever* get reunited with them. That was never the end goal. I think this was all about the slow torture and destruction of me and if what he did to Margaret and Matthew Jason is anything to go by, I think it's all ultimately leading to him killing my family in front of me."

The tears fell from my face just as they started to form up in Psychic's eyes.

"Jake... A few hours ago you were saying you were not going to accept never seeing them again. This is too big a chance at..."

I shook my head again. "No. No. Don't say any more. I've got to do this. I've got to end this *now*. And I need you as far away from here as possible because if it doesn't go down my way I don't want you to get caught up in it. I want you to go and help Emily deliver your baby girl and then give the both of them a kiss from me."

"Please..." Psychic stammered. "Just..."

I reached over and pulled Psychic's head towards me. I kissed him on the forehead and let him go as tears streamed down his face.

"That sprint down the A1 in the middle of the blizzard?" I smiled. "That was the best possible adventure for us to end on, my friend. You were superb... You've *always* been superb!"

"Jake, I..."

"You were the greatest friend I could have ever asked for, but you need to do as right by your family now as you've always done by me."

I tremulously climbed out of the passenger seat and shut the door behind me, trudging off through the snow towards the turn-in up ahead where I knew Jeff Petersen's warehouse to be situated.

I stood outside the main shutters of the warehouse as the snowfall started to ease. Pulling the mobile phone from my pocket, I looked at the clock on the front screen and saw the numbers shine out as 11:57.

"Son of a bitch," I smirked to myself. "We made it with time to spare."

I approached the door off to the side of the shutters and saw that it had been propped ajar. Cautiously opening it I was immediately bathed in the bright lights of the full panel beams from inside the warehouse as I stepped through.

Right in the centre of the unfurnished, completely empty warehouse space was a small barrel with a lid across it as a fire burnt away inside. To the left of that was a small stool and barely touching the surface of that, or at least struggling to, was the tottering feet of someone strung up by the neck with a cable that ran all the way up to the rafters above then back down again to a secured wheel on an adjacent pillar.

My eyes rose up from the feet to the legs, past the torso, to the strained and dishevelled face of Andy Andrews.

He looked like he'd aged twenty years since he'd last sat by my hospital bedside in the aftermath of breaking the Stephanie Jason tragedy wide open and then ostensibly disappeared into thin air thereafter.

He struggled to breath as the cabling rested tight around the skin of his neck and I stepped slowly towards him, anxiously considering my surroundings and what sort of trap could have been laid here.

"Andy?" I stammered as I took in his gaunt face. "What on..."

On the stroke of twelve pm, the sound of clapping started to echo around the warehouse and the owner of the hands making the noise soon stepped out from behind a pillar across the floor, close to where I'd had my confrontation with David Harland last time I'd been in here.

There was Tobin, as we'd christened him, walking slowly towards me. Still clad in his all black attire and finished off with the same white ceramic mask and that weird contraption around his neck, he quickened his pace and delved into a little spin on his feet, followed by a brief jig before coming to a stop next to the secured point of the cabling.

"Well done, Jake Lehman. Welcome to what I am hoping is the conclusion of Round Four. Do you have my money?" He said, having pressed the pad around his neck to start speaking in that grating, digitised voice once more.

I reached into my pocket and pulled out the padded envelope Luke had put together for me the night before, holding it up in front of me.

"Open the grill on that barrel there and throw it in for me please, Jake Lehman. Careful you don't burn yourself though."

"I'm sorry?"

"Open the grill on that barrel there and throw it in for me please, Jake Lehman."

I took a step forward. My confusion was immediately diluted by my anger. I flicked open the lid on the barrel with the cuff of my jacket and dropped the envelope in, then closed it again. Ten thousand pounds regenerated out of the holes on the lid as deep, dark grey smoke.

"I never wanted your money. It was just important to me that you kept yourself occupied. What's ten thousand pound after all? I heard that a film studio recently offered you half a million pounds for your life rights, so this is nothing in comparison, is it Jake Lehman?"

I sighed and dropped my head down for a second, taking pause to regain my composure as my head started to vibrate and my knees began to buckle. I breathed in again and physically straightened myself back up.

"This ends now." I said.

"Excuse me. This is just Round Four."

"No. *This* is the final round." I replied as my mouth began to curl and tense up with a rising fury I knew I was not going to be able to control for much longer. "Take off the mask, show me you are and let's get down to what this has all been really about."

His body started to shake with gusto about a second before the horrifying sound of synthesised laughter followed.

As he laughed my eyes darted upwards for split second and I could not believe what I was seeing: In exactly the same manner in which I had last entered this location with Psychic at my rear back when we climbed in here to look for Baadir Gadiel, the man himself was now silently lowering himself down from the skylight and managing to drop onto the walkway below him without making a sound.

'No Psychic! No!' the voice in my head screamed. 'What are you doing, man? No!'

My eyes locked in on Tobin as he finished fake guffawing so as not to give any sort of clue about what was going on above him.

'You're too far up to jump him, Psych'!' the voice inside of me exclaimed with panic. 'What's your plan here? He's too well angled for you to get to him from behind!'

"You have no leverage. No leverage whatsoever. How dare you disrespect me just because your resolve is fading? Have you learnt nothing so far? How many more people have to die unnecessarily to wake you up to your requirements to me? Your wife? Your sons? Tell me, Jake Lehman? Tell me how many more?"

Psychic slowly and methodically made his way along the walkway above, angling to get himself down via the rear ladders at the back of the warehouse without making a sound.

"No one else dies but you!" I growled, advancing forward towards him!

"WRONG!" screeched the enhanced voice at an ear-splitting decibel as Tobin punched out at the cabling wheel secured on the pillar, freeing the cable itself and sending it whirling in a frenzied manner.

"JAKE! JAKE!" shrieked Andy painfully as the cable around his neck cut off his air supply. "I FOUND MADELINE! LISTEN TO ME! SHE'S SAFE, OKAY? SHE'S SAFE. I PROMISE YOU SHE'S..."

The cable tightened at such a speed that it audibly pinged as Andy was sent shooting upwards, the sound of his neck snapping resounded across the expanse of the empty warehouse.

I rushed at Tobin but he effortlessly side-stepped me, grabbing my hair as he did and slamming the butt of a gun he'd swiftly pulled from the back of his trousers into the centre of my forehead, splitting it open with ease and sending a fountain of my blood upwards.

I fell backwards onto my rear end in a semi-stunned state.

"Please excuse me for one second, Jake Lehman!" the voice vibrated as its owner spun on his feet and fired two shots towards the ladder leading down from the overhead walkway at the back of the warehouse, immediately followed by two more.

I could just about see through the blood pouring into my eyes that Psychic had been at the top of the ladder as the second and third bullets hit him in the centre of his upper back, causing him to emit a horrifying grunt. His body dropped backwards away from the rungs and he silently fell, the only sound being the ungodly crack as he impacted hard with the floor below.

I screamed but no sound could come out. My entire body seemed to become enflamed. I pulled myself to my feet and no sooner did I do so, a heavy boot hit me in the side of the face and swiped me straight back down to the ground.

I grabbed out at Tobin's leg and dragged him down with me. I was desperate to get positioned in a way where I could fling a punch – any punch – but instead he effortlessly shook me off and the best I could do was to grab out at his mask to try and pull it free. I just about got my hands around the contraption on his neck and pulled it furthest away from where it was held in order to see skin underneath.

The sight of a neckline with a deep, entrenched hole surrounded by scar tissue caused me to freeze in horror and Tobin took full advantage of this to prise my hand back and snap my fingers.

I screamed in agony as he kicked me away from him with the greatest of ease and repositioned his voice pack.

"Stop making me go off plan, Jake Lehman. I do not like it. Now I have to consider a sanction this late in the game worthy of such infractions and I'm really not happy about this. If you want a final round in order to see what is left alive of your family, you've got to educate yourself with the information needed to endure it. So take yourself to Mayor Hetherington's infamous party location at 4pm and indulge yourself as much as you see fit!"

I tried to move. It felt like I was dead from the mouth down. No single message from my brain to the rest of my body seemed to be getting through.

"I no longer offer you any reassurance regarding the safety of your family and you have brought that on yourself. I only offer you the promise that your end now approaches."

He slowly started stepping backwards and through my blurred vision I saw him disappear into seemingly nothing.

'Get up, Jake! Get up!' Jane's voice was now screamingly hysterically. 'Get up and get to him! You have to save him!'

Psychic wasn't moving. I squinted and wiped at my eyes to try and improve my vision. From everything I could visually muster, it definitely appeared that he was deadly still.

I propped myself up on my good arm and began to distressingly crawl towards him.

[24]

or

31st August 2013.

"You bloody buggered this right up the minute you let them in here!" Danny shouted at his father.

"Belt up, boy. *I* didn't wave them in, did I?" Sid screamed back as he pointed over to Harv'. "This fuckin' drongo here and his fat galah of a workmate let them in, gave them *my* bloody name and pushed them right onto me!"

My eyes started to flicker open to the sound of the argument around me that appeared to have been going on some time whilst I'd lain unconscious.

"You didn't need to give 'em a bloody bed for the night though, Sid." Jim countered, half out of breath. "You should have left them to ride straight into the sandy nip and end up buried upside down on the side of the road or something."

"I wasn't giving them a fucking bed to play host, you stupid bastard – I was *always* going to go and shoot them whilst they slept later on! I shouldn't have to explain every single thing to you lot!" Sid screamed. "This bitch was sniffing around the road train. I didn't buy her bullshit for a second!"

My head was ringing and felt like it had gained two ton in weight. I struggled to lift it and look around to see where Rachel was.

"Enough with the earbush, for Christ's sake. Let's just get them stripped down and throw them down the hole!" Alf hollered way back from what seemed like the corner of the container.

"No. No. No. Pull your head in a second Alfie, you two pot screamer." Sid shot back as he paced in front of me. "Am I the *only* one thinking straight here? You're all fired up with a gutful of piss. I'm not having the blue heelers turn up looking for dickless tracy here and her pommy fucking sidekick and starting sniffing around, do you understand?"

"So what the hell are you suggesting then?" Jim replied.

Sid sighed and rubbed the sides of his temple. "I want it to look like they were never bloody here because they never *were*, you all get what I'm saying? We get Ron patched up and he puts a call in to his mates who rented the jeep out in the first place, okay? They'll probably prefer to get the car back anyway, so he asks them to tear up the paperwork and give it a clean over once we run it back down to them."

"That's pretty bloody trusting, Dad. We should just crunch it, man." Danny proffered.

"And pay off Ron's mates down in Nullarbor for the lost jeep? Stuff *that!*" Sid snapped. "The jeep goes back and go take these two out into the back of bourke and throw them into the never-never!"

"That's *it?*" Jim shouted. "That's your grand plan? Dump them a few miles out? Are you playing the blood larrikin here or what?"

"Chris? Mick?" Sid barked as my vision started to clear. "You know that waterhole you two like to go hunting 'roos at up and over as if you're heading towards Ex Earaheedy? You could cut these stickybeaks up and leave 'em for the dingos, yeah? That way the only place they'll be found is in the belly of..."

"Dad, come on. This is..."

"Don't interrupt me, kid." Sid shouted over to Danny. "I didn't bring up no wuss. You want to be a fuckin' sook you go piss off over to Alice Springs and cry on your aunt. *This* is the plan."

"I still think putting them down the..." Alf started.

"I don't want no knockers, Alf. I want bloody doers, mate. You hear me? The wind should curl in our favour and then I want them gagged, roped and taken off site. Yes? Make it look like they've wandered off into the never-never and got into bother."

"With no vehicle?" Danny proffered.

"Who knows how they got out there? Nothing to do with us, is it?" Sid. "Because they were never here, were they?"

Chris and Michael looked at one another.

"Mick's seen a couple of crocs up near the waterhole where you're talking about Sid." Chris said.

"Bullshit!" sneered Jim.

"Truth!" Michael shouted. "I totally have. We could cut them and let the crocs take them at the water edge?"

I lifted my head a few inches and slowly turned it to my left.

"He's up!" screeched Alf, causing Michael to stride towards me and with a flash of pain across the side of my head I was unconscious once more.

The unyielding and obstinate bounding of the surface beneath where I lay was what first stirred me back into the world. I came around from no dream or flashback, just shaken from an unconscious state of complete *blackness.* The first thing I came to notice was my restricted inability to breath properly as my mouth was taped over with thick, coarse material and my hands were bound above my head and fastened tight to a metal ridge atop of me.

Then through the gap in my arms I could just about make out that Rachel was lying alongside me, her mouth and arms taped and tied in the same manner as mine. After that, it was the whistling noise of the wind screaming by that I noticed. Along with the waves of sand and dirt that bounced up and slashed against my bare skin on random parts of my body. I blinked repeatedly and as the surface beneath me ricocheted up again and again I came to understand I was in the rear of an open-backed truck speeding recklessly through the darkness.

I turned my head achingly as best I could and just about made out the sight of the back of four heads squeezed into the front cabin of the truck. I had no idea as to who each belonged to.

Minutes passed. Lots of them. They rolled into what must have been hours because the dark sky lightened over our heads and the sandstorm started to fade. Through my one non-swollen eye I watched Rachel keep pulling and twisting at the ropes that bound her. Eventually she freed up some length on the binding that held her to the metal ridge and brought her hands down just enough to pull the tape from around my mouth.

I gasped desperately to inhale air properly, forgetting about my surroundings and involuntarily gulping down large clusters of passing sand. I began to violently cough.

Rachel started to say something indecipherable through her gag.

I desperately tried to stop coughing.

"I shouldn't... have... dropped... the gun!" I stammered whilst choking on sand.

"Pull over!" shouted one of the voices up above us in the driver's cabin. "He's getting loose!"

The truck came to an aggressively sudden hard stop, skidding out on its back end and the front doors either side of the cabin burst open.

"He's not loose, you daft galah!" came another of the voices. "His gag's just fell off!"

"Fuck it!" sighed a third voice. "Just pull them out here and do them!"

The original voice stepped around the truck behind Rachel and I could make out that it was Michael Merindah leaning on the side of where we were bound and held. "We're still well over eighty clicks out, mate. There's nothing out here."

"*Exactly*!" replied Young Lowanna as he came to stand alongside him. "Nothing! We could do them here and let the smell bring the dingoes in to finish off the work."

"That *could* work!" Jim added.

"I'm not calling this one and having Sid on my back!" sighed Michael as he walked off. "You want to pull half-a-job, bust a gut and go for it. It's not on me."

Laughter followed and the sound of the back hatch getting dropped was heard echoing out into the red dawning nothingness around us. Chris Marlee and Young Lowanna climbed up and towered over the top of us as they worked in tandem to untie our arms from the metal ridge.

Rachel wasted no time.

As soon as her arms became free she punched upwards with both hands entwined together and smashed Chris in the testicles, doubling him over as he lost his balance in pain and fell off the side of the truck. She yanked the rest of her arms free and then kicked out at Jim where he stood at the base of the truck.

Young Lowanna turned to grab her hair and I frantically pulled myself towards his leg and sank my teeth deep into his calf. He screamed and fell backwards on himself. I seized the opportunity and wrapped the slackened rope around his throat and started to pull tight.

The tussling and the hollering died out instantly and I felt the cold, small, circular nub of a rifle press against the side of my head.

"Slow down boy!" Michael smirked. "Let him go!"

I froze.

"Let him fucking *go*!" He repeated more aggressively.

I did as he demanded.

"Now slide down the truck, get out and get on your knees, pom!" He instructed.

I slowly and nervously did as he asked, passing a gasping Young Lowanna as I did so. Dropping down into the dirt, I could see a bloodied Rachel lying flat on the ground with Jim's foot on her head.

I looked around me into the great vast nothingness that surrounded us all. There were a couple of damaged, splintered old poles stuck up out of the ground about twenty feet away from us that looked like they had once carried electricity or telephone signalling a long time ago. But other than that, there was nothing except rough, orange soil as far as the eye could see. My eyes focused in for a split second longer on where the ground seemed to drop out off to my right.

"Re-tie them both!" barked Michael.

Young Lowanna set about doing just that to Rachel.

Jim did the same with me.

I watched as Chris approached Michael with a smile and whispered in his ear. I could tell from the smirk that was starting to form across both their faces what suggestion had been made. It made the sick bubbling in my gut start to expediate its journey upwards.

Chris turned and walked over to Rachel. He wrapped her long, dirtied red hair around his hand, coiled a fist and yanked her head right back.

"Are you still so smug and certain you're getting out of here without a gang-bang, darling?" he laughed, leaning down and kissing her on the cheek against her will.

Jim and Michael started laughing too.

"Hang on. Hang on. Who says you get first jump?" Jim grinned.

"Get in line and stop your flappin'!" Chris replied.

"I'm always going after you with the really gorgeous ones!" Jim griped.

"Then don't fucking *go*, pal!" he snapped, throwing Rachel down onto her back in the dirt and then violently starting to pull at her belt and trousers.

Rachel kicked out and Chris pushed one leg down, held it there and then slammed a fist straight into her face, spraying her blood up into the air.

'No!' I exclaimed inside my head, finding the fire to push myself up onto my feet and drive Young Lowanna down onto the ground. I began to pound my tied fists into his already damaged face over and over again, reopening the wound he'd suffered back in the container bar at my hands and spreading abundant discharges of blood all over his face. He tried to shout but blood started to spill into his nose and mouth.

I spun around and took a run straight for Chris. Jim stepped into my path and body-slammed me off balance, careering towards Michael who spun his rifle in his hand and smashed me across the head with the butt like he was swinging a baseball bat for a clear, backboards-striking hit.

I struck the ground and the moment I did both Michael and Jim took to stamping repeatedly on my shoulders and back. I felt like my spine had come through my stomach and as I opened my mouth to scream in agony two teeth from the back right of my mouth slipped out into a bloodied puddle on the dirt beneath me.

Jim grabbed me by my hair and my collar and dragged me unsteadily to my feet. My legs couldn't hold me so Michael gripped the other side of my arm and pulled me on.

I passed by Rachel, who's gag was now loose, and her trousers completely removed. She was fully and indecently exposed from the naval down.

"Don't look, Jake" Rachel sobbed. "Look away!"

"Leave her alone!" I yelled as everything blurred around me.

"You don't need to see this, Jake!" she bawled.

Rachel screamed and Chris began to thrust.

I tried to brace against Jim and Michael but I had nothing.

Jim whipped his belt from around his waist as the three of us landed in front of one of the damaged old poles. Michael propped me up against it whilst Jim forced part of his belt buckle through a protruding steel clip jutting from the wood.

"My turn!" I heard Young Lowanna slur back where they'd dragged me away from.

"Are you having a laugh? *Look* at you?" Chris could be heard to giggle. "Don't be bleeding all over her okay? You'll piss Jim off!"

Jim turned and saw what was going on back there. "Don't you jump in ahead of me, Young 'un! I'll smash the rest of your face in!"

He then turned and together with Michael lifted me slightly off my feet and on to my tiptoes and then tied the rest of the belt around my throat, pinning me against the pole and cutting off the circulation to my brain. I desperately fought to breath.

"You got a knife?" Michael asked.

"Of course I have." Jim replied.

"Stab his legs through then. Get the blood going for the dingoes."

Jim nodded and Michael walked away.

I didn't have enough air getting through to push out audible screams of pain as Jim proceeded to stab me in the calves and feet. I silently coiled as much as I could with the physical distress, but my head was trapped from going anywhere and every time I moved my feet so much as an inch, I choked myself further.

The only sound that could be heard was the sound of tussling, thrusting, laughing... and the pained, anguish sobs coming from Rachel.

Just within the blurred reach my vision could still make out, Chris Marlee appeared in front of me pulling his jeans up and wiping blood from his hands on his already dirtied vest.

"I expected a fight from *her* because she's an Aussie but *you*?" he smiled. "*You've* impressed me. I want you to know that, mate. I thought you poms were a bunch of soft-arses but you *really* put up a good go of it, you know?"

I gasped out.

"I've been bitten by a dingo before." He continued. "It isn't nice. *Savage* little biters they are. Your blood is already in the air to them. They're *coming*. I'd pray that you have already garrotted yourself by the time they get here and start tearing your legs off - except... you know... I don't want to."

He smiled, turned and walked away.

I could not angle myself properly to be able to see clearly as to where Rachel lay. I just heard Chris say "Are you done? You sure?" and then "Step out the way then!"

He stepped back enough to appear in my line of sight and I could see he had the rifle pointed down towards Rachel's position.

"N... No... o... ooo!" I gurgled barely audibly through the restraint.

Two shots rang out into the desert vista around us.

And then silence.

"Well done, you utter fucking dill!" shouted Michael. "How many bloody dingoes do you know that are wandering around out here with a hunting rifle? It wasn't meant to look like a straight up murder, for Christ's sake."

"By the time the wildlife has had their time with the both of them there'll be no bullet wound to consider. Calm *down*." Chris sneered. "Pick her up!"

My eyes started to flicker. I could see blackness edging in from the corners of my eyes as the last thing I managed to make out was Rachel's lifeless body being carried one end each by Jim and Chris over to where the ground seemed to drop out of sight. They threw her away like a piece of rubbish as my eyes closed shut against my will.

[25]

or

"I Don't Know What A Day Looks Like Without You In It, Mate".

The ever-expanding puddle of blood pouring out from beneath Psychic's crumbled body and acting as a reflecting pool for the light panels above was the first clue that this was bad. *Very* bad. I'm no medical professional. I took three attempts to get through my basic First Aid training course (and even then, I had to cheat by writing what 'A-B-C' meant on the inside of my hand). But I had at least a fundamental understanding that keeping your blood inside of your body was *good* and that this much of your blood pooling around outside of your body? No. That was *not* good.

I desperately crawled towards him with everything I could possibly muster, drawing nearer and realising that I'd have to pull myself through his blood if I was going to get close enough to him.

I could see his eyes were distraughtly flickering as his chest struggled to rise with each pained breath he pulled in. Tears poured down my face because of just how very, very <u>not</u> good I knew this situation was right now.

"Psych? ... Psych?" I murmured through my weeping as I pulled myself alongside him and dragged him into my arms, my jeans becoming almost instantly drenched in his blood.

Psychic blinked a little more furiously.

"Jake? Ja... ke?" he stammered painfully. "I can't... can't... I can't... see."

"I'm here. Don't worry. I'm here." I desperately reached inside his blood drenched pocket and pulled out his mobile phone. The screen was cracked and I pressed at it anxiously to get it working but it was showing no signs of life.

"Don't... tell... Emily I came... in here... by choice." Psychic gurgled. "She... She'll be... so mad."

He tried to force a smile. It clearly hurt too much.

"Tell her... you... made me. And... take... the hit. It's the... least... you... can... do."

I stemmed the pain coursing through my own body by looking back through the agonising haze and focusing on the first case Psychic and I ever worked together:

A cheating spouse job we were barely going to turn a profit on because the old dear that was our client barely had a pot to piss in financially but she sat crying in our office effectively enough that I felt sorry for her.

Psychic had really wanted to impress me on that job. He knew I was taking a chance on him despite not having a background in investigation. He was going all out to prove he was naturally gifted and capable of being an asset in this line of work. He was really overcompensating, and he knew that I knew it. He'd even researched all the possible entry and exit points for the housing estate we were completing surveillance on to a ridiculous extent and proposed dual contingency plans for all of them. And most of his plans were straight-out-the-gate *good* too.

It was trial by fire in terms of bonding on that job because we were sequestered together in a surveillance vehicle for a *long* time and if his craic had been terrible than it could have been an awful, drawn out time. But it wasn't. He bantered brilliantly and more than held his own - he busted my balls about what he considered to be my awful taste in music, had some of the best 'bad one night stand' stories I'd ever heard and was prepared to go into serious deep-dive discussions about the merits and demerits of 1980s action heroes.

"How many years old were you when you realised that Arnie, this gargantuan man we all quite literally looked up to as a kid when watching his movies whilst thinking he was this man-mountain of a specimen, was actually only five foot ten and wore lifts in his shoes or stood on boxes in scenes against other men to look taller?"

"That's not true!" I'd gasped.

And then Psychic sealed the deal by backing his statement up with *hard* geek evidence. He'd researched various co-stars heights (who ever needed to know how tall Jim Belushi was for God's sake?) and compared their eyeline with Schwarzenegger's. He was also able to quote at least three or four instances from the movie The Running Man where Arnie's height seemed to go up and down against some of the 'gladiators' he's facing off against in the same scene.

It got to a point eight or nine hours in on this job where I felt I was becoming quite sad that it was going to have to come to an end because I was enjoying his company *that* much. And I knew there and then I wanted to hire him. I just couldn't *afford to* seeing as I was barely taking a wage myself.

Thankfully though, Psychic didn't see a lack of payment as a barrier and kept showing back up regardless. This was something I was secretly glad about because my barriers were up completely after what happened in the police and what Andy Andrews did to me. But between you and me I did kind of *miss* having a friend and Robbie 'Psychic' Dayer definitely had all the hallmarks of potentially being a pretty great one.

"You've... got to... go Jake." He spluttered, pulling me back into the here and now. "You've... got... to. Or this... was all... for nothing."

"I've got to get help." I sobbed. "Just hang on, please."

I struggled in removing my coat, rolling it up and pressing it against Psychic's chest as hard as I could to try and stem the flow of bleeding. He groaned as I did this.

"You got... your wish... though... mate. I got... way... more fucked... up... than you this time." He wheezed out half a laugh. "We... had... a hell of a... run together... didn't... we? Especially... seeing... as we were... never not making it all... up... as we... went... along... just to... get by."

"It's caught up with us now though, Psych'." I cried.

"No... Just me... Not... you." Psychic stammered.

The distant sound of police sirens entered the surrounding atmosphere for the first time. I pulled him tighter and pressed harder on the coat against his chest. They were definitely drawing closer.

"You've just got to hang on, mate. Please just hang on."

"You... you've... got... to... go." Psychic said as tears began to fall. "You... have... to stay in... the game... For Jane and... and... the boys... and... and... you hold my baby girl... and you kiss her... for me..."

He began to choke on his sobs as his eyes flickered faster and his breathing became harder. The police sirens were drawing closer.

"I... really... wanted to... meet... her... I can't... believe... I fucked... up."

The sirens were now right on the other side of the warehouse shutter and the ocean of blue flashing lights was intermittently illuminating our surroundings.

"You're *going* to meet her, Psychic. I promise. You just need to hang on. Please buddy. Help is coming. I can hear it."

"You... have... to... go... and get... him."

"I'll get him. No matter what. I'll get this bastard. But I'm *not* leaving you. I don't know what a day looks like without you in it, buddy. And I'm not going to find out. We're in this to the end together - and this *isn't* the end."

The shutters rolled up and the side door burst open as a wave of armed response police officers flooded into the building.

"They're going to pull me away from you!" I shouted to Psychic over the noise of the police commands to lie down with my arms out to the side. "But I'll still be here. I promise, Psychic. I *won't* leave you."

Paramedics started making their way towards us.

Guns were trained down on me.

Through the bustle and the lines of people, DS Lisa Clarke emerged at the exact moment paramedics set about working on Psychic and two police officers grabbed me and painfully threw me face down to the ground, spraying up more blood from out of me in the process.

DC Gareth Mitchell arrived by her side and looked down at me.

He gasped a little.

"Jesus *Christ*!" Clarke exhaled.

[26]

or

"The Big Dramatic Turning Around Of Jake Lehman's Fortunes".

At some point I had clearly lost consciousness and finally been deemed worthy of the urgent medical attention I so very obviously needed. Because when I came back round from passing out on the ground of Jeff Petersen's old warehouse with some police officer's knee agonisingly pressing down on the centre of my back, I was in a hospital bed – handcuffed to the bedside rail.

As my head cleared and I blinked into my surroundings I was immediately awash with panic and anxiety – How long had I been out? The sheer agony throughout my body had been replaced with a throbbing ache and I was such a veteran of post-beating hospital care that I knew I'd been pumped to the eyeballs with morphine, even before I spotted the drip in my hand and the liquid bag hanging up on the rack above me.

"What time is it?" I shouted groggily to the blurry figure at the side of my bed.

DS Clarke leant forward. "Just before two, Lehman. Try to relax."

"I can't." I murmured, trying to move myself off out of bed but finding it impossible to do so with my plethora of injuries and one arm handcuffed.

"I really recommend you try." She replied.

"I have to be somewhere at four on the dot."

"That's looking unlikely." A voice to my right said.

I turned and found DC Mitchell sat to my right, playing with his phone.

I exhaled anxiously. "I know that you are all probably dead-set on keeping with this narrative you have about me where I've been murdering my way around the city and then breaking out of police custody but you've got to believe me, there's a psycho out there with a grudge who's framing me and…"

"We've *heard* about this footage." Clarke interjected. "It's apparently with our boss as we speak. Personally delivered by none higher than Chief Constable Lane herself. We've not seen it ourselves though – because we were too busy responding to an anonymous tip-off that you were down in Shiremoor shooting up a warehouse."

"You need to go look at the footage and then you need to get back here and uncuff me and let me get to where I have to..."

"We intend to watch the footage, don't you worry." Clarke said.

"But I don't think it's going to move around the cogs half as quickly as you're expecting them to, Lehman." Mitchell smiled. "There's a lawful process and it takes time and it requires..."

"Just unarrest me as quickly as you arrested me and let me go save my family. Please." I groaned as I finally found a semi-comfortable and achievable way to sit up and swing myself to the edge of the bed whilst handling the handcuff.

The door to my private room opened and, from around the side of the uniformed police officer standing guard outside, Chief Constable Jessica Lane emerged in civilian attire with her colleague Detective Chief Inspector Marsha Beverly. Both walking with purpose into my room, closing the door behind them.

Clarke and Mitchell jumped to their feet.

"M'am!" Clarke nodded.

"Detectives!" bellowed Beverly assertively. "We have updates."

Lane took Mitchell's seat from beneath where he stood and moved it closer to my bed. She placed it down next to me and smiled. With a wink she pointed at my handcuff.

"Let's get that off, please folks!" Lane said.

Beverly nodded at Mitchell, who quickly fumbled forward and unlocked the cuff from my wrist before stepping back to where he stood.

"Merry Christmas, Mr Lehman." Lane grinned. "Hell of a way to start the festive season, huh?"

"Jessica," I started. "Psychic? He's..."

"He's in intensive care." She replied. "He's being very well looked after."

"He's *alive*?" I gasped.

Lane nodded. "He's in a *very* bad way, Jake. I need to prepare you for that. But yes, he's alive and they're working on him as we speak. And you've had quite a run of 'accidents' yourself over the last twenty-four hours..."

Mitchell stepped forward with my medical notes from the bottom of my bed. "... Thirty-nine stitches to the head, broken ribs, internal bleeding, hairline skull fracture and..."

"Yes, *thank you*!" Lane snapped, pulling the notes from out of his hand.

I leant forward a little to speak more quietly to Lane. "Listen, now's not the time but I need to talk to you about a favour?"

"Really, Jake? *Really*? You don't think you've well and truly dried out that well?" she smirked.

"Let's get down to business here!" Beverly growled as she came to sit on the bottom of my bed with no regard for my legs whatsoever. "I've seen the footage from yesterday evening that captures the murders of Margaret and Matthew Jason. We've also noted the comments that were made by the individual you recorded. But you're going to have to help us here, Lehman..."

"Do you have any idea who is doing this Jake? Or what they have planned next?" Lane asked.

I sat silent for a few seconds and gathered my thoughts.

"In terms of what's next? All I know is that I have to be at Mick Hetherington's house at four pm today."

Clarke checked her watch.

"What?" gasped Lane.

"That's all I know. I don't know whether Jane and my children are going to be up there. I don't know *anything*. I just know that if I'm not there to answer another phone call at four pm than my family are most certainly dead. And as for who's doing this?"

I sighed and rubbed my eyes, swallowing down to suppress tears.

"I'm reaching here but... I grabbed that guy and pulled off the voice device he's got strapped to his throat. I could just about make out that his neck is all scarred and there's a pretty hefty hole there. That set me off thinking."

"Okay..." Lane said tentatively.

"Just over ten years ago I was out in Australia," I began. "Now's not the time for the whole sorry saga but I was working with an Australian police officer investigating the disappearance of a lass from Tynemouth along with a few of her friends. We zoned in on the men responsible out in the desert and they murdered the officer. A woman called Rachel Casey. I just about survived and in the process of defending myself I shot one of the men, a guy who I believe was called Chris Marlee, through the neck with a bolt gun. I shot him right where that guy earlier tonight had a hole and scarring..."

Clarke looked over at Beverly with concern.

"Those guys and what they did? Their names are etched inside of my head until my dying day and I'm pretty damn certain that the bloke I have spent the last twenty-fours being controlled and manipulated by *is* Chris Marlee! I was always led to believe that he and all the others died. I was *told* they all died. Where the confrontation took place there was an explosion... and... and... there were fires in the outback and... well... and it all got out of control. I was told there was no survivors except me. I was obviously misinformed because Chris Marlee survived and he's *clearly* pissed off."

I swallowed hard again as the voice in my head whispered, 'Tell yourself the lie for long enough and it eventually becomes your truth, Jake'.

"And you think that this Marlee fella hasn't just survived the altercation with you but has lay in wait for over a decade, ready to get revenge?" Lane asked somewhat incredulously.

"Maybe he was gaining his strength back? Maybe it took him this amount of time to find me? I don't know. But this twisted son of a bitch has a personal grudge against me and a scar on his neck that indicates he is Chris fucking Marlee!"

"We need checks ran on an Australian national by that name - stat!" barked Beverly.

Mitchell nodded and started to walk out of the room.

"There was a guy out there at the time, DCI Geoffrey Novak working for Sydney police... He might be retired now. I don't know. He knows all about this though."

Mitchell nodded and opened the door.

It burst further open, knocking Mitchell's hand from the handle and in walked Acting Chief Constable Cary Falk in full formal police dress with Police Commissioner McKinley by his side.

"What the hell is going on here?" Falk shouted.

"Cary, listen..." Lane began.

"Excuse me!" McKinley forcibly interrupted. "Didn't I suspend you last night?"

"No," snarled Lane with contempt. "You asked me to recuse myself from this situation - *pending* you moving ahead with cha..."

"Yet here you are!" snapped McKinley.

"Visiting a *friend*!" sneered Falk. "You need to leave, Jessica. This is not good."

"Why has his handcuffs been removed?" McKinley said, pointing at me.

Beverly stepped forward as a tentative peacemaker, addressing Falk. "Sir please, if I may? You have to allow us to brief you on the latest developments here."

Falk took half a step back and eyed Beverly suspiciously. "Very well."

Beverly hit the ground running and covered everything - what I'd been accused of, what evidence existed that proved someone else was responsible, what the latest request was by this nefarious figure I knew now to be Chris Marlee...

"I can't speak to the Arkin Dentz murder," Beverly continued. "But my team have a time of death for Robert Maitland that is prior to Lehman entering the building where the murder took place. Grey Street CCTV provides confirmation of somewhere between forty minutes to an hour's difference. At the time we're told Robert Maitland died we can place Jake Lehman passing through various camera points in the city to get to his place of work. This, plus the recording that Chief Constable Lane has acquired via Lehman himself, shows there's something else afoot here a lot more complicated than just Jake Lehman going around killing people."

"And unless we change course now, more people are going to be at risk and more people are going to die." Lane feverishly interjected. "If this comes down to you wanting my job Cary, then fuck it you can have it. But if you authorise putting the handcuffs back on Lehman and doubling up security outside his room it won't do jack-shit to stop the next wave of murders and whatever else is planned from happening. I will guarantee that."

"You'll *guarantee* that?" smirked Falk.

"I'll guarantee it, yes." Lane replied. "I'll guarantee *three* murders right now - Jane Lehman, Jack Lehman and Jonathan Lehman!"

I physically winced.

"If Jake isn't at the next destination by four pm then the whole thing takes an even bigger turn for the worst. And seeing as we were yanking explosive devices outside of mosques last night at the same time we were crawling through a bombed-out wreckage in the centre of town, I genuinely don't think we can afford to take that turn."

Falk went quiet.

"You cannot seriously be considering what she is saying here?" jeered McKinley. "Cary, think about the overwhelming evi..."

Lane wasn't giving her a single inch. "Cary, think about how and why you and I ended up where we are within this police service. Think about the fall-out from Hadenbury and the field day the press had knowing so much had been covered up and so many people were looking the other way. We *have* to be on the right side of this and we don't know if we have full control of this footage..."

"You *don't*." I smirked. "I just want to put that out there."

"It's already leaking that we have Jake in custody for crimes we're all aware of by this point he hasn't committed. More murders occur, more carnage bursts out all over the city... on Christmas Eve *no less*, and the media gets wind we knew beforehand someone else was responsible and we didn't do everything in our power to stop them? Well, you wouldn't want me stepping out in front of a microphone thereafter, that's all I'm saying."

"I'm seriously going to enjoy formalising your removal from..." McKinley began.

Falk held up his hand.

"What you do when the dust has settled on all of this is entirely your prerogative, Janet." Falk interceded. "But now? Right *now*? We need to be incredibly careful about the potential for... for... *overreach*, if we can call it that?"

He sighed and put his hands on his hips.

He looked down at his feet then up to the ceiling, deep in consideration.

"Lehman has to be at a set location by four pm or..." Lane offered before Falk's hand shot back up once again.

"I'm thinking, Jessica! I'm *thinking*!" he snapped. "What's the location?"

Lane bit down on her bottom lip. "Mick Hetherington's old estate!"

McKinley rocked back on her feet. "*What* did you just say?"

"The site of all his... *gatherings*!" I snarled. "By four pm. Or my family die."

McKinley looked across to Falk in shock.

Clarke looked over to Beverly and shrugged.

Lane and I stared intently at Falk.

Eventually he spoke.

"Well, he's certainly not going without a full bloody police escort!"

[27]

or

31st August 2013.

"When you come back you make sure you come back proud of what you achieved out there, proud that you were thought highly enough of to be selected to go out there in the first place and then you use that pride to reinvigorate yourself back to the man you know you are at heart. The man I *love.*" Jane smiled as she leaned over and kissed me post-sex, on our last night together before I left for Australia.

I nodded and when she finished kissing me, I leant back in to caress her but my hands felt locked down beneath me and my head wouldn't move forward. The more I pushed to try to free it from this invisible force blocking me from doing so, the more I choked and the more alarmed Jane began to look.

Suddenly I gasped and found myself not at all in bed with Jane the night before I left, but in fact still strung up on the old pole in the middle of the senselessly searing Australian desert.

Both my eyes were very nearly swollen shut and my mouth was dried out and painful to move. I found that, whilst unconscious, one of the Brennan men had rebound my hands at the wrists. Not so well that I couldn't agonisingly pull free but stripping layers of skin from my hands and forearms in the process, like they were just sliding off.

With my hands finally freed I slowly raised my arms up and took hold of the belt around my neck, forcibly pulling forward with all of my might as the wood creaked behind me and I searched blindly to find where the buckle was that held me in place against the steel clip jabbing into the back of my skull.

Unexpectedly the wood around the clip splintered and I fell free onto the ground below, leaving me to feverishly and frantically pull at the belt around my neck so that the buckle was now front facing and I could undo it. I gasped and swallowed anxiously for air even though every wide-mouthed gulp tore more of the cracked skin around my mouth.

Australia has *really* fine dirt. I don't think television and film really capture that.

I landed in it so hard on my knees and forearms, pushing what little substance there was still inside of me up and out of my innards into a bloodied gloop of vomit and saliva on the ground below. My wrists were torn up, my fingers were numb and the strap around my neck had left the beginnings of an open wound. Not all of the blood from my head and facial wounds had dried in the baking heat it seemed. The dirt clung to them.

Remember when you used to get an ice cream as a kid and getting it 'dipped' was such a treat because they'd roll the ice cream in sherbet or sprinkles or whatever and it would all just *magically* cling on and coat the surface? That's what happened to my hands and head.

I tried to dust it off as I began to attempt to crawl.

It was so fine and thin to the touch.

I pulled myself to the edge of the ground where I'd last seen Rachel disappear out of sight and I could see that the terrain declined downwards into a ditch roughly fifteen feet deep.

I just about made out the shape of her. I tried to shout her name but my lips felt heavy and crusted, like they'd dried into a hardened seal across my mouth. I saw her chest struggle to rise. Once it did, it rapidly moved up and down for a few seconds and slowed down again.

'She's alive! She's alive!' I screamed internally.

I pushed myself delicately out over the edge of the decline but quickly slid out of control, crunching into the base of the ditch in a cloud of dust and pain. I couldn't allow myself to pause because I knew a momentary hiatus would ultimately be a hard and permanent stop. I pulled myself instead as best I could using one good leg and a couple of fingers and eventually came to flop down next to her.

Dark coloured blood pumped out of her mouth and her left ear. I knew she was in trouble. Biology was never, ever my strong point, but I knew enough to know that something that opaque must come from deep within the body and if it's pouring out of her mouth and ear it *couldn't* be a good thing.

"Rach... el..." I stammered and slurred, my voice crusted up with dehydration. "I shoul... not... drop... gun... I am... sorry... I dropped... gun."

I kept stammering the word *sorry* over and over, each use of the term generated a tiny modicum of saliva that I feverishly licked around the edges of my mouth. I watched her chest struggle to rise and then quickly fall no sooner than it had. I could see deep red blood ooze from two bullet wounds to her upper chest as I gently attempted to pull the edges of her torn and gore-drenched shirt down over the naked and exposed bottom half of her body in a futile gesture of decency.

I attempted to tell her that I was going to get help and that she was going to be okay. She reached out falteringly to grab at my hand, missed it and redirected what little energy she had left to grab at the side of my face instead and drag it closer to her.

"It's... days in... in... every other direction except... except back to *them*." She'd stuttered through her pain. "You have to... go *back*... go back to *your sons*... so you have to go back... through *them*... You know that... right?"

I started to look down at her myriad of open wounds and injuries, frantically trying to get my head round where to start in helping her and keeping her alive.

"Get up... Please... *get up*... And get back there..." she gasped. "And when... when... you do... you burn it... to the ground... with every one of them in it... You promise me that... Promise me that... Jake... Promi..."

She fell into silence.

"Rach.. el. Listen... to..."

She weakly tapped my hand with the tips of her fingers.

"There's people... in the mines... I heard... them... say... that... when... they were... binding... us." Rachel struggled. "Burn... it... down... so flames... so high... every... one... comes... to... look."

I squeezed her fingers.

"You... sing with me..." she semi-smiled as the light in her eyes started to fade and her breathing slowed. "*Plea... se?* We can... build this... thing... tog..."

"Standing st... str... ong forever..." I strained out in a pained whisper.

"... runs... out... lovers... we still..."

"Have each... other." Hot tears fell down my face, the skin on which had become hardened with dirt. "Nothing's gonna... stop..."

She gurgled. "... Mum? ... *Mum?*"

Her eyes filled up with tears and her breathing finally gave out.

I said her name quietly three time, praying each and every time she'd respond somehow, in some way.

Rachel's head lolled back; her eyes left wide open staring out at the sky above us.

Something inside of me broke loose. I found the ounce of strength required to pull her lifeless body onto my lap and I wrapped my arms tight around her, screaming wildly through my pain, up and out into the great emptiness of the desert around us both.

I don't know how long I'd passed out for, but I knew it was long enough for my face to twist and become frozen in an expression of pure, psychotic fury and for the colour to have completely drained from Rachel's entire body.

She lay in my lap - cold, white and stiff.

I gently eased her off of me and kissed her softly on her icy blue lips.

Digging my fingers into the dirt in front of me I began the slow, agonising pull and crawl up out of the ditch and back onto the even terrain where Rachel and I had been tortured and left for dead.

I took a few seconds to regulate my breathing and then staggeringly pulled myself to my feet, wincing from the open knife wounds in my calves and feet as I slowly stepped forward. The pain in my back was so excruciating I felt like I was having to learn to find an entirely new way to walk again that reduced the pressure and agony.

I fell down next to Rachel's trousers, callously discarded where Chris had first removed them. I set about tearing them into pieces as best as I could with what strength I had, fashioning improvised bandages for the bleeding holes in my feet and legs. A long piece of wood lay splintered from the pole I'd pulled myself free from. It was the best I could hope for under the circumstances as crutches go so I baby-stepped over and picked it up, bolstering myself straight into a supported standing position.

I looked all around me.

I was, for want of a better expression, absolutely *fucked*!

I had no bearing on where I was or what direction I needed to go in. I knew that from what Rachel suggested about "days" under ANY bearing, regardless of how inaccurate she may have been in her condition, I didn't have the strength nor the hydration level to survive.

But I had to *try*.

I had to see my children again.

My line of sight caught the roll of thick black smoke just above the cloud line way, way in the distance. I convinced myself that this must be the fires off in the territories so I turned myself around and forced myself to buy into the notion that straight in the opposite direction would take me back towards Brennan.

This was half-baked at best but I needed the hope to drive me on.

With each step I pushed myself to walk a little further through a wall of pain like nothing I'd ever experienced before. I could see every now and again a flurry of movement a few hundred metres out on my left and right against the great expanse. On the occasions I forced myself to stop and wipe the dirt and sweat from my eyes, I could just about make out that the shapes belonged to the dog-like creatures I assumed to be dingoes.

Were they *real*?

Was I hallucinating?

Were they really encircling me, tightening in around me and getting ready to attack or was it all in my imagination? I must have been giving off one hell of an appetising scent to them if they *were* a reality.

The sun lowered slightly in the sky and I took this to mean that the night was coming. Had I really survived out here that long? My footing stumbled and I stumped down on my left foot as it numbed up, pushing more blood out of the wound which seeped out through my makeshift bandage.

I swallowed and blinked. Both my throat and my eyes felt so heavy and unmoveable. When my eyes opened again I was back in that bar up by St James Park on my first date with Jane. Walking towards me was a younger version of myself, bringing drinks over to the nearby table. I licked my lips staring at that pint of Heineken with the condensation dripping off the chilled glass.

Younger me sat down and started asking Jane how her head was from the injury she sustained at work earlier that day. I'd noticed it was starting to heal over now, but she was still trying to self-consciously cover it with her hair. She asked if I'd like to feel it because she thought it was going to heal all raised and ugly. I watched myself stroke my index finger across that tiny scar on the corner of her forehead and my finger kept going, brushing the hair back behind her ear and letting my hand fall to the back of her neck. Jane smiled, bit her bottom lip as she leant forward towards me and we clashed teeth as we kissed for the first time. I watched the two of us pull back and our nervous laughter shook me back to the reality of the auburn desert surrounding me.

I tightened my grip around my haphazardly constructed wooden support and tried to straighten up the direction I was heading in, worried that I was going to wander deeply off course even though I held no certainty that I was walking where I needed to anyway. It was so hard maintaining a straight direction when my feet felt numb from the shins down.

The terrain around me started to turn green.

I blinked furiously and suddenly the dirt was now grass and I looked down to find I was no longer standing but in fact lying flat out on it with Jane's head in my lap. I let my gaze widen out to the skyscrapers and the buildings around us and I realised I was in Central Park in New York City. This was an early family holiday we took with the boys. I knew what to do...

I looked no more than five or six metres to my left and there was the both of them; Jack running around with a penny-floater football as Jonathan, who'd only been walking for six months or so at this point, doggedly staggered after his brother as quickly as his little legs would let him.

I broke into a huge wide smile.

My mouth hurt because of the formation it made through my dried up, cracked and crusted lips. Jane sat up and shouted over to the boys. 'Shall we walk down to the café for ice cream?' her voice echoed with a heavy reverberation around my head.

Then suddenly it was deadly *silent*. The hustle and bustle of the city was *gone*. I stared all around me, panicked that someone had been able to turn every sound off in the whole of NYC and then my ears picked up the slow, distant resonance of a car engine against faraway crunching gravel.

I lost the steadiness of my gait and blinked manically only to find myself once again back to the true reality I was facing.

With what little my eyes were able to focus I saw a small dot on the horizon in front of me. It drew closer and closer the more my strength faded.

'They're coming back, Jake!' Jane's voice said inside my head. 'They're coming back. You need to get ready to fight. You have to come back to me and the boys and you've got to be ready to fight through Hell and out the other side to be able to make that happen. Fight Jake! *Fight*!'

I widened my stance as what I now realised was a truck loomed closer towards me. I picked up my wooden makeshift crutch and prepared it like a weapon to swing and...

... Then I realised I was watching myself do this through a blurred haze and my actual body crashed down into the dirt, unconscious and *finally* completely broken.

A gunshot rang out and resonated across the expanse as my eyes fell shut.

[28]

or

"Ghosts".

I zoned out on the drive out of Cramlington Hospital and further up into Northumberland. I slouched down as best I could against the head-rest in the rear seat and closed my eyes a little whilst Mitchell argued with Clarke up ahead - something about how she'd promised him he could grab a sandwich before they left the hospital and yet they'd sped off without him getting anything and now he was hungry.

"We've not eaten since late last night!" Mitchell whined.

"You had the option to go home." Clarke countered. "You could have got some rest and got a bite to eat and..."

"*You* opted to stay!" he fired back.

"Yes, I did. I wanted to see this through. You're your own man. You could have gone home if you wanted."

"Well if I'm my own man then I want to stop for something on the way up!" he snapped.

"Fine. Cool." Clarke smirked. "I'll just radio in to the unit ahead and the armed response team behind us and tell them we're pulling into McDonalds on the way up to our destination because DC Mitchell is 'hangry'. How's that?"

I started to forcibly drown them both out at that point.

My mind immediately drifted to thoughts of suicide. The resolve had faded and I no longer thought of this situation as one I could beat. I started to get panicked at the possibility Chris Marlee had waited so long to come over here and get his revenge that maybe his ultimate act of revenge was going to be to murder my family and leave me to cope with the sheer agony of life without them.

Well the joke would be on you Marlee, because there was no version of this life that I'd be prepared to live where I wasn't kissing Jane every day. Or arguing with Jack about the merits of the Die Hard franchise over the Fast & Furious movies. Or just slouching down on the beanbags in Jonathan's room and playing racing games on his console with him as a subversive way to sneak in conversations with him about his day and what he was up to.

It hurt too much to think about all of that though, so I pushed myself to change the course of my thoughts. Instead I fell back to ruminating on the conversation with Lane at the hospital. She brought me a fresh change of clothes from a charity shop in the foyer of the hospital entrance. A pair of jeans and a thick woollen jumper, both of which fit miraculously well and which I'd paired much to her disdain back up with Luke's bloodied, torn and battered Superdry jacket that he'd leant me last night.

It was five minutes to three pm as I stood leaning against the bed, Falk and McKinley long since gone, whilst Mitchell re-cuffed my wrists (one cuff delicately placed against the new support brace on my right arm) and Clarke conferred in the corner of the room with an armed response sergeant.

"You know that I walk in there with handcuffs on and these guys by my side, it's game over straight away right?" I had sighed to Lane.

"We need to make do with the best we're being given to work with, Jake. It's a phone call, okay? They'll be extra quiet and stay back wherever possible. What do you want me to say? Falk hasn't agreed with DCI Beverly about lifting the charges and I'm a week away from McKinley wiping out my career."

"Yeah, about that. What *is* her problem?" I'd asked. "She's the Police and Crime Commissioner and she's acting like she *owns* the whole bloody police service."

"To some politically involved people she sort of does. That's the way it's all aligned nowadays. Political parties push through their preferred candidate and then manipulate the police service to suit their agenda through the role. The issue with her though is that she's *very* connected to 'big money' over any one major party and that makes me very wary of what lies behind a lot of her decision-making."

"You can say that again - she was very pally with Bill Collins, you know?" I'd replied.

Lane had nodded. "And she kind of slept on dealing with Hetherington and Hadenbury because they were friends too!"

"She totally *knew*!" Lane and I sang out in unison.

"As for what her problem is other than that? Well, it's *you,* isn't it Jake?" Lane continued.

"Really? *That* simple?"

"*That* simple!" she had laughed. "Somewhere between you and your little crack team of investigators and reporters locking up her well-connected and rich friends and you being... well... disagreeable, you'll find your very simple answer."

I'd shook my head. "I thought I was getting to be more likeable as time went on?"

"I don't know who told you that." Lane had grinned.

"Hey, listen." I'd whispered conspiratorially hoping it would fly under Mitchell's radar. "I really need to talk to you about *that* favour when this is all over."

"Oh. You're still pursuing that? I thought I'd blown that off?"

I had looked to gage whether she was serious or not.

"It depends what you're going to be asking for, Jake." She'd continued. "Because by the time this is all over, I don't think I'm going to carry much sway once McKinley and her cabal have finished with me."

I'd never been back to Hetherington's gated mansion since my days stalking him up on the incline above his property. It felt like I *had* from watching that clandestine footage Stephanie Jason had recorded of the sordid and criminal acts taking place up there, but I hadn't and I certainly had no stomach to either.

The estate had taken a kicking over the years for obvious reasons. On his death it reverted to his only living relative – a younger sister who lived down in London, apparently – and the intention was always to sell it and sell it at a loss if necessary. The problem was it had been such a deep focus of such detailed media attention in the aftermath of what Emily, Psychic and I exposed that no one in their right mind was ever going to buy it.

I mean, come on? *'Here's the main foyer that leads up to eight bedrooms and four bathrooms and if you just look left you can see where all the child-rape parties took place – and behind that is the home-cinema room!'* No chance. There was talk for a while about it being reconverted into a home for abused children. There was a backlash against that. Then there was rumours Northumberland County Council were going to buy the land, raze the place to the ground and develop it into a small park. That didn't go anywhere either.

Instead it was simply left to go to ruin. Abandoned for people to smash up, break into and damage, allegedly hold seances and (on three separate occasions in the last two years) start fires. None of which caused enough structural damage to make any sort of difference to taking down the eye-sore once and for all.

We drove through the gates in a mass convoy and Clarke radioed in for everyone to pull immediately left on the drive. She got out with Mitchell and walked over to talk to the other officers who joined her in a circle around the armed response vehicle. I initially strained to listen and gave up almost immediately on realising I had no chance of hearing a single thing being said.

I instead took note of the rusted, broken gates to my rear that we'd just passed through and the wild, overgrown bushes that lined the rest of the small driveway up to the house itself. Time - and local angry mobs, judging from the smashed window and spray-painted graffiti on the brickwork up ahead - had not been kind to Hetherington's home.

Mitchell moved around to the rear of the vehicle, opened the door and gently helped me out whilst protecting my head from the car's door frame. This was appreciated.

"This is how it's going to go," he said as he led me away from the car towards where Clarke and the rest of the police stood. "DS Clarke and I are going to walk you in and take a look around. We'll play it totally silent inside and just gather whatever we can to back up this claim about this madman playing puppet-master with you. Sergeant Niro and his men are going to cover the perimeter. If you fuck with us in anyway, if this is a set-up and there's any sort of ambush that leads to you attempting escape, you will be shot. Is that clear?"

"That's clear." I nodded.

"I don't like running..." he attempted to continue.

"That's also clear." I smiled.

"Fuck you! I don't like running so if you make me chase you in any manner I am going to kill you. Okay?"

"Okay. Quick counter question though," I replied. "You can see the state of me, yeah? What makes you think I'm running anywhere?"

Mitchell sighed and walked us both on.

The main entrance door to Hetherington's property had been forced ajar by the time I approached it. Whether that had been done by police now or looters/vigilante types in the past I had no idea. I do know however that a cold sweat presented all over my body as I passed through the door; the ghostly residue of so much internal hatred and acknowledgement of all the disgusting, hateful crimes that had been committed here by the man that destroyed my life and also the lives of so many others.

"If you're right about this guy then what's his connection to Mick Hetherington?" Clarke asked me as we walked through the dirt and cobweb covered foyer that had gone to ruin very quickly in the last couple of years through exposure to the elements, resultant from every window on the ground floor being smashed through.

We walked via torch light shone by both Clarke and Mitchell as they worked to illuminate every corner and dark recess.

"There isn't one to my knowledge." I responded. "No more than there was to the Jason family or Aafeen Taif, his mosque and Mr Gadiel. Or Bobby Maitland, you know? The only known connection I can muster is to Arkin Dentz and that's extraneous at best."

"What is it?" asked Mitchell.

"It was Arkin Dentz' daughter who went missing in Australia. He was my client. He hired me to go over there and look into her disappearance and that's what put me in the path of Chris Marlee and his friends."

"And Dentz owned the building on Grey Street that you ran your private eye firm out of, right?" Clarke clarified.

I nodded.

"So, he killed Dentz because ostensibly he was the one who kicked off this whole sorry saga in his twisted view, is that what you are suggesting?"

"Maybe?" I shrugged. "But it doesn't account for the other connections and how this man knows so many deeply personal things about me."

We rounded a corner into what I presumed was last used as a large dining area. There were two workman's lights on metal stands propped up either side of a huge long wooden table. Clarke and Mitchell's torch beams slid over the surface as we briefly caught glimpses of mounds of paper, files, SD cards and memory sticks, photographs and a couple of computer monitors that seemed to be hooked up to nothing.

"Don't touch anything. It could be ri..."

Clarke didn't get to finish her sentence before the whole room lit up as a result of Mitchell reaching over and switching on one of the workman's lights to his right.

She shot him an angry glance and finished her sentence regardless. "… rigged! Everything could be *rigged*!"

I stepped forward as she spoke and instantly froze on sight of the first few photographs that fell upon my line of sight.

There were photographs of me - *surveillance* photographs - as recent as a month ago. I reached down just as Clarke tried to stop me and I picked up a pile of them, leafing through them and dropping them down as I went. There were photos dating back three years… *five* years… There were photographs of Psychic and I out on a job, some whilst working the Stephanie Jason case. There were photographs of Jane and I together on a 'Date Night'. There me and my boys playing football together on a field or walking through the centre of town as a family.

I began to feel the sick rising up my stomach and towards my throat.

"Jesus fucking Christ!" I gasped.

"There's memory sticks here that are labelled." Mitchell offered, drawing my attention to the right of the table where a pile of such sticks lay with string tied to them and little cardboard labels that, as I picked each up and studied them, said things like 'Lehman - Solo Therapy: 2019' and 'Lehman - Marriage Counselling: 2022'. My eyes bulged and my jaw dropped on sight of one that said 'Hetherington - Meetings'.

"What the hell is this?" I gasped, holding up the latter to Clarke's face.

"I don't know any more than you do Lehman." Clarke offered. "All I can say is we'll carefully bag everything if it looks safe to do so and we'll check it all robustly back at the station to assess its value evidentially."

I continued to look through the array of materials laid out on the table in front of me. I found photographs and printouts of my emails that dated as far back as 2017, it seemed. There were copies of investigations I carried out where it appeared to indicate the client had been a 'fake front' for Chris Marlee to get closer to us via a proxy. There were screenshots of Psychic and I from the TV documentaries we'd featured in and my face had been scribbled over on some and clearly stabbed out with a sharp implement on others. There was even a series of covertly taken photographs of me on public transport that had been taken over a series of *years*.

"You know that feeling you get sometimes where you think you're being watched?" I muttered out loud to no one in particular. "Well, in my case it turned out I was right becau…"

My eyes fell on a small handheld video monitor that played SD cards and just alongside it was a small plastic case containing one such SD card. The case was labelled 'McKinley – Meetings'. I reached down, picked the case up and studied it to make sure it said what I thought it said.

"If it's any consolation you do get thinner as the years go on but seriously you've got to stop touching stuff, Lehman. The last thing you want to do is to worsen matters by leaving your fingerprints all over shit." Clarke said.

"I'm beginning to see now why 'Hero Boy' here has his DNA and fingerprints all over major crime scenes around the city." Mitchell smirked.

I pointed over in the direction of the pile of memory sticks. "I really want to be looking at that one marked 'Hetherington – Meetings' but there's no means of playing it here, right now, is there? Whereas this…"

I unclipped the case and removed the SD card, pushing it into the holding on the side of the handheld video monitor whilst turning the power for it on at the same time.

"Stop! Stop!" exclaimed Clarke.

I pressed play on the first of what looked to be several video files listed on the monitor's front menu screen. A grainy video started playing, shot covertly from the chest of whoever Janet McKinley was sat opposite. They were in what looked to be the comfy seats of a plush hotel room. Mitchell went to speak. I shushed him.

The camera person's voice was strained and gravelly, very clearly indicating a damaged voice box. I pushed the camera close to my face as Clarke arranged herself next to me to watch over my shoulder:

McKinley: "… I'm just glad that Mick was able to introduce us as he did before everything that happened to him."

The Voice: "It was sad what happened to him."

McKinley: "His murder was a tragedy. I think our mutual friend Jake Lehman and his reporter friend used a longstanding grudge against the man to stoke public ire. What am I saying though? You yourself will know more than anyone how powerful a longstanding grudge can be, I imagine? That's why you're sat here, right?"

[McKinley laughs. There's an awkward silence.]

McKinley: "Now, I'm not saying Mick was *entirely* innocent. He always did lean a *little* young when it came to who he wanted to entertain himself with, if you will. But the whole thing was massively blown out of proportion and I always thought had he not been murdered he would have gotten his day in court and the truth would have come to the fore. Up to that point it was obviously important for the greater good of what we are trying to achieve as a collective that I distanced myself from his accusations and was seen to speak against Chief Constable Hadenbury. In line with what the vast majority of the community wanted me to do. Did you ever meet Graham?"

The Voice: "I did not."

McKinley: "Now, I have to be honest with you up until Jake Lehman did what he did to Mick I had no awareness or knowledge of the man at all. I obviously know of him now and I speak for a few individuals within the shared circle when I say that he does make us *nervous*, shall we say? I will face a re-election campaign for my position soon and Lehman's disclosures and his journalist friend Emily Ashley's reporting of it along with continued digging around in the connections regarding it all <u>do</u> scare me greatly."

The Voice: "I understand."

McKinley: "So obviously when I was told by friends you were looking to… shall we say 'deal' with someone who I fear could be problematic to my re-election, I was always going to be interested in a… *conversation*. I have many questions though."

The Voice: "Such as?"

McKinley: "That scarring? He did that to you and your throat?"

The Voice: "He did, yes. I got off lightly. I survived. Others didn't."

McKinley: "And all of this? All of this is because he did that to you and your fri…"

The Voice: "All of this is because Jake Lehman walked into my life and took everything away from me. He then jumped on a plane, came back over here and carried on with his life like nothing happened. As if there were no piles of bodies left behind, burning in the Australian outback. He went on to be lauded, doing apparent good in facing down evil when he is just another form of evil himself. Why does that man get to pick and choose who is bad and who deserves his brand of vigilante justice without any consequence brought back upon him? They're putting him on television and celebrating him as some sort of hero. He's a murderer…"

McKinley: "So why haven't you killed him by now? You obviously feel very strongly about the man. Why haven't you ki…"

The Voice: "BECAUSE nothing so *simple* is good enough for HIM! He got away with what he did to me and my friends by cowardly hiding in the shadows and taking them out when they weren't expecting it. He skulked around in the dark like a weakling. So I want to play like for like. I don't want to kill him - I want to *destroy* him. I want to slowly step out of each and every shadow he passes by and take something from him and when I'm ready I want to turn up the dial and crush him."

McKinley: "I see. Okay, I get that. You want to take it slow. Fine. But I just don't see where I fit in?"

The Voice: "You have powerful connections, I'm told. You still have people within the police service who worked for yourself and Graham Hadenbury. Correct?"

McKinley: "I obviously have to be very careful about what I say."

The Voice: "I want introductions to them. I am going to need help over the coming months to put the final stages of my plan in place. Certain people close to Lehman are going to have to die and I'm going to need assistance in planting things at the scene that are going to fit my narrative. I believe you know who the best people are for that. Most importantly, when the dial hits its maximum, I am going to need you to do what you can with the platform you have to renounce Jake Lehman and use your position to push police resources in a manner favourable to my plan."

McKinley: "I want you to be very clear here about what you mean when you say certain people are going to have to die?"

The Voice: "Everyone he's ever cared about or who's death can be used to manipulate him however I see fit."

McKinley: "That's a little too opaque for me."

The Voice: "I can provide you with a list if necessary but the list is not negotiable."

McKinley: "Let me be a bit more direct here and the only reason I am being this straight-up with you is because I doubt very much there is any value whatsoever in you incriminating me when I am so useful to you..."

The Voice: "Correct! And you should remind yourself that should you speak of this conversation to anyone or hinder me in any way now you're aware of it, you will appear on any list I write."

McKinley: "You don't need to threaten me. I am not grey-toned here. My position on where I stand is a bright, shining white. I wouldn't have taken these meetings otherwise. As I made clear, I am part of a collective of people who are looking to change this city for the better. It's a collective of knowledge, influence, money, ambition - all designed to reduce the impact and presence of a certain class type and certain races of people in the region and move the North East in a specific direction… A more *superior* direction, if you will. You've met with other members of the collective. They clearly think you are of value to me and I to you or we wouldn't have been put together to talk. My personal plan does not rest and stop at being Police Commissioner. It was only ever meant to be used to bolster my reputation and standing before others funded me as an MP and I moved down to Westminster to continue our initiative. Jake Lehman could very nearly have disrupted that plan and it scares me he could again in the future, so you *know* I am not going to have a problem with assisting you in order to alleviate that concern. But it worries me that you take down Lehman and you leave behind his acquaintances who may be as interested in vengeance in his memory as you yourself are towards your murdered friends. So if you want me to make introductions and the like to people beneficial to your plan I'm going to need reassurances from you that when people start getting… erm… *removed*… in order to facilitate your destruction of Jake Lehman, then this would specifically include someone like his associate Emily Ashley so that no journalistic digging goes ahead in his memory. Does that make sense?"

The Voice: "For what you can grant me in return I have absolutely no problem adding other names to my list."

The phone in my pocket started to buzz first and then ring. I hit the pause button on the video monitor and desperately grabbed at the zip on my pocket in order to free the phone whilst Clarke stood looking at Mitchell in a state of shock.

"Shit! You heard all that, right?" exhaled Clarke, pointing at the monitor as I put it back down on the table in front of us.

Mitchell nodded.

I shushed them both and clicked on the call.

"I'm so disappointed Jake Lehman. And so late in the game too." The voice began instantly. *"I accept I have had to reconfigure your levels of respect and reluctantly offer lenience in order to push you further along in the game than you would have got without them, but this behaviour here and now is completely unacceptable to the point that I cannot see past it I'm afraid."*

"Cut the shit, Chris." I snapped. "I'm here at your little lair. I'm seeing what you want me to see. I get that you've been hiding out and watching me for years like some sort of creep that..."

"Excuse me. What did you call me?"

"You heard - Chris Marlee! I know exactly who you are. It's been a long time but I saw what I saw in that warehouse. I did that to you and..."

"It saddens me that you are not as astute as I thought you were, Jake Lehman. And please don't belittle what I have achieved – I haven't been 'hiding' and 'watching'. I have been slowly draining your entire life of every valuable and meaningful detail so that it could be used against you for your destruction. And for a man who works in the dark arts of surveillance you really were a very, very easy mark. I bugged your home. I bugged your phones, your computers... I've listened in on your private conversations with your wife, your therapist, your children. I've taken your DNA and your fingerprints. And you never saw a thing. I have rejoiced in lying above you in your attic whilst you sleep, knowing that I could simply step down and massacre your entire family on a whim should I have wished. And you were never even close to being wise to this for one single second."

Whatever pain medication I'd been given at the hospital was no longer a match for the fury in my body that diluted it and which caused my head to ring with dizziness and my entire torso to course with agony.

"I really thought you would get through to the final round, I honestly did. It upsets me enormously that I won't get to murder your family as you watched like I intended. Alas, I have to live with the disappointment my game was only close to perfect. But at every stage I did warn you that if you alerted anyone to our contact your wife and your children will die, that if you did not come alone to any described location your wife and your children will die and if you showed disobedience or disrespect to the game your wife and your children will die. I offered leniency with regards to the last one. I cannot and will not with the first two."

"No. Wait." I shouted. "I have done what you asked and I..."

"You alerted others to our contact, you recorded our private conversations and shared them, you did not come alone to your current location. Don't try and make a mockery of me, Jake Lehman. It's too late. I need to go now. I have to make the unenviable decision as to whether I'm going to rape and murder your wife in front of your children first or make her watch me whilst I murder them and then rape and kill her. It's difficult. I need time to think about it..."

"You gave me your word. You said that your word was good." I screamed.

"My word was good as long as you played the game correctly and within the parameters of the rules I set. You have not. Therefore, my obligation to you in terms of your family is void. You knew there was a risk in trying to find the 'Jake Lehman' way out of this instead of giving yourself over to me completely. Your risk did not pay off. Goodbye Jake. It's been fun. I'm sorry we didn't get to see this all across the finish line. I will obviously leave a wild card entry into the final round open but... it feels very pointless at this juncture."

The line clicked dead.

"What the hell was *that* all about?" Mitchell gasped.

"Do you remember outside when you said you don't like running?" I asked, slowly backing away from the table. "And how if I made you chase me you'd kill me? Well, *I'm* going to start running now because..."

The first blast landed outside the patio doors across the other side of the dining area where we stood, pushing through a ball of flames and the twisted body of a burning armed response officer. The second blast almost instantaneously followed from upstairs causing the ceiling above to instantly crack and then crumble down large shards of flaming plaster and insulation.

The three of us started running for the door as fast as we could.

The handheld video monitor dropped from my hand in the panic and Clarke quickly dived back to grab it, stumbling over on herself as she did. Flames ripped up all over the floor next to her. I rushed back and took hold of her, dragging her as best I could onto her feet.

"GO!" she screamed.

I yanked her alongside me as best as I could whilst still being handcuffed to the front and we made it towards the front door just as another blast erupted in the foyer area. Clarke was forcibly thrown through a glass window with the explosion and just as I was about to stumble face first, I caught sight of Mitchell as the ceiling beam above him cracked and dropped down towards where he himself was staggering.

I threw myself at him and just managed to connect as the beam hit the floor, rugby tackling him out of the way and through the front entrance door frame as flames licked up all around us.

We landed on the ground with a hard crunch into the gravel layer on the pathway outside. Mitchell was quick to his feet, grabbing me by my collar and yanking me further along the driveway as the house burned intensely behind us. A bloodied Clarke appeared by his side and threw herself under my arm to apply further support.

The three of us did the best we could to gain more distance but it was too late - the final blast rang out, razing the entire property to the ground and sending us all face first into the dirtied stone surface beneath our feet.

[29]

or

"Well This Isn't Looking Good For Anyone Right About Now, Is It?".

The dense and profuse black smoke continued to billow out from where Mick Hetherington's palatial abode had once stood. It was a thick enough blanket of smog that it seemed to almost cut off the gentle cascade of snow that continued to fall. Surviving armed response team members rallied to pull their badly burnt colleagues to safety whilst Sgt Niro stood screaming into his radio for assistance from emergency medical and fire services.

Clarke crouched with her head in her hands as blood from the glass cuts to her head and face seeped through her fingers. Mitchell sat between the two of us. None of us seemed to pay any notice to the freezing cold, wet mound of white we had collapsed down into and was now starting to drench our clothing. Eventually she stood up slightly, leant over him and handed me the smashed remains of the handheld video monitor.

"I'm sorry, Lehman." She said loudly.

Mitchell took it from her hand and drove it hard into the ground between his legs, splintering into even more pieces and pulling from the debris the SD card I had placed inside.

"Who gives a shit about the playback monitor?" he screeched, handing the card back to her. "*This* is what we need to be praying still works because if I heard correctly in there before everything went all Backdraft and shit, our police and crime commissioner is on here ordering you-scratch-my-back type assassinations on Lehman and his pals!"

My ears continued to ring.

Clarke's radio crackled and she put it to her head. A message was coming through but she couldn't hear it through the commotion. She turned the volume up as high as she could and clicked to speak.

"This is DS Clarke! Is someone trying to reach me? Over!"

"Clarke, this is Beverly! Are you free to speak? Over!" the radio crackled in response.

"I'm able to speak, yes. Over!"

"*Privately*? I need you to confirm you are alone? Over!" effervesced Beverly.

"Standby! Standby!" Clarke replied as she struggled up onto her feet and walked away from the two of us.

Mitchell, clearly just as deafened as I was by the blast if the manner in which he continued shouting was any indication, looked at me and gave my shoulder a hard nudge with his own.

"You've been blown up a lot, right?" he shouted. "Your hearing comes back, doesn't it?"

I lip-read as best I could and bellowed back. "I've not been blown up as much as you're probably thinking. There was that thing down in Heaton with the Knights of George bomb, but I mainly just attract solid beatings. And bullets... You'd be surprised how easy it is to get your hands on guns round here, it would seem."

"Didn't you blow up half the Metrocentre a few years back though?" he screamed.

"You know, don't believe *all* the bullshit about that okay? That one has been grossly exaggerated." I bellowed. "Now listen, I like that we're bonding and shit, but I've got to pull something out the bag here because I think this fucker is going to murder my family any minute now, if he hasn't already and... I'm fresh out of ideas here. Have you got any?"

"Ideas?" Mitchell shouted. "Nothing. No."

I bit down hard on my bottom lip as my eyes filled up with moisture. I blinked and the sting from the smoke set in almost immediately even though the tears were very much formed from the distress beginning to overcome me.

"This can't be it, you know?" I said with my lips trembling. "It can't just go like this - me sitting here, clueless, waiting for notification to come through as to where I need to go to identify the bodies of my wife and children."

I furiously and anxiously rubbed at the sides of my temples.

'Think, Jake! *Think*!'

"I don't believe for one second it has been ten years in the making for Chris Marlee and it all ends like this. I *refuse* to believe it." I continued.

"I think from the size of the bloody explosion, *that* is how it was meant to end!" Mitchell reasoned whilst pointing back at the flaming rubble where Hetherington's property once stood.

Clarke approached us from behind, looking remarkably even more pale than she had just a second ago. She stepped across Mitchell and stood towering over me, looking down at me with a grave expression on her face.

"Lehman?"

I looked up at her.

"I want you to stay calm, okay? No matter what I say, I want you to stay sitting down and not make any sudden reactions that make Sergeant Niro over there think you're having an outburst that needs… *dealt with,* promise?"

I gulped down hard as my throat painfully swelled. "Have they found my family?"

"Sort of…" she replied nervously. "Listen to me carefully. There's a *situation* evolving right now on the Tyne Bridge and… well… Okay, I'm just going to give you the full brief, so you have all the facts that I have…"

I started to struggle to my feet. "For God's sake, just tell me…"

"Thirty minutes ago, a minibus stopped on the Tyne Bridge along with other vehicles in the centre of the road. Cars on the north and south entrance stopped too creating a barrier effect. The drivers all got out and absconded, apart from the minibus allegedly. *That's* in lockdown. Small explosives have gone off and a call has come in via 999 stating that your family are on the minibus, it has an explosive device primed on it and it will go off should anyone make an approach towards it!"

"You're not fucking serious?" I exhaled with shock.

"I'm giving you what I've got." She replied before starting to cautiously look around. "Now I *get* that this Chris Marlee fella knew about the covert recording from Hark Royal and our babysitting of you up here because of what has obviously been leaked to him by his friend, Janet McKinley but…"

"But what?" I growled.

"But he's obviously aware you survived his bombs going off up here because he has said that the only person that can approach the vehicle is *you.* And that if you're not there by six pm then he's going to detonate the bus."

"What time is it?" I asked.

Mitchell came to stand next to me and looked at his watch. "It's four forty pm now."

"And Jane and the boys are definitely on there?" I clarified.

"I don't have definite confirmation of that. I know only what I've just told you. They're setting up observations on top of the Sage and the Vermont Hotel and opening up a Gold Command on one of the premises at Swan House roundabout… and I've been asked by DCI Beverly to get you down there as quickly as possible!"

We landed at the sequestered premises of the new bargain-basement, all-you-can-eat buffet restaurant on the 55 Degrees North site at Swan House roundabout which had been completely cordoned off at every junction. The last time I'd been inside this building was many years ago when it was The Purple Peacock and Jane ended up needing fireman-carried back to our car because their resident 'mixologist' allegedly "tried to kill [her]" with too strong a drink.

Mitchell had drove us on full 'blues-and-twos' all the way from Northumberland in a hazardous driving style that matched the weather conditions surrounding us, with no regard for the lives of the car's occupants whatsoever, but I didn't care because he got us to where we needed to be in just shy of thirty minutes.

He and Clarke lead me through the doors of the eatery, still handcuffed, into a sea of complete and utter pandemonium as officers ran around like headless chickens screaming into radios, tables were being hastily commandeered and filled out with technical equipment and over in the far corner of the room stood Jessica Lane, DCI Beverly and Falk amongst a cluster of others.

Monitors were being set up and activated. Thirty conversations seemed to be going on at once and the intense look on Falk's face doubled on sight of me being led towards him. Lane smiled weakly at me as I approached.

"*Great*!" sneered Falk. "Just what we need added to the mix - recklessly high emotion!"

"Thanks for getting down here so quickly!" Beverly said to her two officers before turning her attention to me. "Mr Lehman, I assume you've been briefed on what we know so far?"

"I think so?" I said, barely audibly. "Are my family up there?"

I pointed with a shaking hand outside the building towards the Tyne Bridge.

"We're still working on getting that affirmed." Falk interrupted. "Until it has been, I don't think it is appropriate for you to be in our central command unit. We *are* going to need you nearby, however."

"The information we've been given by the person behind this has stated that your family *are* on that minibus in the centre of the Tyne Bridge, yes." Lane said softly. "Until anything is presented to us contrary to that then that is what we will have to go with as fact."

Falk shot her an angry look.

"We'd be looking normally at getting a heat reading from inside which would give us an idea of the number of people on board, their position and the like..." Beverly explained. "But what we're being told by our units assessing the scene directly is that the windows are blocked up and there's some form of heat panelling purposefully fixed on the interior sides and it's running upwards of possibly fifty degrees..."

"So, are you saying they're in there and they're being slow-roasted alive or something?" I clarified.

"What I'm *saying* right now is that it's creating what is clearly a deliberately intended haze of heat that is making it indecipherable for our teams to get an infra-red read or similar as to who is in there or what is going on inside!" she replied.

"I've got to get up there and take a look!" I nodded.

Falk looked immediately panicked.

Lane and Beverly shot glances at each other. The latter nodded to the former who tentatively stepped forward towards me whilst affixing herself with that 'reassuring' smile she hoped would be of benefit to me.

It wasn't.

"Jake, we don't know what we're facing up there." Lane offered. "We don't *know* that your family are up there yet. As much as we're being told our move has to be to send you in there, we don't know that this isn't just the final elaborate trap in this man's game and the minute you step close to the bridge he blows it and wipes you out."

"We need to slow things down." Beverly backed her up.

"You don't have time!" I said, raising my voice as I spoke.

Within my eye line a uniformed officer went and whispered in Falk's ear and whatever he had said, the acting Chief Constable reacted badly to it.

"*What*?" he screamed. "Can someone please tell me how I'm told the weather conditions are too adverse for me to put my <u>own</u> aerial units up but there's news helicopters circling above the bridge already?"

He looked around the room.

"*Anyone*?" he screeched. "Can ANYONE explain this to me?"

Beverly was handed a piece of paper. She looked at it, considered the content and reached across to Clarke to hand it over to her.

"Unless Chris Marlee is a member of the walking dead then that *isn't* Chris Marlee out there!" Beverly stated. "His death was confirmed resultant from our enquiries with Australian police – September 2013!"

"And DCI Geoffrey Novak appears to have died in a car accident in Sydney in 2016 it seems!" Clarke added whilst studying the paper she'd been given.

"We're creating a reserve space across the road at the Stemkazi Law offices on the bottom of Pilgrim Street." Falk barked. "Take him over there please and remain on standby. When we have anything more to add we will let you know."

"You're moving at a speed that suggests you have *time*!" I shouted. "Time is what you *don't* have, for Christ's sake. If what we know now is correct, he's going to blow whatever he's got stacked up there on the bridge at six pm if I'm not standing there. What is it about what's gone on so far that makes you think he's bluffing about this?"

"If the dust sat in my underpants from the house that just exploded on top of my head is anything to go by, I can confirm he isn't bluffing, sir!" Mitchell added.

Falk stared at Mitchell, contemptuously eying him up and down before looking back at me and sighing.

"You need to understand, Lehman, that this isn't time for you to do your 'thing'." He breathed. "You know, for a lowly private investigator you seem to think you're really rather integral to a lot more than you actually are. Regardless of the personal connection, you will follow what..."

"Personal connection?" I screamed. "My *family* are up there! If that doesn't make me bloody integral to what's going on here then I don't know what the fu..."

"We don't know that yet!" he shouted back. "We don't know whether your family are sat in that hot box up on the bridge any more than we know there's three mannequins yanked from the underwear department in Fenwicks propped inside of there instead!"

"Are you *certain* that Jane and my boys are not up there? Because as of twenty-four hours ago you were certain that I was a murderer and..."

"You have not technically been de-arrested for the crimes which..." Falk attempted to counter.

"JESUS FUCKING CHRIST!" I yelled as I looked across to Lane. "This guy makes even *less* sense than when McKinley has her hand up his arse, working him like Orville the bloody duck!"

"GET HIM THE HELL OUT OF HERE!" shrieked Falk.

"There's less than fifteen minutes left!" I hollered right back at him. "Fourteen bastard minutes if that clock on the wall there is anything to go by! Do you really believe you're going to have made the right judgement call in that time?"

"Officers? Remove him!" Falk shouted, looking past me.

"*ANSWER ME*! ARE YOU GOING TO MAKE THE DECISION THAT SAVES MY FAMILY - HE SAID THIS IS THE FINAL ROUND SO EVERYTHING ENDS HERE! ARE YOU GOING TO LET ME SAVE MY..."

Two uniformed officers attempted to take hold of me. Clarke stepped in the way.

"We've got this! Let him go! *We* have got this!" she said assertively.

She grabbed hold of my arm and as she did, she took a step forward and pushed the SD card containing the McKinley meeting directly into Lane's hand.

"Good to see you again, M'am!" Clarke said as her eyes widened in the direction of what had just been passed over.

Mitchell spun me on my feet and the two of them pulled me out of the eatery and into the freezing cold early evening, trudging us all over to Pilgrim Street. Crowds of people who were out drinking on the last weekend ahead of Christmas, even as the blizzard came and went around them, had started to congregate at the ends of the cordons. They all stood, freezing their arses off with camera-phones all hanging off the end of extended arms hoping to catch some 'drama' they could sell to a news outlet or an online viral video site.

We walked on past one bar on the other side of the pavement from Gold Command which had been emptied out of its patrons but who's music still played on regardless. In this case, the music happened to be one of the greatest Christmas songs ever recorded.

That's right:

Darlene Love's 'Christmas (Baby Please Come Home)'.

"♫♫...*The snow's coming down. I'm watching it fall. Lots of people around... Baby please come home. The church bells in town. All singing in song. Full of happy sounds... Baby please come home. They're singing "Deck the Halls". But it's not like Christmas at all. 'Cause I remember...* ♫♫"

The music faded out of earshot almost instantly once we were clear of the bar as the noise from the crowds drowned it out. Clarke stopped in her tracks right outside of the doors of Stemkazi Law. I could see a few police officers inside, drinking coffee and running additional admin requirements for the higher ups across the way.

"What? What's up?" Mitchell asked, looking at her with concern.

Clarke exhaled hard and turned to look at me directly.

"Do *you* really believe your family are up there in that minibus?" Clarke asked.

"I do, yeah. Do you?"

"I *think* I do, yes. So..."

"So...?" I queried.

"Let me see if I can guess where your head is right now - You've come *too* far and endured *too* much to stop now and you want to get up there on the bridge and be with them regardless of the bombs because if you're going to go you want to go *with* them."

"Pretty much that, yeah." I said.

"So, what's your plan?" Clarke smirked.

"What do you mean?"

"What's your *plan*? How are you going to make it happen?" she replied.

"I'm not sure."

"Seriously? You're not *sure*? I thought you were the *legendary* Jake Lehman - you blew up the Metrocentre by driving a car off its roof or something then you chased down a metro full of explosives and jumped on the back of it." Clarke said, in a way I could not quite work out whether it was mocking or not. "In the last twenty-four hours alone, you outran the police in a motorway chase, drove off the side of Tynemouth Priory and, from what I'm hearing, survived multiple attempts on your life... What do you mean you don't have a *plan*?"

Clarke stepped in front of me and pulled me off to the side into a doorway next to the law offices we were meant to go inside of. Mitchell stared at her with a look of confusion as she reached down and started to unlock my handcuffs.

"Wait," he exclaimed. "What are you *doing*?"

"There's not a lot of time so let me help you jump ahead past the point where you punch me in the face, kick him in the balls and steal my handcuff key, okay? Because my boy here is a total bitch and he'll only end up crying for the rest of the night and..."

"Lisa, what the fuck do you think you're *doing*?" Mitchell reiterated.

Clarke remained fixed on me. A grin started to form. "Now, I'm not on the same level as the mighty Jake Lehman or anything so don't be too hard on me if this is shit but here's what you could *possibly* do... There's a paramedic quad bike back there, have you ever ridden one before?"

I shook my head.

"No, me neither. I hear they're a lot of fun though." Clarke continued. "Anyway, that one over there still has the key in the ignition so the daft-arse responsible for it has everything coming to them basically. You could steal that and double back round through the bus lane, dodge the cars set up as barriers on the bridge entrance and get yourself across to your family before anyone here would know what to do. Certainly before Gareth or I were able to press the panic buttons on our radio because, you know, we'll have just come around from being knocked out... Or *something*?"

I smiled. "Why are you doing this?"

Clarke shrugged. "I don't know. Maybe because you've come too far and endured too much to stop now and if you want to get up there on the bridge and be with your wife and children no matter what than you should."

Mitchell exhaled hard and stepped forward. "For fucks sake..."

He reached into his jacket and pulled his police asp and his cannister of CS spray from the covert holster strapped under his arm. He handed them to me.

Clarke smiled.

"Why are you giving me these?" I said somewhat shocked.

"Because it's Christmas!" Mitchell replied. "And we're apparently your 'Secret Santa' this year it would appear."

"And because you're not one of the bad 'uns, Jake Lehman." Clarke added.

We stood in momentary silence.

"Just promise that when they start asking questions about how you got hold of those things, you back me up that I put up a hell of a fight against you before you got them off me. Deal?" Mitchell said.

I let out a little laugh. "Deal."

"Go!" pushed Clarke.

"You'll get those cuts on your face checked out, promise?" I smiled at her.

"*Go*!" she whispered.

I quickly staggered back through the snow towards the emergency service quad bike on the corner of Pilgrim Street, mouthing 'Thank you' at them as I went.

I didn't take a moment to pause upon arriving at it in case it gave anyone enough time to stop me. No sooner had I walked up next to it then I was sat right on it, revving out of the spot in which it had been abandoned, praying every step of the way that this thing was as easy to operate as it always looked on TV.

A small chorus of screams rang out from the paramedics stood tucked away in a nearby doorframe, seemingly sneaking a quick smoke. The crowd lit up cheering even though they had absolutely no clue what was going on.

This thing was clearly built for the very sort of arduously slippy surface that coated all of the roads and pavements because it made mincemeat of driving across it. I kept pushing the speed as I wove in and out of police vehicles and hit the marked slip-road for the Tyne Bridge. The burnt-out wreckage of a couple of vehicles lay in my path and I manoeuvred around them and up towards a line of four cars that had been abandoned as makeshift barriers, blocking easy entrance onto the bridge itself.

I knew five or so metres out from the bumper-to-bumper placement of the vehicles that there was no way I was going to fit through, so I yanked the quad bike to a hard stop, skidding through the snowy sludge beneath me. I quickly stumbled off the thing as out of the corner of my eye I could see uniformed officers running towards where I'd stopped.

I slipped through the improvised barrier on the north side of the bridge and started running as best as I could, wobbling under the painful strain of my broken ribs and the blurred vision I could just about muster. Speed was not something my body was capable of mustering. I just had to hope that I could put some distance between myself and them as I wove in and out of the stretches of abandoned vehicles in the road up to the minibus.

The police froze at the line of cars and abandoned the idea of passing through the barrier of cars after me. I skidded precariously to a stop outside of the minibus with the blacked-out windows and the wave of severe heat permeating from inside of it.

I looked to my right up towards the south side of the bridge and saw another temporary barrier of cars along with a few scattered vehicles here and there leading up to where I stood just the same as the route in I had passed.

I took a big deep breath and at the top of my voice I screamed "I'm here!"

[30]

or

2nd September 2013.

My crusted and swollen eyes blinked suddenly and rapidly as the beam of sunlight shone directly through into where I lay. I started to delicately feel around me as my eyes came into focus. I wasn't dead. Surely not? This was not the 'other side' because - not that I'd been before or had a frame of reference - surely neither Heaven nor even Hell would smell *this* bad?

I started to realise I was lying on a tattered mattress with a threadbare blanket draped over me up to my chest. I slowly started to move my head to get a better sense of my bearings, becoming aware that my wrists and legs were bandaged and the skin on my head felt tight and sore where the open wounds had once been. Yellowed newspapers, discarded tins and plates, broken up and rusted tools and various pieces of metal surrounded me. The width of where my bed was positioned gave me a strong indication I was in a caravan somewhere.

"G'day mate. You're up? Good!" said a voice from across the other side of this sweltering tin I lay inside of. The body it came from was slouched on one side of a fixed breakfast booth, smoking disgusting smelling rolled cigarettes and drinking a bottle of VB. "You're lucky I found you when I did. I picked off a dingo ten feet from you. Licking it's lips and tying on a slop-bib, it was!"

I strained to converge my sight on who this figure was, but they were sat within the beam of sunlight forcing its way in through a badly covered tiny window and my vision remained blurred. Thankfully they twisted in their seat and leant forward to bring themselves closer to where I lay and I could finally work out that Goodjob Walt was sitting in front of me.

I braced backwards as much as my exhausted and agonised body would allow which wasn't much. Walt slowly raised his hand out and held it up, gently waving his closed fingers side to side.

"Chill, pom. Just chill." He smiled. "You're good. You're *all* good. I've not mended you just to kill you, okay?"

He took a draw on his cigarette.

"I've not much mended you full stop to be fair. But I've done the best I could. Especially considering you were as good as cactus by the time I got to you."

"Where... am I?"

"You're at my place. You're safe. We're miles out from Brennan. Sid and the boys know me well enough now to accept I'm too old to be getting involved with killing bloody coppers. Things are fucked up enough up there as it is, you know? They're used to me going and keeping my head down after they've had one of their 'blow-outs'... *This*? This was a blow-out too far though. I've told them I'm taking off and going to see my sister in Kalgoorlie for a bit. I've done that before. They're not going to miss me. They wrote me off as a washed-up, old bludger years ago."

Walt sucked on the last of his cigarette, exhaled on the burning embers of the lit end and crushed the remnants between his chewed up, leathered fingertips.

"Why did you... come... back for me?" I stuttered as I tried to raise myself up from where I lay, struggling to lift as much as a single shoulder as I did so.

"I came back for you *both*." Walt replied. "I'd lost a taste for this shit long ago but killing coppers? It's too much, as I said. Once Mick let slip they'd dumped you as early out in the woop-woop as they had I thought there was a chance I could get to you both and get you to safety. By the time I found you there was a buckley's fucking chance of *you* lasting much longer and the red-headed Sheila was *definitely* long gone."

"Her name was *Rachel*." I sneered through my pain. "Detective Constable Rachel Casey."

Walt slowly nodded before reaching for a jug of water on the table in front of him and passing it over to me.

"Here! Drink this!"

"What is it?" I queried with disdain.

"It's true blue piss! What do you think it is?" Walt smirked. "It's water, bloody oath eh? I've been dripping it into your mouth here and there for over a day now, but you need to start getting more in you, pom."

I snatched the water jug, smelt it and then desperately started pouring it into my mouth, frantically lapping it down as the cold wet liquid fell around my neck.

"Slowly. Slowly." Walt warned.

I paid no heed.

"You said over a day?" I gasped. "How long have I been here?"

"Two days, thereabouts. I did the best I could for you with what I've got. I used to be an Army medic way back in a whole other life but... well, you were pretty cactus mate and my hands aren't as steady as they used to be. I've stitched your head and your feet and all that. I've had a look at your back. It's pretty buggered up. You need to rest that. I can't do much with it but you're moving around a little now I see so at least you're not a head on a stick, eh?"

"What about Rachel?" I asked slowly.

"I didn't leave her out there if that's what you're asking? She's in my storage shed outside. I've wrapped her up right, kept the crap off her. That was the decent thing to do."

"The decent thing to do... would've been... to never let this... go down in the first place." I tentatively replied with a growl.

"What could I have done? I put my two bit forward to stop you both getting thrown down the hole. I thought that would buy you more time."

"Gee thanks!" I said insincerely.

"Hey. I didn't *need* to do that. I didn't *need* to come and drag you up from the back of bourke either, pom. I'm trying to do *right* by the both of you. You two blue heelers come wandering up here on your own – a couple of stickybeaks well out of your depth without the right back up and..."

"I'm not a policeman." I interrupted.

"What?"

"I'm not a copper. You keep saying that. But I'm not. I'm nothing but a private investigator."

"Fair dinkum?"

"Yeah. And not a very *good* one either. This was one of the rare jobs I actually managed to book and look where I've ended up? I came out here looking for a missing girl and..."

"Who's the girl you're looking for?"

"Her name was Maya Dentz?"

"I don't know why I asked, pom. I'm shit with names. You got a photo or something?"

"I did. It's back in my bag which... well... fuck knows where that is right now. But she was travelling with two other girls and a Swedish guy."

"*Wait*! I remember them, yeah." Walt muttered before falling momentarily silent. "Well you can't be *that* bad a private detective, pom. Because you pretty much found her... What'd be left of her by now anyway. Which one was she? Not the little round-faced one with the black hair?"

"That sounds like her, yeah... What do you mean 'What'd be left of her'?"

He stared down at his feet and dusted off muck from the knees of his pants.

I tried to pull myself into a sturdy seating position but floundered. Walt caught me and helped me get to where I was intending to go on the bed. Once he'd accomplished this, he reached above me and brought down a bottle of half-drank whiskey.

"Here, get a mouthful of this."

"I can't." I replied. "I don't drink."

"Deadset?"

"I'm an alcoholic in recovery."

"Bugger!"

"What?" I said.

"I wish I'd known that before. I've been forcing the grog down you, lad. It's been used as an anaesthetic, an antiseptic and a ruddy body wash on you."

I stared at him.

"... Sorry?" Walt smiled. "I'll not tell anyone though if that's better for you?"

"The only thing you need to start telling me is the truth." I sighed.

"The truth about what?"

"You fucking *know* what!" I snapped.

"Brennan didn't go to shit because BFI ground us out of the game. If that was the case, we'd have been strangled to death in the early 1990s." Walter said as he made himself more comfortable in the breakfast booth, poured himself a large whiskey and set about rolling himself a few cigarettes. "Brennan went to shit because my business partner Charlie died, and his boy Sid took over."

He lit one of his cigarettes.

"*That* was a bad year, that year. I lost my Anne at the start of it. I lost Charlie Berenger a few months later and Sid took over and ran a very different ship and... he never liked steering it alongside me. That was *really* bloody clear."

I sighed with impatience.

"The thing you need to know about Brennan is that the lads up there are all about the hard yakka, don't get me wrong. But they know as well as anyone else they've *got* to put the work in because they're not going to get on a job anywhere else. Those are *bad* people up there, pom. REALLY bad people. Over the years, the Berenger's haven't been going and head-hunting the best of the best from Bagnall-Farina if you get me? These are guys out of prison with a trade beneath them and nowhere to apply it. Sid saw them as cheap labour because no one else would touch them. I resisted his approach as best I could, but we were losing men hand over fist to the big mines and... and... about a year after Charlie went, I got myself in a bit of bother with the law up in Darwin."

I was becoming more and more agitated. None of this brought me any further to understanding where Maya Dentz was within Brennan and why Rachel had to suffer how she did.

"I thought this girl was older than she was. I was drunk and alone up there. It was a bad judgement and... I ended up having to do a bit of time and... well I brought a whole world of shit down on myself." Walter sighed. "And Sid exploited that. By the time I got back down here he forced me out, paid me under what I was owed for my stake and stuck me down the mine as 'staff' until my back didn't work right anymore."

"Take it to a bloody employment tribunal!" I snapped. "Get to the point."

"You want my point, boy?" Walt huffed. "This shit Sid's men did to you and your pal out there? That's *nothing*. It might not feel it to *you*, but Brennan's been a lawless wasteland for a long, long time now and these fellas *love* that. They work hard, they play hard and they live without consequence. Do you understand?"

"Once again – Get. To. The. Point!" I snarled.

"The point *is* you butted heads with men that have raped, robbed and done all sorts before landing at Brennan. And now they're completely unchained, do you know what I mean? You count yourself lucky you came out the other end and..."

"Listen to me *very* carefully," I said. "Those men up there? They didn't just not take to outsiders. They were so fearful of outsiders getting too close to *something* that they dragged Rachel Casey and I further out into the desert, tortured me and left me for dead. Then raped and *murdered* her. And I don't think that had fuck all to do with preserving their secret deep mining techniques. Do YOU understand ME?"

Walt downed his three fingers of whiskey and poured himself another before pushing on, talking with his face pointed towards the floor.

"Sid was getting a lot of knocks off the boys about the lack of women up there. I don't know what they were expecting but the two week breaks over on the Gold Coast or off in Perth where they were sticking it to anything that moved wasn't enough. So, Sid put in a request with one of them agencies out in the cities, ones that found outback bar work for backpackers. My brother-in-law ran a watering hole in Kalgoorlie, and it worked a treat for him. Some young skirt from one of the agencies came up here, looked around and... well... you've been to Brennan, right? You've seen it. No one in their right mind is going to sign off on sending young 'uns up here. We don't have a proper place for them to stay let alone a real bar for them to work in, fair dinkum?"

I sat silent, staring hard at him as he distracted himself whilst he talked – pulling at the dirt under his fingers, picking tobacco bits from his teeth, pouring yet another few fingers of whiskey as the bottle neared its end.

"So of course that didn't work out. Then Sid goes off to Malaysia on business. He's meant to be out there on the beg to find companies for us to export to and instead he comes back with this seedy, piece of shit plan after drinking with wrong 'uns over there for too many nights in a row. There were thousands a head to be made in pulling women off the roads, bagging and gagging them and shipping them out through contacts at the ports up in Darwin to go overseas and work in the brothels there. Hundreds of girls from abroad come here and get lost every year. It's a big, dangerous place out here in the woop-woop. You've seen it. *You* know. The plan was to scout along the Nullarbor Plains and places like that and look for tourists that fit the bill. Sometimes we'd venture into the cities and..."

"So... you started sex-trafficking?" I exclaimed as the cloud started to lift. "Coal mining was bottoming out so you started kidnapping women and selling them as sex slaves?"

Walter stared silently down at his hands as they began to shake.

"Was Maya Dentz trafficked overseas?" I asked.

"I was never in on this from the start. I want to say that. For what it's worth anyway. It took a *lot* of convincing for me to do it. The wages out of Brennan just weren't there. I was starving and struggling and I'd been out too long in the dust to go get civilised, so Sid suggested I drive a couple of the deliveries and..."

"WAS MAYA DENTZ TRAFFICKED OVERSEAS?" I screamed.

Pain shooting through my body as I shouted, like I'd just received an electric shock.

He slowly shook his head.

"The trade died years back. Long before her and her pals got brought up here."

"I don't understand." I said. "Why were they taken and brought to Brennan at all then?"

Walter sighed. "Before the bottom dropped out on Sid's Malaysia deal, we were making some serious fiddly from it all. He had a bloody *road train* running across the length and breadth of the country, man. We were bringing in girls, turning them around and shipping them out sometimes at a higher collective weight then the black stuff we were pulling out the ground. That's when Harv' and Rodge had the idea to burrow through a corridor a hundred feet down where our main work was and create a 'holding area' for them all. And that's where it all went to shit."

"Oh. *That's* where it all went to shit?" I muttered. "Having to dig a prison for them underground, not actually kidnapping them in the first place or..."

"No, you big galoot. You don't understand. You were never going to get men to stay focused on the hard yakka when a few feet along was a pit with twenty gorgeous Sheila's tied up. And before you knew it, every one of us was nipping in there to sample the goods before they were sent off. And... And... the fall-in wasn't down to an excavation gone wrong. It was down to the ground giving out under a bloody orgy."

"*What?*" I gasped.

"Most of us got out. The girls didn't. Ten grand a head... Twenty heads... Do the maths!" Walter said, shaking his head, totally unaware of how crass and cruel he was coming across.

"The whole thing went to shit not long after." He continued. "The trade agreement died. Sid's son, Danny, came up here and he tried to get his old man to clean up a little bit but that only lasted a few months at best. Next thing you know, Ernie and Alf are bringing girls up from Nullarbor, having their way with them and Chris and Mike start doing them in down the abandoned hole. And *that* became the new thing."

"What do you mean 'the new thing'?"

"Well, you don't lose your hard-on just because the cave falls in on twenty women, do you?" Walt shrugged. "So now, when the boys wanted a fuck, they treated it like they were ordering tucker to be delivered. They snatched them off the roads or whilst camping in the nature reserves surrounding us, used them sometimes for a few weeks at a time and then threw them away."

"Down one of the mines?" I clarified.

Walter nodded. "They *all* got thrown away in the end, mate. They weren't *girlfriends*, you know?"

"How many will be down there now?"

He waved his hand indifferently. "I don't know, pom. On top of the original twenty? I don't know. I never counted. But I've seen a lot of Sheila's come into this place. How about that?"

"And Maya Dentz will be down there? ... Long past dead?"

He nodded.

"I chucked her myself." Walt said quietly, almost to himself.

"What?" I gulped.

"I helped to get rid of her and her pals. They were the last ones I ever touched... Not 'touched' like *that*. I've not been able to do that in a couple of years. But they were the last I put out of sight, if that makes sense?"

My mouth curled in anger and contempt.

"Who killed her?" I snarled.

Walt shook his head. "Come on now, I'm an old man. Do you know how many the young fellas up there are dragging off the road every couple of weeks? It all blends into one after a while – same groping, same shouts, same garrottes and knives... If you had to really push me to say, I think the last two who were with your girl specifically were Ernie and Ron, maybe?"

"So, have you done it a lot to poor bastards like what you did to that Swedish bloke Edvin Sixten? Go around the country, framing them for the disappearance of all these women and then making it look like they killed themselves with guilt?"

"No," sighed Walt. "I much preferred it when they snatched a car full of just the Sheila's, you know? Because I never had the stomach for what some of the lads did to males that got caught up in getting grabbed. You can't fuck 'em. We're hardly going to eat 'em. So, what do you do with 'em? String them up and smack 'em around a bit and then they go down the hole too, yeah? That's it... Ernie fucked one poor boy once though, just for a laugh, but it turned all our stomachs and he ended up taking so much shit for it, pardon the pun eh? ... Finding all girls is a rarity and a hassle now. Especially with the figures being what they are nowadays for folk going missing out here."

Walt didn't register a single element of irony in the last part of what he just said. Instead he simply shook his head and continued on.

"But that thing they did with the Swede was *nothing* to do with me. I thought it was bloody daft, if you ask me. What a load of nonsense. It was obviously what brought you and your copper pal up here in the end too. It was Chris and the bloody Kalinda boys who got panicked. They were looking through all the belongings, seeing if there was anything worth swiping and Chris clocked that the kid had been taking photos left, right and centre of the journey so far and he got paranoid that he'd been sending them on. Apparently, you can do that now with your phone and the Face-Twitter and all that, you know? There was even apparently a photo of Ron and Ernie and the road train in the background after they'd first turned up to help them."

"What do you mean 'help' them?"

"Come on, we're not talking about sophisticated methods here – we'd tamper with their vehicle when one of us clocked them at a picnic spot or getting petrol or something, go to their rescue when they conked out and then grab them. But Chris clocked this photo the Swede had taken, and he gets paranoid. He had far too much grog after a night with the three girls and came up with this plan to load their car up in the road train and dump the bloke and it over the other end of the country. I told him he was going troppo but no one up there listens to me one little bit. The suicide note was completely stupid. Just totally stu..."

"Why are you telling me all of this?" I interjected in a guttural whisper.

He shrugged.

"I'm old. I've not got long left; I can feel that when I move." Walt moaned. "And I don't think atoning is going to cut it alone, pom. I think the man upstairs is going to expect me to put a *bit* more graft in than that, eh?"

He shook his head, slowly becoming lost and bewildered in his own thoughts. He bit down on his lip and his eyes filled with tears.

"I'm a monster." He said quietly. "I am, aren't I?"

I nodded and sluggishly, painfully eased myself forward. "Yes. You *all* are. And you *all* have to pay for everything you've done."

Walt looked at me. He blinked and a single tear fell from both eyes.

"Do you have a gun here?" I said.

He shook his head.

"Do *they* have guns up there? More than the one your man Chris was wielding?"

"They do. There's a locker full of hunting rifles and a couple of handguns up there. The lock is busted though... I take it *you're* the one planning to take payment for all our sins here?"

I let my left lip turn upwards in disdain.

"That's right, yes."

Walt eyed me up and down. "Boy, you can't stand, and your legs have more holes in them than that posh cheese. You can't see straight and there's one physically fucked up *you* and thirteen mentally fucked up *them*. I get that you want to crack the shit and bring heaps of pain to Brennan's men but you have to be cra..."

"Shut up!" I snapped. "I want you to answer me only one thing."

"What's that, pom?"

"I want you to tell me the truth – including yourself, everyone up there? Every man? They *all* took part in this... this... *thing*? I'm not talking about just driving the trucks up to Darwin or whatever. I want to know if *every* one of the fourteen of you played your part in one way or another in raping or disposing of the people brought into Brennan, if not both."

Walt sat silent.

He stared out of the window, then down at his hands. He poured himself another whiskey and cleared it in one big gulp before exhaling hard and running the hair back off his face with his hands.

"No man there will get the big ladder up when their time comes!" he finally said.

"Don't give me that shit." I spat. "I don't want you talking to me like you're reading out the inside of a fucking fortune cookie. Give it to me straight!"

"*Every* person, myself included, will have to answer for what we've done up there. Every... *single*... one... of us." Walt snarled. "Is *that* clear enough? There's those that can say they weren't strong enough to resist the peer pressure or whatever but what they really mean is they were too *weak* to turn away the opportunity for young pussy, regardless of how it was served up!"

I held up my hand.

"Enough!" I barked. "That'll do for me."

Walt slid himself out of his chair, turning instantly to a small waist high cupboard on his right. He opened it, reached inside and came out gripping a long-handled axe in one hand and a dark metallic gun-looking contraption with a cylinder attached underneath and a hose of some kind running loose from it. He dropped both on the table.

"Well, if you're going to go down that route, let me help you go!"

"What's that?" I asked, pointing at the metal contraption.

"That's a high-pressure bolt gun. You can get about ten to fifteen feet with that. *Proper* high velocity stuff. It's the best I can offer you."

I slowly nodded and pointed at the axe.

"And that?" I clarified.

"That's an *axe*!" Walt smiled helpfully. "Jesus, pom. You may be more out of your depth than I thought."

"Just an axe?"

"Yeah, *just* an axe. It's not a magic axe. It's not an axe-gun. It's *just* an axe. You... well... you just swing it and... You know what an axe does, right?"

"I know what an axe does, yes. What about this?" I said quietly, pointing at the bolt gun.

"Really simple!" Walt exclaimed as he slowly reached forward and set about connecting the pressure hose to the main body after which he turned a dial and air forcibly loaded its way through the tubing. "There's twenty solid steel bolts in there. That's the maximum it'll hold. Heavy, *heavy* duty bolts too. They'll punch the back out of a cow's head from fifteen feet, so they'll make mincemeat of a human at an arm's length."

I nodded.

Walt started to stand. "You're going to need all the help you can get so..."

"What do you think you're doing?" I snarled. "*You're* not coming with me. Why would I trust you to stand alongside me?"

"*I'm* not going to fight *alongside* you, kid." Walt said calmly. "I'm going to take my ute and drive as fast as I can to get you *proper* help. I'll confess everything. I'll tell the police all that they need to know, and I'll take them down the mines and show them where the drop from the fall-in is. You just need to give me a head-start so I can give *you* a fighting chance."

He started walking towards the door.

"Walt?"

"Yeah?" he replied, turning back to look at me.

"How would I get back to Brennan from here?"

"Fifteen miles straight that way, over the hill. But I'd be amazed if you made one mile on foot in your condition so it's best you just sit tight here, yeah?"

He turned to leave.

"*Walt?*"

He slowly turned to face me once more.

"You could have taken your truck and driven as fast as possible to get help at *any* point before now couldn't you?" I said. "When the sex-trafficking started, when the fall-in happened, when all the kidnapping and murders for sexual kicks began? You could have driven off to raise the alarm then, couldn't you?"

Walt stood taciturn, staring right into me.

I slowly raised my hand and gestured for him to return to the table. After doing so I lifted myself up and took two or three agonising steps from the bed over to the booth, flopping down into the seat opposite where Walt had been sitting.

I cautiously reached out and took hold of the handle of the bolt gun and turned it carefully, so the barrel faced away from me.

Walt remained motionless.

I gestured once more for him to take a seat which he eventually did.

Tears were falling down his face as he looked down at the bolt gun then back up at me.

Eventually he spoke.

"Listen, pom. I believe you when you say you've got killing in mind. A whole *lot* of killing. And who the hell knows whether you're going to get to see it all through as much as you'll probably want to, eh? But I know from the parts I've played in the shit up here over the years, that sort of stuff sticks right to you and it seeps into your bones, you know? You carry it like concrete around with you every fucking day for the rest of your life. Trust me. So, let me lessen that weighted load for you okay? It isn't much. But it's one less. Let me do that... okay? Pass me the bolt gun and I'll sort myself out."

"How do I know you're not going to just spin that thing and shoot me dead the minute I hand it over to you?" I asked.

"Two reasons, kid. One, that would rain a whole stream of piss right down on all the stitching and the bandaging I've just wasted my time doing on you. And two, as I said, it looks to me like you've got killing on your mind... and every single one of those men up there deserve to *die*. No less than I myself do. I have absolutely no intention of getting in your way."

"I don't trust you, Walt."

"No wucka's, pom. I understand."

"What does 'wucka' mean?"

"Worries!" Walt smiled. "No wucka's means no worries!"

I nodded.

We sat silently staring at one another.

"The keys for the ute are on the sideboard by the door. Wait until dark, okay? After two they'll all be pissed up and flat out in their beds with the night crew down the hole."

I nodded once more.

Walt smiled and closed his eyes.

I pulled the trigger on the bolt gun and the entire thing made an elongated *psssss-tt* noise and recoiled heavily in my hand. The bolt discharged so fast I never saw it leave the barrel even though it was bigger and weightier than a bullet. Instead the first I knew it had successfully exited was when Walt's entire upper body slammed hard into the back of his seat and his head recoiled backwards with the impact.

Blood spat instantly out of a newly formed hole in his chest, right where his heart would be. He gurgled as his head fell forward and blood streamed out of his mouth and into his lap. He struggled to raise his eyes to look in my direction. I gently reached over and pushed his head back. He was blinking rapidly as I took hold of his hand.

"Their names... were Maya Dentz and Detective Constable Rachel Casey!" I said as I gently nodded my head ever so slightly.

His eyes closed and his breathing stopped.

[31]

or

"The Big Grand Reveal That All We Can Do At This Point Is Hope This Has Been Worth Your Time".

I had Facetimed with Jane enough times over the years to be extremely familiar with the distinctive sound that is made when an incoming video call comes through. And that very sound was ringing out from inside the minibus I stood outside of.

Fuck it!

I stepped forward to the door at the same moment my own voice started to immediately chastise me. I guess my brain does know what I'm going to do before I do it. *Sometimes.* So suck it, Psychic.

And Jane.

And Jane's parents.

And Kate, my Narcotics Anonymous sponsor.

And Barbara, mine and Jane's therapist.

And… you get the picture!

'Don't you pull on that door, Jake!' it whispered. 'Don't be stupid. You don't know that it's not primed with exp…'

I pulled on the door and it instantly and effortlessly hissed, folding in on itself and opening straight up. A wall of heat roared straight out from inside the minibus, eliciting a rapid stream of sweat from every pore on my exposed skin. It served as an immediate reminder to me and my body of what it felt like to be warm. Something I can assure you I'd not felt since I walked out of my office yesterday morning and crossed the street to go see Bobby Maitland.

I cautiously stepped up onto the stairs leading into the minibus and whether by accident or some sort of sensor, the door closed behind me and shut me in with the intense heat and pretty much complete darkness resultant from every window being painted black. The only glow seemed to illuminate off of the heat panels crudely fastened to the interior sides. That and the lit-up screen from an incoming FaceTime call on an iPad screen that was propped up on the back seat of the minibus.

There wasn't much light overall but there *was* enough for me to be able to register that I was alone, and my family were not here.

I steadily knelt down in front of the iPad and clicked on the green button to accept the call. It connected immediately and there instantaneously on the screen in front of me, taking up all of the space the camera would allow, was the white ceramic masked face of my relentless tormentor.

"I never ever expected the wild card entry into the final round would be utilised!" the digitised voice crackled out over the video call. *"Yet here you stand. I have underestimated you, Jake Lehman. I have truly underestimated the resolve you are prepared to dig deep, find and depend on to be reunited with your family again. You really are proving hard to kill. This would be a good place usually for me to invoke Mark Rippetoe's famous quote 'Strong people are harder to kill than weak people and more useful in general.' But the thing is you've actually outlived your use to me... and I'm conflicted as to whether you're actually strong, or just pig-headed."*

I stood silent, staring intently hoping that he would move his head back just a few inches and expose some of the background as to where he stood, giving me any sort of clue - even the smallest - as to where he could be.

"What? Have you finally run out of quips and zingers to throw at me? Have I actually truly achieved the grand objective of running you down to empty and having you stand here before me broken physically, mentally and emotionally? That really could be quite something, Jake Lehman."

I could feel my mouth curling again with anger as the sweat poured down my face, stinging my eyes and getting into the cuts and abrasions around my head. I refused to allow myself to wince with the pain.

"I will tell you one way you have disappointed me, Jake Lehman? One way I clearly overestimated your investigatory abilities and your capacity for drawing conclusions from available facts like your much-lauded reputation suggests? And that was the assumption I stupidly made - that you would come to know who I am and why you must answer to me long before I actually wanted you to. Then I quickly reminded myself you had amassed far too many enemies to be able to dissect any sort of shortlist within the time I gave you. What does that say about you amidst your many other personal flaws, Jake Lehman? That you could be so hated by so many you don't know which interaction I am holding you to account for."

The masked figure stepped back from the lens for the first time and my attention was so initially drawn to the brick wall and rusted orange bracket behind him, along with the second long flash of what looked to me like the bound shapes of my wife and my two boys, that I did not realise he was unclipping his mask in front of me until the first side of it dropped.

I have the face etched into my mind of every man who I encountered at that coal mining facility in the outback of Australia. They'd lived inside of there for over a decade, each face flashing out to me in both my strongest and weakest moments - alongside the blurred haze of their chalk-written name; their blood, their widened look of shock, their gasps all refusing to leave my psyche no matter how much I medicated. Nor what I chose to medicate *with.*

The face staring back at me through the iPad screen was not Chris Marlee.

I knew the face regardless though. It had weathered with time and slightly shifted in shape due to the manner in which it had awkwardly healed from injuries sustained. But I *knew* that face.

Danny Berenger stood smiling back at me whilst his eyes betrayed the fact that true happiness did not course through him, no matter what position his mouth took.

"Vengeance is sweet. Vengeance taken when the vengee isn't sure who the venger is, is sweeter *still.*" Danny smiled, curling up the scarred tissue around his mouth and rising up a thick clump of barely constructed neck muscle as he did. His voice no longer electronically disguised, instead just croaking with all the difficulty of someone who's voice-box was now barely functional. "A guy called Gary D. Schmidt said that. There's something to it, I have to say. Because right now my belly feels like it is full to the brim on cake and candy."

I opened my mouth. Nothing came out.

"The infamous Jake Lehman finally meets the man who made him." Danny said.

"You didn't... *make*... me." I finally matched to eke out.

"Sure I did, Jake Lehman." He smiled. "Certainly the version that stands before me now. The *real* you - broken, empty, exposed and alone. Where are your little friends now? Where are your enablers?"

Danny stared through the lens of the iPad and appeared to be working to keep a true, furious rage from overtaking him.

"The *other* Jake Lehman? The lauded celebrity righter of wrongs, riding a wave of growing fame because of his alleged heroism? That's not who you *are.* Is it? Truthfully. It's not is it? You didn't earn *that.* You can tell yourself and anyone sorry enough to listen to you over the years that you did, that you were entitled to it and so on. But you didn't and you weren't."

Danny ran his hands across his face, wiping sweat as he did. He was only just getting underway it seemed. "You think you're the real, true *hero* of this city now, is that it? The documentaries and the film rights and all that? People don't give a *shit* about you at heart, Jake Lehman. Do you know how easy it was to hire people to work against you as fake clients gathering information for me? Do you know how quickly I could locate police officers willing to assist me with my plans? Therapists and counsellors prepared to record your most private sessions in return for a few pound? Fuck, it only cost a couple of hundred pound per person to get people to drive bomb-packed cars onto *this* bridge and dump them tonight! What does that *say* about human nature in this day and age? What does all that say about how truly well regarded YOU are to these people? You broke yourself many times over apparently fighting for the truth as you saw it or trying to save this city - and this city in various forms sold you down the river the minute I opened my wallet!"

Danny smirked and cleared his rasping throat. "You've always been a terribly easy subject, Jake Lehman. I've listened in on your most confidential conversations, I've watched you make love to your wife, I've sometimes sat in the back of rooms whilst you've spoken of your addiction details, I've followed you on your cases - I've *even* been the silent client behind some of them. You're so conceited and self-involved you never once suspected or noticed a thing. The master investigator and surveillance agent *extraordinaire* and you never even saw your own alleged skillset being used against you. I was able to lift fingerprints from your own home as recently as one week ago and put them wherever the hell I chose to. When the true facts of ALL of this go wide, do you have any idea how stupid you will look? You have no idea how easy it was to frame you because whilst you were sat crying to your wife about how misunderstood you were and how much of a better life you feel you deserved, I was wrapping your fingerprints around bomb parts and knife handles like I was doing a crafting project with your children! If that doesn't all show you to be the clueless fraud you truly are then we need a brighter spotlight over your head, don't we? Because no longer will I allow you to wear the mask that hides who you really are... A murderer! A psychotic who killed four..."

"And what are *you*?" I snapped aggressively. "What are YOU? Just one of a horrible, sweaty gang of sex trafficking rapists who had the misfortune to survive justice catching up with you?"

"You? *You* were justice? Is that what you think?" growled Danny. "*Who* gave *you* that authority? You, this hypocritical disgrace who vows to be the public face of taking down corruption and fighting to expose the truth but when the truth reveals you to be a psychotic murderer you take every corrupt deal going in order to have the facts hidden. Who told YOU that a man of such contemptable character could be judge, jury and executioner over me and..."

"You and who?" I shouted. "Your rapist mates? Your dad? Is that what this is all about? You are out for revenge because I chopped your fucking dad's head off? Is that what all of this comes down to? You blew up half this city and murdered innocent people just becau..."

"JUST BECAUSE?" Danny interrupted, "Just because vengeance is a form of reciprocity in which each deed begets another. Each act of vengeance is a response to a previous wrong. Do you know who said that?"

"Bruce Lee? I don't know. Who gives a shit?"

"I give a shit!" Danny snarled. "Because thinking like that affords you and I an explanation as to how we became ensnared in such reciprocity - you coming and sticking your nose in my business affairs, psychotically murdering my family and my friends after deeming us worthy of your misbegotten vigilante justice, me having to avenge such behaviour. On and on it goes... '*Vengeance is a form of reciprocity in which each deed begets another. Each act of vengeance is a response to a previous wrong.*' It was James T. Siegel who said that, by the way."

"Cool." I replied. "Did you buy a book of these quotes at the airport on the way over here? Did you read them on the plane? Make notes in the margins? What about this one? '*Revenge is a dangerous motive*'? Do you know who said that?"

Danny stood silently staring at me through the lens. He'd lowered the camera slightly, giving me the opportunity to seize another look into the background. I could only just about steal half second-long glimpses at a time. But I was sure enough I saw Jane and at least Jonathan. They were alive.

"Who said that then, Jake Lehman?"

"It's from the original 1989 UK poster for the Jean-Claude Van Damme film, Kickboxer!" I responded. "Your turn!"

"I see you're finding your *quirky* personality again, Jake Lehman." Danny said. "I don't like it. You're acting like you're some sort of character in an action film. This isn't who you *are*. I have been with you for a long time now and I never thought I would ever have hated you more, but I most definitely have learnt to over the last two years, especially. I liked the *real* you. The broken you who no one had any interest in because you were... you in fact *are*... just a pathetic addict so desperate to be thought of as special and significant that you're willing to travel to the other side of the world and murder to achieve such regard!"

"Look who's talking, you sick fuck!" I spat. "You didn't just travel to this side of the world and start killing innocent people in order to set a specific narrative against me. You lay in *wait*, hiding away, recording me and watching me like a creepy, twisted, pathetic..."

"And though the villain 'scape a while, he feels. Slow vengeance, like a bloodhound, at his heels." Danny sighed. "That's Jonathan Swift."

"Again, cool. Whatever. I don't know what you want me to say... Well done on googling quotes about vengeance? What? I mean, I'm not even sure that last one even bloody worked in the context of what we're talking about."

"Vengeance is mine; I will repay. How about that? Leo Tolstoy. Is that better?" Danny croaked with faked sincerity as his voice started to struggle.

"Better!"

"I've enjoyed bonding with you, Jake Lehman. More so over the course of this conversation than over the previous rounds of the game but alas the final round must be drawn to its conclusion so... Excuse me a second!"

Danny disappeared from view. The iPad screen jostled and bounced around before steadying itself at his end as he propped it up properly against something, giving me my first clear and stabilised look at the background in which he stood in front of.

I *knew* that brickwork. I knew the cluster of orange-seeming metal brackets sticking out of the wall because I remembered well enough what used to hang on them until my boys started getting old enough to ask questions and we had to ask for the rifle to be taken down and locked away properly.

Suddenly Jane was planted down in front of the screen in front of me.

My eyes burst their banks and tears instantly cascaded down but before I could say a single thing my breath was stolen at the sight of Danny gripping her aggressively and pushing a large blade against the skin next to her eye.

"It can't all be fun and games." Danny sneered. "We have to start wrapping this up. So, here we go… Everyone must know of the true monster that lurks beneath the much commended and respected veneer you've sold them into believing is the real you when in fact you are a psychopath who spuriously mischaracterises people's actions, judges them, hides in the shadows and murders them in the dark of the night because he deems them to be deserved of his… *bloodlust* but is too much of a COWARD to face them properly!"

"I've lost track of who we're talking about here," I said. "Who did I mischaracterise, exactly? Are you saying you *weren't* kidnapping, raping, selling and murdering innocent women? Are you saying you had nothing at all to do with those forty odd bodies pulled out of that mine and…"

"THIS ISN'T ABOUT ANYBODY BUT YOU!" screamed Danny as his voice broke high and the twisted flesh around his neck throbbed.

I watched the blade push harder into Jane's skin and a small circle of blood materialise underneath the knife.

'Shut the fuck up, Jake! Shut the fuck up NOW!' I screamed internally to myself.

Danny inhaled and took a moment's pause.

"Look up now. You will see a camera fixed above the row of seats. Confirm to me that you see what I am referring to."

I looked up as asked and saw a small black box camera screwed into the ceiling of the minibus above the rear window.

"I see it." I confirmed.

"In nineteen seconds this camera will start recording you. It will stream live across a website I have enabled. The link for this website has already been pre-circulated with a variety of different media outlets both here and in my home country. You have the opportunity to finally confess your sins and take the weight of the truth you've refused to carry or I will stab your wife through the head right now in front of you and then force you to watch as I take the heads of both your children."

The tears continued to fall and my throat eventually gave out, releasing harrowed and agonised sobs.

"Thirteen… Fourteen… Twelve…"

"I'll talk. I'll talk." I cried.

"And in return for doing so I will allow you to properly and sufficiently converse privately with your family one final time." Danny smiled. "Because at the end of the day, I'm *not* a monster."

I watched as Danny sat back in a chair behind him, a chair I myself had sat on during many family visits up to this very place.

He pulled Jane down on top of him and readjusted the blade, so it rested deeply across her neck.

"Eight... Seven..." He continued.

I took a deep breath in and looked up at the camera above my head.

The red light on the bottom left corner flicked on.

[32]

or

3rd September 2013.

Goodjob Walt's truck crunched through the desert terrain just after half two in the morning, its headlights bouncing out into the darkness to provide what little illumination it could to light my way. As I reached the apogee of the dusty hill with Brennan itself shining out of the black murkiness a couple of miles down at the base of this crumbling, dusty hummock I pulled to a slow stop, activated the handbrake and switched off the engine; plunging myself and all around me into complete silent darkness.

I sat alone, looking into the corner of the truck's rear-view mirror, and accidentally caught sight of my own eye line. I'd never killed anyone before. Walt was right. Worryingly so. It sits *heavy* on you. And I still had thirteen to go.

I'd sat and watched him die.

I'd sat and watched the light go out in his eyes and for his face to slacken and that last death gurgle to come. All things that were completely new to me. It disturbed me greatly – that I had proven capable of taking the life of another so coldly.

It sickened me that I knew I couldn't stop now.

Something inside of me drove me on whilst the reasoned voice in my head tried to call me back. I knew only that to see this through I would need to detach myself from my actions and not linger in any moment like I had with Walt. I pushed Rachel and her final moments to the forefront and found the reticence lessened.

'It's not too late,' the voice in my head whispered. 'One is not as bad as fourteen. You can stop now and you can maybe find a way to...'

'They *have* to die. They *have* to die violently.' My thoughts interrupted themselves. 'They *have* to die for *her*.'

My breathing was laboured and heavy. Certain areas of my body were swollen and sore. I pushed myself to think back to only a few hours earlier when I'd waited for the sun to set by forcing myself to practise walking under the sheer agony emitting from my spinal column. First, I tried shuffling up and down inside the caravan, small steps at first. Then I opted for a piece of wood Walt had used to hold up a broken sunshade as my makeshift crutch, stepping outside and trying to walk a little faster with bigger and quicker steps. The pain was excruciating.

With each practise attempt I forced myself to find a way to use the suffering as fuel and to adapt how I held myself to lessen the physical anguish, curving my spine at the top or leaning further forward than I normally would to take the pressure off the base of my back – *anything* that reduced the pain.

As the sun looked like it was setting off in the distance, I crumbled down on the floor of Walt's caravan and started to work the dials of the shabby and ancient CB radio set that still flickered dully with a modicum of life in it. After several minutes of failed attempts, a cracked and barely audible voice was heard:

"Repeat call sign and say again? Over!"

"I need Sydney police!" I rasped, clicking down on the mic button.

"This is Alice Springs PD. Who is this?"

"Is this the police?"

"You're through to Alice Springs Police Department. Repeat, who is this? Identify yourself?" came the reply.

"This is a message for Detective Chief Inspector Novak of Sydney police. You need to relay this urgently. I repeat, relay the following message to Detective Chief Inspector Novak of *Sydney* police: Rachel Casey is dead and the Brennan facility is burning. He needs to send everyone he can. *You* need to send everyone you can."

"Are you radioing out of Brennan?" the voice crackled back. "Who is this? Identify yourself?"

I dropped the mic, switched off the radio set and sat back with my head in my hands.

By the time night had fallen, I had downed what was left of Walt's whiskey and taken the bolt gun and axe out to his truck, looking back only once to the area where I knew Rachel lay. I sat now, looking down at the axe and the bolt gun on the passenger seat. I'd fastened a makeshift holster to the long wooden handle of the axe using weathered binding I found in Walt's caravan and I'd loosened the clips on the canvass loop attached to the high pressure bolt gun so that I could ostensibly wear it around my waist but have enough slack to be able to pull it up and use it like a machine gun if necessary.

My eyes now narrowed as the pain in my head intensified. I looked away to Brennan off in the distance, most of it shrouded in darkness other than for the high beams of illumination streaming down from the two lighting masts above the mining point along with the flickering glow coming from inside the watch tower perched nearby to both.

Rachel weakly tapped my hand with the tips of her fingers.

"There's people... in the mines... I heard... them... say... that... when... they were... binding... us." She struggled. "Burn... it... down... so flames... so high... every... one... comes... to... look."

I squeezed her fingers.

"You... sing with me..." she semi-smiled as the light in her eyes started to fade and her breathing slowed. "*Plea... se?* We can... build this... thing... tog..."

"Standing st... str... ong forever..." I strained out in a pained whisper.

"... runs... out... lovers... we still..."

"Have each... other." Hot tears fell down my face, the skin on which had become hardened with dirt. "Nothing's gonna... stop..."

She gurgled. "... Mum? ... *Mum?*"

Her eyes filled up with tears and her breathing finally gave out.

I violently shook my head and brought myself back to the now, feeling the pain shoot up my jawline and into my already throbbing head. I'd involuntarily clenched my jaw so tightly shut in an ineffective attempt to stop the unwanted memory flooding over me.

I released the handbrake and let Walt's vehicle slowly and silently descend down the hill towards Brennan. Behind me the skyline was so black yet smelt so bad that I could no longer tell what was the night and what were the thick clouds of smoke from the raging outback fires that seemed to be continually creeping ever closer.

I brought the truck to a stop at the top end of the facility, tucked away not far from where Rachel and I had last left the jeep when we first arrived here. A whole other lifetime ago. I left it facing down towards the mining point with the watch tower on the left. I made sure to drive through the gap at the back of the compound as slowly as I possibly could, sticking to the sheets of shadowy darkness wherever feasible. I sat still and silent in the complete black of the truck's cabin, watching and waiting to see if my entrance had been seen or heard; looking around with darting eyes to gage whether anyone was approaching me. The only sound was the heavy, empty clanging coming up out of the darkness from the mine two hundred or so metres down from where I sat.

"Kill her!" Chris had shouted.

"Drop the gun! Final warning!" Sid screamed.

"Don't you drop that gun, Jake!" Rachel had cried. "If you drop that gun, we're *dead* twenty seconds later. *Both* of us."

"Fuck it!" Sid exhaled as he drove the blade a little deeper into the side of her neck and blood started to drench the collar of her shirt.

I anxiously and furiously banged my fists together and silently screamed as I forcibly dragged myself back into the present. With one deep breath I alighted from the vehicle and pulled my 'tools' out with me. The axe was slung over my shoulder like I was throwing on a school bag and I clipped the bolt gun into the position I wanted around my waist, setting off on a slow and cautious walk along the shadows afforded to me by the line of containers. The bolt gun bounced gently against my thigh without a sound as I walked.

The ladder up to the tower looked intimidating. It was so rickety that it probably would've been daunting regardless of my injuries. Was this thin metal ladder really utilised so frequently by these not-exactly-dainty men day in and day out? It barely looked like it could stay attached to the wooden beams that it was questionably fastened into.

I began a slow, painful but methodical climb up each rung and noiselessly pulled myself onto the wooden walkway outside the cabin once I'd eventually reached the top. The final minutes of Asia's 'The Last To Know' played out from a beaten up old stereo system tucked away in some corner of the cabin.

"♫♫ ... the first one to really know your name. And you were the first one for me. But everyone knew but me. You were the first one to ever let me down. And I was just the last to know... ♫♫"

The big guitar solo crescendo played out as I slipped into the cabin through a tattered doorframe that held no door. Alf Cloke sat tilted back in a chair facing away from me, playing air guitar in front of a radio control panel and a computer console that looked like it had tapped out in the 1990s.

I took one tip-toed step forward.

And then another.

My face twitched with the agony of each controlled step as the pain in my back was now dialled up into the stratosphere from the ladder climb.

"♫♫ ... I was the first one to really know your name. And you were the first one for me. But everyone knew but me. You were the first one to ever let me down. And I was just the last to know ... ♫♫"

I raised the axe off to the side of Alf's head with the intention of swinging it straight into his skull. Asia's 'The Last To Know' faded out and the old cassette inside the stereo picked up UFO's 'Doctor Doctor' as the next track. A majestic, almost ethereal guitar solo opened the track and I watched as Alf nodded along in approval to the track choice.

He suddenly spun in his seat and caught sight of me, catching me off guard by a millisecond. I swung the axe and he raised his hand to catch the handle, the blade itself embedding straight down amongst his fingers and chopping off the back half of his hand down to the wrist bone.

He froze in horror as blood spurted up onto his face.

Just as he was about to scream out in agony, I pushed forward and pressed my hand against his mouth to muffle him. He tried to fight me off at the same time I tried to pull the axe free from the point in his wrist bone that it had come to be lodged.

'Jesus CHRIST Jake, you've got to get smoother at it than *this*!' I heard Rachel's voice whisper to me inside of my head.

'Cut him some slack!' Jane's voice echoed out in there somewhere. 'This is his first time murdering someone!'

Alf started to wrestle me off as best he could. I dropped my arm down to the bolt gun hanging from my waist and released the valve. There was the sudden, rushed sound of air loading into the main chamber and Alf looked down in shock just as I pulled on the trigger and blasted a bolt into his groin at extremely close range.

He recoiled heavily from the blow and I kept pressing down on his mouth to gag him from screaming. After a few seconds, I reminded myself I needed him to work in line with the plans I had forged before he very obviously bled out so I took a step back and pointed at the radio.

"Call them up!" I whispered.

"Wh... at?" he stammered.

"Call them *up*!"

"Who? Who are... yo... u... talking... ab... out?" Alf gasped.

"The night crew - call them up and get them out of there!" I said.

"I can't do..."

I finally yanked the axe free from his wrist bone, causing him to shudder and let out a surprisingly low-level shriek. I raised it above his head and he in turn extended his good arm and started stammering.

"Ok... Ok... What... do... you... want... me... to... say?"

"No codes. No code words. Tell them there's a problem and Sid wants them all out of there!"

Alf reached his good arm over and grabbed the microphone board off the desk. He clicked it and spluttered out over the airwaves.

"Ern'? Come... in, Ern..."

The radio crackled.

"He's further down, Alf. What's up?" came a voice soundtracked against a background of heavy noise.

"John... you... all need... to come... up... now." Alf replied.

"What's going on Alf?" John Kalinda replied.

"Just... get... up... here... *now*. All of... you... Sid... says."

There was a momentary silence.

"Okay. Copy that. Standby."

Alf dropped the microphone down into his lap and winced as it banged off where his testicles used to be.

"What... now?" he asked just as the axe slammed into the side of his head on the final syllable of the final word he spoke. He convulsed in his seat to such a ferocity that he flung himself to the floor, landing awkwardly with the axe handle sticking back up out of his head. I placed my foot down in the centre of his shoulders, pinning him in place and then pulled as hard as I could to free the axe from the slightly obliterated skull.

The vomit rose up in my throat. I swallowed it down as best I could but it wasn't good enough, spraying up onto the wooden floor where I stood.

I picked up Alf's twisted pack of cigarettes from the desk, along with his plastic lighter and I turned away, stumbling immediately out of the cabin and climbing slowly and carefully back down the ladder to the ground below.

I crossed the dirt path towards the mining point as Chris Marlee's voice entered my head:

"Are you done? You sure?" I heard him say.

"Step out the way then!" he followed up with.

I could hear myself gurgle "N... No... o... ooo!" just as two gunshots rang out, waking me back to the here and now just as I arrived at the rusted fence line wrapped around the lift shaft.

A few metres away lay a couple of stacked barrels. I took the one with the giant red 'flammable' sign on the side, tipped it over and rolled it towards the lift shaft just as the whirling cogs next to me and the sound reverberating up from below indicated the lift cage was moving upwards.

I stood patiently, waiting. Once the cage came up into my line of sight through the darkness beneath me and I could just about make out the clustered shape of four men penned in together, I lifted the axe and smashed it down into the emergency control panel near to my feet. The rusted cogs lost life instantly and the lift pully shuddered and froze, jarring the men below to an unexpected stop twenty feet down from me.

There was no way they could get back down. They were completely penned in. The only way out of where they were stuck was to release the metal cage roof and start trying to climb up the lift pully. I didn't give them the chance to consider that option.

I pulled the clipped stopper free from the lid on the barrel and let the contents pour out rapidly into the lift shaft to a chorused bellowing of *"What the fuck?"*, *"Jesus Christ!"* and *"What's going on?"*

I reached into my pocket and removed the plastic lighter whilst taking hold of the lining of my jeans pocket and ruthlessly yanked at it until the material tore free. I lit it on fire and once the flames had sufficiently built, I dropped it down into the shaft, a brash partition of orange light flashing back up as the walls of the lift shaft exploded and four ungodly screams filled out the night air.

The screams were still permeating up and into the surroundings of the Brennan compound as I slipped back into the shadows, limping my way over to the nearby petrol pump next to the watch tower.

I could hear commotion coming from the portacabins up on the dark unlit end of the facility as I turned the big iron wheel around on the side of the pump, slackening the access valve and prizing it open. I didn't connect anything to it. Instead I quickly stepped back as the contents of the pump started to spray out unfettered onto the ground below.

I slipped in behind the pump and made my way along the back of the containers. Limping and staggering painfully with each step. I paused to look from around one corner as I saw Chris Marlee, Harv' Taylor and a wobbling Ron Petrie (with a newly acquired crutch) pass me as they rushed towards the flames burning up out of the lift shaft back at the mining point.

I continued on and eventually got parallel to where I had left Walt's truck. I checked left and right to make sure the coast was clear and stepped out of the darkness, straight into the path of Michael Merindah as he rounded a corner and landed sight of me immediately.

"What the *fuck?*" he gasped as his eyes strained in the darkness to make me out.

He suddenly rushed forward and I lifted the bolt gun at my waist, gripped it tight with both hands and fired twice. He got just about five feet from me with his arms outstretched when the top of his head split in half from the force of the bolt and he fell to his knees in front of me. He looked at me in a state of complete shock as his eyes expanded and blood poured cleanly from his ears and mouth.

Two seconds later he fell face first into the dirt and I stepped over him, pushing on towards the truck as the sight of Rachel, fully and indecently exposed from the naval down, entered my head whilst Chris tussled away on top of her.

"Don't look, Jake! Look away!" I could hear her scream. "You don't need to see this, Jake!"

I pulled the petrol cap free on the side of Walt's truck and used the mud-coated hose abandoned on the open-backed boot to suck free the fuel in order to get it pumping loose out from the tank. The hose itself then became a multi-purpose tool when I moved round to the front of the vehicle and tied the steering wheel straight with it. I released the handbrake and desperately began to push out on the driver's doorframe to get the thing moving.

There was no strength in me of a high enough volume to push down with my legs. The pain in my back shut down any attempts to dig down deep and I collapsed in agony as the truck slipped out of my grip, miraculously and slowly rolling away down towards the other end of Brennan. It disappeared into the dark leaving nothing but a barely visible trail of exposed petrol behind it.

"You know we belong together. You and I forever and ever." I quietly sang to myself as I pulled the lighter from my pocket and started to flick the dial to ignite it once more. "No matter where you are, you're my guiding star."

The tiny flame ignited, and I lowered it down to the ground, exploding out an immediate flash of fire that caused me to roll back in shock and save myself from being burnt on the spot. The fire took hold and followed the trail of petrol, speedily chasing after the truck it was being poured out from.

I agonisingly pulled myself to my feet and carried on singing, barely audibly to no one but myself. "... And from the very first moment I saw you. There was such emotion. I'm walking on air, just to know you are there!"

I stood up straight, using the axe as a crutch to hold me still for a second. I continued singing as the flames ripped along the main dusty road in the centre of Brennan. "Hold me in your arms. Don't let me go. I want to stay forever. Closer each day. Home and..."

The entire compound lit up in a giant flash of yellow and orange, quickly followed by a deafening bang as the perfect marriage of the flame trail, the truck and the petrol pump all met up with one another and exploded off in the distance. The shock still knocked me down into the dirt on my backside and I stared as the silhouetted figures of three or four men ran frantically around against the backdrop of the flaming ignition and two men ran screaming off in the distance, engulfed in fire, before collapsing to the ground.

I picked myself up and staggered off into the shadows between two portacabins. I could see through the window of one that I was next to Sid's office area where Rachel and I had stood days earlier. I could see the chalkboard off in the corner and I saw near to that there was a fairly modern hi-fi set up that seemed to have wires flowing upwards and out to connect with the giant, weathered speakers I had noticed earlier propped on the roof.

I smiled to myself as off in the distance I could hear Sid and his men screaming at one another.

"WHAT THE HELL HAPPENED?"

"I DON'T KNOW MAN; I DON'T FUCKING KNOW!"

"THAT'S WALT'S UTE, SID! THAT'S WALT'S..."

"THIS WAS NO ACCIDENT! SOMEONE'S BURNING UP THE MINE!"

"YOU BETTER HAVE WATCHED THAT POM AND THAT COPPER GET TORN APART BY DINGOES WITH YOUR OWN BLOODY EYES BECAUSE..."

"HARV AND RON ARE GONE, MAN! THEY'RE FUCKING BURNT TO SOOT!"

I climbed in through the window on the side panel of Sid's portacabin and took a moment to steady my breathing – fourteen men had to die on this day; Walt lay dead back in his caravan up the road, Alf was dead in the tower, Michael Merindah was lying out in the dirt with half his head missing, Harv' Taylor and Ron Silver are apparently dead and with them I had to assume were the four members of the night crew, burnt alive in the lift shaft... I quickly tallied the numbers – *nine* down, *five* to go.

There was suddenly a cavalcade of more panicked screams and a thunderous and vociferous crash as the wooden tower gave way and plummeted down to the ground, adding more fuel for the raging fire to burn its way through.

I leant forward and clicked the hi-fi system on and grinned as I saw what track dialled up on the screen for the CD player. I pressed play, turned the volume all the way up as far as it would go and made my way back out of the window as the opening guitar chords of "Layla' by Derek & The Dominoes blasted out.

By the time I flopped down on the orange dusty ground outside, the song was kicking in and the sound was shaking out across the flaming vista representing what still stood of Brennan.

"♫♫ ... What'll you do when you get lonely. And nobody's waiting by your side? You've been running and hiding much too long. You know it's just your foolish pride ... ♫♫"

Fire seemed to be creeping up the grounds away from where the explosion originated. The trail left from the petrol ignition was certainly building up in size as I edged out to the corner of the container to take a look at where the remaining Brennan men were positioned.

No sooner was my head out a mere inch than I was grabbed by my collar and painfully dragged out and slammed against the external container wall by Danny Berenger. He wrapped his dirt strewn hand tight around my throat and pressed down whilst screaming out behind him.

"Dad! It's him! It's the fucking pom! I've got him, Dad! I've *got* him! It's the pom - He's bloody *alive*!"

"GET THE GUNS! GET THE FUCKING GUNS NOW!" I heard someone shout.

I tried to struggle free. Danny blocked me. I tried to raise the axe, but he grabbed the shaft with his other hand and started trying to pull it away from me.

"CAN SOMEONE SWITCH THIS BLOODY MUSIC OFF, FOR FUCKS SAKE!"

"♫♫ ... Layla. You've got me on my knees, Layla. I'm begging, darling please, Layla. Darlin' won't you ease my worried mind. I tried to give you consolation. When your old man had let you down. Like a fool, I fell in love with you. You've turned my whole world upside down ... ♫♫"

I pointed the bolt gun upwards and pulled the trigger. An enormous *pfff-t* threw out a bolt straight up through Danny's chin and out the side of his face. He stumbled backwards with the force of the impact and clutched at the entrance and exit holes. He desperately screamed out in agony, so I pointed the bolt gun back at him and fired two more straight into the upper part of his chest, causing him to recoil backwards and fall twisted into a line of building flames where he lay motionless.

I took a step back to get in between the walls of the containers just as a gunshot whizzed out, barely audible over the sound of 'Layla' but ricocheting off the metal surface of the container next to me with an awful ping and a clang.

"♫♫ ... Layla. You've got me on my knees, Layla. I'm begging, darling please, Layla. Darlin' won't you ease my worried mind... ♫♫"

I got myself around the rear corner of the container and out of sight of whoever was firing at me. Young Lowanna came charging towards me out of the darkness. He was still a good few feet out from me which gave me enough time to raise the bolt gun and pull the trigger.

The chamber jammed and I furiously pulled at it again and again as Young Lowanna's battered and bloodied face loomed towards me, closer and closer. I spun the axe handle in my hand and lobbed it as hard and as fast as I could, just like I'd seen many an Apache Indian do in Westerns with tomahawks hundreds of times over.

It would seem that reality adds an extra layer of difficulty than that which exists in the movies though – that or axe-throwing requires a greater degree of practise than just being able to nail it the first time you ever try it?

The axe landed at Young Lowanna's feet and he dove backwards, allowed for the impact and pulled it from the ground in front of him all in one fluid moment. Then with an almighty guttural scream he threw the axe right back at me.

I ducked and the axe flew just above my head as I fell back into the dirt. It crunched down and embedded behind me as Young Lowanna came towering over me. I grabbed at the axe handle and managed to free it from the ground just as he came jumping down on top of me.

I pulled my hands forward and he seemed to freeze in mid freefall. He gasped out and his eyes darted and as I pushed back against him, he fell to the side and I could see that the blade of the axe had embedded into where his shoulder met his neck.

He lay, clawing at the edges of the blade as it stayed affixed to the area surrounding his collar bone.

"♫♫ ... Let's make the best of the situation. Before I finally go insane. Please don't say, we'll never find a way. And tell me all my love's in vain. Layla. You've got me on my knees, Layla. I'm begging, darling please, Layla. Darlin' won't you ease my worried mind... ♫♫"

I stood up and, as he choked away anxiously behind me, I lifted the bolt gun to try and get a measure on why the chamber had jammed. I had no idea what I was doing so I pulled casually to make sure the hose was still correctly fastened and just as I aimlessly banged my hand on the side of the main body, a bolt clanged out at a reckless speed and entered into Young Lowanna's right eye socket, splattering his brains out the back of his head and all over the dirt.

I walked on, edging my way along the back line of the compound towards where I last knew Sid and the remaining men to be. Just further up, perched out on the corner of one of the portacabins I could make out the shape of Chris Marlee facing away from me and clutching a long hunting rifle.

I slipped quietly and closer to him through the shadows with the intention of shooting him through the back of his head. Just as I raised the bolt gun he turned and the bolt fired through the side of his throat instead and blasted him backwards into the side of the portacabin. He clutched at his throat and fell to the ground, staring up at me as the rifle fell beside him.

"You *raped* her. You *murdered* her." I snarled quietly as I kicked his hand away from his throat. "Her *name* was Detective Constable Rachel Casey."

I fired two more shots, both blasting holes into his chest.

Blood spurted everywhere.

"♫♫ ... Layla. You've got me on my knees, Layla. I'm begging, darling please, Layla. Darlin' won't you ease my worried mind. ... ♫♫"

Before I could finish him off completely or draw pleasure from watching him die slowly, several shots rang out over the sound of the blasting music and the reoccurring scattered explosions of varying sizes. I ducked and tried to run but my legs were failing me.

I dived behind one portacabin just as another shot rang out and I heard Sid shout from the darkness. "You head down that way. I'll wrap around and pick him off he gets past you. He's got to come back your way or burn."

I heard footsteps getting louder and closer as they crunched towards me through the dirt. I stumbled forward to move down between more portacabins and arrived in the space where the road train and truck parts were clustered together. I could just about make out Rachel's jeep parked off in the furthest corner as a pickaxe swung out from my right and I threw myself down to the ground to avoid its blow.

Jim Clancy came striding towards me and raised the pickaxe above his head.

"You burnt my mate to death, you piece of shit!" he screamed.

I raised the bolt gun in his direction. "I've burnt a lot of people tonight. Which one was he?"

I pulled on the trigger at the exact moment he side-stepped to his right, twirled the pickaxe down and around himself and flung it in one fluid swing that smashed the bolt gun clean out of my hands.

He slammed the pickaxe down, missing the side of my head and I lashed out with the axe and slit down one of his legs. Jim screamed and doubled over on the ground. I attempted to pull myself past him and get free, but he grabbed my jeans and pulled me at the waistline back into the position he wanted then proceeded to rain blows down upon me.

As my face swelled up and bloodied with each punch, he reached to the side and grabbed his pickaxe; pressing the long steel handle into my throat and cutting off my air supply.

"Why won't you just fucking *die*?" he shouted as the flames started to roar up and take hold of the edges of Brennan's circled properties.

He started to smile. "She was good. Your girl? She was *good.* I saw it in her eyes – she was *enjoying it* by the end. Fair dinkum mate."

I desperately fanned my hands out, reaching anywhere and everywhere across the dirt to find where the bolt gun was in relation to where the strap was on my waist. I felt the very edge of the handle just as my vision started to badly blur and my air supply become non-existent.

I grabbed and scratched around the handle, furiously pulling and reaching as my strength faded. And with the last ounce of consciousness I had I started to feverishly yank repeatedly on the trigger – releasing repeated gaseous *pfff-t* after *pfff-t*, over and over again. The pressure around my neck slackened and I reeled upwards into a sitting position, gasping for air through my bloodied nose and mouth.

Clarity returned after a few seconds and I come to see Jim was lying in a puddle of red matter, his face completely pulverised to pieces from multiple steel bolt impact shots. I pulled myself upwards and checked the gun itself. I checked the hose line and pulled on the trigger, but the main chamber just whirled empty.

I sighed, let it drop down to my side and slowly reached down for my axe.

I staggered out around the truck area and back down towards the main open stretch of the mining facility as the first signs of a rising sun started to emerge up on the horizon through small pockets of black smoke.

The main petrol pump explosion continued to rage on to my left and the upper part of Brennan lay to my right. The big, grand guitar / piano solo that plays out 'Layla' just broke in as the fire began to pop and build, taking hold of the wooden portacabins and slowly circling itself around me.

The sound of Derek & The Dominoes began to crackle and fade slightly as the fire clearly burnt out some of the speaker lines. A gun shot rang out and sprang dust up from the ground by my feet. I looked down in a daze, acknowledged all too late I was being shot at and slowly raised my head to see Sid standing in the centre of the compound holding a large, new model rifle.

He locked in his aim and went to fire again. Nothing happened. He dropped it down from his shoulder and studied the chamber before trying again. Once more, it didn't fire.

I walked a couple of steps forward.

"Has it fucked up on you?" I slurred.

Sid looked at the rifle, sighed and threw it down into the dirt before shrugging and starting to walk towards me.

I pointed down at the bolt gun hanging from my waist.

"Mine has too." I said, unclipping the band for it from around my belt line and letting it fall down to the ground. "I shouldn't have dropped the gun."

"What?" spat Sid.

"I shouldn't have dropped the gun!" I shouted. "Back in your shitty little bin of a drinking den – I shouldn't have dropped the gun!"

"I don't give a shit. Where's my boy?" he snarled.

"Your boy's Danny, right?" I said, spitting blood out onto the ground and wiping my nose on my arm to free up enough of an airway to be able to breath better. I pointed back up past Sid's position towards the top end of the compound. "He's cooking somewhere up there. I'm going to head up in a minute and throw another few shrimps on him if you want to join me?"

I saw Sid's face contort in agony. He let out a twisted half-laugh as a smile formed across his face beneath a pair of eyes that glared evilly across at me. His stride towards me was broken off by his own portacabin bursting into flames and killing the music, even though there was probably only about forty seconds left on 'Layla' anyway.

He reached into the rear beltline of his dirty trousers and pulled out a long blade of the 'Crocodile Dundee' variety. It glistened against the fire circling around us.

"You were wrong to come here, sticking your nose in our hard yakka." Sid exhaled as he restarted his walk towards me. "What we do here is none of anyone's business. Especially not to some gangly fucking pom, over here taking a blue heeler's job from a true, honest Aussie!"

I tightened my grip on the axe handle. "I'm not a police officer."

"Deadset?"

"Nope. I'm just a private investigator out of my depth, mate." I smiled wearily. "And if you didn't want anyone sticking their nose in the sick shit you've got going on up here then you should have run a more sophisticated operation. Because for anyone who *wanted* to look, you were *very* easy to find!"

"You think? Do you *know* how many pieces of skirt I've exported out of here? Do you *know* how much money I've ran through this place? And *you* think we're *easy* to clock, huh? We've been doing this for years, mate. *Years*! Where have you *been*?"

"Listen, Mick Dundee, I took this fucking job two weeks ago. That's how easy you were to spot. I got you on a bloody mileage discrepancy within a fortnight... A *mileage* discrepancy!"

Sid shrugged. "They got Capone on tax evasion so..."

I spun the axe in half a circle within my grip and smiled. "I guess that makes me Elliott Ness then, pal!"

"You got a Sheila back home? Kids? Stuff like that?" Sid smirked.

I half-nodded.

"Let me know now where to post your bloody head back to them, okay pom?"

Sid moved fast and precipitously with his last two steps for an old fella, slashing out at me as he did and catching me up from my stomach and up across my chest with his blade. I recoiled in pain as a deep shower of blood splashed out and I instinctively swung the axe from left to right, catching him on the very corner of his chin and slicing off a small piece of his face on the jawline.

He winced, staggered back and immediately re-positioned himself in a crouched position ready to come at me again.

I grabbed a double-handed grip on the axe handle and swung out as hard as I could as he charged me once more. The head of the axe landed deep into the side of his stomach at the precise moment Sid landed against me and drove his knife straight through the top of my upper arm.

We both screamed in shocked unanimity. Him gripping me tighter and pulling me closer onto the blade of his knife. Me pushing harder in with the axe. He blurted blood up out of his mouth and all over my face. I recoiled backwards, yanking the axe free from his stomach and causing him to agonisingly squawk as he fell backwards onto one knee.

I staggered forward and used the axe handle to push him down from the position he'd balanced himself. He fell flat onto the ground. Again, with the axe handle, I moved him, so he slumped over onto his back.

"How many people are down that hole?" I growled.

Sid looked up at me with a bloodied grin and spat "Not... enough... *poms*!"

I slammed the axe down hard into his neck, bursting it open and pumping a look of pure agonised horror onto Sid's face. I pulled hard on freeing out the axe from the wound it was wedged in, causing his entire body to convulse.

"Her *name* was Detective Constable Rachel Casey. And she has exposed what you did here!"

I inhaled as best as my lungs would allow and I slammed the axe down once more. What little was left holding Sid's head in place snapped clean under the impact and his decapitated cranium rolled a few centimetres free of the rest of his body.

I teetered backwards and promptly vomited up all over the ground, the contents of my insides immediately mixing with copious large droplets of blood and discoloured sweat. As the fires raged up around me, engulfing me in a swath of thick, black smoke, I dropped down to my knees and thought not of Rachel Casey or Maya Dentz in that moment but instead of my wife and children back home.

It no longer felt realistic to me that I would ever see them again.

'I'm sorry, Jane.' I sobbed. 'I'm so sorry.'

[35]

or

"A Cardigan And A Comfortable Pair of Slacks".

I looked back up at the camera lens above me for the first time since I'd started speaking. My battered face was strewn with tears and I sat there, *empty*. Who knew for certain whether Danny Berenger was being serious about live-streaming all of what I'd just said out onto the internet? But I had to believe he was speaking the truth and that there was no going back now – the so-called 'cloak' and 'mask' I wore as far as he was concerned had now been pulled from my person and the *real* me was exposed.

I was so tired.

I was in so much pain.

The goddamn police van crash down on the Coast Road seemed an entire other *lifetime* ago, let alone everything else that had come after it. I swallowed hard and blinked away tears, freeing them to fall, as a slow and sarcastic clap rang out from the iPad.

"You've had your revenge." I said quietly. "Let them go."

Danny sipped from a glass of water and smiled at me through the screen. "Barbara Deming once said 'The trouble is that in most people's minds the thought of victory and the thought of punishing the enemy coincide.' I think there is *so much* truth in that, don't you Jake Lehman?"

I sat silent.

Broken.

"I feel my punishment intended for you is evolving exactly how I want it to and I feel victorious as a result."

"Let them go." I said quietly.

"What's that Jake Lehman?" Danny smirked. "You don't want to quote anymore Van Damme films at me? You don't want to throw some half-cooked action one-liner at me? No?"

"Let them go." I said more forcibly.

"No. Sorry. But, as promised… you *can* have a moment with your wife."

"And my boys?" I wept softly.

"No." Danny exhaled. "Sadly not. You see, you never afforded me the courtesy of saying goodbye to my father properly, did you Jake Lehman? So that I cannot offer to *you*. Would you like two minutes with your wife or not?"

I slowly nodded, wiping away my tears.

Jane appeared alone on the screen in front of me. Her face looked tear-stained and exhausted. Her hair was tousled and messed out of shape from the gag that was now hanging down from her mouth.

"Hey baby?" I said tenderly.

She smiled faintly at me.

"Things aren't good." I started.

"You don't say, Jake." Jane smirked.

"Remember how you said things left unspoken and unresolved have a tendency to catch up and blow up eventually? Well, it's looking like I left that Australia thing very much unspoken and unknowingly unresolved for far too long."

She nodded.

"I know I've always promised you with all the mad shit I've done, especially in these last few years, that in my mind I held the certainty that I was one or two steps ahead of it all and I knew what I was doing but..."

I swallowed the lump in my throat down.

"... Not *now*. Not this time. I haven't got long so I just wanted to say that I'm sorry. I'm *so* sorry. I didn't want the last time we saw each other to be how it was. I'm sorry that I let my ego get ahead of me these last few months and I made you feel like there was *anything* more important to me than you. You *and* my boys. And I don't know whether I'm going to end up in Heaven or in Hell, but it feels like I'm in the latter right now anyway and if I get to experience the former then it IS going to be hunkered down in some quiet village somewhere, waking up to you by my side... I don't know why I ever got so distracted that I lost sight of conveying that to you. I love you so much, Jane."

"I love you too, Jake." Jane smiled through her tears. "You're a dickhead, but you're *my* dickhead. And do you remember when you first came back from Australia and you relapsed and you lay crying on the kitchen floor? Do you remember that night?"

I nodded.

"Do you remember what I told you?"

"You said you were never going to leave me." I cried. "You said that we were entwined and that the good thing about roots that are entwined is that they are stronger than roots that grow alone."

"That's right." Jane smiled, wiping her cheeks. "And I'm not leaving you now and you're not leaving me either. This *isn't* how it's going to be. Do you understand? I don't want the last argument we ever had to be one about clam chowder. Do you *understand* me, Jake?"

"I understand but he's not letting me say goodbye to the boys, Jane. I think this bus is going to go up with a bang the minute he's finished monologuing and I'll never get to tell them what I..."

I faltered out and froze.

Jane was staring at me wide-eyed and expectant.

The brainwave equivalent of a fist banging inside my skull screaming *'Think McFly! Think!'* started up, rattling away. You all remember the 'clam chowder' incident from mine and Jane's honeymoon, right? Do you remember how that incident bled into "clam chowder" being the 'code words' that Jane or I would use for her and the kids escaping if there was the possibility of danger to them? Do you want me to wait here whilst you go and refamiliarise yourselves?

Do you all remember how a few months after getting back from Australia - at the height of my night-terrors and a heavy re-introduction to Jim Beam and Pabst Blue Ribbon - Jane indulged my fears that friends or relatives from those men from Australia would come over here looking for revenge. And ten years later it seems those fears were *far* from irrational after all, huh? I mean, this *is* the perfect "I told you so" moment but... No. Sorry. Read the room, Jake.

Anyway, if you'll recall we devised an 'emergency plan' to placate me and a 'bug-out' bag was put together for Jane and the kids. Should Jane ever receive a phone call from me in which I ask her "how the clam chowder is" or some variation of that, she knows to get the kids and get to her parents as quickly as possible. From there she'd dump the car in a nearby supermarket car park and then have her father drive her up to her aunt's cottage situated in Cove, a little village on the Scottish borders.

That brick wall background? I *knew* that background. I sat in her aunt's comfy chair by the fire right in front of that brick wall for weeks on end whilst detoxing the second time around and "getting some air" to process what had happened in Australia. I *knew* that rusted metal clip sticking out of the wall because there used to be a very old rifle hanging up there until my boys started getting so old that they wanted to know more about it, touch it, play with it etc and Jane's aunt had to store it away somewhere else. Nothing went up in its place.

They were just over an hour and a half north in Cove.

I had no idea how they'd got there or why of all the places he'd taken them there. Only that I'd talked about it as a 'safe place' in several cognitive behaviour therapy sessions over the last few years and that, knowing what I know now, this was obviously fertile ground for Danny Berenger to exploit emotional connections. Where better, after all, for my wife and my two boys to be found dead than in the very location I regarded as my 'safe place'?

I slowly started to nod my head, looking left and right and taking in a deep breath.

"Okay, okay. Listen," I said. "Are Jack and Jonathan alright? They're there with you now, yeah?"

"Yes. They're here. They're okay. I promise." Jane smiled as her eyes welled up with more tears and she brushed the hair back from her cheek. "You know the night you walked in to that pub I worked at when we met for the first time? I wasn't even *meant* to be working that night. Fate demanded that I did so that we could meet and we could have a life with Jonathan and Jack in it."

"Fate has different plans for us than *this*, I know that much." I nodded. "I don't think our story ends with me getting blown up on the Tyne Bridge, Jane."

She smiled and wiped her eyes.

"Put *him* back on." I snarled.

"Who? Jake, wait. We still have..."

"Put him back on, please. I love you and I'm going to see you soon."

Danny Berenger appeared on the screen as Jane was shoved out of the way.

"You didn't want to take the full two minutes? That's *cold*, Jake Lehman." He smirked.

"Danny," I smiled. "If I'm going to die in a ball of flames up here on the Tyne Bridge any second then so be it but is that *really* how you saw this going? Honestly? You didn't want to get right up close and concentrate on the terrified whites of my eyes as you lopped my head off like I did with your daddy, no? You don't have the stomach for that, huh?"

"Are you trying to provoke me to press the button early so you can be put out of your misery? Is that what your intention is here?"

"No, my intention is to see this done *correctly*. Holly, Leigh, Catrina, Margaret, Matthew, Bobby, Arkin... they'll all have died for even less purpose than I originally thought if we don't do this right, Danny." I said.

"How do you know what is correct or right? How do YOU know *anything* about what my plans or intentions are for you? This whole thing has been..."

"I know this," I interrupted. "I know that big alpha-male father of yours would be disappointed you hid off somewhere and pressed a button to do away with me like some bullshit coward rather than get up close and see the lights go out in my eyes intimately. You accuse me of having skulked away in the shadows. How are you *any* different?"

Danny's already deformed mouth began to twist into a malformed state of anger.

"Maybe your dad's watching you now from Hell and he's thinking to himself *'Hey, my son's a total fucking pussy!'* you know? Maybe he's sat there with Hitler, Bin Laden and Cilla Black shouting *'This Jake Lehman fella? You know the one that cut my bloody head off? Well he's offering to face down my boy and die in front of his own kids for the opportunity and this so-called son of mine has opted out. What the fuck is that about?'* And I don't know Danny, I just cannot bring myself to believe this whole thing has been ten years in the making and you're not seeing it through with a big, old-fashioned fight to the death. Are you scared or something? This is the worst act of Australian related decision making since they decided to take 'Neighbours' off tea-times on BBC 1 and put it on Channel 5 at... Well, can you ask Jane what time and what day 'Neighbours' is on nowadays?"

'I hope to God you know what you're doing, Jake?' Jane's voice whispered to me inside of my head once more.

I took a breath and studied Danny's face intensely through the screen. I could see his eyes flickering with a fury he was struggling to control within himself. He was clearly unprepared for this sudden fight back, no matter how faked it all was and it was visibly throwing him off centre. I had actually resigned myself completely to the fact that I was going to die any moment and the bodies of my wife and children would be found up in Cove hours later. But I had to go out fighting. I *had* to. I knew that this was everything Jane would expect of me.

All I'd ever done since Mick Hetherington stole my career was fight for an inch in order to keep getting by in life – to keep *enduring* it. I knew she was as tired of me fighting for those inches as I was actually having to do it and I knew now why she saw a whole other life down the line where we no longer had to. But I also knew she'd agree with me that the fight didn't end right here in this moment.

"*This* is the final round." Danny snarled as he appeared to try and leave the frame of coverage the camera lens was giving him. "The *final* round!"

"Marciano versus Walcott. 1952." I gasped.

Danny stopped and looked back. "What?"

"Municipal Stadium, Philadelphia. September 23rd 1952. Rocky Marciano versus 'Jersey' Joe Walcott. It's considered to be one of the greatest, if not *the* greatest, fight in the history of boxing. But do you know what many people don't realise about the reality of that fight? After the final bell and the radios got switched off and the TV cameras stopped rolling, Marciano and Wallcott got into a dispute on the routes back to their changing rooms about the decisions made in the fight and who the *true* victor was. They both tore off their gloves and their hand wraps and then went toe-to-toe in a fucking stadium corridor, smashing the shit out of each other with their bare knuckles in front of maybe fifteen people at best. Full on docklands brawling. Until only one man was left standing."

Rocky Marciano did fight 'Jersey' Joe Walcott at The Municipal Stadium in Philadelphia on September 23rd 1952. And it is considered to be one of the greatest, if not *the* greatest, fight in the history of boxing. But everything else I just said?

Yeah, you guessed it – total and utter *chuffing*!

I leant back and stared hard at Danny.

Danny silently stared back, seething.

"I'll go stand in the corridor, Jake Lehman. But I don't think you're ever getting out of the ring!" he snarled as the screen clicked black and half a second later an almighty bang rang out from the north side of the Tyne Bridge and a flash of fire rolled up into the sky. A fire so intense it was still visible through the blacked out windows of the minibus.

I quickly stumbled up onto my feet and ran to the door, feverishly yanking it open and falling out into a freezing blast of fresh snow and high winds. Off to my right a wall of fire blocked the exit off the bridge back onto Swan House roundabout.

On my left another colossal bang was heard from the south side of the Tyne Bridge and an immense fire blasted up into the night sky.

Twenty-five metres up in both directions the abandoned cars on both sides exploded in unison creating a connected storm of flames. Then another twenty-five metres up from them? Another explosion and more blistering heat on each side. With me standing in the middle, waiting to be submerged by the fires when they meet.

I looked desperately around me.

I wondered whether the minibus had a key in the ignition that would allow me to drive the thing out of there and… 'Don't be STUPID, Jake. That thing is as good as rigged to blow as everything else on here!'

Jane always likes to praise me for what she calls my "weird autistic savant like tendency" to hear things or smell things that go under the radar of "most normal humans" and then start deep studying them, poking and prodding until I uncover or discover something no one else had noticed. That, in her eyes, is what makes me the good investigator I am. Then Benedict Cumberbatch had a shitty 'mind palace' variation put out on display in those awful modernised Sherlock Holmes dramas on the BBC and Jane's praise swiftly switched to mocking me and sometimes calling me 'Shit Sherlock'.

I only interrupt the dramatic proceedings right now to tell you this so you'll have the necessary context to understand how amidst the sounds of the explosions (and the heat coming off them), the emergency sirens on both sides of the bridge and the screams coming from down on the Quayside below, I was *still* able to clock the unexpectedly apparent and persistent clanging of a metal chain against the steel girders on the side of the Tyne Bridge, ringing out like a buoy in a sea of madness.

My eyes fell on it and through one of the small grates on the side of the girders I could just about make out that there was something very long and white flapping wildly in the wind whilst strapped against the length of the bridge.

I ran behind the minibus and over to the edge, quickly peering over and looking upside down at what was a huge sign stretching out across most of the Tyne Bridge itself, advertising the upcoming Quayside New Year's Eve celebrations throughout the city.

I stared down at the gathering crowds, hundreds of feet below on the edge of the Quayside. I could see they were all pouring out of the pubs and bars down around there to come look up at all the flames and explosions going off above them.

I could hear Andy Williams' 'It's the Most Wonderful Time' blasting out from some outdoor event down there somewhere.

Who the hell is coming to an *outdoor event* in the middle of a goddamn blizzard?

"Jesus Christ, Jake son. What are you doing?" I muttered to myself as I slowly started to climb up onto the side of the bridge. "What the fuck are you *thinking*?"

'Calm down. You've done stupider shit then this, buddy.' The voice in my head said.

'No, I'm really not so sure about that.' Jane's voice countered.

"♫♫...It's the hap-happiest season of all. With those holiday greetings and gay happy meetings. When friends come to call. It's the hap-happiest season of all. There'll be parties for hosting, marshmallows for toasting... ♫♫"

Two more explosions were unleashed blowing the vehicles that initially contained them skywards and spreading more flames both upwards and towards me from the north and the south. The proverbial flaming net was closing in on me.

"You couldn't just go with a quiet Christmas for once, huh? You couldn't just bank all the times you've cheated death, be grateful and go live in some motherfucking Postman Pat type village?" I started to audibly rant at myself as I lowered over the side facing across to the Sage and desperately grabbed out at the sign. I pulled furiously at the metal chain on one corner that held the sign in place. It wouldn't budge.

"♫♫...And carolling out in the snow. There'll be scary ghost stories. And tales of the glories of Christmases long, long ago ... ♫♫"

"You couldn't have just got yourself a cardigan and a nice pair of comfortable slacks and counted your blessings each morning? No, you couldn't, *could you*? No. No. Not *you*! YOU have to go climbing off the edge of the Tyne Bridge in the middle of a blizzard and then... and then... God only knows what THIS is, idiot!"

The flames rolled closer.

'I love you so much, Jane.' The voice in my head whispered quietly.

"♫♫... It's the most wonderful time of the year. There'll be much mistletoe-ing. And hearts will be glowing. When loved ones are near. It's the most wonderful time of the year... ♫♫"

Half a second later the final blast rang out from inside the minibus itself, connecting all the various pockets of flames along the Tyne Bridge and expanding out a wave of flames in every direction.

The explosion this close to where I hung was just enough to throw me back, snapping the chain I desperately clutched and tearing the sign partially clear from its holding as I plummeted.

I frantically gripped as tightly as possible around the thick, weather-proofed material the sign was made of as I fell through the darkness towards the waters of the River Tyne below. Suddenly the sign reached as much of its free run as it had and sprang to rigidity, flicking me back upwards and in the direction of the north side of the bridge before swinging me violently off to the other side once more.

As the swinging slowed, I wrapped my legs around the sign and peered down to the depths below me as balls of flames raged above.

I still couldn't make out just how far off the surface of the water I was but I heard lapping movements coming from below and the odd crunch as the river slammed against nearby wooden platforms and frozen, muddied sludges on the banks.

'That's a sign, right?' I thought to myself. 'If you can hear it than you can't be far away from it so if you…'

The thought would remain incomplete as the sign I clung to snapped clear with a clean and unexpectedly instant tear.

I fell into the freezing water below.

I think the cold hit my senses before the sensation of the water on my skin did.

I remember bursting back up out of the water almost instantly with a sensation that felt like three layers of skin had been stripped from my head and my eyeballs had exploded.

I knew I couldn't waste time and I started to anxiously pull myself through the ice cold water as my shoes and jeans filled up and became more and more weighted. My jacket and jumper started to harden as I reached the muddied, snow-blanketed banks and crawled as best I could through to the small wooden ladder nearby.

The jostling and cheering crowds from further down the Quayside seemed to rush on mass towards me and a few sets of arms reached out and started to pull me up the rest of the way.

"Jesus Christ!"

"Fuckin' hell, kidda!"

"Are you alright?"

"Get his coat off?"

"Does anyone have a blanket?"

I tried to push past the people that swarmed me but it was impossible. I felt my lips start to harden and my teeth chattered ceaselessly. The blue lights of a police car flicked straight into view as it screeched around the corner and skidded to a stop, scattering a few of the crowd in various directions as Chief Constable Lane threw open her door and pointed at the back seat.

"Climb in!" she shouted as she got out of the passenger seat and ran to the boot, pulling out a thick material drape and a pack of emergency foil blankets and throwing them on the back seat.

I staggered over and climbed achingly inside.

The car sped off as she barked unyielding and inexorable instructions at me - take off my coat and jumper, wrap the foil blanket around me, cover myself on top of that with the coarse sheet next to it, tell her what the hell I was thinking, talk to her, tell her I can hear her, where is Jane and the boys, where are we going... on and on and on and on.

My eyes attempted to roll back into my skull but I blinked fast and rolled my jaw, slurring as I spoke. "They're in... He's got them... in... They're at Cove... They're in... a... They're in... a family... cottage... in Cove."

"Cove? Like up past Northumberland way? *That* Cove?" Lane shouted before turning to the young officer driving. "You better put your foot down, son. We've got a long drive and only a short amount of time."

Lane looked back to me in the rear of the speeding police car and pointed at the driver. "That's PC Monkman, by the way. He's new enough in the job not to have a problem with helping me hand grenade my career."

I half nodded as I threw my wet jumper and jacket down on the ground and wrapped myself tightly in the foil blanket.

"I was settled down in the corner of Gold Command, watching a very interesting selection of video files involving Commissioner McKinley - we'll talk about that more in a minute - and then I decided to go for a drive to clear my head and just as I was passing under the Tyne Bridge I looked up and thought to myself 'Oh. Look? There's my friend Jake Lehman. What's he doing?' and..."

"I was... just... hanging... around." I smiled through my chattering teeth.

"Oh no, Jake. *No.*" Lane beamed. "Don't lower yourself to that. You're better than that!"

I gulped down a little.

"Am... I... am... I on the... internet?" I slurred. "About... Australia... was that...?"

Lane bit down on the bottom of her lip and slowly moved her head affirmatively before I could finish my sentence.

"Apparently so." She said softly.

"Then... I need... to... definitely... call in... that... favour."

"Judging from what I saw on that SD card I sneaked a look at, I'd say it might be *me* who owes *you* a favour but go on?"

I coughed wiped the frozen clumps of hair from off my forehead then pulled the foil and the blanket tighter around me.

"Your brother… still… works for… the… National Crime… Agency, right?" I stammered.

[34]

or

"Vengeance To God Alone Belongs; But When I Think Of All My Wrongs My Blood Is Liquid Flame".

or

"The Long Walk Of Daniel Bradley Berenger".

If Danny Berenger was truly honest he probably loved the legend of his father more than he loved the man himself. They'd never had a particularly close relationship as father and son when Danny was younger. Sid worked away in the mines and only came back to Alice Springs for the odd weekend here and there. When he did he mostly spent his time drinking it up with the locals and flashing his cash around the dustbowl town Danny lived in with his mum and his Aunt Gilly. Occasionally he'd take Danny out hunting kangaroos, teaching him how to shoot and kill. But contact was generally minimal regardless of how much Danny wished every night in bed for it to be the opposite.

In his late teens Danny's mother died of cancer and left him in the care of his Aunt Gilly and her new boyfriend – a weathered and hairy Aborigine called Old Culludie. Danny detested living with them, eventually pushing himself to steal a battered red ute belonging to Old Culludie's drinking buddy, Kamma, and driving it out into the desert in search of what he'd been told was the Berenger family's mining business.

The drive out to Brennan - which Danny's grandfather owned, Sid Berenger was always quick to point out - was long and arduous. For Danny it was ultimately futile too because any hopes of happily reuniting with his dad and getting hooked up with a job in the family business were dashed with immediacy. Sid, in fact, looked suitably embarrassed to see his weedy son from a marriage he liked to pretend didn't exist and turned Danny's arse around back out of there faster than a travelling boomerang.

Danny couldn't face the humiliation of heading back home or the beating he'd probably take for stealing Kamma's utility vehicle. So instead he took up his dad's offer of some petrol tins to "see [him] home" and pushed the truck on all the way to Perth. Eventually moving down the coast to Bunbury – with a few stops to steal more fuel along the way.

After a few weeks of sleeping in the open-back under the stars, scratching around for work here and there and robbing his way around to getting money to feed himself, Danny cut his losses and walked into the nearest army recruitment centre.

Everything after that was a haze.

Bootcamp blurred into trade-specific training, which bled into specific testing and interviewing. Before Danny knew it, he was being told that he had "the right temperament" and the sort of "resolve" that would make him a pitch perfect applicant to try out for the Australian Defence Force's Special Operations Command.

They weren't wrong and Danny sailed through the selection process and the gruelling training that followed. He came to love the life - the structure, the discipline, the camaraderie and bonding, the learning and, what surprised him the most, the *killing*. He learnt to do it hand-to-hand, with a variety of different firearms and, through his studies in explosive ordnance disposal, he was able to reverse-engineer the knowledge to learn how to do it with bombs too. He was so good at it that it that it sort of turned him on when he did it.

So much so that Danny struggled with the downtime - the hanging around bases, stupid bloodless training exercises, the cleaning of the equipment that never seemed to get used anymore... He missed the operational stuff that set him loose to do well what he was good at.

In time, his penchant for taking lives became a concern to all around him. Most definitely to the rest of his unit, who saw themselves just one more trigger-pull by Danny's finger away from getting their arses dragged into a war crimes investigation. So they broke ranks and reported their concerns up the line.

The betrayal fractured something loose inside of Danny Berenger.

And his world most definitely came crumbling down only weeks later when his units' choices and the impending investigation against him as a result caused Danny to snap during stand-down on a base out in the devil's armpit of Afghanistan, far away from where all the real action was going down.

His appointed legal representatives wanted him to claim it was "PTSD-related" but it wasn't. Danny knew that. He legitimately did try to stab his Sergeant in the head with a combat knife. For no other reason than he didn't like the stance he was taking against Danny's assertion that the rest of the unit were "cowardly, bullshit-spouting, back-stabbing scum". Had such scum not been there to pin Danny down and get the knife out of his hand, the Sergeant would have had an extra hole in his skull to use as he saw fit.

Danny used the time in the military stockades to get a handle on his 'anger' and his 'issues'. By the time he was dishonourably discharged he made a promise to himself that he was going to "get [himself] sorted" and go "into private security". Instead, within a week later, he had disappeared down to the bottom of many a bottle of vodka and didn't come back up for air until he was 97 miles outside of Brennan. Now totally his old man's independent mining facility. He set off, weaving the stolen car all over the dirt road on his way to facing off against Sid Berenger once more.

Sid took one look at his son, with all his military-grade muscles and tree-trunk sized neck, and realised that there might be a place for him up there in the woop-woop after all. The biggest problem he saw though was that Danny kept drunkenly rambling about "learning the business", "studying coal" and "inheriting the mine" like Sid had done from his own father – but the truth was that coal-mining was such a small part of what they did up in Brennan nowadays.

So Sid loaded up the ute, threw a few tins of grog in the cooling box and took his boy out to the desert to go shoot 'roos just like they did when Danny was a small, rake-thin teenager. There, sat together on a grainy mound of dirt overlooking one of the most fertile hunting plains Sid knew of, Danny had it explained to him in detail about "what was imported out of Brennan had changed over the years", how they were all "delivery drivers for horny men overseas" these days and just how much money there was in getting in on "this new type of work".

Danny wasn't as disgusted as his father was probably expecting him to be.

The boy had done far worse in his 'adventures' with Special Operations Command. Who was he to judge? And the sort of money Sid was talking about nearly took Danny's head off in shock.

"Boy, you don't want to inherit this. Trust me." Sid had said to him, four beers down. "You want to *milk* this. Me? I've worked it, I've owned it and now I'm milking it as much as I can before the bottom drops out. I've got my money stashed up in a holding box back in the Springs and when the time comes, I'm heading out there to pick it up and fly on over to live out my days face deep in Asian pussy, son!"

Danny went to work side by side with his father and the men he had employed at Brennan.

They all knew what they were doing was kidnapping and sex-trafficking. But no one ever called it that. They all had their own little nicknames for what it was. No one ever let it be addressed by its actual legal definition.

The bottom did indeed drop out of the sex-trafficking operation Brennan had running with the mining company as a front. It dropped right out at the same time Danny Berenger had come to find a thoroughly uncomplicated, twisted monk-like existence out there in the desert. He got up each day, ran through some paperwork for Sid, went out hunting wildlife that would go on to be food stuff for the employees, drank hard, occasionally took a trip down the mine to cover a shift and often sampled the 'goods' that came bound and gagged onto the compound whilst he was down there.

Danny liked blondes the best.

Sid didn't keep to his word though. He didn't take early retirement and go off to some Asian country with his big bundle of money. He kept overseeing fruitless and negligible coal digs, putting down 'dry' month after 'dry' month for the team in terms of actual wages. Allowing the whole operation to become some disgusting site for raping and murdering instead, minus any actual trafficking.

Danny was desperate for his father to see sense in his original plan and knock this shit on the head: Let the Brennan men tear the place apart like some seedy cannibalistic Caligula. Meanwhile he and Danny could be miles away enjoying the fruits that the facility had eked out in all its forms over the generations.

Then Jake Lehman and his gorgeous red-headed police detective sidekick arrived.

Nothing would ever be the same again.

It all got out of hand so fast. Everyone was so quick to act without thinking and Danny found himself drowned out, more so by his own father over everyone else. He tried desperately to reason with Sid and everyone else that killing an Australian police officer could bring a whole heap of attention and hurt on everyone in Brennan that no one wanted. No one listened. Even though reason was coming from someone like Danny – who, despite a penchant for murder, could see that this was madness. He was so conflicted though; he understood they could cause a lot of trouble (if not the end of this whole thing!) if left alive, but murdering them was going to rain down the storm of storms.

At the very least he couldn't comprehend why his dad was so averse to throwing them down the well like everyone else was suggesting. It had served well as a method in covering up nearly fifty other murders. What was two more?

When Sid gave the order that Jake Lehman and the detective lady were to be taken out into the deepest parts of the desert and left for the dingoes and the crocodiles at a desolate waterhole, Danny begged his dad to go out there and make sure that the murders were done properly so there could definitely be no consequences.

"You like your killing, don't you son?" Sid had sneered as Jake and the woman were loaded up into the back of a truck, bound and gagged. "You told me once you were good at that shit, right? Well you get yourself out there with them. You're the expert."

Danny didn't take his father up on the offer.

He lived with a sick ethical balance in his life. One where he had found a way to justify what he did with the girls often brought into Brennan against their will. But not killing them. Not killing anyone ever again if he could help it. That's why after a while he stopped going down the mines anymore. He didn't want to take any part in the disposal of the girls, regardless of how much some of the men called him a 'hypocrite'. And on top of that? Every time he did go down there he could feel their ghosts watching him and reaching out for him.

He probably *should* have gone out there into the never-never with Chris, Michael and the other two. At least then he would have known for definite that the job was done right. At least it would have saved Danny himself being shaken awake from his drunken slumber a few nights later by the sound of an explosion and the sight of a handful of Brennan men sprinting past his cabin door in the early hours of the morning.

"WHAT THE HELL HAPPENED?" Sid was heard to scream.

"I DON'T KNOW MAN; I DON'T FUCKING KNOW!" A guy called Jim shouted back at him as Danny ran over to them.

Chris, one of the men up in Brennan he was probably least close to despite their proximity in age, screeched "THAT'S WALT'S UTE, SID! THAT'S WALT'S..."

"THIS WAS NO ACCIDENT! SOMEONE'S BURNING UP THE MINE!" Jim had shouted. "THAT PUMP WOULDN'T HAVE JUST EXPLODED!"

Sid had started looking around furiously and desperately. His eyes squinting into every corner of the darkness before turning to look at Chris. "YOU BETTER HAVE WATCHED THAT POM AND THE COPPER GET TORN APART BY DINGOES WITH YOUR OWN BLOODY EYES BECAUSE..."

He was interrupted by Michael Merindah, one of Danny's closest pals, running over to the group from the most intense area of the raging fire.

"HARV AND RON ARE GONE, MAN! THEY'RE FUCKING BURNT TO SOOT!" he screamed with tears in his eyes.

Danny watched as his father barked instructions at each of the men. He knew as every instruction landed that Sid was more concerned about the prospect of Jake Lehman or the Australian police officer's return than he was about the fire raging out of control around them. Minimal direction was given to attend to the explosion as it slowly ate its way closer to them all and chewed up the portacabins and containers with their whole lives inside. Instead Sid wanted everyone to fan out and make sure the facility was definitely clear of anyone that could have started the fire deliberately.

Most men scattered of into the night. Sid grabbed Chris before he could leave and in front of Danny he stuck his nose right into the man's face and spat out the words "Swear to me on your life you watched those two die in chopped up pieces left for the dingoes in the back of bourke?"

"I swear! I swear!" Chris had replied.

Danny knew he was lying.

They fanned out and started checking every corner and makeshift corridor between the buildings where someone could be hiding. It couldn't have been more than a couple of minutes of searching, if even that, before Danny instantly spotted a head poking out from behind one container wall, way up from the fiery mining point explosion.

He ran across the dirt path between one side of Brennan and the other, instinctively reaching behind the corner and grabbing onto whatever he could. He yanked Jake Lehman out of the shadows and wrapped his hands around his throat to pin him in place.

Danny would never forget the sight of Jake Lehman as he stood contained before him. The man looked like he had died, lay six feet under and then fought his way back from the afterlife to avenge what had been done to him and his friend. Danny had taken many lives before. He knew what dead people looked like and this looked like a dead man who had inexplicably returned.

The shock caused Danny to stutter the first time he attempted to shout down to the bottom end of Brennan but he got it all out in the end, screaming "Dad! It's him! It's the fucking pom! I've got him, Dad! I've got him! It's the pom - He's bloody alive!"

"GET THE GUNS! GET THE FUCKING GUNS NOW!" Jim was heard shouting back from further down the container line.

Jake started to struggle with a tenacity Danny did not expect him to have. They started to fight with each other and it became imperative to Danny that he got that axe out of Jake Lehman's hand.

Suddenly there was a white hot flash of heat and the side of Danny's face exploded, causing his entire sight to go completely red. He had never felt pain like it. He couldn't control his body but he knew from the blood pouring at force out of the side of his face and down all over him that he had been shot and he was bleeding out. He desperately tried to raise his hands to his face and stem the bleeding but the messages from his brain to the rest of his body weren't working as they should.

Then it all went black.

It was black again when Danny awoke. Only this time the black was a physical one as his face lay pressed into the soot of a fire that had burnt itself out. His head was emitting agonising waves of pain down all of his body and as he slowly reached his hand up to his face he felt the skin around the exit wound to be hot, soft and gooey like it had been freshly and painfully cauterised shut somewhat accidentally.

He tried to sit up but he couldn't at first. He pushed himself to with the same physical determination that had seen him through his Special Operations Command training and selection. He discovered he was pumping blood from two quite large and deep entry wounds in the upper part of his chest near where his pectoral met his shoulder.

Danny got to his feet, just. He had to walk on a tilt that kept his head lolled downwards on the side where part of his face seemed to be missing but he just managed to get the distance needed to stagger upon his father's decapitated corpse. He tried to scream but no sound came out. The more his jaw extended out in a ferocious and feral silent scream the more the wound opened up in his neck and clumps of blood dropped loose.

He saw blue lights off in the distance. Way off in the distance. But he knew they were heading this way. There was no way Danny wanted to be the Brennan spokesperson, covering the topic of what lay rotting down one particular caved-in section of the mine. He was pretty sure he could hear helicopters too.

He pushed himself over to the area where he himself had dumped the female detective's jeep out of sight, whilst Sid had promised to consider all of the options. Danny slumped against the side of the vehicle, whilst trying to configure his body to do what he needed it to do through the pain and the mismanaged messages from his brain. Ordering himself to get inside the jeep and get the hell out of there.

Danny got the engine started eventually and tore out of there, bursting through the rear fence line and off in the opposite direction as to where the blue lights and helicopters had been seen and heard. He knew almost instantly that he was in serious trouble though as the blood loss was too immense.

He couldn't see properly.

He couldn't breathe properly.

He knew he was dying and his only salvation lay hours away.

[35]

or

"The Long Walk Of Daniel Bradley Berenger – Part II".

Danny knew a girl out in Yulara. This had been a whole other lifetime ago when he had thought about sticking a pin in the map and settling down there. Yulara is a town in the Southern part of Australia's Northern Territory, tucked away inside an unincorporated enclave within the MacDonnell region. He'd known of it as a kid as a place that existed somewhere between his childhood home in Alice Springs and Brennan, the site where his dad worked out in the desert.

Through a whole heap of convoluted circumstances that involved him trying to impress his dad by travelling out there one weekend to network new business connections, Danny met a girl called Katie in a dive bar and their one-night stand turned into something a little more. Soon he was travelling out there every weekend and slowly falling in love and finding a state of peace within himself just by being near her. When she fell pregnant he knew he'd found a life that would dial down the turmoil in his head and pull him away from the stuff at Brennan he no longer wanted to be a part of. When Katie miscarried everything quickly fell apart just as soon as it had come together and Danny fled following one drunken altercation too many.

But now Danny landed back there for the first time in years. His prayers that Katie still lived at the same address were met when he collapsed through her front door no sooner than she had cautiously opened it. He fell to her floor a blood-soaked, dirt-strewn mess with half his face missing.

They say that time can be kind but it didn't seem that way with Katie and her willingness to help him had to be coerced with a knife. She came around in the end though and every time he returned to consciousness from blood loss, she was still there helping him and tending to his wounds. Katie was no medical professional though and other than stemming the bleeding she didn't know what to do about the open wounds to Danny's chest and neck. She certainly had no clue as to how to stanch the infection that was very clearly already building up in the latter.

By late afternoon news coverage was in abundance regarding the "explosion" at Brennan and how there were no survivors. Katie obviously knew he worked there and could see from the raw burns down one side of Danny's body that there was a strong indication he'd been involved in said explosion.

By late evening the coverage had turned and news reports were coming in about the discovery of bodies in the mine chambers. Katie started asking too many questions. Especially about why Danny didn't want it to be known he had survived or why he didn't want to be connected in any way to Brennan. But she just kept pushing and pushing and no explanation or excuse seemed good enough. It was agonising to talk anyway and his voice was slowly fading out each time he did. So he killed Katie, left her body face down in her bathroom and emptied her house of pain medication. He took her car off her driveway and headed the 187 kilometres along the Lasseter Highway, further into the Northern Territory where the Imanpa Community lay, two-hundred kilometres south-west of his hometown in Alice Springs.

Aunt Gilly and Old Culludie had moved down to Imanpa a few years back, seeing out their years in a rusted, old, aluminium bucket of a house on the edges of the never-never. Danny knew that this would be a safe place to stay for a multitude of reasons. Gilly being "off her rocker" nowadays with no concept of the real world was one. Old Culludie's extensive history of hating and shooting at police was another.

Danny landed there just over two hours later, now completely blind in one eye and feeling the life fade from him fast. Old Culludie was long out of 'that way of life' but held onto enough knowledge to know on sight of Danny dying on his doorstep that this was a man both in (and running from) serious trouble AND that he had enough contacts in neighbouring townships who could help try and save 'the kid' as a personal favour to him.

It took nearly a year for Danny Berenger to come even close to full recovery. More so because the folks working to 'fix him up' were all of the old, retired and doddering variety long since out of the game. And because he had to learn to do everything again whilst fighting off an infection that desperately wanted to eat his face away. He struggled to walk properly for the longest time. His sight was eventually fully regained but there was part of him that wishes it hadn't been because he was left nauseous every time he looked in the mirror and saw the state his face had been left in.

Danny's voice box was shot to shit and he had to teach himself to find a way to talk that didn't agonise him each and every time he sounded out a word. In the end he stuck to letting himself sound out a slow, low, rasped and croaking whisper because it was the most pain-free.

Over the course of the early part of his recovery, the media reports intensified. Danny kept a white-knuckle grip of fury on the arms of his chair as he listened to the radio in Aunt Gilly and Old Culludie's rusty shack. The excavations up in Brennan were finishing and the police started to detail the sheer amount of "non-mining personnel" corpses that were being brought up to the surface. The media claimed it was "one of the worst atrocities in the country's history" with "close to fifty bodies found abandoned in the mine", some later identified as long-missing backpackers.

This wasn't what fuelled Danny's anger though. What did that was the steady flow of information released by the police to present a specific narrative that Danny and Danny alone knew to be **lies**: Suddenly the story told was that Detective Constable Rachel Casey and UK based private investigator Jake Lehman had come to Brennan to make enquiries in relation to the missing person case of one Maya Dentz and that the men on site blew the whole compound after a shoot-out with Casey and Lehman in order to destroy evidence and avoid capture. Between the explosion and the encroaching territory fires there had been "barely any chance of survival for anyone". Lehman was apparently the only survivor and was being lauded by Australian police as a hero. Detective Constable Casey was posthumously being decorated.

'That's not what happened!' Danny screamed at the radio as Old Culludie looked on with concern and Aunt Gilly sat staring out the window, completely doped into oblivion. 'That pommy fuck blew the place. The boys aren't lying there burnt to a crisp. They're lying there axed to pieces with cattle bolts through their heads!'

Danny's head reverberated severely with all of these lies and the news that Jake Lehman had survived. He felt something bubbling up inside of him that was far more intense than when he'd lashed out at his Sergeant back in his military days. And way more blinding than when he lost all sense of his surroundings and came around to find Katie dead at his feet. This was different. This was an awakening. This was a... thirst he had to satiate.

There'd been no mention of Danny Berenger in the news nor his escape / survival. He assumed that was because for all intents and purposes there was no actual real record of him up there on the Brennan site. In the same way there was no discernible record of who any of the working men there were. It would be months before all of Danny's old colleagues were fully identified via dental records and partial fingerprints.

'This could work to my advantage!' he thought to himself since there were no ties to him and what was being reported. He set out under the cover of darkness one night to head up to Alice Springs. He kissed Aunt Gilly and told her he'd back in a day or so. But he never returned. The drive gave him time to torture himself with more questions he had no real answer to. Mainly concerning how all of Jake Lehman's savage murders were being covered up in the manner they were, and why.

Danny landed in Alice Springs and stayed just long enough to break into Sid Berenger's lock-up and blow out the safe he had stashed inside. Danny took the mounds and mounds of money piles contained within and fled. Only to find once hunkered down inside of a cheap motel on the outskirts of Alice Springs that his father had $527,349 squirrelled away. He just couldn't begin to comprehend why Sid had all of this money yet remained living in abject squalor whilst continuing to pursue such a sordid, twisted lifestyle in the back end of nowhere.

The news reports and interviews with DCI Novak and his designated lead, DI Noah Russ, weren't dying out any time soon. Danny Berenger watched, listened and used them as fuel to push himself on and find the strength required to right the wrongs committed against him and his colleagues. To expose the real truth about what went on at Brennan as he saw it and avenge his father's death at the hands of Jake Lehman.

He bought a cheap $200 ute in cash and drove out of Alice Springs and across to Anatye, through Boulia and Winton before arriving in Barcaldine. Where he hooked up with an old military pal, fobbing off his current physical appearance with lies about being severely injured by a bomb whilst doing private security back out in Afghanistan. He was lucky that his old contact had re-trained in the civilian sector as a pilot. Which is how for $500, no questions, Danny got himself a flight over to Coffs Harbour where he could meet up with a couple of underworld fellas his father knew from finding work at Brennan for their men once they'd got too 'hot' out on the streets.

He had to pay an elevated price for the urgency of his request but they sorted him out with high-end fake credentials and a passport. Danny set off in a hire car he rented just to stress-test his newly purchased identity. Having driven the length of the Pacific Highway down into Sydney, he spent a few weeks setting up a base in the city that would allow him to stalk and assess the vulnerabilities of his two immediate targets.

Danny killed DI Noah Russ first. For no other reason than he believed the man was the one who set Casey loose with her private investigator pal to pursue the investigation that ended with his father's brutal murder. He strangled him in a cheap hotel room and made it look like an auto-asphyxiation sex act gone wrong. Then he waited weeks, very nearly a month in fact, just to see if the rest of the Sydney police force bought his fakery. Danny made sure to draw as much information from Russ before killing him, in order to move on to the next target. This is how he came to learn exactly which part of the United Kingdom Jake Lehman was based in and who the client was that Lehman had been representing.

Danny moved onto DCI Novak next and began to find a magnetism and allure in the slow, covert stalking of his subject. He drew it out much longer than he did with Russ and then, when he was bored one night, he simply ran Novak off the road and smothered him at the scene. An instinctive and immediate burst of action that bellied against the six months he'd been lying in wait.

In the winter, Danny booked a flight to London and then a train ride up to Newcastle Upon Tyne under the identity of Joe Thorin. With £254, 121 in his possession and the intention to spend every penny of it on slowly bringing about the destruction of Jake Lehman and anyone close to him.

His objective was to kill Lehman within six months but the tracking and shadowing of him became an obsession. He started to delight in observing the man's pathetic struggles and playing a covert part in orchestrating obstacles to fall in his path each and every time it looked like Jake Lehman was catching a break in the face of them.

Six months turned into a year and a year turned into two. Danny became fanatical and possessed with finding new ways to infiltrate his target's life. Upping the ante each and every time by crossing more personal boundaries, occasionally testing himself to see how close he could get to Jake Lehman as he moved around his own hometown, yet never be seen by him.

By the middle of 2020, Danny had fully embraced the 'hunt'. Along the way he'd educated himself on so much of who Jake Lehman was and what lay in the man's past that he was able to present himself before mutual enemies and coerce them easily into the plans he had for Lehman's destruction.

Jake Lehman could not just die.

Death was not enough.

Danny Berenger thought back to his own spiritual awakening out in the desert as he bled out of his various wounds and seemingly died and was reborn several times over. He thought about how before he could find the resolve to go on through the long journey out of Brennan, into what he classed as recovery, he had to have his reserves completely depleted against his will both mentally and physically. This was a devastating and agonising process and the journey to filling them back up each time even more so.

He yearned desperately for Jake Lehman to feel **exactly** that.

He wanted Jake Lehman to feel lost and confused and slowly drained of every one he loved and depended on and then... once broken by the utter enormity of what he had been mentally and physically put through... and ONLY then, would Jake Lehman's life be removed from him.

[36]

or

"The Lehman Family Reunion".

Cove Harbour in Cockburnspath is one of the best kept secret spots in the whole of the region. Not so much anymore now I've laid it all out here as documented fact to you. But it kind of is - the small, beautiful and rustic beach, the view of the sea, the great walks around the area and, of course, the 'pirates' tunnel!

We were really lucky to have had Jane's aunt and uncle own a cottage right on the walkway down to the sand with an old, torn-up causeway as their front path. It was a fantastic place for us to come as a family for long weekends over the years and, yeah as I said, it became an invaluable place for me way back when I was trying to recover and survive both physically and mentally in the spring of 2014 from the unrelenting trauma stemming from Australia.

Uncle Billy had died not long after Hetherington had me kicked out of the police and Aunt Marion died just under a year ago. Jane's dad inherited the cottage and, in time, Jane herself would from him.

After pulling in off the main road, a long, steep walk down a gravelled path led towards the beach. Near the bottom was Aunt Marion's weather-beaten cottage and behind that, leading out to sea and around like a reverse '7', was a battered stone causeway looming about twenty-five feet out of the water.

PC Monkman crunched the car to a stop and left the engine running with the windscreen wipers working at full speed to ward off the never-ending cavalcade of falling snow. It was pitch black outside and the wind shrilled and shook the car the three of us were sat in.

Lane twisted in her seat to look at her driver. "Three things! First of all, take off your coat and give it to him!"

Monkman looked at her with an expression of reluctance but eventually unclipped his seatbelt and started to remove his police-issued winter coat once it became apparent she wasn't moving on until he did.

He passed the thick, black coat emblazoned with the word 'Police' on the back over to me and Lane smiled. "Secondly, you're going to stay in the car and wait for my signal which will be a flashing torch beam from just down there!"

She pointed off into the darkness towards the bottom of the path we were about to venture down.

"This isn't a *'stay in the car but then say "Fuck it!" and come running down there to play the late arriving hero'* type instruction, okay?" she continued. "This is a *'stay the hell in the car, do as you're told or the big boss lady is going to make her last act in the job the sacking of you'* type of deal. You get me, yes?"

Monkman nodded.

"When you see my signal, you hit the emergency button on every radio in here and you call everyone in on this location - *Everyone*! Clear?"

"Clear!" Monkman said, nodding some more.

"And, this is *really* important PC Monkman, everything we've talked about on the journey up here - and I mean EVERYTHING - remains completely confidential. Is that clear? Should any information we've discussed get out, it's on *you*. Do you understand? You didn't hear anything... That was the third thing, by the way!"

"I got that." He smiled.

"Aren't you clever?" Lane grinned. "Didn't I pick well in commandeering you back up at Swan House roundabout?"

That third thing was a big ask, in my opinion. We'd essentially spent most of the ride talking about the contents of the SD card removed from Hetherington's house prior to the explosion. Lane had given more of it a cursory viewing than I'd obviously had the chance to so now knew a little more than I did about Police & Crime Commissioner Janet McKinley and it wasn't good.

I pulled back on going into detail regarding my favour from her and the possible connections her brother might offer through his work in the NCA. I wasn't taking any chances because right then it felt to me like even if I was granted the miracle of coming out the other side of this with my family still alive, there was nothing left for me and my *swing* with Lane's well-connected brother as my proverbial bat was looking like my only lifeline.

Nothing left for me but trouble anyway, if my confession about Australia saw the whole Brennan incident reviewed.

I was going to need every helping hand I could reach out and grab a hold of.

"When this is done, she's next." Lane had said about Commissioner McKinley as the police car sped through the blizzard and further up north. "She thinks she's going to oust *me*? I'm going to *arrest* her!"

"Are you going after Commissioner McKinley?" Monkman asked as he drove. "Can I get in on that? I hate that woman!"

"You keep your nose faced forward!" Lane replied.

"It's never done though is it?" I said from the back seat. "There's *always* a next. It should never have been up to me to expose Hetherington and Hadenbury yet I did and what happened? Bill Collins and his Knights of George stepped up in their place. What happens after I lock that shit down? I'm having to scuttle off to bloody Switzerland to make sure Collins faces the justice he deserves. Me – a fucking two-bit private eye for Christ's sake. You lop off a head, another one rises up out of the wound..."

Lane shrugged. "Maybe there's something in the fact McKinley is a connecting tissue between all of those people though. Have you thought of that?"

"As was Hetherington... and Hadenbury. As was Collins." I'd pulled the foil blanket tighter around me still and exhaled hard as the chattering of my teeth finally started to slow. "Depends how big her 'collective' is though, don't you think? The only thing I do know is I don't have what it takes anymore to keep digging away at the crap in this city. Danny Berenger wanted to strip my resolve down to nothing. I think he's succeeded."

The police vehicle switched off its blue lights and made a silent approach along to where we needed to stop.

"The fact that you're here, Jake? The fact that you got off that bridge how you just did? All of that tells me that he *hasn't* succeeded at all!" Lane smiled.

We trudged and tramped side by side with one another through the thick, fresh snow down the path towards the family cottage. It was completely black and we kept our steps small in order to safely judge what could be ahead under foot as the snow submerged us up to around our knees – and higher for the rather diminutive Lane. The only light emitting from anywhere around was the flicking orange glow inside of the cottage. As we drew closer and closer, I began to make out the muffled sound of Curtis Stiger's 'People Like Us' playing somewhere in the property.

"♫♫ ... Baby I know, you hear a lot of talk about the bad times ahead. That I'm the wrong kind of man, what you need is a doctor or a lawyer instead. Well I know that I'm not made of money. And God knows I'm a fool... ♫♫"

I reached down into the still soaking and rigidly stiff jeans pocket and felt the outline of Mitchell's police asp jammed away in there. His CS cannister was long since missing in action it would seem. Lane reached the front door of the cottage first and found it slightly ajar. She looked at me. I at her.

She shrugged.

I nodded.

She pushed on the door gently and it slowly swung open, the song growing louder and a small gust of heat pushing out towards us as a result. We stepped cautiously inside.

"♫♫ ... People like us got no business in love. Yeah, that's what the people say. But people like them got nothing better to do, than chase our dreams away. Well I've finally found you and I won't let go ... ♫♫"

I sniffed the air. Something didn't quite smell right from the instant I was inside but I couldn't place it exactly. It sort of smelt like petrol but... *not*? I'd taken such a battering over the course of the last twenty-four hours that my senses were ruined. I certainly wasn't seeing or hearing properly so why, I figured, could my nose be trusted?

"Do you smell that?" I whispered.

"Stinks, doesn't it?" Lane nodded.

(Sorry for doubting you, nose!)

We rounded the small brick hallway and I spotted Jonathan and Jack straight away, sprawled out on the living room floor in front of an open fire. Both of them were bound and gagged. Jane was nowhere to be seen.

I rushed as quickly as I could over to them and dropped down next to Jack first and started to frantically pull at his gag. Lane did the same with Jonathan and we manically set about trying to untie them.

"Dad!" gasped Jonathan.

"Dad, he took mum!" sobbed Jack. "He took mum!"

"When? Where?" I cried.

Lane helped Jack to his feet.

"♫♫ ... things may not get better, before they get worse. They've all got their reasons why we can't survive. They'll quote you chapter and verse ... ♫♫"

"It wasn't that long ago." Jack replied. "Ten minutes maybe?"

I pulled him into my arms and held him tight, kissing him repeatedly on the forehead.

"Erm… *Jake?*" I heard Lane exclaim as she grabbed at Jonathan and started pushing him backwards towards the route we came in.

I looked at her and found her pointing at the cottage window that faced towards the old causeway. Off in the big black expanse of what was out there I could see a small, flickering orange trail of fire growing in size and intensity as it rushed against the blizzard's harsh winds to charge towards us from the far end of the causeway.

"GET OUT!" I screamed, grabbing Jack and throwing him towards the door.

The four of us got outside and were just about clear when the entire cottage went up in an intense burst of flames. There wasn't any grand explosion akin to anything that had happened on the Tyne Bridge. Just the enormous roar that came from an open flame meeting a large quantity of ignitable substance. The popping and the explosion would come much later.

I pushed Jack up against the snow bank on the furthest side of the path and protected his head from the rising flames. Lane did the same with Jonathan. As the fire built the noise indicated it was escalating itself up to explode. Off in the distance at the far end of the causeway, the flames glimmered and spluttered out into the night against the heavy, building wind and illuminated the shape of two figures out there.

I grabbed at both boys, smothered them with kisses and shoved them back up the pathway towards where PC Monkman was parked.

"Get them out of here!" I screamed at Lane.

Lane started pulling them away from the fire.

"Dad!" Jack and Jonathan screamed in unity.

"Dad, don't go! Please!" sobbed Jonathan.

I smiled at them and said "I love you both so much!"

I walked purposefully to the left of the fire trail burning through the middle of the causeway. I slipped and slid along the frozen stone surface as waves blew up out of the darkness, smashing against the sides, spraying me with ice cold sea water and stinging the open cuts on my skin.

The closer I got the more clear it was to my eyes that Jane was knelt down on the ground at the very edge of the stone jetty, facing towards the ocean with her hands bound as the sea intermittently burst up on impact with the causeway and soaked her down.

I could hear her sobbing as I visually followed the trail from her to the gun pressed against the back of her head, the arm holding it and the maniacal look of evil glee on Danny Berenger's sopping half-mutilated face.

"I can't believe you made it!" he crowed with his mangled voice.

I pointed back over my shoulder to the raging fire at the end of the causeway behind us.

"I *really* liked that cottage." I sighed.

"Ja.. ke?" sobbed Jane.

"The boys are safe. The boys are safe, Jane. It's okay." I smiled.

"Who won?" smirked Danny.

"What?" I said.

"Marciano against Walcott. September 23rd 1952." He replied. "The corridor brawl after the main event. Who won?"

I shook my head slowly whilst wiping the sea water away from my eyes.

"Who gives a fuck?" I exhaled.

"I guess it ultimately *isn't* very important," Danny concurred. "Not to the conclusion of *this* grand plan anyway and..."

"You know," I sighed once more whilst edging a little further forward. "I've been meaning to say this to you – *you* really have to stop calling it 'big' and 'grand' and all that. It's not for *you* to ascribe it that way, you know? Especially considering it... well... it just wasn't *that* fucking grand was it?"

"Really, Jake Lehman?" he sneered. "*Really*? I invaded every single facet of your life. I killed every single person that enabled you or supported you. I destroyed your home and your business. I have wiped away any future you could have possibly had if I was going to allow you to live and..."

"You're not getting it, are you?" I laughed insincerely. "You spent what? Six years? Seven years? What was it again? All living out of the shadows of my life, slowly twisting your knife and look what's happened in the last two of them? I've fucking *flourished*! ... I've become *more* respected. I've found *greater* inner strength and peace. Hell, up until two nights ago, they were planning on making a bloody *film* about *me*. You had to murder all of my friends just to stop me succeeding in *spite* of you. So, let me ask you this..."

I took another step forward as I saw his grip tighten on the gun and the barrel end push tighter into the back of Jane's skull.

"... Was it worth it? Was it worth it all? Six, eight, *ten* years of your life doing this, becoming consumed by me like the little pathetic sick fuck you are and having to watch me get stronger and better whilst you kept trying to crush me down?" I continued. "All because you couldn't cope with your sordid little sex trafficking and murdering enterprise getting exposed. Why? Was it because it was the only way you were getting your dick wet?"

"Is this meant to impress me, Jake Lehman?" Danny psychotically rasped and squeaked through his bulging throat. "That you can show such cavalier disregard and disrespect in your final moments? Because it doesn't! It *really* doesn't!"

"You know what doesn't impress *me*?" Jane bawled through her tears and against the sound of the wailing wind and smashing waves. "I'm sat here listening to you Jake, and you're like some actor at the Oscars who gets up there to accept his award and forgets to thank his wife. Because you know what, guys? I'm really not here to be playing the damsel in distress. Have either of you ever thought that the reason Jake's been able to find strength, keep going and get better enough year after year in order to shit all over your *grand* plan is because of one reason and one reason only? He has..."

Jane abruptly heaved herself to her left, curling round and landing on her back. As she did she threw out a large clump of rock she'd pulled from the edge she knelt at and hid in her bound hands. She flung it with enough force it smashed into the 'good' side of Danny's head and sent him reeling backwards.

"... ME!" she screamed.

Blood burst from the side of Danny's head and the gun went off, aimlessly firing out into the ground. He gathered himself and pointed it desperately towards Jane. I started running as fast as I could at him. He got another shot off in her direction causing her to recoil and fall backwards over the edge of the jetty, away from the second bullet as it ricocheted off the stone surface between where her legs had been. The last thing I saw of Jane was her grabbing out at the stone edging and locking in a tight grip with her bound hands in order to hold on tight and stop herself from falling.

I never got a chance to see anything after that.

Because I was plummeting out over the edge of the causeway with Danny Berenger in my arms, down into the freezing black and contorting surface of the wild sea below.

The both of us landed hard against a submerged part of the jetty, crunching into it on impact as the sea engulfed us. I felt my arm snap backwards and my shoulder crack. I screamed out in pain as my lungs filled up with ice cold, salty water.

Danny floated up from in between my legs and pulled me back down no sooner than my mouth had got inches away from the surface above. He threw punches that were all slowed by the force of the water against his effort. They did not land as well as he probably hoped they would.

This, Jake Lehman, is your fight to the death.

I pushed hard with all of my might and burst up out above the waterline and frantically gasped for air before being yanked back down again. Danny was now above me, using all of his weight to press me against the wall of the causeway underneath the waves and hold me there even though the forceful and unpredictable pull of the current had its own plans for us.

He wrapped his arm around my throat and pulled me in against him, squeezing with all of his might. I used my so-called good arm to frenetically plunge away at my jeans pocket and free the police asp from inside of there.

I could feel myself fading and as soon as I felt the grip of the asp handle so much as a centimetre free from my pocket, I jabbed upwards behind me through the water at where I felt his head would be. I clearly hit something of worth on the third attempt as Danny's grip around my throat slackened and he reeled backwards.

I seized the chance and swam upwards, hitting the surface with yet another desperate gulp of air just as a sub-zero wave smashed into me and sent me careering backwards, tumbling into a small ridged thicket of broken off causeway that was standing alone a little further out in the sea.

I clawed at it, anxiously pulling myself up with my non-broken arm, which now felt like the only part of my body still functioning in any capacity. I could hear Jane screaming desperately back out on the main jetty. I lay backwards and inhaled deeply just as Danny burst from the water and grabbed a hold of me.

I thumped and flailed at him as he punched back whilst trying to pull himself up onto the same stone remains I had been thrown onto. He gained higher ground and started to push himself on top of me. With his forearm pressing down against my throat, cutting off the air, he leaned in and started to smirk through his shivers.

"You know, Jake Leh…"

I didn't let him finish. I raised the police asp and slammed it into his eye then used it to push him off and to the side of me with it when he recoiled in agony. I flipped myself as best I could on top of him and started to furiously and repeatedly jab at the healed but indented area on his neck.

He gagged hard and I hit him again.

He wheezed and I hit him again and again.

The blunt end of the asp slammed into the fragile area and blood soon started to eke out of the wound I was now reopening beneath his chin.

Danny was choking badly and I grabbed at the hair on his head and pulled him close into me, using everything I could muster to drag my broken arm into play.

"Shut the fuck up!" I stuttered as I wrapped him tight against me and snapped his neck within two attempts.

I watched Danny slide out of my arms and disappear down into the dark depth below me.

"I should never have... dropped... the gun!" I gasped, just as another wave smashed into me and sent me scattering backwards off the edge. The sea spun me around against my will and back in the direction of the causeway.

I started to lose consciousness but was pulled back from the brink by the truly agonising sensation of my damaged arm being yanked hard. I screamed as I was hauled hard against the stone steps at the very bottom of the jetty.

Jane could be heard screeching "You've got to help me, Jake! Please baby. Please use your legs!"

I flopped down onto the first couple of steps, coughing and gagging but unable to prop myself up. The only warmth I could feel was the remote and distant sensation of Jane's hands cupping my face as she pulled me closer to her body.

"Stay with me, Jake." She shouted.

"I'm not... going... anywhere... without you... I promise." I slurred as my eyes flickered.

"I don't know where we're going to go anyway, baby." Jane half-laughed whilst crying heavily. "That bastard has blown up our house!"

"How... do you feel... about... the Lake... District?" I stammered as the hill back up on the main land lit up with a sea of flashing blue lights. "I'm so sorry... Jane. I'm... so... sorry. I can't... believe... I nearly... lost you all."

Jane leant down and kissed me gently on the mouth.

"I know this is hardly the time but you really look like shit, Jake."

I nodded and tried to raise a smile.

"I've... really... had... quite the... time... of it... if I'm honest."

"I guess you'll be expecting me to come sit by your bedside and hold your hand again?" Jane sighed as she stroked the hair out of my face.

"I don't... know." I stuttered. "After... your antics back... there... I don't... think... the... role... of the... dutiful wife... works for... you anymore."

"I know, right." Jane giggled. "Did you *see* me? I was flinging rocks and busting heads and all that shit!"

[37]

or

"Cups On A String".

Now, if I'd had *my* way I'd have stayed in that hospital bed up in Northumberland doped up to the eyeballs on morphine and fully embracing what it felt like to be both warm and no longer soaked through anymore. But I *had* to see Psychic. I couldn't shake the strong need to get by his side, to see Emily and apologise to her from the very bottom of my heart.

Jane and the boys had been thoroughly checked over for hypothermia and the like and were now in the good care of hospital staff and her parents. I myself carried a volume of injuries that had now been collected up over the last couple of days and re-dealt with in one big omnibus session of care-giving. So as the sun started to rise on Christmas morning, I waited out the required amount of time for the fresh casts on both of my arms to set and I began the process of trying to 'chuff' my way out of there and back down to the Royal Victory Infirmary in Newcastle where Psychic apparently was.

Chief Constable Lane, however, decided to throw in a curveball.

"McKinley and Falk are holding a press conference at eight am. I'd like to stop that from happening." She said with a smirk. "What's that thing you did with Hetherington back in the day? The 'Gimble'?"

"The Kimble!" I smiled, flashing back to that wondrous moment when Mick Hetherington's world first started crashing down around him as audio recordings of his own voice, detailing his own crimes, played out to his party guests at a local authority event a few years back.

Lane nodded.

I looked at the clock on the wall. "Not enough time and plus, she'd see it coming a mile off if you ask me."

"Well, I'm going to go disrupt the shit out of their press conference anyway."

"Just once, I'd like to get my arse kicked and then get to stay in the hospital bed afterwards at least long enough for the mattress to get warm, you know?" I sighed.

"What are you talking about? I never said you had to come with me?" Lane replied.

"It was kind of inferred, wasn't it?"

"No. Although it might kind of kill two birds with one stone by taking you down there and getting you de-arrested for the murders of Dentz and Maitland whilst we're there, tearing apart McKinley and Falk's little performance."

"Then they can arrest me for the Australia thing whilst I'm there too."

"That's not generally how it works, you know? Let's see what the police out there have to say first and *then* start to worry..." Lane replied.

I nodded, slowly at first and then with a little more gusto as my mind went into overdrive.

"I think we should let the press conference go ahead." I grinned. "But I do have an idea how we can offer up a helping hand to those that are going to be attending it."

I started to delicately ease myself up out of my bed.

"You know Lehman," Lane smiled. "You're like the coyote in those Road Runner cartoons aren't you? You just keep blowing yourself up and throwing yourself off things but you just don't know how to lie down and quit, do you?"

"I'm done chasing down my great adversary though, I can assure you of that. It feels like they keep changing week-to-week but fuck it... I'm done!" I sighed as I painfully stood and hobbled away from my bed.

"Not *yet* you're not though, right?" Lane smirked.

I stopped and frowned. "No... Ok, you're correct. But I'll be done once and for all *soon*!"

We arrived at police headquarters on Middle Engine Lane with a solid half hour to spare. The downstairs media suite was all set up and both local and national press were starting to arrive, milling around in the foyer and waiting to be let in. Up there on the top floors, Falk and McKinley were being briefed and flanked by press officers and legal advisors, clearly getting their stories straight about the "attack" on the Tyne Bridge and how that ties in to Jake Lehman no longer being 'public enemy number one' for the crimes they suggested as per their narrative the night before - but how maybe he did worse ten years ago in another country and...

This was all going to get VERY *complicated*.

Lane slipped us in through the back door and into the lift on the other side of the building from where the press conference was imminently about to take place. I rustled as I walked, wearing a fresh variation on the same style paper suit that I'd left Forth Street police station in whilst under arrest two nights earlier. I could've worn the clean clothes Jane had arranged for me. But I opted for this. For the *effect*. Even though I was freezing my arse off, quilted jacket around me bedamned. We were going to add handcuffs for *additional* effect only we couldn't get them to fit around the plaster cast on one wrist and the sling covering the other.

Lane did not fuck around one bit as the elevator doors pinged open and we strode along the corridor and past Falk's PA. Well, *she* strode. I walked with the pace of a man very much carrying a set of broken ribs, two broken arms – one of which was in a tight sling across the non-dislocated shoulder that had been freshly popped back into place - various sets of stitches to his skull, swelling to his eye socket and cheekbones, mild hypothermia and a severe aggravation of both his longstanding arthritis and his athlete's foot.

We must have ruffled some feathers when the door to Falk's office flung open as all and sundry fell into immediate silence on sight of us; Falk in full formal tunic dress, the head of the police's legal services, a press officer and there at the back of the room, Janet McKinley herself.

Falk took one look at me as I slumped down in a comfy seat in the corner of his room within seconds of getting through the door and without waiting for permission. He stated "Obviously the interruption is far from appreciated Jessica, but I'm also really not entirely sure it's wise for *him* to be here."

Lane smiled. "Really? I was thinking you could have him for the climactic cameo appearance at the end of your presser?"

"Wouldn't that be wonderful?" McKinley sneered contemptuously.

"It could be like the end of Iron Man?" I grinned. "Only instead of Samuel L. Jackson turning up as Nick Fury to confirm he's starting the Avengers Initiative, it could be me just popping in and saying *'Hey, guess what everyone? It turns out I'm innocent after all!'* or something like that."

"You throw that word around – 'innocent' – but I'm not entirely sure you actually know what it truly means." McKinley smirked insincerely. "We've all seen your… I don't know what to call it. Your '*confessional*', shall we say? And obviously that throws up a whole host of information that's going to have to be given over to the Australian police and…"

"... and that's why I think it's best that we place Mr Lehman back into police custody, just for the time being, whilst we speak with the Australian authorities about the information he has put out on the internet." Falk interrupted.

"You know, whilst we're throwing around things we're not exactly sure what they really mean, how about we talk quickly about your role as Police and Crime Commissioner and how you seem to be working right outside of its boundaries constantly, and often for the good of yourself and your own agenda?" Lane said to McKinley as she stood off from leaning against a nearby table, placing down her bulging leather Filofax behind her as she did.

"Woah! Woah!" Falk shouted.

McKinley smiled coldly. "I think those sort of comments need to be formalised and backed up with evidence. I certainly have no intention of responding to counter-allegations to distract from your own acts of misconduct in a public office, Chief Constable Lane."

The press officer stepped forward and started whispering in Falk's ear.

Lane took another step herself and reached into her pocket. It was time for the Russian nesting dolls of 'chuffs' – a chuff inside of a chuff, inside of another chuff, inside of... You get it, right?

I stood up delicately and with difficulty from my chair, and decided to get in front of Lane's intended move against McKinley and block it.

I looked at McKinley and smiled weakly. "Can we talk? Privately?"

She looked me up and down and began shaking her head.

"I don't see any reason to do that and I would not feel comfortable doing so either." She replied coldly.

Falk nodded. "I agree, Janet. Now listen, I don't know why you've burst in here to interrupt our briefing Jessica, but if it was to suggest Jake Lehman joins us at the press conference to have his arrest renounced I think that is a terrible idea in light of what he has confessed to and which is currently all over the internet right now."

I took a step forward and maintained eye contact with McKinley.

"I would really appreciate talking with you for just five minutes, Commissioner McKinley." I said softly. "I'd prefer to do it alone but I'm happy for you to keep one of the police's legal team in the room with you. However, considering Danny Berenger gave me a message to pass on to you I thought, perhaps incorrectly, you would want to talk in private?"

I watched McKinley's nostrils expand and underneath that thickly applied slab of make-up across her face, I'm pretty sure she was draining of colour too.

"I mean, he's Danny Berenger to *me*." I continued. "He might have used a different name with you. What if I just called him the scarred up Australian? Or what about the man behind the mask? How's that? Either way, I have an important message from *him*."

Falk seemed rattled as he said "Janet?" in a concerned, hushed tone.

She looked to Falk and slowly nodded and then in a barely audible voice she asked if we could have five minutes alone together.

There was a little bit of bustling and hushed whispering but eventually every party other than McKinley and I left the room with Lane being the one to close the door behind them, leaving the two of us alone together.

"I think the name Danny Berenger means more to you than it does to me, wouldn't you say?" McKinley said quietly as she stepped forward.

"I don't know about *that*." I replied. "It was enough for you to clear this room out."

"So what's your intention here, Mr Lehman? Because I really don't have a lot of time. Is there another button-hole camera tucked away inside of there somewhere, hoping I say something you can try and use against me? I don't have anything to say to you full stop, let alone anything remotely harmful to my professional standing."

"In time you're probably going to wish you were as cautious about Danny Berenger's covert recording capabilities as you are mine." I smiled as I reached up and pulled down the zip front of my police-issued paper suit, exposing my battered and bruised torso. I unhooked the sling from around my neck painfully and awkwardly, removed my arm from it and threw it down on the ground next to her. "There's nowhere to hide one even if I wanted to, there's no pockets for me to hide my mobile phone either and…"

I stopped myself as I saw her overcautiously start to study Falk's office.

"… And listen, Commissioner McKinley, I'm fucking *good* but I'm not so good that I could have bugged the Deputy Chief Constable's office, okay?" I concluded.

"*Acting* Chief Constable!" McKinley sneered.

"Of course, right." I grinned facetiously. "But getting back to what I was saying – if ever there was the time and place for us to have a completely off-the-record, straight-up-and-honest conversation about your part in what happened to me these last couple of nights, now's the time. I mean, come on. You and I both know that I'm probably going to end up locked away in an Australian prison once you've orchestrated whatever it takes to get that case re-opened. How about just a little bit of closure?"

McKinley frowned, sighed and let out a little laugh.

"I don't think so." She said before turning on her heels and heading for the door.

"Danny Berenger recorded every meeting he had with you. Every meeting with Hetherington too. He recorded every payment you took from him and every piece of information you misused your office to get your hands on, and passed on to him to help in his campaign against me."

McKinley turned back to face me. "Bullshit."

"You're going to wish it *was*, trust me." I replied as I gently removed a small, squared piece of paper from just inside the rim of one of my plaster casts.

I unfolded the paper delicately and took out the SD card that was inside of it.

"This? This is *everything* Danny Berenger had on you. Every meeting you personally ever had with him. Chief Constable Lane thinks she has the one and only copy. She doesn't. I switched them out before leaving to come down here and I'll hand it to you now for you to walk out of this room with."

McKinley tutted. "You *really* expect me to believe any of this? One, do you really think I'd believe you would throw your dear friend Jessica Lane under the bus in such a manner and two, I think I know what your game is - I reach out and take that SD card from you and you start shouting, the door bursts open and you try and argue that my taking of the memory card is a flagrant admission from me that such meetings with this Danny Berenger took place… which they did *not*."

"Wow. You've very, very mistrusting and very keen to believe you're ahead of the game." I laughed. "But trust me, there's nothing any more complicated about any of this whole thing then this…"

I threw the SD card down at her feet.

"No shouting for the cavalry. No big grand reveal. *Nothing.* I love Jessica Lane with all of my heart for everything she's done for me but I know what's on that card right there. I know what you did. I know that you were made fully aware of who was going to have to die as part of Danny Berenger's plan and the risks that were going to be put into play with bombs around the city and everything. You knew *all* of that ahead of time. And on top of that you specifically asked for Emily Ashley to be included as a target when she was never originally going to be and you maintained that request as recently as four months ago despite knowing she was pregnant which is *really* monstrous but... well... and... Listen, I'm a clever fucking guy and I pride myself on being one step ahead of the people out there trying to screw over the less powerful, but as to *why* you did all of that? I'm totally stumped. I'm genuinely at a loss as to why you would do that and play any part in innocent people getting murdered. I'm not *even* throwing you that memory card and asking for the return favour of you making the Australia thing go away before it starts back up. I don't even think *you* have that powerful a set of connections."

I took a deep breath and slumped down into the chair behind me again.

"The truth is, Commissioner McKinley, if I've got to betray Chief Constable Lane and throw away my winning hand to get an answer to all these why's before I'm screwed into serving fourteen consecutive life-sentences or something, I'll do it. I *will.* Because I've *got* to understand..."

McKinley bent down and picked up the SD card but before standing up straight she darted forward in a manner I was not expecting and dropped down at my feet, gripping both arms of my seat and penning me in where I sat.

"*Because* Mick Hetherington didn't deserve to be burnt to death in some shallow grave in the shitty little country park where all the benefit junkies in North Tyneside go for fucking picnics!" she hissed contemptuously. "Bill Collins doesn't deserve to be sat in some Danish jail cell awaiting trial on trumped up charges you and your little reporter friend conjured up! And all because of *you*? A bottom-of-the-barrel, grieving-parent-chasing nobody who apparently tanked out of making it as a police officer and has held a grudge ever since? Those were *great* men. Great men with fantastic insights and aspirations to make this shit-hole of a city a better place, not *for* the beer-swelling jobless masses but in *spite* of them."

McKinley looked behind her to the door and turned back with a deep smirk across her face.

"Do you know *how* great men like Hetherington and Collins were? They looked at the likes of Graham Hadenbury and myself and they saw *potential* – potential to do what it takes to make this city great for the people that matter! Not for the lazy, low-class, don't-want-to-work-for-a-living majority or all the 'ethnics' that have essentially seized control of the entire west end of this city. No, I'm talking about the people that have something to *offer*."

She grinned as she fixed the side of her hair. "I was a bloody secretary to a headteacher of a Grade 4 school down the coast six years ago, with not a single bit of experience in law or policing. No interest in either too. Look where I am now and you just *watch* where I'm going to be heading... and once I get there you'll understand why I don't like you, Mr Lehman. You are a *nobody* who doesn't understand he has zero right whatsoever to being a *somebody* regardless of how much he aspires to be. And you and your reporter friend behaving how you both have has made myself and a few of my associates very nervous as to whether you were ever going to just shut up and go away before you derailed our entire ambitious collective plan."

She stood up, straightened her skirt and buttoned up her suit jacket, sliding the SD card inside her inner breast pocket.

"I'll say this too – I couldn't give one single shit about what went on in Australia, ten years ago or whatever. I really *couldn't*." McKinley smiled. "Obviously I do now because I honestly think it's going to be your downfall once and for all, one way or another. But the overall truth is that I really don't care whether you chopped off some man's head or what that man's son did to a friend of yours out in Adelaide or Sydney or wherever it was. But I can absolutely assure you that when someone comes before me and asks for my help off the back of such an incident, and in return they're willing to remove you and your little friends as a cause for concern to me and the professional journey I'm on, you can bet your bottom dollar I'm willing to *pretend* to care and offer my help how I can... Of course, that's not to say that I ever *did* receive such an approach by anyone regarding such a thing or offered any help in return. I'm just hypothesising that I probably *would* if I was approached."

McKinley smirked, turned and opened the door to Falk's office.

"Now, I bet you wish you'd got *that* all on tape too eh, Mr Lehman?" she smiled broadly whilst patting the area of her breast where the SD card rested. "If that doesn't give you the closure you seek then... I don't have anything else for you."

I got up and walked across to where she stood. She looked me up and down once more with a sneer forming on her face.

"I'll never understand what it is about you that is just so hard to... permanently remove?" she said as she started to walk away.

I smiled and stepped out of the office with her. "I'll walk out with you. Chief Constable Lane's waiting for me downstairs anyway and you're heading in that direction."

"I'd get used to not calling her that, you know?" McKinley replied as she strode along past Falk's PA and down the corridor towards the lift.

"Can I tell you something?" I said as I did my best, limping along, to keep up with her. "I've came close to death a couple of times in the last God knows how many hours since this all kicked off. Not close enough for *your* liking, mind you. But close. And what really shocked me was that those moments you have shared with your loved ones that flash around in your head at such a traumatic moment are not always the ones you'd probably expect them to be."

McKinley side-eyed me as she walked up to the button for the elevator and pressed it.

"For example, I thought that the memory that would flash up in relation to my youngest boy would be me teaching him to ride a bike or us camping out together, something like that, you know? But it wasn't. It was me, sat on his bedroom floor making telephone cups." I continued. "Did you ever do that? I don't know if you've got kids or whatever but did you ever make cups on string with them? And then you'd stretch them out across the hallway or the whole of the upstairs or something and shout messages to each other, pretending that the voices were travelling through the string? ... Weird, huh? That *that'd* be the memory that flashed up?"

The lift doors pinged open and McKinley stepped inside, turned to face me and pressed the button for the doors to close just as I attempted to get in with her.

"I think you should wait for the next one. It really wouldn't be good for us to be seen together." she winked.

She fucking *winked.*

"Cups on a string!" I shrugged.

She looked at me with momentary confusion as the doors closed and I was left standing in the main upper floor space of the executive offices at police headquarters.

On the wall was a brightly coloured seating area, circled around a wall-mounted flat-screen television that appeared to be live streaming the press conference that was about to start downstairs.

I limped over to the area and slumped painfully down into one of the seats and tilted myself back to look up at the television screen.

Now *rewind...*

Take yourself right back to the moment in Falk's office where Lane is giving it both barrels to McKinley and she says "You know, whilst we're throwing around things we're not exactly sure what they really mean, how about we talk quickly about your role as Police and Crime Commissioner and how you seem to be working right outside of its boundaries constantly, and often for the good of yourself and your own agenda?"

Remember that bit, yeah?

Do you *also* remember how as she was saying it, Lane stood up straight from leaning against a table in Falk's office and placed down her bulging leather Filofax behind her as she did. Well, stashed inside of that Filofax but with the microphone end barely sticking just out of the top, not at all visible from view, was Lane's personal mobile phone.

You're now sat there thinking *"Oooooh, I bet it was secretly recording everything after all!"* right?

Come *on*, man. I'm better than that.

I'm Jake *fucking* Lehman, at the end of the day.

No, Lane's personal mobile phone was in fact connected through to her work mobile phone - which at the time she walked out of Falk's office was 'on hold' in her trouser pocket. Whilst Falk reconvened outside his office with the strategising legal and press people, Lane simply walked away and took the lift downstairs to the media suite - where she promptly took it 'off hold' and placed the call onto speakerphone in front of the small pool of reporters, cameramen and the like.

McKinley and I were then immediately audio-streamed out to the throng of news-hounds thereafter, live for all to hear.

A real life play on the good ol' cups on a string, huh?

Or... you know... just *actual* phones?

And that SD card in her pocket? Lane gave me that. It's blank, apparently.

Whoever McKinley thought her 'associates' to be, they clearly considered her to be absolutely expendable on the grand schemes of their "collective" plan. Because her mobile phone never rang to warn her about our private conversation being broadcast out, no one came bursting through Falk's door to shut her up... *nothing*. They didn't even stop her later walking into the media suite itself. It says a lot as to how arrogant and conceited McKinley was that she walked through several waves of police personnel downstairs who all dropped their eyes or scattered from her path and she never picked up on this once. Whoever the 'collective' were, they let her hang herself out to dry on an open telephone line broadcasting into a bank of microphones before a sea of hungry journalists.

If it hadn't have hurt to high heaven for me to do so, I'd have pulled my hands back behind my head and rested it easily on them in front of the entertainment that rolled out on the television above my eye line:

Commissioner McKinley strode out in front of the press and took her seat behind the small typed name plate bearing her details. She smiled at the gaggle of press, adjusting herself as she waited for the other attending members to walk out behind her. They didn't. There was a deathly, painful and awkward silence. She looked to her left and mouthed something indecipherable. The camera streaming this footage scanned over to where she was looking and just caught Deputy Chief Constable Falk susurrating *"Get up! Janet, get up!"* for the briefest of seconds before scanning back to her as one reporter was finally heard:

"Commissioner McKinley, are you here today to address the lazy, low-class, don't-want-to-work-for-a-living majority, all the so-called 'ethnics' that have essentially seized control of the entire west end of this city or *both*?"

Complete commotion broke up as other reporters then started shouting questions at her too. Most of them seemed to focus in on her knowledge of people's death before they were murdered and attacks on the city before they were carried out. McKinley looked deeply and immediately panicked. She frantically stood and turned to leave just as DCI Beverly and DS Clarke appeared either side of her.

"Janet McKinley?" Beverly said "Through powers afforded to me under the Serious Crime Act 2007 I am arresting you for the offence of intentionally encouraging or assisting an offence; encouraging or assisting an offence believing it will be committed; and encouraging or assisting offences believing one or more will be committed. You do not have to say anything. But, it may harm your defence if you..."

The screen went black.

"Damnit!" I sighed.

"Cups on a string eh, Lehman?" Lane was heard to say from behind just as she arrived beside me and sat down in the chair to my right. "Cups on a *bloody* string!"

I smiled and held out my plastered hand.

She gently patted against it in an improvised fist-bump sort of gesture.

"Pretty good, huh?" I grinned.

"I don't know," Lane laughed. "I think I preferred 'The Kimble' if I'm honest."

I feigned mock outrage.

"You need to go home and lie down anyway Jake." She continued. "You look like you're about to drop."

"Oh I plan to," I nodded. "But first I was hoping you and I could maybe make that phone call to your brother?"

[38]

or

6th September 2013.

The last thing I truly remembered was falling to my knees amongst the blood-stained orange desert surface of the burning Brennan compound as unrelenting, thick, black swathes of smoke consumed the area around me. I could barely see past the hand on the end of my arm and I had been struggling to breath easily anyway long before I found myself in this predicament. I couldn't see a direction to move in as the raging fires built around me. There was a whirling engine up above me and the smoke plumes seemed to suddenly and frantically oscillate away from the noise.

'I'm sorry, Jane.' I sobbed. 'I'm so sorry.'

I gagged, coughed and then faded into unconsciousness. The final sensation was how hot and fine the dust felt as my face landed against it.

When I miraculously came back around I was in a sterile private hospital room, breathing through an oxygen mask and barely able to lift my head for how swollen and aching it was. I was so incredibly thirsty and my lips felt like they'd been sealed shut. I clawed anxiously at the mask on my face and tried to sit up as best I could when suddenly DCI Novak appeared by my side and gently lay me back down.

"Calm down, kid. It's okay. You're safe." He smiled.

"Wa-ter." I gasped.

He nodded and reached for a cup off a nearby table and gently placed the straw from it in the corner of my mouth.

"Little sips!" Novak said.

I tried to nod.

Man, this water was cold – and **so** good!

He sat back down in the seat by my bedside and let his head fall towards the floor. The boisterous man I last saw him as in his office back in Sydney seemed to have long since left and this before me is what remained.

"Where am I?" I asked.

"You're back in Sydney now, mate." Novak nodded. "You've been out a couple of days. We got you to an outpost hospital over in Kaltukatjara initially because the medics didn't think you were going to make too long a trip, yeah? Once you were stabilised, we got you down here."

"But... Rachel..."

The tears fell instantly from Novak's eyes and he looked away with shame as he wiped them from his face and cleared his throat. "We've got her... You kept muttering something every time you came around... We sent some local boys out to check and..."

He coughed again.

"She's coming... home." He nodded painfully.

"She was the bravest person I've ever met." I said as a painful lump formed in my throat.

Novak kept nodding and his eyes welled up. "She was better than all of us."

"She *deserved* better." I replied.

He leant forward in his seat and looked me dead in the eye. "You mark my words, Jake. Until my dying day and most likely on the other side of it too, I will never ever forgive myself for being part of the pack mentality against that girl. That she took you out there alone and exposed like that, desperate to prove something she should never have had to prove? I could have put a stop to that ever needing to be her mindset long ago."

I stared at him.

"She shouldn't have been out there at Brennan any more than she should have been down there in that basement doing thankless work." Novak said as his voice broke. "And now she's dead and we're all one less of the very sort of person this world needs whilst old fucks like me..."

"This may well ease your conscience saying it now," I painfully exhaled my interruption as I adjusted myself into a sitting position in bed. "But I was in your office that day, remember? I heard what you said. I saw how you looked at her."

Novak nodded, wiping tears from his eyes. "It's all the worse because she never did anything *to* me, you know? The shit rolled down hill that she was someone not fit for the service and needed worming out of the job and... and..."

"You towed the line?"

"I towed the line," Novak whimpered. "I towed the line despite her being a ruddy mate as well. And she lost her life as a result."

"She lost her life *horrifically*. You need to know that. She lost her life in a truly horrific way." I replied.

"Is that why you did what you did up there?" Novak said.

I fell silent.

This was the moment where I had to face up to the prospect there was no way I could get away with writing off everything that happened up there at Brennan as a 'bad dream'. I hadn't passed out in the desert and hallucinated what happened next. It was coming back now like a flood – I actually *had* made my way back there.

"It's a mess up there." Novak said quietly. "There's so many burnt and disfigured bodies we don't have numbers yet."

"Fourteen. I killed fourteen." I barely murmured.

Novak pulled his seat closer.

"Well, just put a cork in that for the minute okay?" He muttered. "How about you start at the beginning and go from there, alright?"

"Before I do," I groaned, "you need to order the excavation of that mine and get my client's daughter out of there... along with the bodies of what could be a hundred more women for all I know."

"... *What?*" gasped Novak.

I told him everything.

I left out nothing.

I clinically spelt out every beat of the decision-making process Rachel and I had taken from the minute we left his office and I laid it on hard that we would never, ever have taken the drive up to Brennan from that town in Nullarbor had she not been so desperately consumed by a desire to prove herself once and for all to a police service that had so callously abandoned her for such despicable reasons.

I cried my way through what happened in Sid's ramshackle bar and thereafter out in the desert, whilst sweat poured out of every part of me. I sobbed uncontrollably as I recounted holding her as she died painfully in my arms, calling out for her own mother.

Novak broke down in tears as I spoke about Rachel's final moments, his eyes widened and his jaw dropped as I informed him of the details given to me by Goodjob Walt regarding the true secret nature of what went on up in Brennan and had done for several years, and then he clenched his teeth and nodded along with every detail as I described returning to the mining compound to seek justice for what they did to Rachel and all those other women.

"... Strewth!" he exhaled as he sat back in his chair.

We sat in silence for the longest time until eventually Novak cleared his throat, checked that the door to my room was firmly closed and then leant as far onto my hospital bed as he could to get his face close to mine.

Then he spoke very quietly and very quickly - that there was going to inevitably be a major investigation into whatever is found down the Brennan mine columns, that a lot of police services are going to be getting looked into as to whether they ever did enough in all the missing persons cases around the country and that the murders of fourteen men in the outback by a visiting Brit should never be allowed to "distract" from what is recovered out of the mine and what went on there.

Novak said he didn't want Rachel's memory, professional or otherwise, to be any further besmirched and he wanted the 'narrative' to reflect the true nature of her abilities. What if, he suggested, with my assistance Rachel had spotted an unexplored line of enquiry specifically in the Maya Dentz case and she and I had been officially tasked with exploring it. He would do everything required to make sure paperwork 'existed' regarding "interfacing with local police departments out there" and put a "believable background to it". And what if, he continued, Rachel and I followed the line of enquiry out to Brennan and the men there tried to hide their guilt regarding a massive series of murders and history of sex trafficking by blowing the compound following a shoot-out that Rachel single-handedly faced down with my unarmed assistance.

Novak then sat back in his chair and sighed. "Between their *self-created* explosion and the territories fires, no one stood a chance. Your radio message can fit in with this and I can work everything at our end regarding causes of death and the like. Rachel doesn't just die a *hero*. She dies as the *face* of exposing a disturbing and large-scale operation of serial killing and sex-trafficking if what you're saying turns out to be true."

This was a poisoned chalice, make no bones about it.

A corrupted deal really no different than the one Mick Hetherington offered out to my colleagues that ultimately served to kill my police career. Novak's offer was designed to save his neck as best possible, I could see that.

I wasn't that naïve.

But at the same time I really wanted to go home. I wanted to kiss my wife and hold my boys. I didn't want to be here anymore and, to put it simply, this was sounding like the fastest route to making that happen AND also giving me what I wanted more than anything right then - which was justice any which way I could take it for Detective Constable Rachel Casey.

"There isn't anyone alive out of there but you, Lehman." Novak whispered conspiratorially. "I walked that facility as the soot hardened myself. In terms of who's to say what happened up there, the 'who' is *you* and *only* you. Detective Constable Rachel Casey deserves better than being regarded as someone who took a reckless chance, went off the reservation, got out of her depth and lost her life as a result. She deserves far, far, *far* better than that."

I slowly nodded.

"And I'm prepared to throw the original investigating officers into the proverbial fire pit to make sure she gets it. Her family will hang medals above their mantel in her name for this. They *have* to. I'll see to it. But I need your help to do that."

I asked for time to think about it.

He rose up out of his seat and started saying something about needing to sit down for a coffee "with the chief" about this all anyway. He asked if I would like him to make arrangements for my wife to be contacted and told that I was safe. He then removed his mobile phone from his trouser pocket and placed it on the hospital table next to me.

"I'll come back for this in a minute." He smiled though his eyes suggested he was in pain as he reached down, clicked a couple of buttons on his phone to switch on the speakerphone as his voicemail inbox kicked in and then walked mournfully from the room just as the beep was heard.

The time and date on the opening of the message indicated it had been left on Novak's phone the morning after Rachel and I had camped out in the cabin, just before we set off on our ill-fated trip up to Brennan.

Her voice rang out around my room:

"... Sir, it's Casey. I know you're expecting us back any minute so that you can throw a rug over all of this and send Lehman packing but... well... we're going to be late returning. We've found something or... I don't know, maybe we've found nothing... I just know that I'm done being hung out to dry and this definitely feels like I'm being set up to fail on whatever this Dentz thing is you've assigned me to. And I'm not playing ball anymore, sir. I don't know whether I'm shooting myself here or handing you the loaded gun to do it yourselves but this Lehman bloke has shaken something loose and... and... you know, I've spent so long fighting <u>against</u> you lot in this job I've actually forgotten <u>why</u> I joined the job in the first place. Does that make sense? We're out here together, me and him, just two misunderstood thorns in the side of everyone else, trying to let the world know we deserve to be treated better than we are right now, you know? There's questions needing answered about this Edvin Sixten thing and I'm out here in the middle of the bloody never-never with an annoying ruddy pom who's done more to inspire me and shake the life back into me in this last week than anyone else has in a couple of years. And I'm thinking I'm going to hang with him for a bit and see if I can get those questions answered. I will check in again if this thing is a thumbs-up. Tell DI Russ, he can take this out of my holiday allowance. And one other thing, sir – maybe if this does all blow up in my face and I'm no longer a copper, you and your wife could come have a drink with me some time just like the old days? ... I'd like that. Speak soon."

I picked up Novak's phone, jabbed hard to switch off the voicemail and threw it down to the bottom of my bed. I didn't know I'd started wailing until my throat gave out and nurses came barrelling into my room to see what the agonising noise was.

I dried my eyes, requested more pain medication and passed out not long after.

Then, upon waking, I took the deal Novak offered me.

[39]

or

"The Long Goodbye".

or

"Seriously? How Hasn't This Thing Ended Yet? Come on, Man".

I arrived at the RVI hospital in Newcastle before they'd even finished booking Janet McKinley into custody at Middle Engine Lane police station. The sky was clear and the snow had eased off. Reports were indicating that the nearly four day long blizzard was done. It timed itself just right, huh? It's not like everything I'd had to face in the last forty-eight hours would've been a whole lot easier if I'd not had to be enduring it in the middle of a fucking *blizzard* but… I digress!

I had said my goodbyes to Lane back at the police station and made a handshake deal regarding my future and how her brother, employed at the National Crime Agency, could abet with it. Then whilst commotion reigned down below us, DS Clarke and DC Mitchell assisted in slipping me out of the side of the building and delivering me to the hospital.

The walk along the corridors of the Royal Victoria Infirmary was a chore at the best of times let alone without my plethora of injuries. The struggle was broken up by the sight of Luke Brody and his girlfriend Jennifer Howard coming walking towards me from the ward that I was actually heading towards.

"Jesus, Jake! You look…"

I didn't let Luke finish.

"Like *shit*?" I queried.

"What's worse than shit?" Luke asked.

"Diarrhoea shit?" Jennifer offered.

We both cast her a look and then Luke shrugged. He looked me up and down.

"Is it over?" he enquired.

I nodded.

"Is he dead?" he pushed.

I nodded some more.

"And Jane and the boys are safe?"

I kept the nodding going.

"So who was he then? What was this all *about*?" Luke asked.

"I take it you missed the live stream out across the internet?" I smiled nervously.

"We've been busy helping deliver babies!" squealed Jennifer.

"That's quite an exaggeration." Luke laughed. "We sat in a hospital corridor. We did get to see your bridge stunt though, Jake. We watched *that* live. That was *phenomenal*."

"It didn't feel it, trust me." I sighed.

"So, come on. Who *was* this shitbag?" he doubled down.

"He was just someone who found me more disagreeable than everyone else." I exhaled. "But I want to thank you. I want to thank you *both*. You saved my life, Luke. You really did."

"Do you know how many times I walked around this city back in the day with everyone laughing at me behind my back because I fucked up my boxing career?" Luke said as he put his arm around me and nuzzled into the side of my swollen head. "But you never did. You *always* saw me right. When neither of us had a pound in our pockets, you shared work my way you couldn't afford to and left me in a position to eat. I don't forget that. I'll *never* forget that."

We hugged and then Luke pulled me away from Jennifer for a second and ever so gently placed his hand on the side of my face.

"I understand more than most what it's like to feel like you've ran from a fight and have to live with the repercussions of that. I did that for years, didn't I? And I know how hard it is to come back swinging too. But look where I am now as a result, yeah."

Luke leaned in close.

"Now let me tell you a secret – They offered me another straight million to go back in for a rematch against that beast as a proper pay-per-view event and I turned it down."

My mouth dropped a little. "Seriously?"

He nodded. "Sometimes you've got to know when the fight is done. Sometimes you've got to make peace with yourself about having done enough."

Luke stared at me hard.

"*Sometimes*, Jake… You've got to *know* when the fight is *done*!"

He tapped me gently on the side of the face and winked.

"I take it we're rescheduling this couple's night out then?" Jennifer shouted over to us.

I arrived by Psychic's bedside to find a very exhausted Emily sat there and a very small hospital-cot pushed alongside her. Inside of that was Gracie Irene Dayer, just over a day old and weighing in at 7lb 3oz. Emily seemed happier to see me than I was expecting her to be. Especially considering the father of her child lay there in the bed before her; his head encased in bandages, tubes pouring out from around his chest area and both of his legs in traction.

Maybe the fact she was relatively pleased to see me had a lot to do with what was on the TV in the corner of Psychic's room - the news appeared to be covering the immediate fall-out of McKinley's appearance at the intended press conference an hour or so ago.

"Impressive! That was really quite something. I'm so glad I got to see it roll out live." she grinned, pointing up at the television. "I'm pretty sure I heard *my* name in amongst that conversation... What a bitch, huh?"

I nodded as I hovered by the door. "I only got to see the live feed from police HQ. It cut off at the best bit."

"When she got arrested? It was *brilliant*, Jake. She screamed. She actually did a full on *shriek* as they handcuffed her. What it is about these people and their inability to shut their mouths about their villainous plans though?" Emily continued. "I'd call them idiots but they got away with so much evil for so long they're clearly not, are they?"

"They all got caught out in the end by me so yeah, they're not *that* clever Em'..." I said quietly.

"You really shouldn't undersell yourself, Jake." She smiled warmly. "Come in, please."

I stepped properly inside of the room and let the door close behind me.

"You look worse than he does and he's barely alive." Emily smiled weakly whilst pointing back at Psychic. "Are you okay?"

I slowly shook my head and started to cry.

"I'm sorry, Emily. This is all my fault."

"Did you make him go in there with you?" Emily said. "Tell me the truth."

I remained silent. Now was not the time to throw Psychic under the bus.

She smiled even though it clearly pained her to do so. "He'd have followed you anywhere, Jake. I've seen that for myself. Even when you didn't ask him to, even when he didn't want to..."

"He shouldn't have been anywhere near this. None of you should have been." I sobbed.

"He's going to be okay, Jake. We will mourn every friend we've lost but we've not lost Robbie. They say he'll make a full recovery in time but it's going to be a long road. But he's not going to be fit for anymore 'adventures', you know that right? Though, I don't know if *any* of us are after this. All of our worlds have changed, one way or another. Ours certainly have..."

She turned and walked back towards the cot.

"I'm pleased he's hanging in there." I said.

"Of course he's hanging in there because he needs to meet his beautiful baby girl!" Emily replied quietly as she reached down and picked up a sleeping Gracie.

"Meet Gracie Irene Dayer. Would you like to give her a cuddle?"

I looked at her, smiled, painfully bent down and kissed her gently on her head then looked back up to Emily and slowly shook my head.

"The first man that holds her has to be her Daddy."

Emily smiled. "What about you Jake? I'm only just catching up on everything and... and... well, where do *you* go from here?"

I looked at Psychic and blinked away tears as I quietly answered.

"Away."

Emily and Gracie went off for a discussion with one of the nurses on the maternity ward and I was left alone by Psychic's bedside. I placed his hand down on top of one of my plaster casts and placed my other bandaged hand over his.

I cleared my throat at least three hundred times or something, struggling repeatedly to find the right words to start. Man, this was harder than any 'share' I ever did at a Narcotics or an Alcoholics Anonymous meeting.

"You've... you've got a very... *very*... beautiful daughter!" I stuttered out of the starting gate. "I can't wait for you to meet her."

"I want to thank you. You know? For... what you did?" I continued. "You're always there for me and... and... I don't know what to say?"

I fell silent as my eyes welled up.

"I remember the day you walked into my office and said *'Hi, I'm Robbie!'* You were giving me the hard sell about taking you on and being willing to work for free and I immediately thought *'Oh, okay. So what's his game?'* because that's just how I was built. I didn't like people anymore. I didn't trust people. And here you were, pushing your way into my life – determined to prove something to me about yourself. You did prove something in more ways than one, Psych'. You proved that you were a superb investigator and you proved that you're a great friend. The *best* friend. You taught me how to trust and *like* people again."

I cleared my throat and rested my head on our hands in order to compose myself for a second. "I always thought I was just bluffing and blagging as a private investigator, you know? I knew I was good at chasing the facts and what not. But in terms of really, truly having a clue about what the hell to do within the trade itself? I was just faking it to get by and hoping that my moral code kept me out of prison so I didn't end up like one of those News of the World gutter PI's from back in the day. Remember them? Then you came along and… I never felt once like I was faking anymore. I felt like me and you, together? We could take on the *world.* And we kind of did in a lot of ways. We took down some very bad people and we got ourselves into some scrapes that no one should be facing, let alone a couple of Geordie private eyes!"

I let out an exhaled half-laugh just at the immediate memory of some of the scrapes Psychic and I had got into over the years.

"I spent so long thinking that I had to put myself at risk to take down bad people and achieve some sort of recognition for it all because that was what would bring me some sort of eventual peace about the betrayals in my past and the Australia thing, and that being acclaimed and playing the 'deep blue hero shit' card was what was necessary to achieve that. But you know what I came to realise over the course of these last two nights? This whole fucking thing from the minute I opened the doors of Lehman's Terms wasn't about me righting wrongs and needing to take down bad bastards. It was about *me* and *you…"*

I started to sob.

"I never thought I was the sort of guy that had anything to offer anyone, you know? I thought I carried so much baggage and trauma that people would just want to keep an arm's length from me. And you didn't just want to be my work-mate, you wanted to be my actual *friend.* You saw something in me that when the shit hit the fan and you watched me walk into that warehouse, you followed me the fuck *in* despite having so much to lose and… and… I don't know how to ever repay you for that, Psych'!"

I paused, took a deep breath and composed myself.

"I have no idea what is going to happen to me next Psychic but I know that I'm done with this city. I *have* to be. The ties that bind me to it are the ties that are pulling me down, ultimately." I cried. "And I don't know how long it is going to take for me to process what happened to Holly, Leigh and Catrina but I know that it's not going to help me being around here while I try to do it. I've got to find a way to not run from any fall-out coming my way but at the same time get the hell out of here and get to a place where I can concentrate on just staring at my wife and my boys for a bit, and doing *nothing* else but that. Does that make sense? I won't be here but at the same time when it comes to you, Emily and Gracie, I'll not be far away. Whatever you need I'll...

"You... better be... shitting... me." Psychic slurred.

"You're *awake*!" I gasped.

"I didn't... get shot... off... a roof... and... crack... my head... open... for you... to learn about... friendship and... trust."

"I was trying to make a deeper point than that and you..."

"You talk... far... too... much." Psychic whispered with difficulty. "I was... sleeping... I wasn't in... a coma."

"Psychic, I love you man." I said as my eyes welled up.

"Promise me..." He struggled.

"Anything, mate? *Anything*..." I cried.

"Promise... me... you've not... brought... one of... your... playlists in... with you!"

[Epilogue - 1]

or

12th September 2013.

I walked through the Arrivals gate at Newcastle Airport and unfortunately didn't see Jane and her father standing there waiting for me before they saw me. By the time I did I could see the shock and horror on their faces as I limped towards them on crutches with an airport attendant pushing my luggage trolley for me. Jane saw my stitched and swollen face, crusted in parts from severe sunburn, bob towards her across the forecourt and I saw her expression twist and burst into one of cataclysmic upset.

We fell into each other's arms as my father-in-law discreetly positioned himself in a manner to support me while the full physical weight of Jane's distress was levelled against me.

The 'night terrors', as the professionals in the Sydney hospital identified them, followed me back to the UK and started there almost immediately. My falling off the ol' wagon swiftly followed too and soon I was going out to the 'office' garage just to sit alone and drink all day whilst staring at the cobwebs in the corner of the brickwork.

One day Starship's 'Nothings Gonna Stop Us Now' came on the radio and I came around two hours later from passing out in a furious rage only to find I'd obliterated the knuckles on my hands from drunkenly pummelling the wall.

Jane tried what she could to get me help and to push me into attending AA and the like. I eventually started to ease off the drink without leaning too hard on needing that. But the only reason I did was because I found a new crutch:

My follow-up appointments at the hospital turned into a cavalcade of physiotherapy sessions and time at the pain management clinic. The latter introduced me to a whole host of different opioids to treat the agonising back-pain and the headaches and, in time, all the other stuff I started to think up in order to get more tramadol and naproxen.

An accidental cross-over of tramadol with a couple of fingers worth of Jim Beam one night to help me sleep undisturbed by more 'visits' from the Brennan boys introduced me to the wonderful possibilities that could be afforded to me by double-dosing my pain meds or mixing them with alcohol. Pretty soon I was messing with them in a bad way and using them to survive the days and the nights.

There was an initial follow-through from Novak's 'inventive reporting' of the facts regarding what happened up at Brennan, especially once it broke about the number of bodies found down the collapsed section of the mine.

Australian and British press vied for interviews and for all of five minutes it looked like there was the possibility I was going to be a 'big deal'. I couldn't reconcile how to feel about this. There was the part of me that desperately wanted me to monetise it however I could because I had a family to support and this sure looked like an easy way of doing that. One Australian gutter-rag offered me $75,000 to sell my story. The fear that held me back was that I would be selling a *lie*; a lie I didn't want Rachel Casey's parents to read in any sort of lurid detail like a tabloid would inevitably report it. I spent so long deliberating about it that my "fifteen minutes" passed and the interest was gone by the time my mind was made up about what to do.

It served well to have held out and swerved the media offers, at least in the short term, as I received a phone call from Arkin Dentz' assistant, Marcus, six weeks after being back in Newcastle.

I'd been avoiding meeting with him and even went so far as to get Jane to ring through to Dentz' office initially and explain that I would be delayed in meeting and invoicing etc. because I was in recovery from the events that took place on the other side of the world. Like a mum would do for her son on PE days because he has an aversion to getting changed in front of the other boys.

The message from Marcus was that Arkin was "in a bad way" and needed to meet "sooner rather than later". I assumed with his emphysema and coronary artery disease this meant that the developments that had come out of Australia were drawing the life out of him once and for all. I assumed incorrectly. None of us were to know he'd go on to live for over another ten years.

We met at his request in Harry's Bar on Grey Street. It was *early* on a rainy morning and I had to double check that Marcus really meant to meet there because it was unlikely to be open at that hour.

"Well Arkin owns the building so we'll make sure it is open!" Marcus had replied.

I clumped in there early on my crutches and found Arkin already there, sat in a corner booth, attached to his oxygen tank and with his wheelchair positioned nearby, reading something that looked complicated on his iPad. He saw me, smiled and removed his oxygen mask as I approached.

On sitting down he reached as best he could and patted my hand.

"My daughter arrived home a few days ago." He smiled.

I didn't know what to say. I offered only a gentle smile in return.

"I knew she was not alive when I sent you out there. I had accepted that if I'm truly honest with you. I never expected you to go out there and reverse the facts." Arkin wheezed. "But my dream was that you could get answers to where she could be so I could bring her home and receive peace that she was buried right. And you gave me my dream, Mr Lehman."

"I think we're on enough of a level now for you to call me, Jake." I smiled.

"You nearly gave your life to afford me my dream result in this abhorrent matter and I owe you a lot more than whatever your agreed rate was at the outset."

Marcus stepped forward and placed a cheque down in front of me.

My eyes bulged.

Mainly because the cheque had my name on it and a whole *host* of zeroes.

"What is *this*?" I gulped.

"This is your agreed rate and expenses for the time you spent on this case and also six months secured salary for your business at the same rate to assist you whilst you recuperate from your injuries." Arkin replied.

"It's too much. I can't accept this."

Arkin nodded. "It's only the first part. I would introduce the second part to you myself but I would never make the stairs. Instead, Marcus is going to take you across the road now and show you your new premises. Rent-free until the day you no longer wish to be based out of there."

"You're not serious?" I gawped. "Thank you? Wait... *are* you serious?"

Arkin smiled. "I am and thank *you*, Jake."

Marcus did indeed walk me directly across the street and up a flight of stairs to the open plan office space which I was now informed were to be the official new premises of my private investigation company, Lehman's Terms. I stared around the big empty space and started to see both potential and professional respectability right within my grasp.

Jane and I set about giving it a lick of paint and buying some furniture for the place so that it didn't come across like there was one guy behind one desk, sat in one chair just begging for someone to give him a job or at the very least come and talk to him.

We even got a makeshift plasterboard partition and door put in by a handyman/tradesman client who did it in lieu of paying his invoice for a personal injury surveillance job I did for him against one of his employees who was taking a lend. Inside of this plastered off area we called it my 'private' office and I placed a desk outside of it to make it look like I had a receptionist – who just happened to *always* be 'out to lunch' any time a prospective customer came in.

We got a couple of second-hand sofas and spaced them out in the main area outside my 'office' to give the outer area the feel of a *real* reception.

By the time we were finished setting it all up I suddenly had this new found enthusiasm to get into work each day. The black coffee and tramadol breakfasts played their part too, however.

Then, one cold and January morning in 2014, I was sat putting the finishing touches to a collision-investigation report I'd been tasked with for an ambulance-chasing solicitor with a terrible reputation – the first *actual* job I'd booked in months, no less – when I heard the door downstairs swing open off Grey Street and feet come clumping up towards me.

I came out of my inner office as the main entrance door opened at the top of the stairs and in walked a tall, good-looking fella with a drooped shoulder.

"Hi, can I help?" I smiled.

"I was just wondering if you have any jobs going?" he asked.

"We don't I'm afraid. We're quite a small operation and we're at capacity." I lied, not wanting to say 'There's just me and I can barely afford to pay myself.'

"Would you accept volunteers? I'd be happy to just get my hands dirty with you guys for the experience. I'm just really interested in getting into this line of work." The man replied.

"I'm sorry, we don't take volunteers on but I will keep you in mind." I grinned as I took a step towards him. "What's your name?"

He stepped towards me and extended his hand out to me.

"Hi," he smiled. "my name's Robbie Dayer."

[Epilogue - 2]

or

"Thirty Months Later."

Monkhouse Isle, Scotland.
59°03'54.0"N // 2°33'59.7"W

Between the islands of Stronsay and Auskerry lies Monkhouse Isle, a small fishing port with a population of 189 that some would say is very nearly lost to the ages. The fishing seasons dictate terms of activity on the island just as much as the weather cycles do and the weather is rarely anything other than cold and wet. You really had to have a certain disposition to want to work here for any season, let alone stay here all year round. The people that did live here though have lived here forever; set in their own ways of doing things and usually incredibly reticent about taking to "outsiders" or "newcomers".

They had no choice about working through such reticence when Lucas Doyle, sheriff of the isle, dropped dead of a heart attack after forty years on the job and his deputy, Dennis Quint, retired pretty much not long after and left the island altogether. The long-timers on Monkhouse Isle didn't think there was a need for a replacement. Doyle did a fine job, they were happy to admit, but that's because he rarely left his little wooden office in the corner of the town and was happy to accept that the islanders here had their own way of doing things and didn't like to be messed with whilst doing them. Their word was not as strong to heed as the law itself though and soon a new sheriff of the isle was shipped over from the mainland - and he brought his family with him.

Frank Galvin arrived on the tail end of a particularly bad storm season with his wife, Jenny, and his two boys, Robert and Charles. Along with them came their beagle puppy too. Jenny took the job as headmistress at the small school on the isle. Robert became a teaching assistant there and Charles was enrolled as a student though his mind was never off fishing. As a family they ingratiated themselves to everyone with their friendly demeanor but Frank, more than the rest of the family, tended to keep himself to himself.

Many thought that had a lot to do with the distance Frank felt he needed in order to be able to police the island because he certainly took less shit from the residents and seemed more invested in the job than Doyle ever did. No more was that apparent then when it came to 'kick-offs' at the island's only pub at the top of the corner hill, six miles north of the main landing dock.

There really wasn't anything quite like a bunch of hardened, alpha-male fishermen depressurising with alcohol after weeks and months at sea in order to "blow off some steam", but a shock was delivered at the very first bar brawl under Sheriff Galvin's watch because everyone came to learn quickly he was not shy in pulling the shotgun from the back of his police vehicle and letting off some rounds to encourage disbursement.

An even bigger shock was soon to follow when Frank let it be known there was going to be zero tolerance on drink-driving throughout Monkhouse Isle from here on out. The more stuck-in-their-way types thought that Frank would "calm down after a bit" and "come round to how it is" here. Other than growing a big thick beard to look less 'wet-behind-the-ears' and more like the locals he interacted with each day, that didn't appear to be the case - even two years in on the job.

Galvin didn't seek this job out so much as a contact at the National Crime Agency put it on a 'plate' and slid it across the table to him when he was at his most 'hungry' and presented it as the best option available to him in the face of what Galvin was up against.

There was the possibility of owning a coffee shop in Castletown-Bearhaven in Ireland but that didn't come with the opportunities Jenny hoped for herself – and plus the Monkhouse Isle job was *much* more in keeping with Galvin's skillset. He didn't have the first clue about making coffee. As far as he was concerned, it only came one way – hot and black… and sweet if possible!

Never did he think for one second that he would take to it and come to love it on Monkhouse Isle as much as he did though. His biggest worry was the impact it would have on his two boys and the seismic change it would be for the both of them but he was able to settle better upon seeing just how much they loved it here too, even though Charles would prefer a "considerably better quality of internet connection that doesn't just disappear because the wind is high". Jenny loved it more than *anyone*. She treasured the clean air, the fact that she had such beautiful walks to work each morning and how everybody knew everybody and got along. For the most part.

Galvin had himself the same routine every morning - he was always up before everyone else and, after his first black coffee of the day, he'd shower and dress in such a manner that lessened a need to spend too much time looking in the mirror. (He'd never made peace with the scarring his face and body carried from a whole other life and his reflection tendered to exacerbate regretful feelings occasionally.) He kissed his wife and children goodbye after laying breakfast out for them and then he would jump in the battered Land Rover that came as part of the job, with his *real* partner by his side - a beautiful beagle he'd named Casey - and drive down through the town centre to his little wooden office tucked away behind the bakers.

There he would take an update from his deputy, Laysie Griffer, who wasn't that good at her job but *was* the daughter of Monkhouse Isle's mayor so Galvin found himself having to ride with it because battles were chosen carefully in a place as small as this when you're all pushed up against each other's shoulders. And after he'd sieved through the (80% irrelevant to 20% relevant) morning briefing from Deputy Griffer, Galvin would fill up his flask with fresh black coffee and take the Land Rover up the hill to his favourite spot.

He always made sure to stop on the old gravel point outside the school on his way. There he would be able to look through the fence and see straight into the headmistress' office where his wife was normally sat at that time in the morning, having seen the school's *thirty* students through the gates.

She was as beautiful to him as she was the first day he ever laid eyes on her across a crowded bar back in the day, her nursing a wound to her forehead from a recklessly thrown pint glass. Sure, she'd gained a little weight and she carried a few wrinkles around her eyes and her dimples but they'd shared a *hell* of a life together by this point. She'd earned them.

Anyway, time had *not* been kind to Galvin himself - and he knew it. It wasn't just the extra 'tyre' around his belly and the greying hair running through the sides of his hair and beard. It was the stiff, painful and hunched gait he walked with nowadays from a few too many years jumping off things he shouldn't and running into people's fists. And yet Jenny still kissed him and made love to him like she considered him to be the most attractive man in the world.

He liked to sit there each morning outside the school, sip his second mug of coffee and think back daily to their first kiss on their first date – how he'd stroked his index finger across that tiny fresh scar on the corner of her forehead and then moved the same finger down to brush the hair back behind her ear. And how she'd smiled, bit her bottom lip as she leant forward towards him, only for the both of them to clash teeth hard. He would catch himself smiling each and every time he did this each day and Jenny would never fail to see him across the way, gently tap on her window and then press her finger to her eye, then her heart and then out in his direction.

Galvin would reciprocate the gesture and then drive on, fuelled for his day.

From there he'd take the car up to the cliff that overhung the main fishing port and he'd set the handset for his police radio on the dashboard, plug in his old discman to the auxiliary point on the stereo system and listen to his CDs whilst watching the boats come and go as the waves lapped around the isle's beautiful causeways.

He found it so incredibly peaceful.

He would sit and absentmindedly run his fingers through his thick, greying beard and just embrace the stillness. Some days he would write out his monthly postcard to his god-daughter, Gracie. It kept her in his heart and thoughts between the meet-ups with her and her parents on the Scottish mainland every three months or so.

Under Casey's watchful eyes and salivating mouth, Galvin would settle in as the first track on his homemade CD playlist burst out and pull a sandwich from the glove box. As he unwrapped the foil he could see Casey's eyes widen with the hope that it was a meat-based filling between the bread.

"Who loves you?" Galvin would say each and every day whilst tearing the sandwich in half.

Casey would raise her paw and place it on his leg.

"That's right, Case'!" he'd nod, popping the sandwich into her mouth for her to devour instantly and then ruffling her belly as she ate.

Galvin was in such a blessed position at this point in his life to have nothing more to prove to himself or anyone.

He could simply be at amity and harmony that he had good to give to others and that he was so unbelievably lucky to have learnt the value in learning to love properly and selflessly whilst receiving such love in return.

He had spent so long in his life putting himself at risk trying to prove that he was someone of worth but he eventually came to realise that he hadn't been put on this earth to be the righter of wrongs or to achieve greatness by being 'that guy' the crowd cheers or whatever.

He was here to be the husband and the father his wife and his boys deserved.

Galvin was just thankful that he came to recognise this before it was too late.

The police radio would cackle after an hour or so.

It *always* did.

Deputy Griffer always had *something* for him.

It wasn't ever particularly high octane stuff but Galvin had no appetite for that sort of thing anymore. But it was work all the same.

He pressed pause on his discman which shut off the music coming through the car's speakers immediately.

"Go ahead, Laysie." Galvin said into his radio.

"... ... and I said to him that you'd stop in and have a word. Over to you." Deputy Griffer blasted out in a manner that was barely comprehensible.

"You've got to keep your finger down from the start of whatever you're saying, not half way through." Galvin sighed. "And it's just 'over'. Not 'over to you'."

The radio crackled.

"O'Loghlin Abernathy up on the Burnby Stretch has been on, boss." Deputy Griffer boomed in her thick Scottish brogue, loud and clear this time. "He says Mrs MacAddair is shooting at the rocks on their property line again and causing all sorts of trouble. He says she's drunk and there's stones flying everywhere. Over and out to you."

Deputy Griffer clicked off.

'*Closer*, Laysie.' Galvin thought to himself. 'We're getting there.'

He turned the engine back on, zipped up his Sheriff's jacket and clicked on his seatbelt.

Turning to look at Casey, he ruffled her ears and smiled. "Don't worry. She's never, ever going to be as good a deputy as you, girl!"

Galvin took one last long look at the beautiful view beneath him and smiled broadly in appreciation of it as if he'd never see it again, despite knowing he'd be back here again tomorrow to indulge in its wondrousness.

He looked at Casey and smiled. "Remember what I keep telling you, Case'? The sign of a great travelling singalong song is that it immediately induces a big, joyous communal smile on everyone's face and it forces everyone to burst into song alongside it with everyone knowing every word and just loving the shared moment..."

Casey barked repeatedly and bounced in her seat.

"No - wait for it, wait for it!" Galvin laughed before reaching over to his discman and un-pausing the song he'd been listening to. He turned the volume up high as he sped off along the country lanes to Mrs MacAddair's cottage:

"♫♫ *... Everybody wants a thrill. Payin' anything to roll the dice, just one more time. Some will win, some will lose. Some were born to sing the blues. Oh, the movie never ends. It goes on and on, and on, and on...* ♫♫"

The End

[Acknowledgements]

I really hope that you've enjoyed this book as much as you all seem to have with the other two. I hope that it isn't a disappointment to you. I'd like to thank you if you are one of the readers who took the time to write a positive review on Amazon, share links to my work on Facebook and Twitter and to buy extra copies as gifts to others. Each and every one of you has, by doing all of that, made it possible for me to be able to see Jake Lehman's story across the proverbial finish line and I am so grateful to all of you.

I'd like to say a massive thank you to Lesley Renwick for working as editor on this book. This time round there were no constructive readers by choice in order to preserve the specific story I wanted to tell so the responsibility of proof-reading, calling 'bullshit' on certain plot developments and providing constructive feedback was all on her and her alone. I am so appreciative to her for giving up her time and helping so invaluably.

An enormous thank you also to Mark Flaherty for once again delivering phenomenal cover art for the book and for helping getting the manuscript all 'ticked off' for uploading. He's an insanely talented and patient fella and it's his work that has drawn people to giving the books a try more than any plot outline on the back cover. Mark runs his own graphic design company, Me & Alan, and I urge you all to check them out. And recommend them to others too please.

I don't believe there is a great deal to benefit from being overly precious as a writer and in the past, with the other two books, each Jake Lehman adventure has been made all the better by one of the constructive readers taking an idea I had and suggesting an add-on or an amendment. It would have been mad not to have taken them. This time round Mark made a last minute suggestion regarding a crucial scene and he made it at quite literally the eleventh hour of finalising the book. I was certainly not going to turn my nose up at something that elevated the particular chapter in question as brilliantly as it did so I took it at ran with it. It improved that section of Lehman's Infamy greatly. So thanks for that too, Mark.

The biggest thanks must be reserved for my wife. Once Lehman's Terms was as well received as it was I set myself the thoroughly unnecessary and incredibly stressful personal target of breaking down, writing and publishing the entire 'trilogy' in one twelve month period. This is / was insane and I do not recommend it. It is an awful strain. And whilst it was successfully achieved (with two months to spare, no less) it could only have been done with the selfless support from my wife and the sacrifices she made. Between the finalising of my second book and the publishing of my third my business expanded, my professional circumstances changed and we had a second child. But my wife steadied the course all the way through and made it possible for me to have concentrated writing time each day. I love you very much, Jen.

When I first set out drafting my first novel, Lehman's Terms, it was always with the idea of having this profane, pop culture drenched, irreverent front as a means to sneak in through the back door a bit of a wider discussion about addiction, corruption, trauma and the like. Once that seemed to be well received by those that read it I finally got over my fears about putting my writing "out there" and set about developing the initial story into the one I wanted to tell overall.

The ending was *always* set from the outset. Lehman was *always* going to end up where he does. Building out from Lehman's Terms, the ambition was also always to jump off the back of that and tell a story about finding peace from your past and reaching a place of understanding that your value isn't drawn from fame, infamy, success, riches and so on but from the *relationships* you have with the people around you. I'm happy to think that I achieved the storytelling objective I set myself over these three books… only with a whole heap of "fucks", tangents about films and *great* music recommendations 'accidentally' thrown into the mix.

Leonard McClane

Printed in Great Britain
by Amazon